I0666720

The Unsuspecting Heather Meyers

A Redemptive Love Story

SHAWNA ROBISON YOUNG

YOUNG AT
HEART
STORIES
PUBLISHING

ISBN: 978-0-578-64505-6
Library of Congress Control Number: 2020902598

This novel is a work of fiction. Any references to
historical events, real people, or real places are used
fictitiously. Names, characters, and places are
products of the author's imagination. Any
similarities to people living or dead are
coincidental.

Scripture quotations are taken from THE HOLY
BIBLE, NEW INTERNATIONAL VERSION®,
NIV® Copyright © 1973, 1978, 1984, 2011 by
Biblica, Inc.™ Used by permission. All rights
reserved worldwide.

Edited by Dori Harrell, Breakout Editing
Cover design by Shawna Young
Image from Canva.com
Author Photos by: K.Newby Photography

DEDICATION

For my husband Jason, my children Karlee, JJ, Kaylinna, and Kallie, my parents Steve and Linda, and my brother, Steve. Thank you for being my biggest supporters and for nurturing my creative spirit.

"Be alert and of sober mind. Your enemy the devil prowls around like a roaring lion looking for someone to devour. Resist him, standing firm in the faith, because you know that the family of believers throughout the world is undergoing the same kind of sufferings."

1 Peter 5:8–9 NIV

Chapter One

Go! Now!

This was Heather Meyers's chance, maybe her only one, to escape a life in shackles.

The bright numbers on her alarm clock switched to 3:44, and her heart leapt. She looked at the empty spot next to her and drew in a deep breath, then blew it out. Her pounding heart drummed in her ears as she rose from the bed and made it.

Everything needed to look as normal as possible.

She grabbed the letter off her desk and put it in her jogger pants pocket then reached under the bed for her old softball duffel bag, and threw in a few days' worth of clothes and toiletries.

She took her worn Bible from the nightstand and clutched it to her chest.

Go!

The word echoed in her head. Sleep deprivation meant nothing. She tossed the Bible into the bag and went to her grandmother's antique cheval mirror and slid down the back panel, exposing the secret compartment where she'd hidden a thick envelope stuffed with cash. She removed it, the love letters between her grandparents, and the old family photos her grandmother had left inside years ago. Heather put the items in her bag and returned to the mirror. She ran her hand along the top of the compartment where her grandfather had etched the words *I love you*. Leaving her most prized possession behind would be her only regret.

She slid off her wedding ring and placed it inside the compartment she'd taken the letters from, then pushed the back panel of the mirror upward. Excruciating pain shot through her right shoulder. She used her left hand instead, but the back wouldn't catch.

"No excuses," she said.

Fighting through the pain, she pressed her lips together and slid the mirror up. It locked in place. She grabbed the bag and took one last look at the cheval glass, then tiptoed onto the creaking living room floor. The shower ran in the guest bathroom, and Sissy had left the TV blaring in her room. Urgency rose in Heather's chest. Why was her sister-in-law awake already?

Heather laid the letter for Sissy on the breakfast bar. Lies. Heather regretted that too, but it was the only way.

Careful not to make a sound, she crept to the front door. The red light on the alarm panel blinked. She halted. The code? What was it? Random numbers with no significance. She'd memorized it yesterday, but a lot of good that did her now.

Wait.

The code was on a pad of paper next to Sissy's bed.

Fighting a cough tickling the back of her throat, Heather crept down the hallway toward Sissy's room. The shower stopped. Shoot. Heather darted back to the front door.

Breathe. Focus.

She closed her eyes and pictured the panel display.

Help me, God.

7-3-8-6-4-9-1-5.

Fingers racing, she pressed the first three numbers, fumbled over the next, then tried again . . . and again. Finally she hit the right combo and disabled the alarm.

Freedom awaited outside the door.

She put her hand on the knob and stared at the black spot in front of her on the doorframe, where white paint had chipped away.

Just open it. Go.

Her limbs weighed heavy on her body, and she turned the knob as the ticking of a clock and her pulse hammered in her ear.

The cool January San Diego morning air hit her face.

She reached under the newspaper sitting on top of the front door mat and snatched the set of car keys wrapped in a piece of paper with *White Honda Accord* written on it.

A cough threatened to reveal her presence, and she held her breath while she ran down three flights of stairs to the side of the building. A lone white car sat parked in the first spot. Quivering, she unlocked the car and flung the door open. Once inside, the cough broke through her lips. She pulled her bloody hand away from her face and reached into the glove box for a napkin, then wiped the blood away. Something was wrong. Really wrong. But she had to get away as far as possible before she could see a doctor. Finally.

Heather's hands trembled on the steering wheel. She hadn't driven for years. She backed up without incident. In her rearview mirror, the silhouette of a person from one of the apartments stood at a window.

Clueless where the road would take her, Heather turned out of the parking lot and rolled down the window. She wouldn't go another day without feeling the fresh air in her lungs.

J. J. Jones moved the five-year-old bald girl's bent knee toward her chest. Three months before, Tara's fall from the top of a slide had led to the discovery that she had not only broken her femur but she also had Leukemia.

She grimaced as he straightened her leg, then laid it down on the table.

"I see you're still hurting a little, but that's normal," he said. "It shouldn't be too much longer until your leg is as good as new."

"Mommy said this is my last session. I'm going to miss you." She looked at the hand-painted mural on the wall behind him. "And the monkeys."

He tapped the end of her nose. "I'll miss you too. And because you've been so brave, I have a surprise for you. Head on over to Missy. I'll be right there."

"You're the best physical therapist ever!" She jumped off the table and ran to the L-shaped receptionist's desk at the front of the building, which faced the waiting area and the open one-room, six-bed physical therapy office.

Her mother touched JJ's elbow. "She's right, Dr. Jones. You are the best. I'd love to show you my appreciation. How about dinner tonight?" She moved closer to him.

He stepped back. "Thanks for the offer, but I'm pretty busy these days."

Tara's mother winked, then swayed her hips as she walked toward her daughter. He grabbed the bottle of cleaner from a nearby shelf and wiped off the table he'd used with Tara.

In front of him on the wall, monkeys hung from vines in the children's corner—his favorite spot in the office. His daughter, Amelia, had helped design it five years ago. She'd suggested one of the monkeys wear a cast on its leg and a smile on its face as it hung upside down from its tail. And she'd insisted on the ball pit in the children's center that way her baby brother could play in it when he grew up.

His heart ached. He missed those days. How had nine months already passed since the last time she'd visited him at his office? Zac, however, came at least once a week and, as Amelia had predicted, spent most of his time in the ball pit.

"Dr. Jones, Tara is all set," Missy announced.

He turned and placed the paper towel roll and cleaner back on the shelf, then made his way to the front desk. Tara's mother leaned on the counter while her daughter dug through a large chest of stuffed animals.

JJ expected he'd see the little girl again, with her type of cancer. Hopefully, it would be later rather than sooner. Her case had been difficult from the beginning. Five years old. One year younger than his son.

He ran his hand across his five o'clock shadow. He did what he could to help alleviate pain and promote healing for his patients. If he could take the pain away and wipe a disease from existence with just a thought, he would. So how could God, if he was real, allow innocent children to be riddled with such an awful disease?

Tara came around the receptionist's desk, squeezing a purple stuffed monkey. "Thank you, Dr. Jones. I love it!"

He patted her head. "You're welcome. Now, you keep up on your physical therapy at home. Missy gave your mom the list of what to work on. Anytime you see that monkey, I want you to remember me and do your exercises."

"I will." She squeezed his leg, and he hugged her back.

Ms. Shoots put her arms around him too. "Thank you, Dr. Jones," she whispered in his ear.

He pulled away. "My pleasure. You two take care."

As they left his office, he took a seat in the waiting room chair closest to the door and rubbed his worn-out hands. Applying pressure and giving massages most of the day took its own toll on his body, but he didn't mind. Every morning he rose eager to help the next set of patients.

"You okay?" Missy asked.

"I wish I'd released her from my care completely healed."

"She is a sweet one, huh? You helped a lot. Remember how much pain she was in before? And you've taught her how to cope."

"She shouldn't have to learn to cope. In our day and time, why can't we find a cure?" He raked his hands through his hair. "I want to fix them all, you know."

"You're a good physical therapist. Imagine if they didn't have you to help relieve their pain."

"I wish I could do more."

"I know you do." She started typing. "Let me finish this, then I'll help you clean up."

"Thank you." He looked around his empty office. Earlier it had bustled with patients talking to him about the weather, the local high school basketball team, and his advice on the latest medicines.

How he wished he had more patients to help. He didn't want to go home where no one, not even his trusty golden retriever, Duke, waited for him.

The front door opened, and an older woman entered with a cane, a black top hat, a matching long coat, and her gray hair in a bun. She smelled like chocolate, reminding him of childhood Saturday mornings sipping hot cocoa with his mom while they watched cartoons.

She smiled and tipped her head forward. "How do you do, sir?"

"I'm well. Thank you. And you?"

The woman touched her hip. "This old girl is giving me the fits. Must be this frigid Indiana weather. I broke it several years ago, and every so often it bothers me. A little bit of PT and I'll be as fit as a fiddle. I don't have an appointment, but since I was in the area, I thought I'd stop in and make one. I've heard wonderful things about this place."

He stood and held his hand out. "I'm Dr. Jack Jones, but please call me JJ."

She took his hand. "Hello, JJ. I'm Anna Ingram. I'd like to get in as soon as possible. The pain is tolerable, but I don't have time to let it slow me down. Can you squeeze me in the next few days or so?"

"I could do a quick consult now, if you'd like, and then try to get you in tomorrow for more thorough treatment." He turned to Missy. "Do I have any appointments available?"

Missy typed, then ran her finger across the computer screen. "You have a nine forty-five in the morning."

"That would be wonderful," Ms. Ingram said. "Thank you."

He moved to the reception desk and leaned over the counter for a clipboard, then handed it to the woman. "Please fill this out while I set everything up."

After straightening the bands, balls, and weights, he pulled up a new patient file on his computer, then returned to the waiting room. "I'm ready now."

She handed him the clipboard, and he placed it between his underarm and side, then held out his other arm for her to take ahold of, along with her cane, while she stood. She grimaced and scooted her feet across the floor.

After he settled her on the exam table, he took a seat on his stool and wheeled it and his computer tray close to her. "Ms. Ingram—"

"Please call me Anna."

"Yes, ma'am. Anna, you said you broke your right hip years ago. How and when?"

"It was a terrible fall. I slipped on a patch of ice on my driveway. I was hurrying and not watching where I was going. Boom. Down I went. Knocked myself unconscious too. It was a long recovery. It happened about twenty years ago, I'd say. It only hurts from time to time."

"No cancer or terminal illnesses contributed to the fall?"

"No cancer." She shook her head. "From what I hear, that's your specialty."

"It is, but I work with anyone who needs physical therapy. How did you hear about me?"

"Believe it or not, we work in a similar field. I'm a hospice nurse. A career choice I started late in life. Working with dying patients can be emotionally hard, as I'm sure you know, but someone's got to do it, right? I want to help my patients pass to the other side with as much peace and dignity as they can." She pointed at him. "Don't you let this old body and wrinkles fool you. I may look like I have lots of miles, but on the inside, I'm just getting started."

He grinned. "No, ma'am. I'd never be fooled. You're a sharp one. I can tell."

"I'll work hard to get this hip back into working order."

"I know you will." He took her hand to help her lay on her back.

He moved her leg up and down, from side to side, and in a circular motion, paying particular attention to her facial expressions at different angles. Each time her face tensed, he made a note of it and eased the pressure. After manipulating her hip, leg, and joints and asking more questions, he massaged the area he'd tried not to torture too badly. He hated putting patients in more pain than need be.

"Are you doing okay, Ms.—"

She raised her eyebrows.

"Anna."

"I'm good. I've heard you're the best in this region and that people travel from all over to see you."

"That's what they tell me. Would you like me to put heat on your hip before you leave?"

"Sure. That sounds nice."

JJ took a warm pack and placed it on her hip.

"JJ, tell me about yourself. I didn't see a wedding ring. Are you single?"

JJ rubbed the spot where the ring should be. He'd not worn it often enough during his marriage, but now that he had no right to wear it anymore, he felt naked without it. "Yes, ma'am."

"You're a heartbreaker, huh?"

"Excuse me."

"I don't mean anything bad by that. A handsome doctor like you, I'm sure you have a long line of woman wanting to date you."

JJ smiled. "I don't have time for romance. Two kids, a practice to run, patients to help."

"Like I said, hearts breaking all over Danburg tonight."

"Ha. Ha. I doubt it."

"What about your children's mother?"

"We're divorced."

"I see. Are you and your kids close?"

The question stabbed his heart. "My son's my little buddy. But my daughter's struggling a bit. The divorce is my fault, and she hates me for it." He cleared his throat, shook his head, and then attempted a smile. "We'll make it through."

Why was he telling her all this?

She touched his wrist. "I'm sorry. I didn't mean to pry. Sometimes things fly out of my mouth before I think. She'll come around, I'm sure. There were two people in your marriage. I'm sure it wasn't entirely your fault."

"No, it was all my doing."

"Your daughter will forgive you."

"I hope so."

"I'll be praying for you and her."

"Thank you, but I don't think it will do any good."

"Why not?"

"It's hard to see the amount of suffering I do and know how many prayers my terminal patients say and that most of them aren't healed. You know how it is—you see it every day. My patients are incredible people who deserve a god's intervention. If he doesn't help them, then why would he help me?"

"It's the sick who need a doctor. Not the healthy."

"Okay? That's obvious."

"It's from the Bible. A reminder that Jesus came for the sinners. No one is perfect. We all need him. We all make mistakes."

"Some worse than others."

"Not in his eyes."

"If the fairy tale is real, he doesn't make sense that's for sure."

"We don't have to understand it, just have faith in it. He is so, so good. Even in the bad times."

"My girlfriend back in high school believed in all that too, but I just can't."

"I'll be praying for you just the same."

He chuckled. "I guess it won't hurt anything, right?"

"It just might help. You never know."

"We'll see." He smiled.

The timer went off, and JJ removed the heating pad. He took Anna's hand and helped her sit up.

"I'm feeling better. Thank you." She hopped off the table and rubbed her hip, then headed toward the door without a limp. She slid into her coat, put on her hat, and waved. "See you tomorrow, JJ. I have a feeling this is the start of a great friendship."

With that she walked out the door, leaving her cane against the wall. He grabbed it and ran out the door after her, but she'd already disappeared.

Chapter Two

Heather pulled next to a gas pump somewhere in New Mexico. She'd let her fancy lead her this far for the last twelve hours, but it was time to stop for the night. Several immaculately landscaped hotels, gas stations, and restaurants lined the street. She stepped out of the car and coughed as cold air blasted her. She rubbed her bare arms. She definitely needed more than the T-shirt now.

The sense she was being followed haunted her, and she looked over her shoulder as she rushed inside the gas station.

The young Hispanic boy, probably no older than nineteen, behind the counter tipped his head at her.

She returned the gesture. "Do you sell coats?"

"Yes, ma'am. Over to the right in the back, near the restroom." He pointed.

Ma'am? She'd never been called that by anyone outside the marines. Thirty-five wasn't young by any means, and her body proved it couldn't do as much as it once had, but *ma'am?* Did she really look that old?

"Thank you," she said as she headed to the back.

Several coats hung on the racks. She checked the price. A hundred dollars. She swallowed hard. Were things really that expensive now? She chose a gray one and a pair of matching gloves, then grabbed a map. After adding a ginger ale to settle her nauseous stomach and a tank of gas, she paid him in cash.

"You don't happen to have a pay phone I could use? Do you?"

He furrowed his brows and scrunched his nose. "Pay phone? Are those even still around? You can use my cell if you want." He handed it to her.

"Thank you."

She moved to the end of the counter and dialed.

"Hey, girl," Sissy answered.

"Hi. I wanted to let you know I arrived safe earlier today. I'm here at the facility. I'm not sure how long I'll be gone."

"I'm proud of you. I will stay here and hold up the fort. Is this the best number to reach you at? It said New Mexico call. Is that where you are?"

"No, I'm north of Los Angles. I borrowed a phone."

"How did you get there?"

"I took an Uber to the bus station." Heather's heart raced. She hated lying to Sissy.

"How brave of you. I can't believe you were able to do that."

"I was determined."

"What should I tell Keith when he calls in a few weeks? Do you think you will be back by then?"

"Probably not. Please don't tell him."

"I love surprises. I will come up with good excuses why you can't come to the phone. Good luck."

"Thank you. You know Keith's going to be pretty mad when he finds out we didn't tell him."

Sissy laughed. "He doesn't scare me. He's all talk. Besides, he will be so happy when he finds out you've overcome your agoraphobia that he'll forget all about the deception."

Heather's stomach knotted. How little her sister-in-law knew. Keith would go ballistic. Search the world for her, but Heather would make sure her husband could never find her. "Thank you, Sissy. Take care. I love you. Bye."

"Back at ya. Bye."

Heather hung the phone up and handed it back to the guy. "Thanks."

"No problem. Ma'am, what happened to your phone? Did it die? We've got chargers if you need one. They're right over there by the books."

"No. I don't have a cell phone."

He scrunched his nose. "Really? Why not?"

She shrugged and headed for the door. "I don't need one. Thanks for your help. Have a nice evening."

After filling her gas tank, she chose the hotel next door and paid cash. The lady at the front desk, preoccupied with her cell phone, barely looked at Heather or her expired driver's license. Thank goodness, because Heather surely didn't still look sixteen.

The woman, without glancing up, handed Heather the room key and pointed to the left.

"Elevators are at the end of the hallway. You're on the second floor. The free breakfast is from six to ten thirty."

Heather snatched the keys and rushed to the elevators and up to her room. She locked the door, then slid a chair in front of it. She looked out the window at the few cars in the parking lot and the laughing couple exiting the restaurant across the street. She shut the curtains, tossed her bag onto the bed, and sat next to it. She pulled out the map of the USA and unfolded it.

She needed a plan. Where should she go? What would she do there?

She could be a nanny. She'd love that. To smell babies' sweet little heads and cuddle them close. Feed them their bottles and sing lullabies.

Or a preschool teacher, someday after she got a degree. Or a social worker so she could work with foster children. Whatever she'd do, it would include kids.

She closed her eyes and circled her finger over the map. She'd leave it to fate. She pressed her finger to a spot and opened her eyes.

Indiana? No. She couldn't go back to her hometown. She needed a fresh start where no one knew her. Up north, perhaps? Or down south? Deep in the bayou. She grinned, imagining herself in the swamps wrangling an alligator. Or a safari tour guide. She pictured herself in a round tan hat, speaking Australian English—why Australian she didn't know—but she'd drive the big Jeep through the jungle of Africa, pointing out the lions and elephants. What an adventure that would be.

She closed her eyes and drew in a deep breath, then blew it out.

A summer working in Africa had been her old high school boyfriend's idea. They never went together, of course. Had he? They'd had such big plans. She shook her head. That was the past. Eighteen years ago. She wouldn't revisit any of it.

She needed adventure. The good kind. The thrilling kind. The kind she'd once dreamed of. The most she'd seen of the world was traveling from duty station to duty station with Keith. It would have been nice to have experienced San Diego, Quantico, and Miramar, California. Imagine her on the beach, basking in the sun, tan, and living the good life. Keith hadn't offered her anything close.

Again, that was the past. No looking back. Now she could go anywhere she wanted.

She closed her eyes and circled her finger over the map again, this time moving her hand away from Indiana.

One, two, three. She opened her eyes.

Georgia. That sounded nice. She took a closer look at the town. Waycross.

Waycross it would be. Why not?

Flutters stirred in her stomach. She ran her finger across the roads she'd take and mapped her course. No one would stop her from doing whatever she wanted now.

She glanced up at Indiana. How could she disappear and not tell her parents why? What if she took a quick detour into Danburg before anyone other than her parents realized she'd been there? She'd show her parents she was okay before any speculations of her disappearance arose.

Her heart ached. And she could tell them goodbye forever.

Chapter Three

Amelia slammed the softball flyer onto her bedroom desk. Would everyone stop trying to convince her to play. She tossed her backpack into her closet, then plopped on her bed. She stuck earbuds in and scrolled through her playlist until she found one that fit her bad mood. She stared at the ceiling and tapped her foot to the fast beat.

Her mom walked in front of her and waved her arms. Amelia took out the earbuds while the music continued to blare through them.

"Your dad called. He wanted to know if you'd like to go to the batting cages after he gets off work."

Amelia rolled her eyes and scoffed. "Can't he get a clue? Can't anyone? I'm not playing anymore, and I don't want to hang out with him."

"Be nice."

"Whatever. I had an awful time with him at Christmas. I stayed in my bedroom the whole time. If you can even call the loft a bedroom. It doesn't even have a door or four walls. It looks over the living room, for goodness' sake. It's so weird." She glanced around. "This is my room. This is my home. Dad's apartment will never be. I hate him."

"Amelia!"

"Don't you get it? I want nothing to do with him. He's scum."

"Amelia Katherine Jones, stop." Her mother put her hands on her hips. "He's a good dad."

"Why are you defending him?"

"Your dad hurt me, hurt you, I know, but I will not let you disrespect him like that."

Amelia rolled her eyes. "Whatever. I really don't want to hang out with him at all, like never again."

"I'm sorry you feel that way, but you have to. He hasn't forced the court order on you because he understands what you're going—"

"How does he understand? Did he catch his dad cheating on his mom?" Amelia raised her voice.

"No." her mother frowned and looked away toward the window across the room.

Amelia's stomach knotted. She shouldn't have gone there. Her dad had done enough to hurt her mom. Amelia didn't need to also. "I'm sorry, Mom. I'm just so mad at him."

"I am too, but whether you like it or not, you have to see him. Try to remember what a good dad he's been."

"I don't care. It doesn't matter now. He had a good life with us, and he blew it."

"He hurt us all, but we have to move on." Her mother made her way over to Amelia's desk under the window and picked up the softball flyer "Are you going to conditioning? I thought you weren't going to play this year."

Amelia shook her head. Softball had been her life since she was like three, something she and her dad had enjoyed together. He'd taught her to pitch, but now she couldn't even touch a ball without wanting to hurl it at something. "I'm not trying out."

"That's a shame, but I guess I understand. If you want to blow off some steam later and want to throw the ball, I can try. I know I'm not your d—"

"No thanks. Besides, it's freezing outside."

"Like that's ever stopped you."

Amelia huffed and threw her head backward onto the bed. "A lot's changed. I will never love softball again." She smirked. "I can thank Dad for that."

It was too much to think about it. Pain sat in her chest. She shoved the earbuds back in her ears and closed her eyes.

Heather drove around the block for the third time and parked in front of her parents' house. As she stepped out of the car, the cold, snowy air took her breath away. She pulled her unzipped coat tight across her chest.

The small ranch-style red brick house still sported the white shutters she'd helped her father hang twenty-five years before. His beloved green-and-white-checkered lawn chair, which her mother hated, retained its spot on the small covered porch, and his red-and-cream 1979 Ford F-100 Lariat sat in the driveway in front a black Toyota sedan.

Heather half expected her mother to be standing at the white storm door watching her through the small square window, but only a winter wreath could be seen through the glass. How had Heather stayed away for this long? She missed her parents more than she'd ever let on.

A yapping cocker spaniel appeared between the front curtains and jumped up and down. He was new.

"Tommy boy, quiet. What's gotten you all in an uproar?"

Her mother appeared beside the dog. Her gray hair, once brown, caught Heather off guard. An ache stirred in her stomach. When their gazes met, her mother put her hand over her mouth and widened her eyes.

Heather lifted a hand.

A smile spread across her mother's face, and she darted away from the window. "Dan! Dan! Heather's here!"

The door flung open and slammed against its frame as her mom raced down the driveway with a slower stride than Heather remembered. Heather rushed up the driveway to meet her mother. She threw her arms around her and clung on.

Her mother took Heather's face in both her hands. "Is it really you?"

Heather nodded, and her mother pulled her into a hug. Heather tucked her face into her mother's neck.

"I've missed you so much." Her mother took both Heather's hands in hers and looked into her eyes.

The dog barked and rapped his paws against the glass.

From behind, a set of arms wrapped around her. Heather turned. Her daddy grinned, then gave her a bear hug. She sank into his arms and laid her head against his chest. The smell of his Stetson cologne surrounded her. She grabbed him tighter. She would never let go.

"Why didn't you tell us you were coming?"

Staying in his arms, she looked up. "Because I knew you'd call in the extended family, the neighborhood, and entire church congregation for a celebration."

Her dad pulled back and winked. "You know me too well. But you haven't been back here for seventeen years. Can you blame me? This does call for a party."

"Please don't. I'm here for a quick trip."

"You're no fun." He laughed while looking around. "How long are you staying? Where's Keith?"

Her stomach tightened, and her heart raced. "He's on deployment. Left on Saturday."

"Did you drive from San Diego all alone?" Her mom's voice rose an octave.

Heather nodded.

"That worries me, sweetie. I know you're a grown woman and you've traveled the country several time, but a mama's always going to worry about her daughter's safety. Lots of crazies in this world! You can never be too careful. I hope you at least carry Mace on you for when you have to stop.

"I can handle myself."

"I know you can. You've always held your own."

How wrong Mom was.

Her mom touched her shoulder. "How did you work it out? Keith always says you all don't have the money to come visit."

"I've been saving little by little." The truth told more than she was ready to reveal.

Her mother stared down the street. "I'm surprised Keith wanted you to drive by yourself cross country. He's so protective of you. Such a good man."

Heather wanted to roll her eyes, but raised them instead. Yep, Keith Meyers. High school quarterback. Marine. Hometown hero.

Her mother gave a gentle smile. "Don't get me wrong. I'm excited you're here."

Her father squeezed Heather again. "Come on in. We have a lot to catch up on."

Following her parents into the house, she glanced behind her. It appeared no one had followed her. She took in a deep breath and touched the doorframe as she entered. She'd done it.

"Go ahead and put your things up. We'll head to the grocery store when you're done." Heather's mother opened the bedroom door for her.

"Remember, you guys promised. No parties."

Her father held three fingers up. "Scouts honor. Lasagna for the three of us."

She stepped into her old bedroom, and her parents went down the hall. The changes felt like a smack in the face. They'd removed everything that had made the room hers. Her old boy band and beach posters had been replaced with framed scenes of bicycles and flowers. A delicate white daybed had taken the place of her captain's bed, and the teal walls were now a light pink. A treadmill sat where her cheval mirror once had. It didn't seem right not having it.

She laid her duffel bag on top of the unfamiliar vanity dresser and unpacked her clothes into the empty drawers. She stared at herself in the mirror. She didn't recognize the woman looking back at her. The girl who'd left this room ages ago held a spark in her eye, a constant smile on her face, a go-get-them attitude. How had she allowed Keith to beat her down to nothing? She shook her head.

"You were a coward."

She placed her hands on the dresser and looked down. She knew better. She'd tried to fight back at first. She'd thought he'd change, had listened to his lies. Then it was too late. He'd cut her off from the money, and she'd lived in fear to even look at him wrong, let alone challenge his no-leaving-the house or calling-her-family rules.

She lifted her head and stared at herself again.

"You did it." She straightened her back. "That was the past. Don't you let him or anyone or anything hold you back ever again."

She grabbed her bag and opened the closet. She placed it on the top shelf next to her old softball trophies. At least her parents hadn't gotten rid of everything. She pulled down the last one she'd received, *Outstanding Freshman*.

"That was a long time ago, huh?" her dad said as he entered her room.

"I regret giving up on that dream."

He kissed the top of her head. "You had a new one. A life with Keith."

Her stomach lurched. "I chose wrong."

"Heather?"

She turned to look her dad in the eye. Shame swirled around in her gut. Her parents would be disappointed in her when they found out what she'd done. She had more skeletons in her closet than anyone knew. Somewhere buried under years of lies, the eighteen-year-old girl she'd left in Danburg fought to resurface.

"Daddy, I have a lot to tell you, but I can't yet. I need time."

She fell into his arms. She couldn't disappoint him. Did her parents even need to know her adult life hadn't been what they would have hoped for her? She'd stayed. She'd allowed it. No, she needed to keep her secrets hidden. She'd tell them just enough. No one needed to know, and she surely didn't want to relive it. Keep it buried. Let everyone keep believing she was the amazing Heather Cole who married equally impressive Keith Meyers.

"Whatever it is, you can tell us." Her father squeezed her tighter.

"I know. For now, just please don't tell anyone I'm here."

He drew her back and looked at her. "I won't. Does Keith know you're here?" His tone was serious.

She shook her head no. One lie revealed.

"Guys, you ready!" her mom called from down the hallway.

"We're coming." Heather grabbed her old softball hat sitting on the other side of her trophies.

He touched her arm. "I love you. And whatever is going on, we will support you."

"Thank you." She put the hat on, then walked toward the bedroom door. She turned to look at him. They would understand. "When I'm ready, I'll tell you guys everything."

Heather stood behind her parents in the checkout line. She pulled the brim of her hat farther down her forehead and made sure her long brown hair framed her face. She had avoided making eye contact with anyone. Thank goodness her dad had suggested going to the store in the next town.

"How did I forget the lasagna noodles?" Heather's mom held her palms up and crossed her eyes. "I'd lose my head if it wasn't attached."

Heather laughed. "I'll go get a package."

She returned to aisle seven and reached above her head for the lasagna. Pain burst through her shoulder, and she dropped the box. She grabbed her shoulder with her other hand and rubbed the muscle, but it didn't help. The tight aching had become almost constant.

A cough rattled her chest. The pain intensified into the rest of her body as if a compactor had crushed her bones. She caught her breath. The damage Keith had inflicted on her throat and shoulder needed treated. She couldn't take any more pain.

Her clothes adequately hid the bruises, but just in case, she pulled the back collar of her shirt higher on her neck and made sure her hair sat neatly over the front and back of her right shoulder.

"Excuse me, dear." An older woman handed the box of pasta to Heather.

"Thank you." Heather kept her face downward.

"Are you okay? That's a pretty nasty cough."

"Yes, ma'am." Heather headed down the aisle toward the cash register.

"I don't mean to be nosey . . ." the woman said.

Heather stopped but didn't turn around.

"Forgive me. You should see a doctor about that cough, if you haven't."

"I plan to."

"Be sure the doctor checks you over really well," the woman shouted down the aisle. "I know you're young, but you never know."

"Yes." Heather turned. "Thank yo—"

The woman disappeared around the corner. The faint aroma of chocolate tickled Heather's nose.

Chapter Four

JJ, sitting in the driver's seat of his SUV, in front of his old house, waved at his six-year-old son bounding down the sidewalk from the front door. JJ's stoic ex-wife followed behind.

Zac climbed into the backseat. "Guess what, Daddy?"

"What, buddy?"

"Mommy's taking me to the movies next Sunday."

"That'll be awesome."

Corrin leaned in the car and kissed Zac on the head. "See you in two days."

JJ looked around. "Where's Amelia?" He wasn't accepting any more excuses.

"Inside. She has a slumber party tonight."

He huffed. Enough was enough. "What time is that over? I'll pick her up."

"She's not coming over to your apartment this weekend."

"Uh, no! That's not the arrangement. I agreed to moving out and the divorce if I get the kids every weekend. I was flexible in the beginning, but this has to stop. Six months is long enough to keep her from me, don't you think?"

"She's busy."

He should go in the house and tell Amelia she was coming no matter what. He had a right to see his daughter. Maybe he should tell her she couldn't go to the slumber party.

Corrin threw up her hands. "It hasn't been six months. You saw her at Thanksgiving and Christmas."

"Really? You think that's—"

Corrin glanced at Zac. "This isn't the right time to discuss this."

JJ handed his phone to his son. "Play a game or something."

He stepped outside and joined Corrin on the sidewalk. "What? You think I shouldn't be angry? That two holidays make up for the rest of it? She didn't even talk to me."

Corrin rolled her eyes. "That's not my fault. You know she wants nothing to do with you right now."

No matter how many times Corrin reminded him, it felt like being hit by a two-by-four. "I know I've made mistakes, but how am I going to fix things when you aren't making Amelia come over? She's fifteen. She doesn't get a choice."

"Like always, it's about you and what you want, not what's best for her." She shook her head. "You'll never change."

Change? What did he need to change? He'd lost nearly everything, and he'd been the reasonable one. He'd given Corrin the house, the cars, the weekdays with the kids, more alimony than mandated, and practically everything she'd asked for in the divorce, including his dog.

Amelia *would* start coming to his house every weekend. The longer he let her stay away, the further apart they'd grow. "I will give her this last weekend, but from now on I will drop her off and pick her up when she has places to go on the weekend. I get that she's not my biggest fan right now, but I love her and I miss her."

Corrin crossed her arms. "I know you love Amelia, but this is really hard on her. She never expected to find her dad . . ." She looked toward Amelia's second-story bedroom window.

JJ followed her gaze. Guilt ripped in his chest. No child should come home to find her dad with another woman. His daughter peeked out from behind the curtain. He waved at her, but she walked away.

"I know I screwed up." He reached into the front pocket of his dress shirt and pulled out a pack of cigarettes, then popped one into his mouth and lit it. "I'll spend my life making it up to you all."

"Maybe if you'd stop dating, she could see how sorry you are."

What? No. He wasn't married anymore. He could see whomever he wanted whenever he wanted. Corrin wouldn't control him. He didn't flaunt those women in his kids' faces. There was no way they could even know he went on dates from time to time.

"What makes you think I'm dating?"

"You always have someone."

"There's no one. I don't have time to date."

"Yeah, that's right. Just time for hooking up." She put her hands on her hips and shook her head.

"We're divorced. I can do whatever I want."

"The problem is, you had the same sentiment when we were married."

Even mad Corrin was gorgeous. Her blond hair hid any grays, and at almost forty she had fewer wrinkles than some thirty-year-olds. How had he, an average pimply-faced seventeen-year-old, won the affections of her all those years ago? They'd had wonderful years together, and he'd screwed it up.

"Corrin, I'm sorry. You're incredible. I'm the idiot." He touched her elbow.

She stepped back. "There's nothing you can do to change it now." She waved to Zac. "I'll talk to Amelia. I'll get her to come next week."

"Thank you."

She nodded, then marched into the house and shut the door. From Amelia's bedroom window, the curtain drew back again, but JJ couldn't see Amelia. Hoping she could see him, he held up his thumb, pointer finger, and pinkie to sign *I love you*. The curtains closed.

Christmas music traveled from the living room into the kitchen, where Heather stood at the sink rinsing flour off her hands. The smell of sugar cookies mingled with a cinnamon-scented candle wafted past Heather.

Her mother, wearing a red apron with a Christmas tree on it, came behind Heather and tickled her sides. "Dad's getting the rest of the decorations down from the attic while we finish up the cookies."

"We don't have to do this." Heather laughed. "It's crazy and it's January. Christmas was over nearly a month ago."

"That doesn't matter to me. Christmas was always your favorite holiday, and I haven't spent one with you in forever. We are doing this."

"You're the boss."

She tucked her arm into the crook of her mother's, and they walked arm in arm to the kitchen table, where another couple dozen Christmas-shaped sugar and gingerbread cookies waited for them to decorate.

Her mother handed her one and patted her hand. "I've missed this."

"Me too." Heather reached across the table for the red icing bag and lined the gingerbread boy's pants red while her mind traveled back in time to a Christmas long ago. Six-year-old Heather sat upon the chair holding up a gingerbread cookie decorated with gumdrop buttons, chocolate chip eyes, and a licorice mouth. She'd used chocolate icing for the nose and other details.

"Perfect." Young Heather placed it on the tray with the other ones she'd decorated. "My gingerbread kids!" She pointed to each one. "One, two, three, four, five, six, seven, eight, nine, ten, eleven, twelve."

Standing behind her, her daddy touched her shoulder. "That's quite a crew you got there. They look delicious." He reached toward the boy with green buttons.

She smacked his hand. "You can't eat them. They're my children."

"Aw, come on, Hethie." He sniffed over the plate. "Just one."

"No way." She pulled the plate toward her. "I see I have to protect you little guys and gals."

"What a good little mother you will be one day." Her mother's voice echoed through the kitchen.

The response from the girl whispered into thirty-five-year-old Heather's ears. "I can't wait."

"What was that, dear?" her mom asked.

The memory vanished.

Heather shook her head, bringing her thoughts back to the present. "What?"

"You said something about you can't wait."

Had Heather said that out loud?

Her father, wearing a Santa hat, popped his head around the corner from the hallway. "Everything's down. Hop to it. Let's do this!"

Her mother hopped like a bunny to the kitchen entryway and kissed him. "Wrong holiday, dear."

Heather laughed. "You guys haven't changed a bit."

Her dad winked, then motioned for her to come over. "This place isn't going to deck the halls by itself. You going to join us?"

She grinned. Her adult life had been a lot different from her childhood. Thank goodness she was here now.

Heather put a different Christmas CD in the living room stereo, then joined her parents at the tree in front of the big picture window. The three of them stood hand in hand looking at it.

"Not too shabby," her dad said. "Looks even better than last month. We make quite a team."

"That we do." Her mom kissed him on the cheek.

He took her mom's hand and spun her around. "You are the most beautiful woman in the world, Mrs. Cole."

"Why thank you. And you aren't too bad yourself."

Warmth filled Heather's heart. She'd forgotten love like that existed.

"I want one of those cookies you two made." Her dad strode toward the kitchen. "They smell delicious."

He came out with a gingerbread cookie. "Can I eat this one?"

Her mother laughed. "Why are you asking?"

"Because I don't want to get scolded by Heather for eating one of her children. Remember how upset she used to get with me."

"Dad, I was six."

"You'd have thought I'd murdered that little cookie by how upset you got after I—"

"You bit his head off right in front of me!"

He widened his eyes. "That's why I always ask."

"Go ahead, Dad. You can eat it."

"Are you sure?" He raised an eyebrow.

"Good grief." Her mother yanked the cookie out of his hand and bit the head off.

The three of them burst into laughter. Heather's

stomach had not hurt this much in a good way for longer than she could remember.

She'd hate to tell them goodbye next week.

"Hey, JJ," a woman said as he walked into the coffeehouse a few shops down from his physical therapy office.

Anna stood at the counter, waving. He returned the gesture, then stepped in line behind her. "Good morning. You getting coffee?"

"Heavens no. I hate the stuff. I'm getting hot chocolate. This is the only place I've found that even comes close to my family's secret recipe."

JJ smiled. "Is that right?"

"Mine's the best, but this will do in a pinch. I'll have to bring you a cup of mine sometime. Do you like hot chocolate?"

"I haven't had one since I was a kid, but I liked it then."

"What do you like to get here?"

"I like a boring, plain coffee with cream and sugar. I need it for these early mornings. I think you're my first patient today."

"Wonderful." The barista handed Anna her drink, then she turned to JJ. "Do you have time to come sit with me after you get your coffee, and we can chat?"

He looked at his phone. "Sure. I've got a good ten minutes or so."

He ordered his drink and joined her on the couch in front of the fireplace. "How are you today, Ms.

Anna?"

"Doing well. My hip's a little sore, but I know that's nothing the good doctor can't fix."

He winked. "I try. Do you think the exercises are too much? I could have you do simpler ones and use the less-tension bands."

"Perhaps. I trust your judgement." She patted his leg. "Tell me. Did you and Amelia make it out to the batting cages?"

"No. She wasn't up for it. She still says she isn't going to play."

"What else could you two do together?" She scratched her head. "What about a movie? Anything out that you'd both like?"

"There probably is."

"What about basketball? I hear that's big in Indiana."

"She doesn't play, but she does like watching the high school team. I'm pretty sure she has season student tickets. I wouldn't be able to sit with her."

Why was Anna worried about helping him with Amelia? The other day they'd spent most of her session talking about his daughter. She'd been the one to suggest he take Amelia to the batting cages.

"A concert?"

"I like that idea." He set his cup on the coffee table in front of him and pulled out his phone. "I wonder if anyone's playing this weekend."

He scrolled through the list of events in the nearby smaller cities and then to Indianapolis, the closest metropolis within an hour and a half. "I don't believe it. Her favorite band is playing Friday night. I wonder if Corrin would keep Zac so I could take her."

"That sounds like a lot of fun."

"Excuse me. I'm going to go call Corrin."

She nodded while taking a sip from her cup.

He went outside and called. "Hey, do you think Amelia would want to go to that New Vibe concert with me on Friday?"

"I'm sorry, but one of her friends already asked her last night. I was going to tell you later. Tara's parents got a hotel, and they're going to make a weekend of it."

He lowered his chin. "She's not coming over again? What if I say she can't go with Tara and she's going with me?"

"Like that will go over well."

"Then she needs to go to dinner with me this week. I'm fed up. I want to see her."

"I know you do. She's got nothing going on tomorrow. I'll let her know you'll pick her up."

"Thanks." He hung up and trudged back inside to the couch.

"By the look on your face, I guess it's a no-go for the concert."

"No, but I'm taking her out to dinner tomorrow."

"That's good."

"She won't talk to me."

"How do you know that?"

"She hasn't spoken more than two sentences to me since . . ." He shook his head. "I'd rather sit in silence with her than not be with her at all."

"That's a start. Be there. Be present. And don't give up."

"I plan on it. I don't know that she'll ever forgive

me."

"Keep at it. She'll get there eventually."

He nodded. "I hope."

Chapter Five

Heather, sitting at the kitchen table, took a sip of hot chocolate and stared out the window at the sunrise. The warmth eased the cough tickling her throat. A cardinal landed on the snowy picnic table. He sang a little song, then flew off. The frozen creek behind the chain-link fence reminded her of the first time she'd met twelve-year-old J. J. Jones. She'd thought he was crazy walking along the ice-covered water. She'd warned him he'd fall through. He didn't listen of course, and he did fall in ankle deep when the ice cracked. That was the start of their friendship.

She took another sip and looked over to the swing set where she and JJ had buried a time capsule underneath it. They'd filled it with photos, their favorite childhood toys, and notes of their dreams and wishes to their future selves. Not one of hers had come true.

"Morning, dear. You're up early." Her father kissed the top of her head.

"I'm going to go to the doctor today for this cough and chest pain."

"Bronchitis? Pneumonia?"

"That's what I'm thinking." She hoped that was all it was, but she was still coughing up blood.

"Do you want us to go with you?"

"No. You guys have work. I'm fine. It's no big deal. I need to get on an antibiotic."

"Mum's still the word about you being here, right?"

"Yes, please."

"Are you ready to talk yet?"

She exhaled. "Not yet."

"Are you sure? I'm worried."

She nodded.

Swinging her legs off the end of the exam table, Heather waited for the doctor to return. She studied the eye chart. Perfect vision. She read the poster on type II diabetes and the weight chart. According to it, she was twenty pounds under her healthy weight. She blew out a breath. What was taking the doctor so long? She started counting the tiles on the floor, when someone knocked on the door and opened it.

Dr. Edwards entered and took a seat on the stool in front of Heather.

"Your bloodwork showed that your red and white blood cells, along with your platelets, are low. The x-ray showed that you do have pneumonia, but you also have several suspicious masses on your lungs and in your right shoulder."

Her heart dropped into her stomach. What did that mean? Masses?

"Heather, I'm sending you over to Dr. Sutter. She's an excellent oncologist in Indianapolis. We set up an appointment with her today at two. She will do further testing to investigate, but from all the symptoms you've described, I suspect it may be cancer."

She held her breath. Cancer? No. That wasn't possible.

"I thought you said I have pneumonia."

"You do. Which is a common infection in lung cancer patients."

Lung cancer? She hadn't smoked a day in her life. She wouldn't. She'd watched both her grandparents die from emphysema. This made no sense.

"Could you be wrong?"

"I hope I am. Go see Dr. Sutter. She's the best. She'll run all the necessary tests."

"I'm moving next week. Should I wait until I get there?"

"No. We are putting a rush on your tests and will know something in the next day or two."

A rush. Why?

"Where are you moving?"

"Georgia."

"Leave your new address with us. I will do research and get you set up with doctors there."

"I don't have a place yet."

"Do you have a support system there?"

Why was he talking like this? As if he'd already given her the diagnosis?

She shook her head no.

"Is this a necessary move, or could you hold it

off for a bit, at least until we know what we are dealing with?"

She had less than three weeks until Keith would have access to a phone. Sissy had promised not to say anything, but what if she slipped or what if people in town recognized her?

"The move is necessary, and I need to go as soon as possible."

"Okay, let's see what the tests say and then go from there. I will help you get all set with doctors in Georgia if it comes to that."

Two guys ran past Amelia in the loud, crowded high school hallway, and a third bumped into her.

"Sorry." He started to walk off, but stopped when his sparkling blue eyes meet hers. He ran his hand through his brown surfer-style hair, then touched her arm. "You all right?"

Butterflies raced inside her stomach. Mark Turnglass, captain of the baseball team, cutest and most popular boy in school was talking to her. "I'm good. Thanks."

His eyes lit up, and he pointed at her. "You're Amelia Jones. You play softball, right?"

He knew who she was! She suppressed a scream. "No. I mean yes, I'm Amelia Jones, but I don't play softball anymore."

"That's too bad. Coach has us conditioning with the girls on Thursdays. That's where I'm headed. Would have been nice to hang out."

Her heart leapt. He wanted to hang out with her?

43

"You played last year for Danburg Middle School, right?"

She nodded. How did he know? He was a junior. She was a freshman.

"You're the best pitcher around since, like, when Heather Cole played ages ago. She's a legend. Have you heard of her? Her senior year she pitched Danburg to an undefeated season by throwing three no hitters and shut out every opponent. She went to IU on a full-ride scholarship."

Had he really compared her to Heather Cole? Had her parents somehow put him up to it? "Yeah, I've heard of her. You can't play ball and not know who she is."

"It's a bummer you aren't playing. The team could really use you."

Despite the compliment and Mark's incredible smile, he couldn't convince her. "Yeah, I don't think I'm going to play. There are lots of great pitchers and other players too. I think they'll have a decent season."

"Cool." He nodded. "I guess I better go. Catch you later."

"Later."

He walked down the hallway toward the gym at the end of the building, and she headed the opposite direction to the front doors. She swallowed hard and shook out her excitement through her fingers.

"Hey, Amelia."

She turned to look at him, and he threw a baseball toward her. She caught it.

"Why don't you come join us anyway? You don't have to practice. Sit in the stands, and we can

44

talk after. I could give you a ride home."

She smiled. Of course she'd stay. She had nothing to do this evening besides a little homework. Her mom said she had to get her room cleaned before the concert tomorrow, but that wouldn't take anytime. She could do that after dinner with her da— Shoot! Her heart sank. Dinner with her dad. He'd be there any minute.

"I can't. My dad's picking me up, and he has this whole evening planned."

Mark nodded. "Have fun. We can do something another time." He pointed toward the gym. "I really got to go."

She waved bye as he walked into the gym. She remained watching even after he'd gone inside.

Mark Turnglass!

He stuck his head around the opened door. "Hey, keep that ball. Okay?"

"Thanks."

He disappeared behind the gym doors again. She looked down. Her heart boomed. A phone number? *Call me.* Really? He wanted her to call him? She hugged the ball. The number didn't need to be written with a permanent marker. It was already permanently stored in her mind.

With a little skip to her step, she exited the school and spotted her dad parked at the curb. Even being forced to spend dinner with him couldn't ruin her good mood. She opened the door and raised her eyes to say hello.

"What's the ball about? Are you going to play baseball instead of softball?"

"No." She opened her backpack and shoved it in.

"It's nothing. Where are we going?"

"How about Mexican? I know you love it."

"Sure. Whatever you want."

"How was school?"

"Fine."

"Do you have any projects or big tests coming up?"

"No."

She was wrong. Being in his presence ruined any good vibes she had going. She put her earbuds in and played the first song on her playlist. She cranked it up and stared out the window.

Her dad yanked her left earbud from her ear, and she whipped her head in his direction and glared at him.

"I was talking to you. That's rude."

Her insides seethed. She should have stood him up and stayed to watch Mark practice.

She jerked the other earbud out. "I had a test in geometry today. One in biology tomorrow. And a book project due next week on *The Hunger Games*. I ate Frosted Flakes for breakfast and drank juice. I had school pizza for lunch, which, yes, is gross. A boy flirted with me and gave me his number. And I don't want to be here right now. Anything else you want to know?"

Her dad clutched the steering wheel and stared out the window. A vein in his neck popped up and down while he drove the rest of the way to the restaurant. She didn't care if he was mad. Now she wouldn't have to talk to him. She looked down at her phone and checked her friends' statuses on social media.

A few minutes later, he parked the car and got out. He hustled to the other side to open her door like he used to when they went on father-daughter dates. She opened the door herself and slammed it. She wouldn't give him the pleasure to act like things were still the same.

They made their way inside, and the thirty-something Hispanic woman smiled. "Good evening. Is it the two of you?"

"Yes," her dad said.

"Give me a minute. I'll get you a table ready."

He gestured toward the chairs in the waiting section, and Amelia sat first, then he took the spot next to her.

"JJ, is that you?" A blond woman touched his arm.

Who was she? One of his flings? She looked his type. Tall, beautiful, blond, and not Amelia's mom.

"Hello, Ms. Shoots. How's Tara doing?"

"She's doing good. She loves that purple monkey. She sleeps with it and carries it around everywhere. She says she has to do her exercises because Dr. Jones says to." The woman smiled at Amelia. "Who's this?"

"This is my daughter, Amelia."

Amelia gave the woman the phoniest smile she could muster.

"Aren't you gorgeous."

"Thanks."

"You look like your dad."

No one had ever told Amelia that. This woman was full of it.

The woman ran her hand up and down his arm.

47

Who did she think she was?

"It's good to see you take care of yourself and stop long enough to get a bite to eat."

"Yep. I'm spending time with my daughter."

"You guys have fun." She waved, then stepped out the door.

Amelia's dad blew out a breath and rolled his neck.

"Who was she?"

"My patient's mom."

"Did you date her? She seemed pretty cozy with you."

"No."

"Then why were her hands all over you?"

"That's how she is."

"You don't mind though, do you?"

"Of course I mind. I haven't given her any reason to think I'm available. Yet, she . . ." He shook his head. "You know what. I'm not dating anyone. I don't want to. I'm not interested. I don't have to explain myself."

"But you do. I don't believe anything you say. I never will."

"I'm sorry for that."

"How could you?" She tugged at her bottom lip.

"I was dumb."

"That's obvious. What were you thinking?"

"I wasn't."

"You don't care about anyone but yourself."

The hostess, holding two menus, stepped in front of them. "Your table's ready."

Thank goodness. Amelia had nothing more to say to him.

Chapter Six

Sitting in a chair across from Dr. Sutter's desk, Heather waited and read the diplomas, certificates, and awards from the doctor's years as an oncologist.

She dug her nails into her clutched fist. There had to be a mistake.

Not likely. Before running more tests, Dr. Sutter had speculated the same as Dr. Edwards. Today Heather would find out.

She stared at her crossed feet rocking back and forth. She was only thirty-five and still had a lifetime to live. She pictured herself holding a little brown-haired girl in her lap. Abi. She'd loved the name as long as she could remember. Every doll, every imaginary friend, every fish, every child she'd dreamed of having someday held the name.

She stood, then paced.

A knock pounded on the door, and her heart sped. The female doctor—face stoic—entered and held her hand out for Heather to take. "Morning. Please take a seat."

Heather returned to her chair, and the doctor took

her place behind her desk.

"I have bad news."

Her stomach dropped.

"You have a very aggressive lung cancer. We also found cancer in your lymph nodes and your right shoulder. The spots found on your back did come back as melanoma. At this point it is hard to tell whether it began as skin cancer and then spread or whether it began in one of the other locations. My best guess is that it started as melanoma and then spread to the lungs, lymph nodes, then the shoulder. You have stage four cancer, and it *is* progressing rapidly. The team and I agree that surgery, radiation, and chemo will not be effective. The cancer will continue to spread quickly."

"Are you saying there is nothing you can do?"

"I'm afraid so."

Her heart pounded hard, and her nerves stung. "How long?"

Dr. Sutter raised an eyebrow. "I don't like to give numbers, but three months. Possibly six. Maybe more."

The doctor continued to talk, but Heather didn't hear her. Why was this happening? She had so many things she'd wanted to do now that she was free of Keith. Instead of an adventure list, she'd write a bucket list. It wasn't right. Why her? Hadn't she been through enough? Why now?

Why not me?

She sat up straight. She'd fight this. Keith took her dignity away. She wouldn't let cancer take it away too.

JJ walked into his office carrying a cup of coffee. String and brass instruments gently played through the speakers, and Missy sat at the reception desk, focused on typing. He waved in her direction, but she didn't look up.

He leaned over the front of the desk toward her. "Boo."

She jumped. "You scared me."

He winked, then pointed upward to the ceiling speakers. "No top-hits radio today? What's this?"

Missy smiled. "Classical music. My anxiety is out the roof. It helps soothe my soul. I thought it could help your patients relax too."

"Or fall asleep from boredom." He laughed.

"No." Her face lit up. "It's relaxing."

"You're right. It is." He put his coffee on the desk and slid off his gloves, then put them in his coat pocket. "Things okay?"

"Yeah. It's Jake. Everyone keeps telling me we aren't right for each other, but I can't give up on the guy. He drives me crazy, but I love him regardless."

"I wish I could give you words of wisdom, but we both know I'm not the right guy to be giving any kind of advice. Be careful, okay?"

"I will."

He took off his jacket and hung it on the coat tree in the front corner of the waiting room, then returned to the reception desk. He clapped his hands and rubbed them together. "What's on the schedule for today? I know you called me in early for a last-minute appointment."

"Yes, Dr. Sutter said it was important that the patient get in ASAP. It's a pretty easy day otherwise."

She handed him the new patient folder, and he flipped it open.

Heather Meyers. A vision of a sixteen-year-old, brown-haired, green-eyed beauty flashed through his memory. Could it be the same Heather? Probably not. No telling where the marines had Keith stationed now.

He closed the file and looked at the clock—6:30. "I'm heading back to my office. Let me know when Mrs. Meyers arrives."

"Sure thing."

He walked to his office at the back right corner of the physical therapy room and shut the door. He sat at his desk and scanned the file. *Heather Meyers. Lung cancer. Stage 4. Metastasized to right shoulder. Age thirty-five. Birthdate—*

His stomach dropped, as if he'd driven over a steep hill too fast. The same name and birthdate? Too coincidental.

He dropped the folder to his lap. Was Heather back?

He raked his hands through his hair. Cancer. She was too young. When he saw stage 4 cancer patients, all he could do was keep them comfortable until the end.

This had to be another woman.

Closing his eyes, he drew in a deep breath and imagined what Heather's life probably looked like. She'd chase her little boy and girl on a beach while her teenage sons stood in the ocean throwing the football back and forth. From behind, Keith would wrap his arms around her waist and kiss her neck.

JJ smiled. Heather deserved that kind of happiness.

The buzz from the receptionist startled him. "Mrs. Meyers is here."

"Thank you. I'll be right out."

He opened his eyes. *Don't let it be Heather Cole.*

Taking in a deep breath, he opened the office door and peeked out at the front desk. Missy smiled and motioned with her head toward his new patient in the waiting area across from the front door. Her pale, skinny arm sat on the armrest, but the rest of her body hid behind the wall that separated the waiting area from the PT room.

His heart lurched inside his chest.

Missy frowned and wrinkled her eyebrows at the computer screen. "Mrs. Meyers, it appears there's a problem with your insurance. Can I see your card again?"

The woman grabbed ahold of the armrest and struggled to pull herself up. "Sure." The deep, raspy voice didn't sound familiar. Thank goodness.

She turned the corner. Long, wavy brown hair framed her frail face, and her green eyes meet his. The black purse slipped from her hand and crashed on the floor.

His heart stopped.

Heather struggled to hold herself upright as another cough shook her body. She lost her balance, but the physical therapist hurried and caught her by the elbow, his eyes looking deep into hers. A familiar jolt of electricity coursed through her elbow into the rest of her body.

Could it be?

He was taller, more lean and muscular, and small wrinkles sat at the corners of his eyes, but not much else had changed. He still wore his blond hair in a crewcut, his skin was still tan as if he lived near a beach, and his eyes . . . still dark blue and captivating. Heat rose to her cheeks.

Had Dr. Sutter mentioned his name? Heather had heard *physical therapy*, but she hadn't heard much else. Jones was a pretty common name. Even so, anytime she heard the last name she thought of him.

"JJ?"

"Heather."

Not taking his eyes off of her, he led her back to her chair.

He turned toward the receptionist. "What's the problem with the insurance?"

"TRICARE isn't recognizing her. I think I input a number incorrectly."

Heather's stomach knotted. Had Keith figured everything out?

Another painful cough tore through her. Black clouded her vision as JJ put her arm in the crook of his and helped her stand.

"Never mind the insurance. Don't charge her."

Heather didn't have the strength to refuse. She let him lead her to an office in the back of the large open room. He helped her into a chair, then he sat across from her behind a desk. A sharp jolt slammed through her eyes and pounded against her temples. She closed her eyes and rubbed her forehead. How fast it had all come on. Yesterday she had walked with no problem, and today she barely had the energy to stand. Only by God's providence had she'd been able to drive and make it inside the physical therapy office.

"Are the lights too bright? I can turn them down." He spoke in a hushed voice.

"No, they're fine. Thank you."

Opening her eyes, she stared at his hands tapping a pencil against his desk.

He cleared his throat. "So . . . it's been a long time. How've you been?"

Where to start? Once upon a time, she would have spilled all her secrets to him.

He laid the pencil down and shifted in his seat. "I can't believe you're here. I mean, here in my office as a patient with . . ." His chin dipped toward his chest. "I'm so sorry, Heather. This is terrible." Leaving his chair, he made his way toward her. "How are you doing pain-wise?"

He reached for her shoulder, but she jerked away.

He frowned.

No man had touched her since she'd married Keith. And only JJ before that. Her stomach flip-flopped. JJ was home to her too. But he'd broken her heart.

She stood and had to hold on to the armrest to keep her balance. Using the wall for support, she made her way to the door. "I can't do this."

A sharp cough brought her to her knees.

JJ's hand touched her back. "Heather?"

She gasped. "I . . . can't . . . breathe."

She coughed up a mouthful of blood, then collapsed onto her stomach. She didn't want him to see her like this. He needed to remember her as young and beautiful, not dying and lying in her own blood on the floor. She tried to put her hands next to her head to lift herself up, but she had no strength.

"Missy, call 911!"

JJ's words were the last she heard as darkness surrounded her.

Chapter Seven

JJ rubbed his arms to keep them warm. The paramedics lifted Heather's gurney into the ambulance. Two stayed inside with Heather, and the other two shut the door, then ran around to the driver and passenger doors. JJ wanted to be next to her, holding her hand, making sure she'd be all right, but it wasn't his place.

The lights swirled and the siren blared, then the ambulance sped out of the parking lot to the main road. It turned down another street, and he could no longer hear or see it.

He went back inside and grabbed the phone on the reception desk.

Shaking, he dialed the phone number he still had memorized.

"Hello," Heather's mother answered.

"Hello, Mrs. Cole." He swallowed the lump in his throat. "This is J—Dr. Jack Jones. Heather was in my office this morning and collapsed. We called the paramedics. She's being transported to Danburg Baptist Hospital."

"Okay. Um. Thank you." Click.

JJ stood frozen with the phone in his hand. Had that all really happened? Had Heather Cole . . . Meyers walked back into his life? No, it had to be a nightmare. How could such a sweet person be infected by such a toxic disease?

Missy took the phone from JJ and set it on the docking station. "Who is Heather Meyers, and why are you all out of sorts?"

"She was my neighbor when we were teenagers." The truth lay somewhere in that answer, but Heather was much more than that. "She's an old friend."

"Do you want to go to the hospital? I can call Ken in to handle your patients today."

Should he? God knew he wanted to check on Heather. Dr. Sutton had referred him, and he could help if the family had questions. But would she want him there? The whole situation was a little awkward. But this was Heather Co . . . Meyers, for goodness' sake, the girl he'd thought of every day of his life. If it were any other patient, he'd at least check on her.

His chest tightened. He had to make sure Heather was okay. He had to ask for forgiveness before . . . thinking the words was more than he could stand.

"Yes, please call Ken. I don't know if I'll be back in today. Anna has her last appointment this afternoon. I'd like to be the one to release her. Please see if she can reschedule for tomorrow."

Grabbing his coat, he ran into the blustery weather. He tilted his head upward, and thick snowflakes landed on his face. He closed his eyes. In his memory, fifteen-year-old Heather smiled with a twinkle in her green eyes. With outstretched arms, she spun while the snow fell on her.

He opened his eyes and balled his fist. He deserved her fate. She didn't.

"Heather, baby, what happened?" Her mother darted through the hospital room door and ran to her bedside. "Dad's on the way."

Smiling beneath the oxygen tube draped under her nose, Heather hoped to reassure her mom until her dad arrived. They would need each other to lean on. She'd kept all her secrets from them long enough. It was time she told them everything. "I'm okay."

"You collapsed at a doctor's office. You aren't okay."

Avoiding eye contact, Heather wiggled her toes under the white hospital sheets. "I probably didn't eat enough." A cough ripped through her. "I haven't had much of an appetite since I've been sick. This pneumonia is kicking my butt."

"I can see that." Her mother kissed her forehead. "Are you feeling a little better now?"

"I'm weak but hanging in there."

Heather's oversized gown slipped down, exposing her right shoulder and back.

"It looks like your gown came untied. I'll get it." Her mother slid the gown up. "I'm worried about you, honey."

"I know, Mom."

Her mother froze, then pulled the gown down.

"Heather. What's this on your shoulder?"

As if moving slow would magically make the bruise disappear, Heather turned her head toward her exposed shoulder and pulled the gown over it. The large, fading yellow bruise looked better than she'd imagined.

"I tripped and fell down my steps a few weeks ago."

"It looks awful." Her mother tied the gown.

"It felt awful."

"I imagine so."

Heather chased down another cough with a sip of water. "Who told you I was here?"

"I don't know. A doctor. I didn't ask questions. I rushed to get here. Was it the doctor who diagnosed you with pneumonia?"

Heather shook her head.

"Is there something you aren't telling me? Everything isn't adding up."

Heather stared at the sheet. The word *cancer* sat on the tip of her tongue, but she couldn't say it yet. Once she spoke the words, it would make it all true.

JJ rushed through Danburg Baptist Hospital's doors to the information desk. "I'm looking for Heather Meyers."

"JJ?"

Heather's dad, all six foot five of him, stepped up to the desk.

"Yes, sir." JJ extended his hand.

Mr. Cole stared at it for a moment before he

shook it. "You're here to see my daughter?"

"Yes. She passed out in my office today. I wanted to check on her."

"Your office? You're the doctor who called?" Mr. Cole furrowed his brows. "Why would Heather come see you?"

"Dr. Sutter referred her to me."

"You're a physical therapist, correct?"

"Yes, sir."

"I didn't realize she'd changed doctors. What's going on? Why is she seeing you?"

JJ's stomach dropped. Her dad didn't know? JJ shouldn't be the one to tell him. "I can't discuss—"

"My daughter's been admitted to the hospital."

"I'm sorry. I can't discuss my patients."

"It must be bad if she went to see you."

"I don't think she knew it was me until she got there."

Mr. Cole's eyes widened. "Hmm, that makes sense. I'm going to go see her now. You can go ahead and leave. Mrs. Cole and I have everything under control. No reason for you to stay."

"Sir, with all due respect, she's still my patient, and I'd feel better if I could check on her. She hasn't been dismissed from my care yet."

"I don't think she'd want you as her physical therapist. Too much history there."

"I know I'm not her—or your—favorite person, but I can help Heather. I can be sure she has everything she needs while she's here, even get her another physical therapist if she wants, but I need to run everything by her."

"There are plenty of doctors and nurses here who

can take care of her. Thank you for trying to help, but I must honor what Heather would want, and she wouldn't want you here."

The words stung. "But—"

"Let her be."

JJ rubbed his forehead as he stared at Mr. Cole's shoes. If a boy treated Amelia like JJ had Heather, he would force the guy to leave too. But that was eighteen years ago. He wasn't still that stupid kid.

He was a doctor now, for heaven's sake. A six-foot-two, muscle-bound athlete, yet he still couldn't stand up to Mr. Cole.

"I'm worried about her." JJ pulled out his business card from his wallet. "Can you do me a favor? After she tells you what's going on, can you keep me in the loop?" He handed the card to Mr. Cole. "I know I made my mistakes, and I've regretted them every day of my life. I'd like to tell her that."

Mr. Cole nodded, then shook JJ's hand. "Is my baby girl okay?"

JJ shook his head no.

Chapter Eight

Scrambled eggs, grits, ham, toast, and peaches sat in front of Heather on the hospital over-the-bed table. The smell made Heather want to vomit, and the sight almost sent her over the edge.

"Are you going to eat any of your breakfast?" Her mother sat at the foot of the bed, rubbing Heather's legs.

"No. I'm not hungry."

"I wish you'd try."

Heather lifted a piece of toast and put it to her open lips, then set it back down. She couldn't do it. She placed a few fingers over her lips and shook her head. "I'm going to throw up if I eat it."

"Do you want me to see if the nurse can get you antinausea medicine?"

Heather nodded as the door to her hospital room opened and her dad entered, speaking in a gentle voice. "What kind of pain would you be in that you went to see JJ for help?"

Like a child caught with her hand in the cookie jar, her pulse pounded against her veins and her legs tensed. "How did you know?"

"He was here asking for your room number."

Her mother took her hand. "Talk to us."

"I don't know how to—"

The door opened again, and a nurse entered. "Good morning. I'm Sherry. I'm taking Betty's place." She checked Heather's IV bag and oxygen tubes. "Let me know if you need anything."

"Thank you."

"Can she get something for her nausea?" her mother asked.

Sherry nodded, then turned to leave.

"Excuse me," Heather's father said, "but when will a doctor be here to tell Heather what's going on?"

The nurse looked at Heather. Now would be the perfect time to try out her telepathy skills.

"The doctor will be by later today. For now, we're doing all we can to keep her comfortable."

"Comfortable? She needs answers." Her father's voice rose.

"I'm sorry, sir. That's all I can tell you right now."

Sherry left the room, and Heather's parents stared at her. "What's going on?" her father asked.

She took a deep breath, then blew it out slowly before letting the words escape. "I have cancer."

JJ entered his apartment door and walked up the stairs. At the top, he turned to the right into his empty dining room. After all these months, he still didn't have a table. He tossed his mail on the breakfast bar that faced the living room, started a log on the grate, and then plopped onto his old leather recliner next to the fireplace.

The silence made the room seem colder. He leaned forward and poked the fire. He needed someone to tell him everything was going to be okay. But it wouldn't. Heather was going to die, his daughter was going to keep on hating him, and he'd never be more than a cheater in the eyes of those who knew what he'd done.

He reached for his pack of cigarettes and stuck one in his mouth, then flicked his lighter. What was he doing?. He stopped the flame, then popped the cigarette out of his mouth and set it in the ash tray on the coffee table. He should be the one with lung cancer, not Heather. She'd probably never smoked a day in her life, unlike him, who'd taken his first puff the second Heather was out of his life. What an idiot. Addicted to them in a week.

He leaned his head against the chair and propped his legs on the coffee table. Back then, what a rebel he'd thought he was. Goody-two-shoes Heather wouldn't tell him what he should and shouldn't do anymore. He'd drink. He'd smoke. He'd finally get him some.

He shook his head. His selfish desires always drove him to wreck the good things in his life. He'd thrown Heather out to the trash because Corrin had given him what he wanted. After marrying Corrin a year later, he'd started running around on her. What a fool he'd been. Blamed his late nights on studying with his college buddies, when he'd really found a girl in his class to hook up with. And that was only the beginning.

He sprung from his chair, grabbed his cigarettes, and rushed to the kitchen, where he tossed the pack into the trash. He reached for a bottle of water from the refrigerator and took a swig.

Heather and Corrin deserved more than he had given them.

So did all those other women he'd used.

He took another drink.

If he could go back and fix it, he would. He would have chosen Heather. He was a good person back then, someone he was proud of . . . until *that* night. He should have fought for her. Instead he'd blown it. She'd lucked out though.

Look at who he'd become. Not worthy of Heather for sure.

No matter how many degrees he earned and titles he put in front of his name, he'd always be a loser in comparison to the marine-hero husband she married.

He closed the cap on the bottle and leaned his elbows against the counter.

But even if Heather wasn't married or sick, she would never want him. He'd known that the second he'd slept with Corrin. He'd made a choice in the heat of a moment and ruined everything with Heather. Back then she'd wanted a boy with views similar to hers. A boy who'd wait until their wedding night. A boy who loved Jesus. Unrealistic foolishness. But she'd found that and more in Keith.

And Keith had become the luckiest man on earth, marrying the most beautiful, loving, sweet girl. No one had ever compared to Heather.

JJ shook his head. Dumb fool. Why, back then, had he not realized how wonderful she was?

He raked his hand from the top of his head to the back of his neck.

And now she was going to die.

After three days in the hospital, Heather settled into bed under the floral comforter in her old bedroom. Shivering, she pulled the covers to her chin. Time was of the essence. She wouldn't be able to leave Danburg now.

A knock startled her.

"Can I come in?" Her mother cracked open the door and peeked in.

"Yes." Heather's voice croaked.

With a coffee mug in hand, her mom sat beside her on the bed. "I made you hot chocolate. Lots of whipped cream. You still like it like that?"

She wiggled into a seated position and reached out from under the covers. "Yes, thank you."

"Are you feeling okay?"

"I'm a little tired and will need help to the bathroom in a bit."

"Of course." With tears in her eyes, her mom ran a hand along Heather's forehead and through her hair. "I'm glad Keith agreed to let you visit. Imagine if you were going through this alone. Have you gotten ahold of him yet? Will they let him come home?"

Heather's heart dropped to her stomach. She had

so many skeletons in her closet, but she'd take them to her grave. No reason anyone needed to know the life she'd lived.

Her mother searched her eyes. She didn't need to know everything, just enough.

"I'm not going to tell Keith."

"Why not? That's not fair to him. Even if you're afraid it will distract him over there, he needs to know, sweetheart."

Heather cleared her throat. "He doesn't know I'm here."

"I thought—"

"I left him." One skeleton removed.

"Why?"

"I've had enough."

"Of what?"

"I . . . he . . ." Heather shook her head.

"It's okay. You can tell."

Unable to look at her mom, she stared at the tan carpet. As a child she'd pretended it was quicksand. How ironic. Back then she never could have imagined what being trapped felt like. After marrying Keith, she'd learned fast.

"He thinks his healthy, obedient wife is waiting at home. And I plan to keep it that way."

"What happened?"

"He defiled our marriage."

"He cheated on you?"

Heather nodded. "And more, but I'm not ready to talk about it."

Her mother looked at her shoulder, then widened her eyes. "That bruise, your fall. Did he hurt you?"

Heather barely nodded. "I was going to tell you

68

guys the day I found out I had . . ." Her heart ached. "I was ready to leave. Start over." She lifted her gaze to her mother. "Come to find out, I'm here to finish my life."

Oh my goodness. I'm dying.

A tear slid down her check. She wiped it away.

Her mother took the mug and set it on the nightstand, then wrapped her arms around her. The gesture broke the dam of pent-up emotions. Heather hadn't cried in years. Hadn't felt for longer. She collapsed into her mother's arms and moaned through her tears as the pain of her life washed over her.

Chapter Nine

JJ's black Mustang slid across the icy parking lot of his medical center. Days like these made him ready to trade in the old car for an SUV, but Corrin's car payment, the house, spousal and child support, and other bills he'd agreed to pay, along with his apartment, made him glad he'd paid off the sports car. Besides, in the spring, he'd rather teach Amelia to drive in a car than a tank, if she'd let him.

Although he wished time could stop and she wouldn't grow another day older. Maybe a Hummer was the better idea. Well, better than rolling her in bubble wrap or never letting her leave the house. How could she be old enough for her permit? She was growing up way too fast. Another reason he needed to make things right with her.

Stepping out of the car, he slipped on a patch of ice, but a hand caught him by the elbow. "Thanks." He looked up at . . . Heather's dad?

Mr. Cole furrowed his brows. "Son, I owe you an apology for the other day."

"No, you don't. I understand now. I have a

daughter. If anyone treated her the way—"

"Never mind that. That was almost twenty years ago." Tears filled his eyes. "Heather finally told us about the cancer. I don't know how much longer . . ." He took in a deep breath. "It's too late for chemo or surgery. One day she thinks she's got a cold she can't kick, and the next day she finds out she's got a few months to live."

JJ swallowed hard. He had never seen such anguish on a man's face. He could only imagine how he'd feel if it were Zac or Amelia with cancer. He placed his hands on Mr. Cole's shoulder. "This whole thing sucks. I mean, stinks."

"Believe me, son—I've thought worse words than that over the last few days."

JJ looked through his driver's-side window and spotted the pack of cigarettes sitting in the cup holder. He'd stopped all of three days. He was stopping again right now. He noticed his gloves on the passenger seat and realized how cold his hands had become. He slid them into his pockets. "Mr. Cole, do you want to go into my office and talk?"

"No, I came by to ask if you'd still take Heather on as a patient. Dr. Sutter highly recommends you. She says you're the only PT in the area with the specialty credentials. Yesterday, when we took Heather the seventy-eight miles to Indianapolis to see Dr. Sutter, Heather collapsed. She can't handle traveling there again in her fragile state. Dr. Sutter has offered to see her here in Danburg instead of us having to go up north. We decided it wouldn't be good for Heather to travel that far several times a week."

"Sir, I'd do anything for Heather."

Mr. Cole rubbed the back of his neck. "Things have gotten worse. She can't even move her shoulder without pain, and we . . . have to carry her everywhere because she's too weak to stand."

JJ lowered his chin to his chest.

"Can you come by the house tonight? We're hiring a live-in nurse, and I'd like you to meet with her to plan."

"A hospice nurse?"

"Yes."

JJ lifted his head forward. He had walked away from Heather all those years ago, but now he'd be there for her. Now he'd help her build a little strength and hopefully alleviate some pain in her final days. "You convince her, and I'll be there tonight after work."

"Six o'clock. Nancy will have dinner ready."

Was this what Heather's life amounted to? A pitiful bag of bones carried from room to room? As if she were a china doll who could break at the slightest bump, her dad laid her on the brown suede couch. He covered her with a white-and-purple crocheted blanket, turned on the TV, and handed her the remote before walking toward the kitchen.

"Dinner smells good. What are you making?" he asked her mother.

Heather didn't hear the answer, but the smell made her want to throw up. Everything made her sick these days, and nothing stayed down.

Keith would've been happy with how thin she'd become. She swallowed down a bitter taste in her mouth. She didn't have to worry about him anymore. She'd be dead before he returned to the States.

The doorbell rang, and she jumped, pain searing her shoulder. She held her breath until the pain subsided.

Her father opened the door and stepped outside. "Thank you for coming."

Heather clicked through the channels, but nothing looked good. She picked up her mother's book from the end table. Romance. She'd stopped believing in that years ago. Give her a good suspense. Or a fantasy to give her a bit of vicarious adventure.

A blast of cold air raced in. She tucked the covers around her and started to read.

"Heather. We have company."

She kept the book in front of her face like a protesting six-year-old. She'd told her parents she didn't want to hire a nurse. No one needed to come to her aid or rack up medical bills. Let the cancer take her.

Her father pulled the book down and stepped to the side. "Heather, look who's come to see you."

JJ, grinning, took wide steps toward her, then raised one hand.

The lights from the rotating ceiling fan danced in his eyes. Her lips parted. She didn't care how good he looked in that gray button-up shirt that fit him a little tight across his . . . muscular . . . arms and chest. And it didn't matter how good and familiar he smelled either. She swallowed. She didn't want him there. She inhaled the hint of redwood—the first smell in weeks that hadn't made her ill. Her heart fluttered and her nerve endings tingled.

He winked at her, and her insides screamed like a schoolgirl with a crush. He'd always had this effect on her.

No. Stop it. You don't want him here seeing you like this.

Shoot, why had she refused to let her mother help her shower that morning? Heather slicked her wild strands of hair back toward her ponytail. She probably looked like a grease mop while he looked like a runway model.

"What is he doing here?"

"Your mother and I have been talking, and we agree that you should work with JJ. He can help ease your pain and build your strength."

"I agreed to the nurse to lessen the burden on you and Mom, but I'll live with the —"

A cough seized her, and agony took hold of her lungs and shoulder. Her father held her up as she swallowed hard. This was her life—unable to cough without help. "I'm okay now."

"Let JJ help you. Please." Her father looked in her eyes.

This had to be unbearable for her parents. She tucked her hands underneath her. She could work with him for them. Forget how uncomfortable it would be for her.

The doorbell rang, and her mother came out of the kitchen to answer it.

JJ cleared his throat. "Should we discuss this

with Keith?"

"He's on deployment." Heather looked down at the blanket.

"Can you at least talk to him?"

She shook her head.

"Heather, JJ's the best, and you deserve the best," her father said.

"Of course you do, my dear," said a gray-haired woman who stood next to her mom and dad.

JJ whipped his head around.

The woman smiled at him. "Hello, JJ. Long time no see."

With furrowed brows, JJ pointed toward the woman. "You? Well, how about that? How's your hip doing?"

"Good as new, thanks to you." She knocked on her hip.

Heather's father cleared his throat. "You know each other?"

"I saw JJ for a few sessions, but not to worry. He really is as good as they say. We made quite a team getting this old girl fit as a fiddle." She held her hand out to Heather and kept hold of it as she spoke. "I'm Anna Ingram, your hospice nurse." She leaned in toward Heather. The scent of chocolate surrounded her. "I see you've meet JJ. We are going to come up with a plan to alleviate your pain and let you live to the fullest. But it's up to you to enjoy what life you have left." She patted the top of Heather's hand. "Will you let us help you?"

Enjoy life? That seemed impossible. She had so little time.

Heather glanced back and forth at her parents'

downcast faces. Her mother attempted a smile, but Heather could read through it. Heather sat up straight. She'd fought through hell and come out of it. She wouldn't give up now.

She nodded.

Chapter Ten

JJ plopped on his couch, pushed off his boots, and opened his laptop. He knew his field backward and forward, but finding the right technique for Heather would take research. Anna had made it sound like the two of them could not only alleviate Heather's pain but also help her live longer.

"Daddy?"

Amelia's voice startled him, and he looked up at her standing at the loft railing from her bedroom into his apartment living room below. She hadn't spoken to him all night until then, and to hear her call him *Daddy* melted his heart. Although, he was pretty sure she wanted something.

"Yes, sweetie."

"Can Susan come over tomorrow? You told me she could a few weeks ago."

There it was. But he'd take it. She was talking to him.

"Sure, but I have to go see a patient midafternoon. Can you two watch Zac for me?"

"Yes. Thank you."

"Why don't you come watch TV with me?"

Huffing, she came down the stairs. She sat next to him, picked up the remote control, and flipped through the channels.

More silent treatment, but he'd take it too. At least she'd sat down.

He placed his hand on Amelia's knee. "I'm glad you came again this weekend. I've missed you."

She glanced at the computer. "Lung cancer? What are you doing?"

"One of my patients found out she has it. I'm trying to find techniques to help her."

"I see. I hope you can help her."

"Me too."

"Dad, do you think I'm pretty?"

JJ closed his laptop and sat up straighter. "Of course I do. Why?"

"There's this boy at school."

He playfully covered his ears. "I don't want to hear this. Boys are bad news. Believe me—I know."

She crossed her arms and let out an exaggerated sigh. "Yeah, you don't have to remind me. I can never trust a boy or you." She jumped from the couch and ran up the stairs. "I hate you."

Heather lay propped in bed with several pillows behind her head. A bright light peeked through a slit between the bedroom curtains, and she blinked a couple of times until her eyes adjusted. The taste of blood swirled in her mouth.

Call her a modern-day vampire.

She barely noticed its pungent flavor anymore. The foul culprit had kept her up most of the night, taunting her from sleep. Cough. Blood. Cough. Blood. Cough. Blood. She could barely breathe without vomiting it. How did Anna and JJ think they were going to get her out of bed without her hemorrhaging?

She huffed. It couldn't be morning already.

Ginger ale would really hit the spot and wash away the bitterness permeating through her mouth. A watered-down glass of it sat on the nightstand. Her dry and scratchy throat called for relief. A wet, moist sip would pacify the need. With every bit of energy she had, she reached for the drink, then raised the glass to her mouth. The muscles in her arm gave out, and she dropped it on the floor.

"Shoot."

She tried wetting her tongue with salvia, but completely dried out by blood, her mouth had none to offer. She pinched her lips together. Should she ring the bell for Anna? Were ginger ale and her dry mouth really worth bothering her nurse? Someone should clean up the soda on the carpet. If she could find the energy to reach for the bell, would she have any left to shake it?

She rested her head on the pillow. She was too tired.

She'd wait until someone came in. The air blew on her from the vent above, and she shivered. It took more strength than she had to pull the cover from her waist to her chest. She'd stay cold. Cough. Blood. Cough. Blood. She stared at the ceiling.

"Rise and shine. It's a beautiful day," Anna sang

as she opened the curtains, illuminating the room with the blinding sun.

Heather squinted. "Ugh, I haven't slept all night."

The odor of cooked meat filled her nose. Anna, wearing a snowman apron and a cheery smile, stood by the opened curtains, holding a plate of bacon and jelly toast on a tray.

"I can't eat that."

"Yes, you can. It will give you the strength you need to get out of this bed."

"Yeah, right. I can barely lean over for a glass without dropping it." Heather motioned to the puddle of ginger ale and broken glass.

"Not to worry. I'll get that cleaned up right away and bring you a fresh glass." Anna laid the food tray across Heather's lap. "Lots of ice to water down the fizz, right?"

"Yes, thank you."

"Not a problem." Anna left the room.

Heather spun the bacon around on the plate and gawked at it. She lifted the toast to her nose and smelled the grape jelly. She gagged and tossed it back onto the plate, then laid her head on the pillow and closed her eyes.

"You do need to try to eat. Dr. Jones will be here soon, and I told him I'd have you fed and ready to go. Nothing better to start your day than with a good breakfast."

Heather opened her eyes.

"JJ's coming here today? I thought we would start on Monday. Isn't he off work on Saturdays?"

Anna placed the new drink on the tray.

"Dear, I don't think that doctor much cares whether it's his day off or not. You can't find a better doctor than one who puts his patient's needs above his."

"I can't imagine JJ putting anyone's needs above his own. He used to be pretty self-centered. I'm sure he's hoping to get something out of it."

"What would he get out of helping you?" Anna raised an eyebrow.

"I don't know."

"Dr. Jones seems genuinely concerned about you."

"It's been a long time since he's regarded anything involving me."

"Sounds like there's quite a story there. But no matter what happened in the past, Dr. Jones has agreed to help you, and it appears to me he's now a good man who's willing to give up a Saturday for *you*."

Had JJ changed? Was it really fair to judge him based on the boy he'd been? She wasn't the same girl he'd known.

Closing her eyes, she remembered back to their teenage years, to the time he'd accidentally bumped into her and knocked her down during a friendly game of two-on-two basketball. He'd extended his hand to help her off the ground. Friends until that moment, his touch had sent warm sensations through her hands into her stomach and down to her toes. As if she were still there in his driveway fighting off the new feelings of a fifteen-year-old, Heather caught her breath and opened her eyes. The gentle way he'd held her arm and back the other day had sent the same electricity through her veins.

She looked at her finger where her wedding ring should be. She shook her head. She was still married. True, Keith had been the one to ruin their marriage, but she'd been the one to walk away. Did she have the right to think of another man? It didn't matter anyway. She was dying, and besides, she didn't want to think of JJ like that. He'd hurt her. But still, she'd never forgotten what they'd once had.

Anna grinned. "Something making you flush, sweetheart?"

What childish foolishness. She touched her hot cheeks. "It's nothing."

"You know what I say. Cherish every wonderful memory you have. I've found the ones that make you blush are the best kind." Anna winked. "Eat, and then we'll get you cleaned up before the doctor gets here. I'll be in the living room if you need me."

Heather raised the bacon to her mouth. Its smell churned her stomach, but she forced one bite. Then another until she'd eaten two pieces and half her toast. After finishing the glass of ginger ale, it appeared everything would stay down.

Thank goodness. She didn't want JJ seeing her toss up breakfast.

"Anna," Heather shouted.

Anna stuck her head around the corner.

"I'm done. Can you help me get ready? I'd like to look as presentable as a dying woman can."

JJ, standing at the edge of the kitchen, grabbed a plate of pancakes and a glass of milk from the breakfast bar and handed them to Amelia as she walked past him. She took her breakfast into the living room and put it down on a TV tray, then plopped onto the couch next to Zac and crossed her arms over her chest.

"Sorry, guys. I haven't gotten around to buying a dining room table yet. We can pick one out tonight. What do you think?" JJ placed Zac's plate on a tray, then tousled his son's hair.

"That'll be cool." Zac shrugged.

"What about you, Amelia? You and Susan up for a trip to the mall?"

Amelia huffed. "She's not coming now."

"It'll be us then."

"Are you even going to ask me why she isn't coming over?"

"Why isn't she coming?"

"Because of you. Her mother doesn't trust you." She pushed the tray away and ran up the steps to her loft. "You ruin everything."

He stared at the loft railing and clutched his fist. Words escaped him. Susan's mother was a prude. He'd been a lowlife husband, but that didn't make him a bad father.

"She yells at Mom a lot too." Zac shoved a big bite of pancakes into his mouth.

JJ put a hand on his son's shoulder. "I'm sorry, buddy. I've made some really bad choices. "

"We all make mistakes. I forgive you."

The pardon pummeled JJ in the gut. "Thank you, buddy. When did you get so grown-up?"

Zac jumped onto the seat of the couch and wrapped his arms around JJ in a sleeper hold. "I don't know. It all happens in the blink of an eye."

"It does, does it?"

"Yep. That's what Mommy says."

With his son dangling from his neck, JJ carried him over to the middle of the floor and pretended to be taken down to the ground. Zac let go and jumped back, bouncing on his toes and holding his fist up. JJ sat on his knees and swung his arms outward while Zac weaseled his way onto his back. JJ wiggled free and body slammed him, then tickled his stomach, underarms, and feet.

Zac's laughter infiltrated JJ's soul.

Stop! Stop!" Zac's voice cracked.

"Ready to give up. Huh? Huh?" JJ poked at Zac's sides.

Zac stopped laughing and looked in JJ's eyes. "Never!" Like a ninja, Zac arched his back and flipped his feet under him. He jumped on top of JJ and knocked him onto his back.

"Dude, that was awesome. Where'd you learn how to do that?"

"Henry."

"Who's Henry?"

"He's a third grader at my school."

"That's pretty cool. Can you teach me?"

"Yeah!"

After about ten minutes of trying, JJ finally landed on his feet. "Not too bad for an old man, huh?"

Zac wrapped his arms around JJ. "I've got the coolest dad ever."

A huff came from the loft. "Or the worst dad ever."

JJ looked up at Amelia. "That's it, young lady. I've made my mistakes, but I've apologized. This attitude of yours is enough."

"My parents are divorced and my life is over! All my friends and their parents know my dad's a womanizer."

"A woman-what?" Zac lifted his upper lip and furrowed his eyebrows.

"Amelia, stop it."

"Why? You can't handle the truth like an adult?"

"If you want to have an adult conversation, then act like one. This is not the appropriate time to talk about this."

She turned her back. "Whatever. I want to go home."

"You are home. Whether you like it or not, this is your home too."

Turning, she glared at him. "Fine. When you go see your patient, I'll ask Mom to come get me."

"You are *not* going to your mom's. You and Zac are coming with me. It's time you get a reality check. You think your life is over? You need to see what that looks like."

She rolled her eyes.

"I'm taking a shower. You get down here, eat your breakfast, and you better be ready to go in an hour." He stormed down the hallway.

"Oooh, Sissy, you're in trouble."

"Shut up, Zac."

JJ closed the bathroom door and stared at himself in the mirror. How would he ever regain his daughter's respect?

Chapter Eleven

JJ knocked on the Cole's front door. Zac wiggled back and forth and played with his fingers. Amelia, with pressed lips, held her arms across her chest and stared at the ground.

Mr. Cole opened the door and smiled. "Why hello. I didn't realize you were bringing visitors."

"Is it all right?"

"Of course."

"I figured the kids could go down to the basement and play pool or video games. There's still a game room downstairs, isn't there?"

Mr. Cole nodded and stepped aside. "Come on in. It's freezing out there."

JJ stepped into the living room first, then Zac. Amelia stood in the doorway, still looking down, then huffed and walked in.

Mr. Cole held his hand out to Zac. "I'm Dan. And you are?"

Zac stared forward.

JJ put his hands on his son's shoulders. "This is Zac. He's a little shy."

"It's nice to meet you, Zac." Mr. Cole looked at

Amelia. "And you are?"

She looked up.

"Amelia Jones. How did I not put two and two together? Of course. You're JJ and Corrin's daughter."

Amelia scrunched her nose. "Pastor Cole?"

He held out her hand, and she shook it.

"Let me go back and check on Heather. Anna and her mom are with her. She didn't sleep well last night. Have a seat please, and I'll be right back."

When Mr. Cole disappeared, JJ asked, "How do you know him?"

"He's over the Christian Athletes club at school."

JJ nodded. "I didn't realize he was still doing that."

Amelia let out a long sigh "How long are we going to be here?"

"It depends on what Heather's up for, but possibly an hour or so?"

"Heather's your patient? Heather Cole? Danburg's softball queen?"

"Yeah. Why?"

"Is that why I'm here? You going to try to convince me to play?"

"Of course not. I didn't even think about that."

Amelia looked around the living room and spoke in a bitter, accusatory tone. "I guess you've been here before, huh? Since you know there's a game room downstairs."

"We were childhood friends. I used to live on this street."

"That's her, right?" She pointed to Heather's

senior picture on the wall.

"Yes. That's her."

"She's pretty. Did you like her?"

"Heather was very special to me. She was actually my—"

"She's awake and ready to see you," Mr. Cole interrupted. "The kids can help themselves to the game room downstairs. Mrs. Cole and I will be here in the living room if they need anything."

"Thanks. I'll show them to the basement, then be back up."

The game room hadn't changed since the last time he'd been there. A pool table occupied the front center, and the back half was set up as a movie area with a large screen and entertainment center. The same red leather couch he'd snuggled close to Heather on divided the two spaces. "Don't be loud, okay?"

"Okay." Zac smiled. "Can we watch a movie?"

"Sure. They're in that cabinet. Amelia, can you help him get that set up?"

She nodded. "Can I meet her?"

"Later if she's up for it."

"But I thought that's why I had to come, so you could teach me a lesson." Huffing, she plopped down on the couch. "I've got Zac. Go help her."

"Watch the attitude."

"Whatever."

"Come get me if you need anything."

With a smirk on her face, Amelia nodded. JJ held his breath, then let it out slow. It took every bit of his willpower to stay calm.

He walked up stairs and met Anna at the top,

then followed her to Heather's room.

Heather sat on top of the comforter and smiled when he walked in. That was a better response than he'd anticipated. Anna must have really worked on her.

Her pants and loose-neck, long white sweater swallowed her. Though pale and thinner than she should be, time had magnified her beauty.

He sat in the chair next to her. "How are you doing today?"

"Been better."

"I bet." Drawn to her as if time hadn't changed anything, he reached forward to touch her hand, but drew it back. He didn't have the right to touch her affectionately anymore. "Here's what I'd like to do. If any major decisions need to be made, I'll give my opinion, but all medical advice should come from your primary care doctor and oncologist. I'm not charging you or your insurance for this, and I'm not logging hours. I'm doing this for you as a friend. That being said, I'm going to treat you like any other patient. I'm going to push you, and you're going to hurt a little. You're going to think I'm a quack and hate me. All of this will have to happen before you'll have strength again."

"Okay."

"Let's get to work."

Heather lay on the bed with her head and back propped up by pillows.

JJ handed her a small yellow ball that fit in the

palm of her hand. "Lift it in front of you as high as you can while putting a little pressure on the ball."

As soon as her arm went higher than her chest, her shoulder burned, and she dropped the ball. He was right. He hadn't made her do much for a healthy person, but being stabbed over and over with a knife couldn't feel worse than the pain burning through her shoulder.

"I can't. I can't do anymore. It hurts too much."

"Okay, Cole, that's enough for now."

Her stomach dropped. He didn't have the right to call her that.

"You're definitely tough." He winked. "Like I didn't already know that."

"I don't feel too tough these days."

"We'll get you there, Cole."

She drew her shoulders up and looked down to her lap. "Please call me Heather."

"What did I say?"

She looked up. "Cole."

His eyes widened. "I didn't realize I said it. Sorry." He sat down next to her on the bed and took her right hand in his.

What was he doing? If using the nickname he'd given her all those years ago—one that meant he loved her—was not acceptable, this certainly wasn't. She started to withdraw her hand, when his thumb massaged her palm.

Heat rose from her toes through her bones and up to her face. She closed her eyes. After a few minutes, he helped her lay back, then moved his hands up and down her arms, massaging them. Sensations she'd forgotten existed coursed through her. Afraid her heavy breathing would give away how much she enjoyed it, she held her breath.

"Relax. Let the massage do its job."

Relax? Impossible with his strong, gentle hands touching her in a way no one had for years. It didn't mean anything. He was her physical therapist, nothing more, but the sensation of his tender touch reminded her of what having a man's hands on her should feel like.

"Not to alarm you, but I'm going to work on the area around and under your armpit, then around the front of your collarbone up to your neck and the front of your shoulder."

"Okay."

From outside her clothes, his hands and fingers rubbed deep into her muscles. Her pain eased under the massage.

"All right, now let's work on your back." He helped her roll onto her stomach before rolling his knuckles into her shoulder.

She moaned. "Oh, my goodness. I'm sorry." Her face burned with heat.

"It's okay. It happens all the time. I know it's about the relief, not about me."

Maybe a little of it was about him. She held her breath and stayed perfectly still. She missed having gentle hands touch her.

"Where are your kids?" JJ asked while he continued massaging.

The question echoed in her mind as her pulse pounded in her ears. "Kids?"

"I thought you and Keith would have a houseful."

The massage couldn't take the pain away from that truth. "No. Keith never wanted any."

"But you love kids."

Heather took in a deep breath, then exhaled. "I do. How about you and Corrin? How many kids did you have? Anna said you brought them with you."

"I did. They're downstairs. We have a fifteen-year-old daughter, Amelia. And Zac's six."

Envy twisted a knot in her stomach. "Tell me about them."

"Amelia's sweet. Reminds me a lot of you at that age. She's tenderhearted. Really mad at me right now, but a super-great kid."

"What did you do? Force her to do physical therapy too?" Her quick wittedness caught her off guard. After years of not laughing, it felt good to make a joke.

He stopped rubbing her shoulder.

"Something like that."

"And Zac?"

"He's the coolest kid you'll ever meet. This morning he taught me how to flip from my back to my feet. He's a little ninja."

"Can I meet them?"

"I'd love that."

She grinned. JJ had always liked kids as much as she had. A quality she found more attractive than his incredibly good looks. A flutter captured her stomach.

What was going on with her? She *did not* like JJ. He'd been the one to ruin the life she'd dreamed of having with him.

I'll always hold him responsible for that. Where

had that thought come from? It wasn't like she'd resented him all these years. In fact, she had thought she'd forgiven him. But seeing him again spotlighted the past, and clearly she hung on to some bitterness. Regardless though, like always there was something about JJ she couldn't resist.

His fingers dug into a tender spot, and she tightened her shoulder.

"I'm sorry." He lightened his touch.

"Are you okay? Did I work you too hard? Does the massage hurt too much?"

Not in the way you think. "No, it feels nice. That last spot was a little tender."

"I'll finish up here, then go get Amelia and Zac if you still want to meet them."

She nodded. He finished massaging her right arm, shoulder, and neck, then helped her sit. He left the room, and she played with a string on the edge of her comforter while she waited.

What was it about Jack Jones? No matter what happened between them, she'd never gotten over him. Life had forced her to bury the feelings. If Keith ever had any inkling . . . She shuddered.

JJ peeked his head through the doorway. "You sure you're still up for meeting them?"

"Yes, come on in."

They entered the room. His daughter smiled, and his son hid behind his father's leg, but she could see the boy's blond curly hair.

"This is Amelia. And this little guy"—he guided Zac in front of him—"is Zac."

Amelia extended her hand. "It's nice to meet you."

"You too." Heather used the little bit of energy she had left to accept Amelia's hand. Then she looked down at Zac. "How old are you?"

He held up six fingers. Heather smiled. He was adorable.

"Wow, are you in kindergarten?"

He nodded.

"What kinds of things do you like?"

"I like karate."

"Your dad told me you taught him a ninja move. Can you show me?"

Zac grinned from ear to ear. "Yes!" He lay on his back, then flipped up.

"Wow. When your dad makes me stronger, you'll have to teach me how to do that."

Heather focused on Amelia. "What are you into?"

She shrugged. "I don't know. School, I guess."

"Softball," JJ said.

"I told you, not anymore. I quit."

"You know, Heather used to play."

"Any girl who knows anything about local softball has heard of you."

Heat rose to Heather's cheeks. What a compliment. She figured she'd been forgotten long ago. "You aren't playing anymore?"

JJ looked at his daughter. "She's afraid she isn't good enough."

Amelia rolled her eyes. "That's not it at all. I just don't like it anymore. Besides, conditioning already started, and I flaked on that."

"What position did you play?" Heather smiled.

"Pitcher and first."

"Awesome. Me too. I bet you're really good."

"She is." Pride rang through JJ's voice.

Amelia ran her foot along the carpet. "Yeah . . . well, it doesn't matter anymore."

"Conditioning isn't mandatory, and off-season practice is good for keeping your arm warmed up, but lots of high school girls take breaks every now and then. My freshman year I broke my wrist sliding into home and couldn't play the rest of the season. My doctors made me rest it for nearly eight months. I came back the next year pitching just as strong. You can do it if you want. I don't have the strength to physically show you anything, but I'd love to give you pointers if you want."

Amelia stared at her feet. "I don't know. Maybe. It's been a really hard year. I don't want to play."

While Heather spoke, she watched JJ observe his daughter with downcast eyes. "I can understand that. Be sure to think about what you want. I stopped playing softball a long time ago, and I regret it now. You don't want to look back on your life someday and realize you gave up what you loved."

"I'll think about it."

JJ rubbed his hand over his mouth and glanced at Heather. Their eyes met. What had life been like for him? Why was the last year hard on Amelia?

"You can come watch her play sometime." Zac jumped on the end of Heather's bed.

Pain rocketed up her back, and she winced. "I'd love that."

JJ pulled Zac off the bed. "Be careful, buddy."

"I'm sorry."

"It's okay. I can't blink without it hurting." She looked at Amelia. "When are tryouts?"

"In a few weeks."

"If you decide you want to try out, come over and we'll chat ball. Even if you don't want to try out, you are always welcome to come and talk about whatever, boys, school, fashion—not that I know anything about that. But seriously, I'm here. I'd love company. And who knows. If Anna and your dad can get me strong enough, we could—" A cough burst out, and a handful of blood followed.

Zac wrapped his arms around Amelia's waist as their father ran out of the room and returned with a towel.

Staring into her eyes, he wiped her mouth and hands. He'd become a kind, compassionate man, but they were both married, and she was practically in the grave.

"Thank you." She put her hand on top his.

"Always."

Standing in front of Heather's house, JJ shut Zac's car door, then ran around to the driver side. He stared at the handle, unable to open it. Leaving Heather didn't seem right. Yes, Anna and her parents were there, but he wanted to sit by her side and hold her hand. He had stayed as professional as possible, using proper techniques to work the shoulder, but massaging her and hearing her moan under his touch sent forbidden desires through him. He'd wanted to kiss her and remind her of what they'd once had. He leaned his head against the roof of the car.

A knock startled him. "Daddy, I'm cold."

He ran his hands across his face and eyes. "I'm coming, Zac. Sorry." After one quick glance toward Heather's bedroom window, JJ climbed into the car and started it.

Amelia, sitting in the passenger seat, reached over and put her hand on top of his. "She's nice."

He looked at his daughter and nodded. That was the first act of affection she had shown him since the day she'd caught him with the other woman. He patted her hand. "Yes, Heather is one of the nicest people I know."

Without a word he drove home, praying Heather's oncologist was wrong and something— chemo, radiation, surgery, a new miracle drug— could be done to save her, but he had read her medical reports. She had no options. Only her god had the power to heal her now.

He pulled into the parking spot in front of his apartment. "You all go on in. I'll be in in a minute."

He held the keys up for Amelia, but Zac snatched them from his hands, jumped out of the car, and ran toward the building. Zac unlocked the door and waved as he went inside.

"I can't believe Heather's dad's Pastor Cole."

"Yeah. He's been there a long time. He's a good man."

"Who is Heather to you really? I saw the way you were looking at her."

"How was that?"

"Like you care a lot about her."

He looked Amelia straight in the eyes. "Heather was one of my best friends and the first girl I ever loved." A single tear rolled down his cheek.

"I'm sorry she's dying. That was pretty scary today seeing her cough up blood. It really shook Zac for a minute."

"It was awful seeing her like that."

"But you sprung right to action and took care of her. Do you work with patients that sick all the time?"

"Not all the time, but the majority of my patients do have cancer or other terminal diseases."

"Is it hard knowing your patients are going to die?"

He nodded.

"Especially Heather, huh?"

He stared at the steering wheel. No one knew how devastating this was on him. But he'd be there for Heather through it all. His heart wrenched.

"I love you, Daddy."

He wiped at his eyes. The words pummeled his heart. He wrapped his arms around her. "I love you too, sweetheart. I'm sorry for everything."

She pulled back. "I'm really, really mad at you, but I do love you."

"I'm going to spend the rest of my life making it up to you."

Amelia took in a deep breath and blew it out. "I don't want to talk about it. Are you going over to Heather's house again tomorrow?"

"Yes, I'll probably go every day until . . ." He stared out the window at the frozen pond between apartment buildings. Heather would be gone by

April according to the doctors, barely enough time to see spring.

"Can I come too?"

Amelia wanted to stay longer with him? It was to see Heather again, but that was okay. "It's up to your mom. She's picking you up around two."

"Daddy!" Zac stood on the balcony. "I'm hungry!"

Amelia opened her car door. "I'll go find him food. Don't freeze out here."

"I won't. I'll be in in a minute."

With one hand on the top of the door, Amelia leaned her head into the car. "I really like Heather. I can see why she was your first love."

The words echoed in his head while he watched his daughter walk away. His first true love.

Chapter Twelve

ow are you feeling? I didn't hurt you too bad, did I?

Like a schoolgirl, Heather smiled at JJ's text. One short therapy visit and meeting his kids was all it had taken. It wasn't right. She'd left her husband less than three weeks ago, but she couldn't help herself. She never could when it came to JJ.

She attempted to type a message on the phone her parents had given her, but she hit the wrong letter. Backspace. Four words accomplished without a mistake. Yay. Oops. No. Backspace.

If Keith hadn't insisted it was a waste of money for her to have a cell phone, and if he'd let her use his phone every once in a while, she wouldn't be clueless. Calling JJ would be much easier and more effective. Who invented this concept? It was like passing notes in junior high, except writing with a pen and using heart bubbles was easier than hitting the wrong letter every other word, watching autocorrect pop in the wrong word, and figuring out what the silly little faces meant.

Besides, she'd rather hear his voice. Finally,

getting it right, she sent the text.

Nah, my shoulder actually doesn't hurt as bad as usual.

The phone dinged with a notification almost immediately. How had he typed that fast?

Good. I know I pushed you really hard there at the beginning, but we've got to do that to build up your strength.

I'm okay. Promise to end every time with a massage, and I'll do anything you ask.

Is that right? ;)

Yep. What's that symbol you sent?

A wink.

Wink?

Yes, I'm winking at you.

I see. Be patient with me. This is my first smartphone. My parents said I needed one.

Really. Where have you been living? Back in the 1900s?

She couldn't hear it, but no doubt he tipped his head backward and laughed at his own joke.

I guess. Keith had a cell phone. He said I didn't need one.

Now I see why it takes you such a long to respond.

;) Did I do that right?

Yes, if you meant to wink at me. I'm glad you aren't hurting too bad. Once we get that shoulder mobile, I want to get you OUT of that bed and walking.

That would probably never happen, but if it did, she'd surely be hurting afterward. Heat rose in her cheeks as she typed out a response.

If you promise to use your miracle hands and give me a full body massage.

Not sure if she should send the text, she stared at the words. Did it sound too forward? What did she care? She had two and half months to live. Dying people could say whatever they wanted, right?

She pushed the Send button and waited. Minutes went by without a reply. She shouldn't have sent it. What if Corrin read it? Or Amelia?

I hope that didn't sound bad. I meant I'll be so worn out and hurting afterward. I'll need relief.

Silence.

Stupid. JJ had a wife and kids. She couldn't say whatever she wanted.

She laid the phone on the bed next to her and picked up the book on the nightstand. She read a page but didn't comprehend any of it. She tried again, but thoughts of JJ and his children permeated her mind. How blessed he was. She closed her eyes. What if she and JJ had ended up together? What would their children have been like? One named Abi no doubt. She smiled. Out there in an alternate universe there was a houseful of children she and JJ should have loved together.

She laid the book down on the nightstand and checked her phone in case she'd missed a text. Nothing. Keeping ahold of the phone, she rested her arm across her chest and stared at the ceiling. Her life had become word puzzles, books, TV, and looking out the window when she wasn't sleeping. Meeting JJ's kids was the highlight of her day. Of her week, really.

Would they come visit her again? Hopefully,

Amelia would take Heather up on her offer to talk softball and Zac would show her more karate moves.

From down the hallway, Anna sang. Her voice grew louder as she moved closer to Heather's room then she opened the door. "I brought you lunch. Are you up for chicken noodle soup?"

"It smells delicious."

"Someone's got her appetite back."

"I guess. I'm actually feeling pretty good."

"Enough to go for a walk later? It's a beautiful day."

Her heart raced at the thought, but how could she?

"I've arranged for a wheelchair. I thought your parents could join us."

A wheelchair? It was better than lying there under a floral comforter. "Sounds nice. But after a nap. I feel good, but I'm a little tired."

"I think that's merited. You worked hard."

A text notification chimed, and Heather snuck a peek at her phone. JJ. She looked at Anna, then back to the phone.

"Is that from Dr. Jones?"

It could have been anyone. Why did Anna suspect JJ? "I think so." What was she saying? Of course it was from JJ, and she needed to be sure he hadn't taken her text the wrong way.

Anna chuckled. "He's a handsome devil, and his kids are adorable."

"His kids are pretty great."

Anna placed the tray on Heather's lap and sat in the chair next to her. "What's the story with Dr.

Jones?"

"What do you mean?"

"Your parents said you were childhood friends."

Heather smiled. "We were more than that, but Dad didn't want to admit his little girl had a boyfriend. JJ and I were high school sweethearts."

"You were?"

"Yes, we dated for three years. Our freshmen year to the summer before we were seniors."

"What happened?"

Heather leaned her head back against her pillow and watched the snowflakes falling outside the window. "We weren't meant to be."

"I'm sorry, dear."

"Even after I married Keith, I wondered what if, but when I heard JJ and Corrin had a baby, I knew God had destined for them to be together."

"God works in mysterious ways sometimes."

"I guess." She peeked down at her phone again. Would it be rude to check the message while Anna was still in the room? The woman sure loved to talk.

"I'll leave you to your lunch. I have a few things to take care of. Unless you want company?"

"No, I'm fine. Thank you."

"I'll be back in a little while to get your dishes." Anna placed the bell on Heather's tray. "Don't hesitate to ring this if you need me. That's what I'm here for."

Heather opened JJ's text before Anna exited.

Sorry I didn't get right back with you. Amelia tried to make grilled cheese sandwiches and accidentally burned them, so I had a smoke-filled kitchen to tend to. As far as the massage, I understood what you meant. ☺

Good. I don't want Corrin to get the wrong idea. I hope she's okay that you're working with me.

She doesn't know.

Oh.

Why wouldn't he tell her? Did they not talk about work?

We actually signed divorce papers about seven months ago.

I'm sorry. What happened?

Long story.

Should she tell him the truth about Keith?

Keith doesn't know about the cancer, because I left him.

What?

Long story too. But after he left for deployment and I knew he was out of phone range, I left.

When do you think he'll figure it out?

Probably soon. I never know when he'll have access to a phone, but I figure if he knew by now, he'd be calling my parents.

What do you think he'll do when he finds out?

Heather shuddered. Take her by the hair and drag her back, then beat her into submission.

He'll try to beg me back, but I don't plan to spend the rest of my life, as short as it may be, with someone who makes me feel like he does.

And how is that?

Worthless and small. Unlovable. She clutched the phone. She didn't want anyone other than her parents to know what she'd allowed Keith to do to

her. She knew better. She hadn't allowed Keith—
he'd broken her. JJ could never know how weak
she'd become.

He cheated on me.

She stared at the phone while she waited for him
to respond. Why had she told him about Keith's
infidelity? Would he understand why Keith had
cheated? She'd never done more than kiss JJ, but
that didn't seem to be enough for him after a while.

He's a fool.

*Keith said I did nothing for him, and he had to
get it somewhere else.*

Why was she revealing so much?

*No. He's obviously got a problem. I could kill
the guy for saying that. It has nothing to do with
you. You're amazing.*

If that had been true, JJ wouldn't have done the
same thing to her.

I wasn't enough for you.

Her finger hovered over the Send button. What
would she accomplish by letting him know his
actions still hurt her? For eighteen years she'd
wanted to hear an apology, but not by guilting him
into it. She wanted a real apology when he was
ready. But why? They were kids back then. Even
so, it didn't take the pain away.

Her shoulder couldn't support the weight of her
lifted hand anymore. As she shifted to make herself
comfortable, her finger swiped the Send button.
Shoot. Was there a way to stop the message before
it reached his phone?

*I was a jerk. You were too good for me. I didn't
deserve you.*

He could have fooled her. Never mind they'd been friends first and shared hundreds of secrets. Once she and JJ were finished, he never spoke to her or looked her direction again. And even though he'd crushed her heart, every morning she'd wake wishing it had all been a nightmare. Because how could the love of her life not love her back anymore? How could the fifteen-year-old-boy she had fallen in love with turn into a complete eighteen-year-old narcissist?

But I wanted you. I would have forgiven you.

Why couldn't she stop telling him all these things? She'd harbored them for so long. Had it taken one afternoon, and she was ready to forget all the heartache and be friends again?

Silence.

Back then her only possible future included him. No matter how much he had changed for the worst, or the stupid things he said, or the insincere way he held her hand and kissed her in the end, she thought she could never love anyone like she did him. He'd been her everything. But then Corrin came along, and he . . .

I'm sorry. I was a dumb kid.

That apology would have been enough seventeen years ago, but so much had happened since then. She laid the phone on her chest and stared at the ceiling.

The phone beeped again. *You still there?*
Yeah.
Can you forgive me after all these years?
I don't know. You really hurt me.
I'd change what I did if I could. I've regretted it

every day.

Then why did you do it?

As awful as it sounds, I was a teenage boy and wanted more physically.

Boys would be boys. That wasn't an excuse.

All I ever needed was you. I've screwed up my life.

He'd needed her? Whatever. He had two incredible kids, was the top physical therapist in the region, and from the car he drove and the clothes he and his children wore, it looked like he had plenty of money to spare. Except for the divorce, he'd done fine without her.

You can't expect me to believe it.

Why?

You never talked to me again even though we'd been friends first.

I was ashamed of myself.

She laid the phone on her chest again. What else was there to say? He wanted forgiveness, but she couldn't give it anymore, could she? He'd thrown her away for Corrin, and Heather had made the worst choice of her life by turning to Keith for comfort. But did she want to go to the grave without forgiving JJ?

Her cell phone beeped.

I did try to call you after you got married. Shelly gave me your number. Keith answered and told me you never wanted to speak to me again, and if I ever tried to contact you again, he'd hunt me down and kick the living daylights out of me.

Sounded like Keith.

I wish you would have called again anyway.

I did. I'd call in the middle of the afternoon, when I figured he was working, to hear your voice, but the few times you answered, I chickened out. I've never gotten over you, Cole.

Please stop.

Why?

Because my life has not been easy, and realizing how much you regretted your choices is tearing me up.

I'm sorry, but it's true. I still love you, Cole.

No. No. No. Why couldn't he have realized that before? No, JJ didn't love her. A boy who loved a girl didn't cheat. Didn't make his lady feel worthless and unwanted. Didn't flaunt it in her face that he'd found someone else. No. She'd been a pretty face whom JJ and Keith had traded in for women who'd given them what she wouldn't.

She turned her phone off. She couldn't hear any more lies.

Chapter Thirteen

T he alarm clock on JJ's phone blared, and he turned it off. He wiped his hand across his sleepy face and sat up in his bed. The reality of what he'd admitted to Heather last night raced through his mind. He checked his phone to see if she'd responded. Nope. He swung his legs off the side of the bed and stretched his arms above his head.

How could he be so smart and so stupid at the same time? What was he thinking, telling her he loved her?

A knock pounded on his bedroom door.

"Come in."

Dressed in pajama pants and a red hoodie with the high school's bulldog mascot, Amelia smiled. "Good. You're up. I made breakfast."

"Did you burn anything today?"

"Nooooo." She rolled her eyes.

He followed her into the living room. Glasses of milk and bowls of Cheerios with cut-up bananas sat on TV trays. Zac slouched on the couch, a brown blanket wrapped around him and over the top of his head.

"Good morning, young Jedi." JJ kissed his son's head.

"Morning, Daddy. Amelia said I had to eat up and then take a bath 'cause we're going to church this morning. Is that right?"

JJ looked at Amelia. "We are?"

She nodded. "Yes, if we are going to be over here every Sunday. I'd like to go."

Would God strike him down for entering the building?

"To your mom's church? I don't know that I can go back there. They don't like me. Remember when that old woman wacked me upside the shoulder with her purse?"

Amelia tucked her lips in as a smile formed at the corner of her mouth. "I remember. You deserved it."

JJ nodded. "Still. That's just not right."

"Will you take us?" Amelia lifted questioning eyebrows. The same look his mother had often given him. Pure genetics, because Amelia had never met her grandmother.

JJ wouldn't deny Amelia anything she needed, no matter how hard. Even if that meant dragging himself back to a church full of people who knew his secrets.

"I can drop you and Zac off if you want."

"No, I want you to go with us, but I was thinking we could go to Pastor Cole's church instead." Amelia batted her eyelashes and smiled.

"If you want to go there, we can."

She nodded.

"Looks like that's what we're doing." JJ smiled, then picked up a bowl and shoveled a spoonful of Cheerios into his mouth as he sat on the couch next to Zac.

"Do you think Heather will be there?" Amelia asked.

"I doubt it. She's pretty weak."

Zac made big eyes. "If Heather's dad is a pastor, then what does her mom do?"

"She's a cashier at Tomlin's Grocery," JJ answered.

Zac pulled the blanket off his head. "Cool. Can she hook me up with free candy bars?"

JJ scrunched his eyebrows and threw him a whatcha-talkin-about look.

"What? I like candy bars."

He ruffled Zac's hair. "You're a character."

"What did Heather do?" Amelia whispered. "You know, before . . ."

"Good question. We really haven't talked in years."

How could he have claimed his love for Heather without knowing anything about her? He'd been positive she'd had kids. Positive Keith would have treated her better than JJ had. What else didn't he know?

"Is it okay if I ask when we go over there later today?"

"I take it your mom said yes?"

She nodded. "I asked if we could stay with you longer."

Zac jumped into a ninja stance on the couch. "But I'm going over to Danny's house later."

JJ pulled Zac's legs out from underneath him and rubbed his knuckles on top of his son's head. "Don't worry, buddy. I'll call your mom and work out the details. You can still go to Danny's."

Amelia cleared her throat. "Heather got me thinking yesterday. I'm not sure yet, but I don't know if I want to give up softball. Do you think we'd have time to throw the ball a little before church?"

"Yes. Of course."

He wanted to wrap his arms around her, but he wouldn't push it. Baby steps.

Amelia swirled Mark's baseball between her gloved hands as she looked out at the icy lake at the park. Wait until he heard who she'd met and that she was thinking about trying out for the team.

"You are crazy, sis, for doing this. It's too cold." Zac shut the door to their dad's Mustang and warmed his gloved hands in front of the vent.

She dropped the baseball into her bag and took off the thin knit gloves. She slid on a softball mitt and pulled out a ball. The laces rubbed against the inside of her palm. Her hand itched to throw it.

Her dad, bundled in a coat, gloves, toboggan, earmuffs, scarf, and boots, squatted to catcher stance. He held his catcher's mitt in front of him. "Give me your best pitch."

She wound-up and released the ball. It soared through the air and landed in her dad's mitt. The air left her lungs for a moment, and a tear slid down her cheek.

"Perfect. Pitch me another one."

She exhaled and hurled another and another. Fifteen minutes later, she couldn't feel her hands, but she had to release one more.

"We need to go." Her dad tossed the balls back. "Church is going to start soon."

She caught the balls and put them in her duffel bag. Heather was right—Amelia didn't want to look back and regret anything. No matter what had happened, it wouldn't stop her love for softball.

"Are you sure you'll be okay here by yourself?" Heather's mother asked.

Heather sat in a pew in the front row. She looked at her mother and Anna and then around the empty sanctuary of her father's church. Lights gleamed in from the stained-glass windows, and rays danced along her arm. The musty smell of the old renovated building reminded her it had been far too long since she'd been in church.

She inhaled the smells again and nodded. "Yes."

Mom gave her a kiss on the cheek. "I'm sorry I have to be in the nursery this week. I don't have anyone else who can fill in last minute."

"I could stay with you instead of going to Sunday school," Anna suggested.

Heather smiled. Life didn't need to stop for her. Her father and mother still had a church to run. "Really, I'll be fine." She held up her phone. "I have this if I need anything."

"Okay. I'll see you in a little bit." Her mother waved as she exited down the aisle and out the door.

Anna took her worn Bible out from under her arm and flipped through it. A rainbow of colors filled the highlighted pages. "I learn something new every time I read this." She closed it. "I can't wait to the get into the Word in Pastor Cole's class. Your father and I have had great talks. I'm interested to see his teaching style."

"He's pretty amazing. When I was little, I'd sneak into his class so I could listen. You better head down to the basement. Class should be starting soon."

"You sure you don't want to go too?"

"Dad offered to carry me downstairs, but I don't want him to have to do that. I'm good."

"Positive?"

"Positive."

Heather needed the serenity inside the sanctuary more.

Anna waved goodbye, and Heather sat alone. She ran her hand across the hymnal sitting next to her, then traced the letters on the front. She closed her eyes and drew in a breath.

How had Heather not spent every Sunday for the last seventeen years in God's house?

If the ten-year-old version of herself could see her now, she'd surely give Heather an earful. Back then she'd known she'd marry a preacher like her daddy. But then she'd met JJ, and everything changed. She learned of a whole new world outside of church and youth group and PG movies. He introduced her to her first cup of coffee, taught her a dirty joke or two, and showed her what mooning was.

The smell of coffee brewing wafted past and sent her stomach into a fit of nausea. She swallowed hard and pushed the sensation away. Thank goodness. She wouldn't have been able to make it to the bathroom alone. She turned her phone on just in case she needed someone.

Her phone dinged, showing she had three missed texts and two missed calls from JJ. Like a bug drawn to a light, she opened his text messages.

Are you there? I'm sorry if I scared you. 2:35 p.m.

Heather, please respond. What can I say? I'm an idiot. I know it was inappropriate to tell you that. But I do love you. 3:00 p.m.

Okay, I'm going to try to call now. Please answer. 7:00 p.m.

As if she liked the way his words tortured her, she clicked the first voicemail, 7:02 p.m. "Okay, Heather. I need to explain. Please call me back."

She should turn the phone off again, but she craved his voice begging for her attention. She tapped the 10:34 p.m. voicemail. "Since the day I meet you, I wanted you in my life. I've been a fool. I love you, Cole. I couldn't go another second without letting you know you were good enough. Screw Keith. I want you, if you'll have me for as long as you have left."

What? He wanted to be with her?

She gasped for air, then forced herself to suck in a deep breath and blow it out slowly. Why now?

117

Why when they wouldn't even have a chance?

What did he expect from her? To date her? What would that entail? Him watching her puke while he forced her to exercise? She glanced at the folded wheelchair leaning against a wall. Him wheeling her around town like a cripple? No. She'd accepted death was her fate. A life with JJ never was.

JJ pulled his Mustang onto the tree-lined drive up the hill to the old white country church. The snow-covered branches reached across the street toward one another, like lovers meeting for a long embrace. Behind one of these trees he had given Heather her first kiss. What he wouldn't give to feel those lips on his again. Every Sunday for three years he'd sat next to Heather, holding her hand in church, waiting for her dad to stop preaching so they could run to the trees and kiss, taking turns leaning against the trunks.

JJ pulled into a parking spot and drew in a deep breath. Guilt slashed his stomach into pieces. He hadn't been back here since the day Heather had found out the truth about Corrin.

The swing set, the last place he and Heather sat as a couple, sat off to the side of the parking lot next to the church. The memory invaded his mind. He'd chased Heather around the trees and caught her by the waist. He'd pulled her against him and kissed her. "I love you, Cole."

"I love you too. We better head up to the church. My dad will be locking the doors soon."

"Okay. Want to race me to the swings? The loser has to do a favor for the winner."

"You're on!" She sprinted up the hill.

He watched her tan legs and bulging calf muscles. He gulped. He wanted her, and more than just a kiss.

She turned around and ran up the hill backward. "You coming?"

"I'm enjoying the view."

She shook her head. "Good 'cause I know how much you love to clean. I've got a list of chores for the Coles' annual deep-cleaning week." She turned back toward the church.

"Hey." He raced forward and caught up to her. "I don't think so." He kicked it in and reached the swings before her. He raised his arms in victory. "I am the champion."

She put her head on his shoulder. "What do I have to do?"

The bright sun hit him in the eyes. "I'll be nice. Get my sunglasses. They're under my driver's seat."

She winked, then dashed to his car, flung the door open, and disappeared. It took several minutes before she stood. A frown on her face, her eyes downcast, and a piece of paper in her hand. "Who's Corrin?"

His heart sank to his stomach and stopped. "What?"

"This letter says she loves you and that she can't wait until your camping trip, where you two can be alone again?"

"I don't know where that came from. Maybe it's

119

Bryson's."

"Don't use your best friend as a pawn. It's addressed to you. I'm not stupid. Don't lie to me."

He stepped toward her.

"Who is she?"

"A girl I meet at my first-aid/CPR course."

"And she's your girlfriend?"

"No."

"Don't lie!"

"She's not. I promise." He took her hand.

Heather pulled away. "Please tell me the truth. If you care about me at all, be honest."

What had he done? He wrung his hands. He couldn't lose Heather, but he couldn't let Corrin go either.

Heather's eyes focused on him. "What does she mean 'be alone again'?"

He ran his hand on his temples. She deserved the truth. "We've been together a few times."

"By we've been together, you mean you guys. . ."

He nodded.

Tears sat on the rims of her eyes.

"I'm sorry." He reached for her arm.

She stepped back. "We have to break up."

Words wouldn't come. He nodded.

She'd straightened her back, had slammed the letter and his sunglasses against his chest.

"Yoo-hoo, Dad." Amelia waved a hand in front of his face. "We going in?"

He shook his head. "Yep. Sorry."

He led his kids up the steps and inside through the double glass doors. Several people stood in the foyer area, talking and drinking coffee. A group of older women whispered and pointed in JJ's direction. When the shortest woman in the bunch caught his eye, he nodded his head and winked. The little old lady whipped her head back to the group.

JJ checked Zac into the kids' area, then returned upstairs with Amelia. At the sanctuary doors, Pastor Cole held his hand out. "JJ. What a surprise. I didn't know you were coming today." He turned to Amelia. "Nice to see you. Heather came today. She's already in there. You should go say hi."

JJ's heart pounded. He had to talk to her. He wasn't wasting another moment.

The crowded sanctuary didn't stop him from spotting her right away. Sitting alone in the front row, she turned her head slightly and met his gaze. Following the fast beat of his heart, he picked up the pace and headed toward her. If Amelia followed, he didn't know. Heather smiled. A good sign. She looked behind him, and her smile grew.

"Hello, Amelia. I'm glad you guys are here. Come sit next to me." Heather patted the pew.

Beaming from ear to ear, Amelia ran around JJ and took the requested seat. With the only option left, he sat on the other side of Amelia. Heather and Amelia didn't speak loud enough for him to hear.

How long would Heather ignore him? His phone showed that she'd recently seen his texts, but had she listened to the voicemail? Did she know he wanted to be with her? Would she want to be with him too? Or maybe she really did want nothing to do with him.

He didn't regret anything he'd told her. She

deserved to know how special she was and that he still loved her. Maybe he was moving fast, but time was not on their side. He'd wasted enough of that already.

She couldn't avoid him forever. After the service he'd corner her.

Anna walked in front of their pew and waved, then took the seat next to JJ. "Lovely church, huh? I love the stained-glass windows. There's something about an old church building that fills a person's soul. Even if you haven't been for years."

JJ shook her hand. "How are you today?"

"Better than I deserve."

She probably meant something biblical by it. Like because of what Jesus had done on the cross or something like that. But for him it meant something else. Heather deserved life. He deserved death. He sniffed and shifted in his seat. "Heather must be doing pretty good since she's here today."

"She is. Yesterday afternoon she got a wheelchair and we went for a walk, or rather we skated down the street." Anna laughed. "With all the ice and snow, we didn't get too far, but it was nice to get her out in the fresh air for a few minutes."

"How did her lungs take to the cold air?"

"She coughed a little, but really with your visit and the walk, she's doing exceptionally well." Anna brought her voice down to a whisper as the overhead music stopped. "She's a fighter."

A twenty-something man with shoulder-length hair and carrying a guitar stepped onto the stage. "Good morning. Let's worship."

Heather remained seated while everyone else stood to sing. Her voice carried over the others even though her frail and skinny body looked as though it might shatter with one small bump. If JJ didn't know better, he'd swear Heather had anorexia.

JJ didn't get it. How could she be full of worship and adoration? God had allowed the cancer. Couldn't he have found a way to reveal it before it reached stage 4?

It didn't make sense how she could worship her god like that.

The song ended, and the young musician made the announcements, prayed, then asked them to stand again. Heather held on to the end of the pew and attempted to stand, but sat back down. Whether he understood it or not, she wanted to stand and give God the little bit of energy she had to worship, and JJ would help her do it. He rushed to her side and wrapped his arms around her waist and held her up. The smell of vanilla filled his nose. He fought the urge to lean in for a bigger whiff.

"Thank you."

He smiled. Needing more support, she wrapped her arm around his waist. To anyone who didn't know, it might look like the two were in a relationship, and he didn't mind that one bit. Let the gossipy old ladies from the foyer wonder why Mrs. Meyers had her arms wrapped around a man who wasn't Keith. Who cared what they thought? Keith had blown it. So had JJ, but he planned to make it up to her and show her how a man should love a woman.

Amelia watched her dad hold Heather up through the worship songs. Sometimes he really was such a great man. Her stomach knotted. Why did he have to be selfish and ruin things with her mom? Amelia missed the man he'd been in her mind. Hating him had been hard, and she could feel her heart softening for him, but she didn't know that she was ready for that.

The last song ended, and the worship pastor asked everyone to sit. Sweat sat on Heather's brow and exhaustion showed in her eyes as Dad helped Heather sit. He winked at Amelia on his way back to his spot beside her.

Shocking Amelia, Heather laid her head on her shoulder. "I'm worn out. I'm sorry."

"You stood for a long time," Amelia whispered. "I don't mind at all. You can rest on me as much as you need."

A deep cough from Heather echoed against the church walls, and her body thrashed violently, as if she didn't have control or the energy to support her own body. Afraid Heather might fall out of the pew, Amelia reacted quick and wrapped her arms around Heather's back and held her through the cough.

Amelia hated this for Heather. It wasn't right. Heather was young and beautiful, kind and once so athletic.

When the coughing ended, Heather whispered, "Thank you." She then laid her head on Amelia's shoulder.

In awe, JJ watched Amelia tend to Heather. Such a thoughtful girl. He hoped this weekend was the start of their relationship getting back on track.

From the corner of his eye, he caught sight of Pastor Cole stepping up to the podium. "As many of you know, my daughter, Heather, is here today. We are asking for your prayers. Recently, she found out she has . . ." Tears choked him. "Stage four lung cancer. She's been given only a few months."

Gasps sounded throughout the church, and whispers spread like wildfire, followed by stares in Heather's direction. A single tear slid down Heather's cheek. JJ's arms burned to hold her.

Take me instead, God. She doesn't deserve this. I do. Punish me. Not her.

The music minister stepped in next to Heather's dad. "Congregation, let's surround Pastor Cole, his wife, and daughter in prayer. Would someone please get the pastor's wife from the nursery?"

A woman ran out the back of the sanctuary as people made their way around Heather. Soon her mother entered, and Mr. Cole met her halfway down the aisle and led her by the hand to their daughter as the congregation parted, giving room for her parents to join hands with Heather and kneel in front of her. People laid hands on Heather and her parents. Others placed hands on the people in front of them. Amelia leaned forward and put her hand on Heather's arm and Mrs. Cole. JJ reached behind Amelia and put his hand on Heather's lower back.

The congregation offered tearful prayers and pleas to heal and save Heather from the disease. Others prayed for wisdom for the doctors to know what to do to help her in her last days.

Yes, JJ needed wisdom, all right, on how to keep her comfortable and mobile, and her oncologist needed to find a miracle.

An older woman prayed for peace for the family and their continued faith in God. The prayers morphed into one large cosmic ball of whispering words bouncing against the walls and shooting toward the ceiling. Prayers layered over the others, sounding like a whooshing geyser flowing straight to heaven.

Taken over by an entity he didn't understand, JJ's words joined the chorus of prayers. Drowned by all the other hundred voices, he could barely hear his own as the words escaped. "Heal her. I will do anything." He swallowed hard. "Please. If you are real. Please show me."

A hand touched his shoulder, and he turned to see whose. With closed eyes, one hand in the air and the other on him, Anna's lips whispered a prayer. JJ closed his eyes.

I love her, God. If you're really there, please let her forgive me. I know I don't deserve it, but let her love me back, and I will honor and cherish her until her last breath.

Chapter Fourteen

Heather's chest tightened. The scent of old-lady perfume and Stetson cologne swirled around her as she received hug after hug followed by well-wishes and words of encouragement. Overwhelmed, she tuned people out. The smells gagged her, but she swallowed hard until the feeling passed. At least all this attention kept her from having to acknowledge JJ, who stood behind the group of people.

Having him here in her dad's church after he professed his love was too close to déjà vu. Although, she wasn't the same naive girl she'd been back then.

From the corner of her eye, Heather caught sight of her old youth pastor, Baker, who greeted JJ with a hug. As the line dwindled, the two men talked.

More well-wishers and more hugs. More tears and more sympathy. All the while, JJ and Baker captured her attention. What were they talking about?

JJ smiled, and the deep creases next to his mouth sent a wave of forbidden memories. Other than his new wrinkles, with her eyes closed she could run her hands along his face and probably recognize every crease, groove, dimple, and scar. She looked away from JJ to the elderly man taking her hand. She shouldn't entertain any sort of reminiscent thoughts, but the flood of memories seemed impossible to dam up. She'd learned with Keith to turn off her emotions and feelings. So why couldn't she do it with JJ?

The old man let go of her hand, and she said "Thank you for the kind words" as he walked away. JJ gestured for Baker to go ahead of him. The youth pastor touched her shoulder, then gave words of encouragement and a hug before leaving.

Now only JJ stood in front of her. Heather looked around. The rest of the sanctuary sat empty. Her father and mother spoke with an elder in the hallway right outside the sanctuary doors. Where were Amelia and Zac? Anna?

"Hey." JJ sat down next to her.

"Hey."

The scent of his redwood cologne invaded her sanity. Somehow she sensed his hands running along her arms even though they remained in his lap, his lips brushed against hers even though he hadn't leaned in toward her, and his words from years ago whispered in her ear. She breathed it in again, reminding her of a time long ago when she felt safe in his arms.

He put his arm behind her on the back of the pew. "So."

"So." She stared at the ground.

"I said some things."

"Yeah, you did."

"What do you think about what I said?"

How could she tell him when she didn't know herself? When they'd ended, she'd understood she'd never be with him again except in her dreams, where she'd hidden all her wishes. The only place she had the freedom to believe her life hadn't become what it was. A tear slid down her cheek. If she could turn back the clock, then she'd pick JJ a million times over. She would have been happy and loved and . . .

A pain radiated through her shoulder. She reached across her body with her good arm and rubbed at the pain. JJ moved her hand down to her lap and massaged her shoulder.

"Are you hurting?"

She nodded.

He searched her face with those piercing blue eyes. His fingers kneaded into the nape of her neck, and she leaned into it. Another tear. What was wrong with her?

He wiped the tear away with his other hand and put his mouth against her ear. His warm breath blew on her as he spoke. "Relax, Cole. Let my hands do their job."

The dam broke. Every good moment she'd stored away sprung to her mind like a movie montage. The kisses beneath the trees, the touch football games where he'd tackled her anyway, the concerts and ball games, the front porch talks before they'd started dating, the first time he'd smiled at her, held her hand, showered her with gifts and flowers. The boy who looked at her like she was the only girl in the world for him.

The same way he'd looked at her every time they'd been together since she'd returned.

No, she wouldn't fall for him again. But she'd never fallen out of love. She laid her head on his shoulder. "I can't be with you."

"I'll wait as long as I have to."

"I'm not going to change my mind. I'm going to die. Why would you want—"

He kissed the top of her head. "Because it's you."

"So?"

"I'm not letting you go this time."

JJ pulled into the driveway of the house he'd bought for Corrin soon after he'd graduated medical school. Standing on the porch in the dark, Corrin waved at him and Amelia as they slid out of the car. "Hey, guys, did you have a good time?"

Amelia nodded. "We did."

JJ handed Amelia her bag. "Why don't you go in so I can talk to your mom?"

"Okay, Daddy. See you next weekend."

"Bye, baby." He kissed her cheek before she went inside.

Corrin's eyes widened. "Daddy, huh? Seems like a lot changed over the weekend. How did that happen?"

"We went to church this morning."

"Wow." She raised her eyebrows.

He swallowed past a lump in his throat. "Then

we went to Heather Meyers's parents' house."

"Why?"

"I'm Heather's physical therapist."

Corrin's eyebrows furrowed. "I didn't know she and Keith moved back."

"They didn't."

"Then what's going on?"

"Heather has stage four lung cancer." His heart felt like it dropped into his stomach.

"Is she going to be okay?" She ran her hands up and down his arm.

"No."

"That's awful."

"She's been given three months. Amelia was sassing me Saturday, so I made her and Zac come with me to Heather's appointment. She and Heather connected right away."

Corrin looked down at the ground and spoke softly. "Amelia wanted to visit her again today?"

"Yes."

"Does she know who Heather is?"

"Yes."

"How did she handle that, all things considered?"

"She was okay with it."

"How are you?"

"Not doing well. Heather's so young." He clutched his fist.

"How's Keith handling it?"

"He doesn't know. She left him."

Her eyes widened, and surprise sounded in her voice. "Really?"

A pair of headlights flashed in their eyes as a

black truck pulled into the driveway. "Are you expecting visitors?"

She shook her head. "No. I have no clue who that is."

The driver stepped out and raised a hand. JJ couldn't make him out in the dark. When he reached the porch, the chest-length beard caught JJ off guard, but underneath the black hipster glasses there was no denying the brown eyes of his childhood best friend, Bryson. Keith's younger brother.

"What are you doing here?" JJ put his arm around Bryson and patted him on the back with his fist. He hadn't seen Bryson since before Heather and Keith's wedding.

Bryson stepped back and slid his hand down his beard. "Have you heard about Heather?"

JJ nodded.

Bryson turned to walk away. "I wanted to be sure you knew."

"Hey, wait."

Bryson stopped and looked at JJ.

"You want to come in and talk." JJ looked at Corrin, hoping she could tell through his eyes he was asking if she minded.

She nodded.

Bryson rubbed the back of his neck. "I don't know, man."

"It's been a long time. It'd be nice to catch up."

Bryson stood silent, staring at JJ.

Corrin opened the door. "Come on, Bryson. Why don't you come in? It's freezing out here."

Bryson nodded and stepped inside. JJ led him

through the foyer into the living room and offered him a seat on the couch. Corrin went into the kitchen off the living room.

Bryson looked around the room and up to the balcony walkway. "Nice place."

"Thanks."

"How long have you guys been here?"

"About eleven years, but I don't live here anymore."

Bryson raised an eyebrow. "What happened?"

"We're divorced."

"Sorry to hear that, man."

"How are you doing? What are you up to these days?"

"I'm not here to try to rekindle our friendship. That was over a long time ago. I wanted to be sure you knew about Heather. I know what she meant to you."

"Thanks. Yeah, I know what's going on. I'm her physical therapist."

"Why?"

"I work with cancer patients, and her oncologist wants her to see me."

Bryson shook his head and clinched his jaw. "My parents are beside themselves. They tried calling the Coles, but they aren't answering. How could Heather come back here, find out she has cancer, and tell no one? We tried to get in contact with Keith, but they told us it would be a few days before he could call. Sissy admitted Heather left California a few weeks ago for treatment for her agoraphobia."

Heather had agoraphobia? She hadn't seemed

like it today at church, surrounded by such a loud crowd.

"Does your sister live in San Diego?"

"No, she stays with Heather when Keith goes on deployments."

None of this made sense. "I'm confused. How long has Heather had agoraphobia?"

"I don't know. Since like Keith's second deployment, so twelve, thirteen years ago."

"Man, I had no idea. She's seemed completely normal."

"Except she's dying and didn't tell anyone." Bryson shook his head. "We don't even know if Keith knows."

Should JJ say anything? It was Bryson, after all. JJ let out a long sigh. "He doesn't. Heather said Keith had cheated on her, so she left him. She'd been sick for a while, and when she finally went to a doctor here, she found out about the cancer."

"Keith is going to flip. She's his world." Bryson ran his hand across his temple, then shook his head. "I can't believe he'd cheat on her. Are you sure?"

JJ shrugged. "It surprised me too, but that's what she said."

"I don't know why she didn't call Mom and Dad. I guess she didn't want Keith to know she'd left him. Maybe she isn't right in the head. Cancer can mess with your brain, right?"

"Yes, but—"

"It's been at least fifteen years since any of us, other than Sissy, has seen Keith and Heather. Did you know that?"

"No. I hadn't talked to her since we broke up.

They never came home for a visit?"

"No, her agoraphobia was too bad."

That wasn't adding up. Heather hadn't been the type to stay away. Had agoraphobia actually crippled her that much? That would make sense why she'd waited so long to go to the doctor though.

Bryson shook his head. "Keith and Heather always did their own thing. And then when her fear of leaving the house got to be too much, Keith became a homebody with her. That's why the cheating doesn't make sense."

"Or perhaps it does. If she wouldn't go anywhere, do anything, maybe he was fed up and found someone else."

"I doubt it. Don't you remember how insanely in love he was with her? He still is."

JJ cringed. He remembered all right. Watching her date Keith, who'd treated her like a princess, had pummeled JJ's ego. It was what eventually drove a wedge between him and Bryson. "You're probably right. It may be the cancer messing with her mind. I'll talk with her tomorrow and let her know your parents want to talk to her."

"That would be great. Dad's ready to storm the Coles' house."

"I'll see what I can do. Other than this, how you been?"

"Doing good. I finally got married a few years ago. We have a two-year-old son, Sebastian. We live in Indy. How are you?"

"Not too great, man. I could really use a cigarette."

Chapter Fifteen

Looking out the window from her bed, she watched JJ pull up in front of the house. He rushed out of the car and darted up the driveway. She smoothed down her hair and rubbed her cheeks, hoping to put a little color to them.

Her door opened, and JJ stepped in with a smile as he made his way to the chair next to her bed. "Can we talk?"

Hopefully, it wasn't about his feelings for her again. She nodded.

"I talked to Bryson last night."

Her stomach dropped. She'd known going to the church meant Keith's family would find out she was in Danburg and that she had cancer. They'd want answers, but she wasn't ready to give them.

"He said some things that confused me."

"Like what?"

"Do you have agoraphobia?"

She clutched the edge of the comforter and stared forward at her closet doors. "Until the day I left Keith, I hadn't stepped foot outside my home for years except for his duty-station moves."

"But you don't seem like you have it."

She shrugged. She *wasn't* going to tell him the real reason she never left the house. "I don't know. I just had to leave. Nothing else mattered."

"You're shaking." He ran his hand on top of hers. "Are you okay?"

"Yes." She hadn't realized she was trembling until he mentioned it.

"Were things really that bad?"

She nodded. "I don't want to talk about it."

"Okay. I won't make you." He squeezed her hand.

"Bryson said his parents are really worried and want to see you."

"I know. Dad talked to them earlier. They're going to be here in a few minutes. I knew I couldn't put it off anymore."

Heather watched the carpet. Keith would know soon enough. Hopefully, she'd die before he'd make it to the States.

Like a helpless baby, Heather's father cradled her in his arms and carried her from her bedroom to the couch. JJ followed behind, then sat next to her. She hated for JJ to see her this way. Why was he staying for the Meyers' visit anyway? He could come back later for her session. Either way it was nice having him there, and his presence made her feel a little braver. Telling the Meyers she was dying was one thing, but to have to look Keith's parents in the eyes and reveal she'd left their son was another. Maybe she wouldn't tell them that part.

The doorbell rang. Her mother opened the door, and her father greeted Mr. and Mrs. Meyers with a handshake as they entered.

Mr. Meyers took a step toward Heather. "My word, girl, you look . . ."

Awful? Skinny? Like death was knocking on the door?

Mr. Meyers froze, but Mrs. Meyers walked to Heather and kissed her cheek. "You look as beautiful as always, darling."

Heather took her mother-in-law's hand in hers. "Thank you."

"Why didn't you tell us about the cancer?" Her mother-in-law squeezed her fingers.

"I was going to. I wasn't sure how to tell you yet."

"Have you gotten ahold of Keith?"

Heather shook her head.

Mr. Meyers cleared his voice. "Diane, why even ask? You know very well she hasn't. Why? Why would you not tell your husband? That boy loves you, and you up and left him." The anger ringing in his voice sounded like Keith's before a rampage.

Drawing inside herself, her mind went blank, and she felt as if her body drifted upward, where she watched the scene play out from above in her hovering body.

Mrs. Meyers looked at her husband. "That's between her and Keith. They'll work it out."

Mr. Meyers said no more, but the anger on his face looked all too familiar. Keith would hold that kind of rage in until he knew no one was around to hear, then he'd beat Heather until she couldn't remember passing out.

Mrs. Meyers's smile fell to a frown, then she spoke softly. "We tried to reach Keith, but his command said it could be another week before we can speak to him. Due to the circumstances, though, they're trying to get a message to him as soon as possible."

Like a spirit taking over an unsuspecting body, Heather slammed back into her body. Fear rushed through her veins. "I didn't tell him anything because I don't want that to be on his mind while he's over there."

"You told Sissy you were going to treatment. You lied. And now you want me to believe that you weren't going to tell Keith for his benefit. Whatever." Mr. Meyers leaned in close to her face.

JJ put his hand on Mr. Meyers's chest. "Hey now. I know you're upset."

Mr. Meyers stepped back and glared at him. "What are you here for?"

"I'm her physical therapist."

"Why?"

Heather cleared her throat. JJ had done nothing wrong. He didn't deserve this interrogation. "My oncologist referred me to him. Not that it's your business."

"It is my business. You're my daughter-in-law, and that young man is your ex-boyfriend. He has no right to have his hands on you."

Her dad stepped in next to him. "Excuse me. She's my daughter, and she makes her own decisions on her care. JJ has been nothing but professional."

Mrs. Meyers put her hand on her husband's chest. "Let's go. We wanted to be sure she's okay, and she is so—"

"She's not fine. Look at her."

Mrs. Meyers looked in Heather's eyes and whispered, "I'm sorry."

Heather nodded. She understood what Mrs. Meyers was saying.

"I have about two and a half months, more if I'm lucky. Tell Keith if you have to, but I'm not leaving Danburg. I'm staying right here with my parents until the end."

"What about Keith?" his father asked.

"What about him? He's made it clear he'd rather me be sick than get me the help I need, so do whatever. Tell him. Don't tell him. You're right. I left him and hoped to never see him again."

Mr. Meyers turned and stormed toward the door. "Come on, Diane."

Mrs. Meyers trudged after him. She turned and looked at Heather. "I'm sorry for what you're going through. We're worried for you and don't understand why you left Keith."

"All due respect, you do know."

"I don't know what you're talking about."

"I'm afraid you do."

Mrs. Meyers looked down at the ground.

"Come on, Diane." Mr. Meyers shouted from outside the door.

Like a trained dog, she obeyed.

Heather let out a long sigh and ran her hand along her temple. Keith would soon know everything. She looked at her parents, then JJ. She had hoped to be dead by then, but she had too much to live for. She couldn't let fear rule her anymore. Bring him on.

Chapter Sixteen

Trying not to wake Heather, JJ crept out of her room and down the hallway to the living room, where the large picture window displayed the night sky. The lamp on the corner end table illuminated the space. The distant voices and studio audience laughter from the TV in Mr. and Mrs. Cole's bedroom carried. He peeked at his cell phone—11:33 p.m. Had he really massaged Heather that long? He hadn't stopped when the session was over, and after she fell asleep, he couldn't bring himself to stop. But two hours? His hands ached now, after the realization.

"How's she doing?" Anna entered from the kitchen and handed him a mug full of a warm dark liquid topped with whipped cream.

"Sleeping." He lifted the mug. "Thank you. What is this?"

"Something I whipped up. An old secret family recipe. An extra dab of this and a little bit of that."

He took a sip. "Is this your hot chocolate you told me about?"

She smiled and directed him to take a seat next

to her on the couch, then took a sip from her mug. "Today wore Heather out. Mr. Meyers is a little overwhelming."

JJ cleared his throat. "I'd never seen him like that before."

"I was glad you stepped in when he got in her face. It frightened me a bit."

"I couldn't believe he did that. I get him being upset about Heather leaving Keith, but that was over the top. All in all, Mr. Meyers is a good guy though. His bark is bigger than his bite."

"How well do you know him?"

"I've known him my whole life. He'd do anything for anybody. He gets angry from time to time, but who doesn't?"

Anna took a sip of her drink. "I guess. Something seems off with Heather. I noticed it more today when the Meyers were here. Perhaps there's more to Heather's story than she's telling."

"I've gotten that feeling too. She's changed. I mean, I know a lot of time has passed and the cancer is taking a toll on her, but she's different. That spark. That silly side of her is gone."

"Almost like she's broken?"

"Yeah."

"Being cheated on can do that to a woman."

Guilt rushed from his toes to the top of his head. He took a sip of hot chocolate and swallowed it slowly. What an ignorant fool he'd been. No woman deserved that. He hated himself for what he'd done to Heather and then Corrin, but it hadn't stopped him from hooking up with women. The attention they gave him only filled the hole in his heart in the moment. Every time after, he'd promise himself never again. If only he could turn back the clock.

He set his mug on the coffee table. "If Heather and I would have ended up together, I'd have showered her with everything I could give her. I'd have made her feel like the most important woman in the world. And I would have given her all the kids she wanted."

"Is that so?" A hint of skepticism trailed in her voice.

"Do you doubt me?"

"Are you the type of man who can commit to one woman?"

His heart stopped, and he opened his mouth. Of course he could. Now. For Heather. He rubbed the stubble on his face. But he never had. Was Anna right? Could he? "What do you know?"

"I know Heather has been through enough, and you professing your love has piqued her interest. But unless you plan to change your ways, she's going to die lonelier than she is now."

"I love her. I was a stupid kid back then."

"But have you changed?"

He stared at the mug in his hands. "I want to be better."

"Be careful with Heather. She's hiding more than you think."

A moan came from down the hallway. JJ started to stand, but Anna said, "Sit. Finish your drink. I'll come get you if I need you."

He leaned his back against the couch. What was Heather hiding? He took a sip of the hot chocolate and closed his eyes. He hadn't realized how tired he was. A few minutes of sleep, then he'd head home.

JJ walked through darkness searching for light. Water dripped from behind him and echoed. The sound of screeching animals came from above. Someone lit a match, and everything came into view. Cave walls touched him on both sides, and a bat hung a few feet above him. The figure of a short gray-haired woman led the way twenty feet in front of him. Anna? He stepped over a stalagmite into a puddle of water. He steadied his pace, careful not to slip on the wet ground. The walls narrowed, and he turned sideways to fit through.

"Come on, boys," called a man's voice from further in the cave. "We're almost there."

"I'm coming, Dad."

A teenage boy raced toward JJ. As if JJ were a ghost, the boy ran through him. JJ froze and his heart stopped. What was going on?

"Wait for me," called a younger boy's voice.

JJ whipped his head in the direction of the voice, and the second boy ran through him. He had to be dreaming.

The gray-haired woman had disappeared, and the boys climbed on their bellies scooting across the cave floor. JJ followed through the tight squeeze that took him outside the cave into the starlit night sky. Crickets chirped, toads croaked, and owls hooted. He stood alone in tall grass. Where had everyone gone?

"I told you to keep up. What was your problem?" The man's voice came from over a large boulder.

JJ climbed over it and saw Mr. Meyers standing in front of the two boys.

Keith?

Bryson?

Mr. Meyers pointed his finger in Keith's face. "What happened?"

"Bryson couldn't make it over the steep incline. I helped him."

Mr. Meyers slapped Keith across the face. "I told you to leave him if he couldn't do it."

Keith rubbed his jaw. "He's nine and it's dark in there. He was crying."

"He would have found a way. You did."

"It took me all night, and I was terrified. I wasn't about to let him go through what you made me."

Mr. Meyers grabbed Bryson's collar. "Do you want to be a man or not?"

Bryson stared in his dad's eyes, his body shaking and his lips pressed hard together.

"Well do you?"

Bryson nodded.

"Then you go back in there and meet us on the other side."

Bryson shook his head. "I don't like bats, and it's dark in there."

"Be a man."

"Dad, leave him alone."

Mr. Meyers pushed Keith down, but he got up, his back straight and fists clutched. His dad punched him in the face, then knocked him down on to his back and put his knee to Keith's neck. "Don't you say another word!"

Keith gasped for air.

Mr. Meyers looked at Bryson. "You go back in there and find your way out in the dark. Do it now, or I will hold your brother down until you do."

Gurgling, Keith shook his head and grabbed at his dad's knee pressed into his throat.

"I'll do it," Bryson yelled. "Now let him go."

"Not until you're inside the cave."

Bryson's lip puckered. He climbed over the boulder, slid down, and went inside the cave.

Mr. Meyers took his knee off his son. "Don't you ever disobey me again!"

Rubbing his neck, Keith nodded.

JJ needed to throw up.

The silhouette of the gray-haired woman appeared at the opening of the cave. She entered, and JJ followed. Bryson sat barely inside, whimpering. The woman touched his small back before she walked down the path and disappeared.

Byson sniffled. "Don't be afraid. You can do this for Keith. Stay low to the ground and feel the path. That's what Keith said to do."

Bryson climbed onto his stomach and scooted between the low ceiling and floor. A bat screeched from above, and he shuddered. "Be a man."

JJ followed behind as the boy made his way through the cave in total darkness. Bryson screamed in pain halfway through, but kept going. When he reached the end, the morning sun had risen. Bryson fell out and collapsed. A large, bleeding cut ran from the top of his cheek to his chin.

A dark cloud descended, and Bryson disappeared

behind it. When the cloud lifted, the night sky shifted and JJ stood in a dimly-lit, small, unfamiliar living room with mismatched furniture. The scent of apple pie wafted past him.

Anna stood in the hallway. He stepped forward to join her and bumped into the coffee table.

"Keith, is that you?" Dressed in a short red spaghetti-strap dress, a younger, healthier Heather came around the corner. "I made you . . ." A frown spread across her face.

Not noticing JJ's presence, she grabbed the remote control off the table and curled up on the couch under a blanket. The phone rang, and she grabbed it off the end table next to her. "Hello. Hello. Anyone there?"

She hung it up, then laid it on the table. Clicking through the channels, she stopped at the *New Year's Eve Special*. A boy band performed, and she tossed the remote on the table.

JJ remembered watching this performance on TV. Corrin had teased about how attractive the guys from the band looked in theirs suits and that they had incredible voices. It had ticked him off. The New Year's Eve party Corrin had taken him to was lame, and he'd had no other choice than to listen to the punks sing.

He missed Heather. If she'd been at the party with him, the two of them would have found a way to have fun. And he wouldn't have needed the beer or the buzz.

JJ remembered wondering what Heather was doing to ring in the new millennium. Most likely having a better time than he was. She was probably living the high life with Keith at a military New Year's Eve party and wearing a tight dress. Keith would kiss her neck, and she'd moan, telling him they should leave the party early, and Keith would lead her out of the party and to their house. Keith was probably enjoying Heather the way JJ never had.

JJ had taken a swig of his beer. He had to hear her voice. He'd snuck away from the party and back to a bathroom, where he'd called Heather . . .

He whipped his head toward the phone she'd lain down a moment ago.

He waved his hands in front of Heather's face, but she didn't see him. He looked back at Anna, who turned down the hallway. What was going on? He followed her, but when he reached the end of the hall, it appeared as black nothingness and she'd vanished.

The dark turned to light again, and he was standing back in the unfamiliar living room. The New Year's Eve special now displayed a five-minute countdown, and Heather had fallen asleep. He picked up the blanket from the floor and covered her with it before sitting next to her. Her hair had fallen in her face, and he reached over to move it, when the front door flung open.

Startled as if he'd done something wrong, JJ jumped off the couch.

Keith stumbled in. The smell of flowery perfume and alcohol followed. He glared at Heather sleeping. "Lazy sack of bones. Get up."

When she didn't stir, he made his way to her face and belched in it.

Opening her eyes, she pushed him backward. "Ew. Keith. That's nasty."

"Don't push me away. What do we have under here?" He lifted the blanket. "Um, um, um. Look at you in that tight little dress. Who you wearing that for?" The anger rose in his voice.

She clutched the bottom of the sofa cushion. "I wore it for you. I also baked your favorite pie."

"You baked a pie? Is it any good?"

"I think so. It's your mom's recipe."

He pointed to the right toward the dining room table lit by red candles and decorated with rose petals. "What's that all about? Why are you making such a fuss over tonight?"

"I thought you'd be home sooner, and we could have our own New Year's Eve party."

Keith stood. "Yeah, well. I had things to do." He snatched a mint off the end table and popped it into his mouth, then grabbed her by her wrist and yanked her off the couch. "You look hot. I'll skip the pie and take a slice of you instead."

With closed eyes, he leaned toward her, and she stiffened. His lips touched hers, and she flinched.

"What's that about? You don't want me?"

"No, I do." She put her arms around his neck and pulled his face toward her.

"Forget it." Keith pushed her down onto the couch. "You couldn't come close to what the sweet little honey did for me. Talk about celebrating a new year."

JJ clutched his hand into a fist. "Why, you loser. How dare you?" No one heard him.

Keith left the room and returned with the pie

she'd prepared in a glass pan. The smell made JJ's mouth water. Keith stuck a fork in it and took a bite, then spit it at Heather. "Yuck. Can you do anything right?"

JJ swung at him, but his fists went through Keith.

Heather wiped the chunks of apple from her face. "What was that for? You're such a—"

"Now I know why JJ traded you in for Corrin. You're lousy in bed, fat, can't cook, and dumb as a box of rocks." He slapped her upside the head with the glass pan.

Wincing, she turned and touched the spot where he'd hit her.

"Look at me, stupid!" Keith grabbed her chin and forced her face upward.

Motionless, it appeared she wasn't breathing as her hollow eyes stared at Keith. He ran his thumb along the trail of blood dripping down Heather's face. "Don't ever try to make my mom's food again." Then he scooped the rest of the pie into the palm of his hand and threw it at her face. He crashed the pie pan against the coffee table, and it shattered into pieces. "Now clean this up. I'm going to bed. Don't bother joining me."

JJ swung at Keith again, but it was useless. Keith stormed down the hallway.

Blood trickled from her forehead into the apple pie. Expressionless, she walked to the kitchen, and JJ followed. She grabbed the kitchen towel from the counter and scraped the food off her, her movements slow and stoic.

Not a tear or moan escaped as she leaned over

the sink to wash her face. The water running down the sink turned red. After drying her face, she wrapped ice inside a towel and put it against her forehead. With one hand she grabbed the trash can and brought it to the living room. Like a robot on autopilot, she picked up the pieces of glass. One sliced her hand, and she cringed. JJ grabbed it. As if she knew he was there, she stared into his eyes. He ran his hand along her cheek. She closed her eyes and leaned into his hand. Could she feel his touch?

"10-9-8-7-6-5-4-3-2-1. Happy New Year!" From the television, people cheered, and the New Year's song played as the room turned dark and Heather faded away.

When the lights rose again, JJ stood in another living room where Heather, looking a little older and with a black eye, sat on a different couch, staring at an assortment of colorful flowers in a vase on the coffee table, next to a *Cosmo* magazine and a note addressed to her. A shower ran from down the hallway.

She opened the letter, and JJ read it over her shoulder.

I'm sorry. I missed you last night. Join me in the shower when you wake up.

She touched her swollen eye and rubbed her finger along a cut next to her eyebrow.

JJ could kill Keith. How dare he hurt Heather like that.

She jumped from the couch and darted to the front door, then held on to the handle as she stared back toward the hallway, then to the alarm panel next to the door.

She whispered, "Go."

"Yes. Go," JJ said.

The shower stopped, and Heather ran to the couch and picked up the magazine.

With a towel wrapped around his waist, Keith swaggered into the room. "I thought you were going to join me."

"I woke up and thought I'd skim through this real quick."

"Instead of joining me?" He turned the magazine up to his view. "Humph, are you taking good notes? There is a move or two you could learn from an article. I folded the page number down. Be sure to read it."

He snatched it out of her hand, flipped through the pages, and handed it back. The title made JJ's eyes widen.

She blushed. "I can't do that."

He grabbed the magazine and threw it across the room. "Don't even bother reading it then! You couldn't do it right anyway." His eyes moved up and down. "Given that body and what a waste."

She looked down. "Maybe I could try." She got off the couch and headed toward the magazine.

JJ stood in front of it with his arms across his chest. She had more class than that. As if she could see JJ, she stared into his eyes, then turned back to Keith. "I'm willing to do anything if you'd agree we can try in vitro fertilization."

A sly grin spread across his face. "A baby? Huh? If you'll do that." He pointed at the magazine. "I'll think about it."

She ran to the magazine and flipped to the page.

Keith laughed. "You stupid idiot. You think an ultimatum works on me? We aren't having kids." He ripped the magazine from her and leaned his face inches from hers. "Get this straight. I don't like kids. I don't want kids. We are *never* having kids."

"But I thought you said we might. We tried for a while."

"Well, I lied. We aren't. About twelve years ago, I got a vasectomy to guarantee it. You aren't ever getting pregnant."

Heather dropped to the ground and clutched her stomach. Not a tear fell, but rage entered her eyes. "How dare you? Why? Why would you do that and not tell me?" She rose and pointed a finger in his face. "You told me I could get off birth control so that we could try. Then you made me think for all these years I couldn't get pregnant. You are sick. I hate you!"

"The feeling's mutual." He punched her hard in the throat.

She clutched her neck and tried to shout, but he punched her in the stomach, and she doubled over then fell on her knees.

She panted for air and Keith entered numbers into the alarm. JJ fell to his knees beside her while Keith reentered the code. Beeping sounded from the panel, and Keith slammed the door as he left.

Heather stared at the door. The beeping increased in speed, announcing only a few more seconds until it would be set.

Clutching her stomach, she rolled onto her back and stared at the ceiling.

Her words came slow and in a whisper. "Help

me, please."

"I'm right here," JJ said.

She looked in his direction.

"Can you see me? I'm here. I'll help you." He put his hands under her to scoop her up, but his arms went through her.

She looked back at the ceiling. "God, please. Please rescue me."

Even though Heather hadn't shed a tear, JJ couldn't stop the faucet. *God, help her.*

Darkness enclosed the room and spun him around until he landed in a third living room.

Heather, thin and pale, sat on a suede couch. Her deep cough filled the room.

"Could you shut up? I'm trying to watch the game." Keith popped a handful of mixed nuts into his mouth.

"Sorry." Her voice sounded raspy, like the one she had in reality—wherever that was now.

"Don't talk either. You sound like a man. I must have coldcocked you in the throat pretty hard this time. I'm sorry about that, babe. But you know how I get when I'm tired and you aggravate me. I don't mean it. I love you." He kissed her neck.

"I know," she whispered.

He put his arms around her shoulder and pulled her against him. "You've been looking hot lately. How much weight have you lost?"

Still whispering, "I don't know. Maybe twenty, thirty pounds."

"Well, keep it up and I might just have to go AWOL instead of going on deployment." He lifted his eyebrows up and down and ran his hand along her thigh.

She stared at the floor and appeared to hold her breath.

He sat up. "What? You have nothing to say. You don't want me to stay?"

"No, it's not that. It's just I know you can't."

"I'd do anything for you. You know that. I'd go AWOL for you. But you—" He glared. "You wouldn't do anything for me. You probably can't wait for me to leave, huh? You've got someone else, don't you? And the moment I leave, you're going to go run off with him. Aren't you?"

He grabbed the collar of her shirt.

"No, there's no one."

"Yeah, right." He ran to the kitchen and rummaged through the drawers. "Who is he?" He came back into the room with a rolling pin.

"No one. There's no one."

He swung at her face with the rolling pin, but she blocked it with her arms.

"Leave her alone." JJ jumped on Keith's back, but again it was as if he wasn't there.

Keith reared the tool back. "I know you do. That's why you've finally lost the weight. You're doing it for him. Well, he can't have you."

She turned to block the blow to her face, and he caught the top of her right shoulder near her collarbone and back. She yelped. He hit her shoulder again and again, every time her screams intensified.

"You sick SOB." JJ jumped in front of her, but the rolling pin went through him and crashed into her shoulder. She tried pushing Keith away with her hands, but he grabbed both wrists with one hand and continued beating her.

"Your feet. Heather, your feet," JJ yelled.

She glanced down and twisted her body enough that she was able to kick Keith in the groin and then in the stomach. He doubled over.

She ran out the door into the night, the alarm blaring. Keith hobbled after her and caught her arm at the top of the stairs. "You want to go. Then go." He let go and pushed her.

She tumbled down the steps and landed with a thud at the bottom. She lay with her eyes closed and not moving.

JJ was going to throw up. This was Keith, hometown hero, the big brother everyone looked up to? What kind of twisted nightmare had JJ fallen into?

Heather sounded like she was choking, and blood trickled from her mouth down the side of her face. Keith ran down the steps and carried unresponsive, not-breathing Heather up the stairs. "I'm sorry, Heather. I love you." He kissed her bruised face. "I go crazy thinking of you with another man."

She gasped, then choked and coughed up blood.

"I'm sorry. I'm sorry. I won't do this again. I'm going to get help. I promise." He cried into her chest. "I promise."

The room faded to black.

Sweating and heart aching, JJ opened his eyes in the

Coles' living room. He rubbed his eyes. Was he still dreaming? He couldn't take any more of the nightmare. Everything looked the same as it had when he'd fallen asleep. His coat hung on a hook near the front door. His partially finished hot chocolate sat on the coffee table, and the Coles' bedroom TV could be heard.

From down the hallway, Anna walked toward him. "Heather's okay, but the pain in her chest is pretty bad. I gave her pain medicine and a sleeping pill. Sorry I didn't come out and let you know sooner. I wanted to sit with her until she fell back asleep. I thought you'd be gone by now."

"I guess I fell asleep. I had a crazy dream."

"You know dreams have a way of revealing truths to us."

JJ looked at the drink that had turned cold. "Yeah. I hope this one didn't. It started with a memory that a childhood friend told me and I'd forgotten."

"Do you want to talk about?"

JJ raked his hands through his hair. "The dream left a knot in my stomach. It felt real. What has Heather told you about Keith? Do you think . . . I hate to even say it . . . that he was abusive?"

Anna nodded. "It's what she hasn't said that's told me the most."

Chapter Seventeen

J J turned off the light in his office and hustled past Missy's desk.

"Dr. Jones, do you want this?" She reached behind her and grabbed his coat off her chair. "Thank you for letting me borrow it."

"No problem. Are you good for locking up?"

She smiled. "I don't mind. Where are you off in such a rush these days?"

"Remember Mrs. Meyers from a few weeks ago? The cancer patient?"

She nodded.

"I'm treating her at her home."

Missy touched his shoulder. "You said you were friends when you were kids. Are you okay?"

"No, but I'm doing what I can."

She came around the desk and held the coat out for him to put his arms in the sleeves. He slid his arms in. She tucked the collar down and ran her hand across the front along the buttons. She smelled flowery, and the desire to kiss her raced through his body. She looked up at him from under her lashes. He leaned in toward her mouth, and she closed her eyes.

Inches from Missy's lips, the words from Anna whispered in his ear. *Are you the type of man who can commit to one woman?*

Why did he do this over and over? He pulled back. "I can't. I'm your boss."

She blushed. "I don't mind." She pressed her body against his.

"What about your boyfriend?"

"We broke up."

He exhaled. "Believe me if this were a month ago, it might have worked out, but I have feelings for someone."

"That hasn't stopped you before." She raised her eyebrows.

He looked out the window. "I know, but I've changed, or I'm trying to change. Heather is worth it."

"Heather? As in Heather Meyers, the patient you are rushing out the door for? Doesn't that cross an ethical line?"

"No, because I'm not treating her under my practice. I'm helping her out as a friend."

She stepped backward. "Isn't she dying?"

He nodded. It was hard hearing those words. He saw Heather fading every day even as she built strength. He wouldn't bring himself to believe that one day soon she'd close her eyes and never wake again. The constant ache in his chest increased. What he wouldn't give for a cigarette. But smoking now seemed like a smack in the face to Heather. Lung cancer. What a sick joke.

Heather sat in her wheelchair in the living room, looking out the picture window at the wet yard, street, and sidewalk. The temperature had changed to an unseasonable fifty degrees that afternoon, melting the snow away.

"Let's go splash in the rain puddles." Anna entered from down the hallway with a pair of rain boots on her feet and another pair in her hands.

Heather giggled. "People will think we're crazy."

"Who cares what people think about an old lady and a woman in a wheelchair splashing around? We want to enjoy life, and splashing in puddles was on your list, right?"

"My list? You mean my bucket list? You read it."

Anna nodded. "It was on your nightstand. I'm sorry."

"That's okay. It wasn't a secret."

"I especially like number one. Forgive those who wronged you."

"That's going be a hard."

"Forgiving people can be a challenge."

"I don't know if I can do it. I've been hurt pretty bad by a few people, and I'm holding a fairly big grudge."

"Don't hold on to it for too much longer. Forgiveness can be freeing and take a weight off your shoulders."

"I've heard that, and I'm going to try. I've got some whoppers to deal with."

"I can imagine." Anna knelt down and slid the rain boots onto Heather's feet. "Let's put these babies on and jump in the puddles."

Heather smiled. Life wasn't boring with Anna around, that was for sure.

Anna wheeled Heather to the front door and opened it. The temperate February air filled Heather's lungs. She drew it in and blew it back out. How nice it was to be outside.

Anna wheeled Heather down the porch ramp to a large puddle in the driveway. Anna locked the wheels, then took Heather by her elbows and helped her stand. Using Anna's arms for balance, Heather kicked the water at her nurse.

"Hey now." Anna returned the gesture.

Laughter rippled through Heather, followed by a cough. A hand grabbed her from behind and helped Anna settle her into the wheelchair. When her cough stopped, JJ stepped in front of her and smiled. He was early. Her heart leapt with joy, and she grinned. She longed for evenings with him. He was the reason she'd forced herself to shower and make herself look presentable, even though it took everything out of her.

She reached for him. "Please help me back up. I'm okay."

Holding on to his strong forearms, Heather steadied herself. They stood toe to toe. She inhaled his incredible smell and got lost in his eyes. Why wouldn't she give in and let herself fall for him? Could she trust him with her heart again? She wanted to spend the rest of her life happy, and she could do that being his friend.

Water splashed all over her and JJ. She looked over at Anna standing in a large puddle, laughing.

"Hey!" Gripping hard to JJ's arms, Heather kicked water at Anna.

Like a five-year-old playing tag, Anna snickered and darted toward the house. "Try and get me."

"Me, get you?" Heather giggled. "Like that's fair. Taunt the dying woman who can't even stand on her own."

"Excuses, excuses." Anna stuck her tongue out, then ran up to the porch and opened the door.

"Where are you going?" Heather said.

"I've got to take care of something. You have fun."

"Chicken."

"Bawk, bawk." Anna flapped her arms. "No seriously, I need to talk to my father."

"Excuses, excuses." Heather laughed.

"Uncle. I give in." Anna winked before going into the house.

"Anna brought you out to play in puddles?" JJ laughed.

"Looks like it."

He kicked water onto her boots.

"Hey." She splashed him in return.

Soon they were splashing each other back and forth and laughing. After a few minutes, her chest tightened and mucus rattled in her throat. She blew out a breath, trying to steady her breathing, but she felt as if she was gasping for air. Afraid she'd collapse, she clutched his arms tighter.

"Do you need to sit?"

She nodded, and he helped her into the

wheelchair.

"Are you okay? I'm sorry I wore you out."

She smiled. "Don't be sorry. That's . . ." Pausing to catch her breath, she looked at him. "The most fun I've had in a long time."

A drip fell from the sky, followed by another and another. She didn't mind the rain. It reminded her she was free and alive and had time to enjoy moments like this. A minute later the rain came down quick, drenching them. He spun her chair around, hurried onto the porch, and opened the door.

"Wait," she said. "I don't know how many more times I'll have to stand in the rain."

Scooping her out of the chair, he returned to the yard and set her feet on the ground. She held on to his arms while she lifted her face toward the sky.

Letting go of JJ, she held her palms upward and spun around. She completed her turn and fell forward. He caught her, and she looked into his eyes. His chest rose against hers as he leaned forward. Her lips parted and grazed his. Her stomach knotted. This wasn't right. She turned away.

She was still married. She wouldn't be that kind of woman. Besides, she'd be dead soon.

Wearing the extra set of clothes he had in the trunk of his car, JJ sat in the chair next to Heather's bed as he waited for her to finish her bath and get dressed. A text notification chimed, and he pulled out his cell.

Hey man. This is Bryson. What's up?

Bryson? Was he wanting to reconnect? JJ hadn't had a close friend since Keith had torn him and Bryson apart. JJ didn't want to get his hopes up, but he sure missed the guy.

At Heather's. How about you?

Not much. I'm still in town. Want to grab a late lunch tomorrow?

Sounds good. McDougal Café?

Great. See you tomorrow. 2ish?

See you then.

JJ placed his phone on Heather's nightstand and rubbed the back of his neck. Tomorrow, JJ would ask Bryson if he knew Keith was beating the living daylights out of Heather. Of course the whole crazy thing might have just been a dream, but it seemed too real for that. He'd never had a vision before, and he wasn't some kind of kook, so why did he believe the nightmare was more than a figment of his imagination? He wanted to ask Heather, but it was none of his business, and he couldn't figure out how to broach the subject either. Would he be able to figure out how to bring it up to Bryson?

Anna wheeled Heather into the room, then propped the pillows for her to sit in the bed. Heather wore a pair of gray leggings and a matching scoop-neck top that exposed a little of her left shoulder.

He shook the yearning for her out through his fingers. "Feel better?" He winked.

"Yes, but I'm pretty tired. I don't know how much physical therapy I'll actually be able to do."

"That's okay. I wasn't going to do much

anyway."

Anna touched JJ's arm. "I'll be in the living room if you need me. I need to talk to my father again." Worry sat in her eyes.

"Is there anything I can do for you? Everything okay?" JJ asked.

"I just have a little unexpected issue I need to deal with, but my father's got it under control. I need to check in with him." Anna left the room.

Heather gave JJ a sly smile. "What's this about not making me do too much?"

"Since you were standing and kicking, I think you earned a break."

"Does that mean a longer massage?" She batted her eyes and stuck out her bottom lip.

He laughed. "If you want. You could convince me to do anything."

"The massage is my favorite part."

Massaging you is mine too. "That does seem to be the part everyone likes. For me though, I'd rather do the exercises and rest my hands." He winked. "Ah, but the life of a PT—no love for me. I give the massages and never get one in return."

"That doesn't seem fair." She patted the edge of her bed. He obliged and sat down facing her.

"No, silly. Turn around."

He raised his eyebrows, then turned.

"Now scoot back closer to me."

His heart raced. She ran her left hand along his back and moved up to his shoulders and neck. The light pressure did little to massage the muscles, but the touch sent him in a fight against his desires. Her hand ran down his arm and back up, and then she moved her hand across to the other shoulder and his neck.

He knew she meant nothing by it other than kindness, but he wanted to turn around and kiss her. Her lips had been so close earlier. He'd thought for a moment she'd given in.

He stiffened his back.

"Everything okay?" She stopped massaging.

"Yes, this feels nice. Been a long time since I've had a massage."

"You deserve it."

He turned to face her. "No, I don't."

"Sure you do. You've grown into a kind man."

"Why do you say that?"

"The way you talk about your kids and your patients." She looked down. "The way you take care of me."

If she only knew the truth. Should he risk their new rekindled friendship to tell her why he and Corrin divorced? No, he'd hide it as long as he could. Hopefully, she'd never find out.

Heather rolled to her side and stared out at the night sky while JJ massaged her shoulder. His hands sent sensation through her body that made her toes curl. She'd found a way to suppress the moans now, but over the last few days, as the pain eased, she began to enjoy the massages for more than simply pain relief. If he tried to kiss her again, she didn't know if she could stop herself.

His hands slid under the loose-neck shirt onto

her bare shoulder. She held her breath.

"Relax."

She exhaled and let her shoulders feel weightless under his massage. She closed her eyes. It was as if life had not happened apart from each other. He made her forget why she never wanted anything to do with a man again.

His hands stopped on her shoulder. "Heather?"

"Yeah?"

"What is this bruise from?"

More than a month and it was still there. Would it ever heal? "I tripped and fell down the stairs before I came back here. I guess it was the start of me losing my strength." The memory of what really happened sent phantom pain through her shoulder.

JJ pulled the back of her shirt down, exposing the whole shoulder. He traced it with his finger. His touch, like a hot branding tool, seared her skin. "This doesn't look like it's from a fall."

She flinched. "I don't know why. I fell down the steps."

JJ rolled her over and stared in her eyes.

"What?" Heather grabbed the edge of the comforter and twisted it between her thumb and fingers.

"Did you go to the hospital?"

"No."

Silence echoed against the walls. He searched her face. "Why not?" He took her hands in his. "Did Keith push you down the steps?"

She clutched the sheet tighter and swallowed hard. She couldn't tell him the truth. He couldn't see her as a weak person who'd let Keith do that to her.

"I slipped."

"Stop lying. I know the signs of abuse."

She stopped breathing. "What are you talking about? Keith cheated on me, but he never—"

He lifted her to a sitting position and pulled the shirt down off her shoulder. "Stop. These are marks consistent with blunt-force trauma from an object, not a—"

"Get out!" She pointed to the door. "You're crazy. I fell down the steps. Why are you fighting me on this?"

He moved a strand of hair off her face. "Because I love you."

She stared at the bed. She hated lying to him, but he didn't need to know what she'd been through. "Then believe me. You're wrong."

"You told Mr. and Mrs. Meyers that Keith would rather you be sick than get you the help you need. What does that mean? You deserved better than that."

She shook her head. "I can't explain it."

"Why not? Tell me the truth. I won't look at you any different. You are my Heather. My Cole."

Her heart thundered in her ear. The truth sat on the tip of her tongue. "I never had agoraphobia. He didn't like me leaving the house."

"Why?"

She closed her eyes.

"Heather, why?"

Tell him. Trust him. He loves you. She drew her lips into her mouth. "I don't know. I really don't. It all started when he caught a guy he worked with checking me out. When we got home that day, he told me my shorts were too short and my top revealed too much. From that point on, I had to ask to go anywhere and I was only allowed to wear sweat pants and baggy T-shirts. Eventually, he wouldn't even let me go to the store or the doctor." She blew out a quivering breath of air.

"Did you go places anyway?"

She shook her head.

"Why?"

"He was my husband and I—"

"That's a load of bull and you know it. Don't lie to me."

She wanted to run away from this conversation. Shame sat in the pit of her stomach, twisting it apart.

"He beat you into submission. Didn't he?"

A tear slid down her cheek. Would he stop interrogating her? She didn't want to admit any more to him.

"No."

"You promise me?"

She looked him in the eyes. She couldn't lie to him.

"Cole, please tell me the truth."

She nodded as another tear fell. He wiped it away.

"He was very abusive."

Chapter Eighteen

Full of a ball of nerves, JJ stepped into the café. He hadn't slept all night, and he needed to confront Bryson about the truth regarding Mr. Meyers, Keith, and his vague memory of the cave incident.

Bryson waved him over to the booth in the back. Two soft drinks sat on the table. When he reached the booth, Bryson stood and gave JJ a hug. "How're you doing?"

"Okay. How about you?" JJ slid out of his coat and took a seat.

Bryson sat across from him. "Fairly well."

"That's good." JJ wanted to get right to it, but he'd ease into it. "Do you like it up in Indianapolis?"

"Yep. I train horses."

"Like for the Derby?"

"I haven't been lucky enough for that yet. But someday, I hope. I do all kinds of training, from races to equestrian sports to training horses to be emotional support and service animals. I even train them to work with the police."

"That's pretty impressive."

"Thanks. And you got your medical degree and are a physical therapist."

"I know. Can you believe it?"

Bryson nodded. "You always were smart. Book smart." He smiled. "Not so smart with the ladies though."

"Hey now. I had more luck with them than you did."

"Exactly. That was the problem. You had a girlfriend." Bryson grinned.

"You're right. I wasn't smart with the ladies. I messed that up twice."

"How *is* Corrin?"

"She seems okay. We mainly talk about the kids. I don't really know anything about her personal life."

"What happened to you two?"

"Me and my stupidity for other women."

"That always gets you in trouble." Bryson shook his head. "I hear that you have a teenager."

"Yes, a fifteen-year-old daughter and six-year-old boy. They are amazing kids."

"That's great. My Sebastian is full of energy. He keeps us on our toes, that's for sure."

JJ couldn't take any more of the small talk. "I was thinking the other day about that scar on your face."

Bryson ran his hand down his long beard. "What about it?"

"You got it when you went with your dad on that cave trip, right?"

"Yeah."

"I kind of remember you telling me that your dad forced you to go in by yourself and find your way out. That he'd hit Keith and pinned him down until you agreed to go in. Is that true?"

Bryson's eyes widened. "Yeah. I'm surprised I told you the whole thing. I normally say I sliced it in the cave and came out bleeding. I leave all the other details out, but you were my best friend back then. We were young, like eight or nine or something."

"I forgot about it until the other day. I don't remember your dad being like that."

"He put on a good show. He wasn't the nicest. Sissy, Keith, and I watched out for each other. Mom tried, but she couldn't do much. Sissy moved out as soon as she could. Keith at least stayed until I graduated."

"Why didn't you tell me?"

"I didn't want anyone to know what my dad was like. I avoided him as much as I could. That's why I was over at your house all the time until Keith and Heather started dating. I owed Keith. He'd had my back and protected me over the years. When he told me you were bad news and to stop hanging out with you, I listened."

Everything became clear. "I've missed you."

"Me too. We were partners in crime, huh?"

"That we were."

"Remember that time . . ."

JJ's mind raced with questions he needed to ask, but how would Bryson answer? Keith walked on water in his eyes. JJ interrupted whatever Bryson was talking about. "Did Keith ever hurt you?"

"No. Never. He wouldn't."

JJ took in a deep breath and blew it out slowly. "Keith abused Heather. That's why she left him."

Bryson raised an eyebrow. "No. He wouldn't."

"She admitted it to me last night. She has a huge bruise on her shoulder from a month ago. She said she fell down the steps, but . . ."

"But what?" The anger rang in Bryson's voice. "Keith would never hurt her. She's his world."

"Heather said she doesn't have agoraphobia and he wouldn't even let her leave the house. That's why Sissy came to stay with her."

"She's lying. He adored her."

"Maybe too much. Like he was obsessed?"

Bryson shook his head. "Not Keith. He wouldn't hurt her. He knows what we went through."

"He also cheated on her over and over."

Bryson rolled his eyes. "Like you have room to talk. I've heard the gossip around town. You cheated on Corrin, and your daughter caught you in the act. I wanted to give you the benefit of the doubt. But you haven't changed at all. You're still that selfish punk who couldn't let Heather be happy. Stop planting ideas in her mind. I already told you I thought the cancer was messing with her thoughts." He stood and threw a few dollar bills on the table. "The fact that she's allowed you to be her physical therapist is proof of that." He walked toward the door, then turned around. "Keith will be here tomorrow to set all of this straight."

JJ's shoulders tightened. "Does Heather know?"

"I don't know." Bryson stormed out of the café.

JJ had to get to her now. He rushed out the door

and dialed Corrin's number. He climbed inside his car, backed up, and sped down the road to Heather's house.

"Hi, Daddy." Zac's voice filled the car as JJ drove through town.

"Hey, buddy. Can I talk to Mommy?"

"Sure. Mommy! Daddy wants to talk to you!"

Come on. Come on. Get off the road. The car in front of him put-putted down the road, slowing JJ to twenty miles an hour. JJ weaved over the center line and zoomed ahead of the car.

"Hey, JJ, what's up?"

"I have to go to Heather's, and I don't know how late I'll be. I'm sorry."

"Is everything okay? She's not—"

"No, she's okay for now. Please let the kids know I'll call them later. Again, I'm sorry."

"Do you need me to do anything?"

"No, but thanks. I'll tell you more later."

He hung up.

Brakes screeched outside. Heather peeked out her bedroom window. JJ? It was three. Why was he so early? He hopped out of his car and ran to the porch.

The doorbell rang, then Anna's and JJ's voices carried into Heather's room. As they got closer, she could finally make out what they were saying.

"Come on back. I don't believe she's sleeping."

The door swung open, and JJ rushed in. Sitting down on the bed next to her, he grabbed her hands.

Drops of sweat sat on his forehead. What was going on?

"Keith knows everything. He's coming here tomorrow."

Her heart stopped, then pounded faster than she thought possible. She had known Keith would find out soon enough, but not this fast.

She searched JJ's face. She needed him to protect her. Her parents, JJ, and Anna all knew the truth now, but that didn't help the fear creeping into her mind. Keith would hurt her, hurt her parents and Anna and JJ. He'd do anything to get to her.

JJ wrapped his arms around her. "I've got you. It's okay. Stop shaking. I won't let him hurt you ever again."

She held on to JJ. Life would have been better with him. "Thank you for being here."

He pulled her in closer. "I'm not going anywhere. I'll always be here."

JJ rubbed his hands together as his insides twisted with fury. He sat in the chair next to Heather, knowing he didn't want to hear what she was about to share. Her parents sat on the end of the bed touching her legs, and Anna stood in the doorway.

Heather reached for her mom's hand. "It's time I tell you guys everything. I know you already know what Keith did, but since he's coming tomorrow, I want you to know how bad it was. I know you believe me, but he can be a charmer."

"Of course we believe you," her father said.

She cleared her throat. "A few months after we got married, we were watching a baseball game. I mentioned the batter had a good stance. Keith went off about how I shouldn't be checking out guys. I didn't understand where he got that idea from, so I laughed. I swore his eyes burned red as if the devil had taken over him. He slapped me across the face and told me to never laugh at him again. He apologized and said he felt awful about it. He didn't hurt me again until a few weeks later, but after that he hit me several times a week, sometimes every day or more. He never let me leave the house alone."

She took in a breath and blew it out slowly. "Sissy came to stay with me during his deployments. He had warned me I was *not* to go anywhere. But after living like a prisoner, I ignored his warning and ran a few errands. I'd thought, what could he do to me while he was gone? Sissy had told him about the few trips I'd made. She didn't know, of course, that when he got home from deployment he punched me for every time I'd left.

"The stomach for running to the grocery store for milk. The face for going to a movie. In the center of my back for a trip to the bank. And my side for stopping for a burger. After that I never dared to go out again."

A tear slid down her cheek, and JJ wiped it. He'd kill Keith tomorrow. "Why didn't you tell anyone?"

Heather closed her eyes. "I thought about telling Sissy once, but I figured she wouldn't believe me, and she told him everything. Who else would I tell? I wasn't allowed to have a cell phone or call anyone from our home phone. Once, I called my mom without his permission, but he figured out what I'd done. Another beating for that. He put alarms around our house so he'd get alerts if a door or window opened."

JJ clutched his fist. He'd show Keith what a beating was. How dare he keep Heather locked up like a captive in a dungeon?

"He tracked anything I did on the computer." She stared at her fingers while she twiddled them. "When he discovered I'd been looking at pictures from IU's website of my softball year, he threw the laptop at me and hit me with it until it broke because he claimed I was trying to live in the glory days before him. He disconnected our internet after that." She took in a deep breath and blew it out. "I thought I was trapped."

"How did you finally get away?" Anna asked.

Heather looked up. "The night he pushed me down the steps, I realized I had to leave. A few days later, a neighbor slid a note under my front door. She'd heard the fights and wanted to help me. She gave me three thousand dollars and the keys to her car. I ran three days later. I wasn't going to come here. I was going to disappear forever."

JJ wanted to wipe every awful memory from her mind. How dare Keith treat her like that? His stomach churned.

She looked at her parents. "But I had to see you guys. I missed you. When I walked through the front door, I finally felt free."

Her mother gasped. "Dan. What are we going to do? He's coming here tomorrow."

"You aren't letting him in this house. That's what you're doing." JJ stood with clutched fist.

Her father squeezed Heather's leg. "I agree."

"No. I want to talk to him. He needs to know it's over."

She had to stand up to him. To show him he may have taken all those years from her, but he hadn't completely destroyed her. She was taking back her life, as short as it might be. And he would never again have control over her.

Chapter Nineteen

Watching *Back to the Future*, Heather sat on the couch snuggled next to her father. He leaned over and kissed her head, then laughed at the truckload of manure dumping into the back of Biff's car. She had missed days like these. If Keith weren't arriving at any moment, she could actually pay attention to the movie.

"What did I miss?" JJ carried a bowl of popcorn into the room. He popped a handful into his mouth as he sat in the blue armchair closest to her father, then leaned over and offered her dad some.

Taking a handful, her dad said, "You missed the skateboard chase scene."

"Ah, man. Love that part."

Heather smiled. It was nice having JJ and her dad in the same room and getting along. During his earlier years, JJ had one thing on his mind, and her dad, watching them like a hawk, made sure the teenage boy and his hormones kept his hands and mouth where they belonged. Now both men had the same thing on their minds—taking care of her.

A car door slammed. JJ ran to the window and

peeked through the curtain as her dad went to the front door. Anna and Heather's mother entered from the hallway and locked arms. JJ joined her father at the door. Heather's army, ready for combat.

Feeling like an anxious paratrooper about to join a mission, her heart sped through her chest. Time to step off the platform and jump. She was dying, but she still had fight left in her.

Her dad opened the door.

Keith scoffed. "What are you doing here?"

His voice sent her nerves in an uproar as if electrocuting her from head to her toe. Hyperventilating, she couldn't catch her breath. Her chest compressed, and a cough tickled her throat. She swallowed it down. Being afraid didn't mean she couldn't fight the monster.

"JJ's our guest," her dad said. "Not that it's any of your business, but he's been helping Heather, and I wanted him here today."

"It *is* my business because my wife is in there. She came here without me, and JJ decided to move in on her."

"It's not like that." JJ balled his fists. "Why don't you just leave, Keith?"

Why was JJ saying that? He knew she wanted to talk to Keith.

"I'm not going anywhere without Heather." He tried pushing his way through the door, but JJ and her dad stood taut, shoulder to shoulder.

"Heather. Heather. Babe. Can we talk, please?"

Since the first time he'd hit her, she'd hoped the man she'd fallen in love with was still in there. She grasped the arm of the couch and pulled herself up.

"Heather?" her mom whispered.

Not sure if she could make it, even with adrenaline pushing her wobbly legs forward, she walked toward the door.

Her dad raised his voice. "No, you cannot come in my house. You are no longer welcome here. I know everything you did to my daughter."

No. She needed to talk to him.

"Sir, I don't know what she told you, but I love her."

"A man does not hit a woman he loves. Go away."

Heather touched her dad's arm. "Dad, I want to talk to him. It's okay."

"No." JJ shook his head.

"It isn't up to you. He's my husband. I want to talk to him."

Her dad looked in her eyes. "I can tell him everything."

"Thank you, but no. I want to do it."

The walk from the couch had taken all her energy. She grabbed her father's arms as she collapsed, and her dad turned, catching her by the elbow. The space between the two men left room for her to see Keith.

Keith gasped, and his eyes bulged. "Oh, my gaw . . . Heather. Are you sick?"

He didn't know?

"Come in, please. Let's talk." Her voice sounded confident, but her heart clogged her throat. She swallowed hard.

Her dad raised his eyebrow.

"It's okay. I *need* to do this. If you can help me

back to the couch, we can talk there."

Her dad scooped her into his arms and opened the door wider for Keith to enter. Frowning, Keith looked at her with downward eyes. She knew in his crazy, demented way, he thought he loved her.

Her father carried her to the couch, then set her down. Keith took the spot next to her, and her father hoovered in front of them. Her mother, JJ, and Anna stood in the middle of the room, staring at them.

"Can we have some time alone, please?" Keith asked gently.

"Absolutely not," JJ nearly barked.

Keith glared at JJ while he bobbed his knee up and down.

Her dad moved to JJ and touched his shoulder. "Honey, I don't feel comfortable leaving you."

"He won't hurt me while you're all in the next room. If he does, you can call the police."

Her father picked up the cordless phone. "Okay, but we will be in the kitchen if you need us."

The women followed her dad, but JJ, with his arms across his chest, didn't budge. She stared at him and nodded toward the kitchen. He shook his head.

"Please," she whispered.

Tightening his lips, JJ pointed at Keith. "You lay one hand on her—"

Keith laughed. "Chill, dude."

"I'll show you chill." JJ took a step toward Keith, but Heather's father, who'd come back to the room, placed his hand on JJ's chest and stopped him.

"Let's give them a minute."

Heather pointed at JJ. "I want you to go in the kitchen. If you don't, then you can leave my house right now. I need to talk to Keith. Alone." She glared at him. "Do you understand?"

JJ huffed. "But—"

"But nothing. Go." She pointed to the front door. "Or leave."

"Don't touch her." JJ walked toward the kitchen.

When everyone had left, Keith leaned forward to kiss her cheek. "I like the way you bossed him."

She turned away. He reached for her hand, but she pulled it away.

"What's that about?" he growled.

"Why are you here?"

"I don't know. You tell me. My mom said it was an emergency and that I needed to come home." He flared his nose and spoke through gritted teeth. "From what I gather, you've decided to leave me and turn your parents against me?"

His family hadn't told him anything?

"Why is that idiot JJ here?" Wild rage that she'd seen too many times sat in his widened eyes. He jerked his head and lifted his hands.

She covered her face.

"What? I'm not going to hit you." He looked toward the kitchen wall. "Why didn't your dad want to let me in? What kind of lies have you been telling them?"

"They aren't lies. I told them everything." She trembled on the inside, but she wouldn't let him see that. Fear didn't own her, and he certainly didn't either. "I don't want to be married to you anymore."

His jaw stiffened. "But I love you."

184

"I don't want to spend the rest of my life with someone who has lied to me, cheated on me, and beaten me."

His clenched jaws softened, and he ran his hand along his mouth. His eyes searched hers. He reached for her again, but she pushed his hand away.

"Stop," she said.

"A man should be able to touch his wife without her worried he's going to hurt her." He searched her eyes. "I need help. I know it. I told you that before I left. I'll change. I can't lose you, babe."

She felt sorry for him, but that didn't mean she'd go back to him. She'd heard his spiel before. Instead, she cleared her throat. "You don't have a choice. You're losing me either way."

"What does that mean? Have you already moved on with JJ?"

"No, he's my physical therapist."

"Your physical therapist? For what?"

"He's helping me build strength and trying to alleviate my pain."

He scrunched his eyebrows. "Why?"

She dipped her chin to her chest. She hated to hear it every time she said it. She looked him straight in the eyes. "I have lung cancer. Stage four."

This time when he reached for her hands, she didn't pull away. "How? You don't smoke."

Heather shrugged. "It's in other places in my body too, like my shoulder. The doctors said it could have started there and spread to my lungs. It's too far along to tell. I have a few spots on my skin too. Dr. Sutter said it very well could have all started as melanoma." She pulled her hand away. "But we'll never know now. If I'd gone to the doctor sooner, it might have been treatable."

"Have you started chemotherapy? Radiation?"

"It's too late for that. I have less than two months left."

He ran his hand along the top his head, and his eyes darted back and forth. "What? No. They have to be wrong."

"They're not. If you hadn't played Russian roulette with my life, then . . ." She pointed in his face "Not once in seventeen years, even when I had a fever, would you let me see a doctor, except to get birth control of course. It was a matter of time before either you killed me or an illness. I'd rather finish my life with dignity than spend another moment with you."

He fell on his knees and put his head in her lap. "I'm sick. I don't want to be like that. I really don't."

She shook her head and scooted over. "I can't be with you. Even if you promise to never cheat or hit me again. You've taken too much away from me."

He lifted his head. "Heather, I want to be here for you. I really do." He stood up and threw his hands on top of his head. "Please let me show you."

"If you love me, then let me go." Adrenaline driving her, she pushed herself off the couch and made her way to the kitchen and clutched onto the doorframe for support "JJ, will you take me to my room? Dad, would you show Keith out?"

"No, Heather. That's not it." Keith gritted his

186

teeth. "Do you hear me? It's not over."

He stepped toward her as JJ lifted her and carried her down the hallway.

"JJ, you better bring her back here. I'm not done talking to her."

Heather looked up at JJ. "I want to say one more thing to him."

JJ turned around.

"Keith, I'm done talking to you. It's over."

Heather let out a big breath as JJ laid her down on her bed. A flood of tears broke through and poured down her face. "I did it."

JJ smiled. "You were strong. I'm proud of you. Now your dad will take care of the rest. You okay?"

She wiped the tears from her face and smiled. "Yes."

JJ returned into the living room. Mr. Cole and Keith stood in the middle next to the coffee table. If Keith didn't get out of this house soon, JJ didn't think he'd be able to control himself from giving him a hard kick out the door.

"Heather was too worn out to continue the conversation with you. I'm going to finish it." Mr. Cole handed papers to Keith.

Keith looked down at them. "Divorce papers? I don't think so. I'm not signing these."

"Yes, you are. You have shown you don't have her best interest at heart. We're not allowing you to make any medical decisions for her. You *will* sign these."

"No. I'm her husband, and I plan to be with her through this."

JJ stepped next to Mr. Cole. "We have no intention of letting you anywhere near her after today. She wanted to talk to you, so we honored that. You *are* going to give her a divorce."

"You may have a PhD and you think you're something, but you aren't going to tell me how this happens. I'll tell you." Keith turned toward Mr. Cole. "I'm taking her to my parents' house. You can fire that nurse of yours and get rid of this joke." He pointed to JJ. "I might let you and Mrs. Cole visit if you stop all this." He threw the papers at Heather's dad.

Mr. Cole pointed his finger in Keith's face. "Get this straight. Your marriage is over. She said if you don't sign these papers, she'll go to your superiors and tell them what you've done."

Keith rolled his eyes. "It's her word against mine. There is no proof."

"There *is* proof," JJ said. "She's had a full body scan to determine where the cancer has spread, and it came back this morning. You know what they found? Years' worth of broken bones throughout her body that never healed correctly because you never took her to the doctor. She told her doctor everything. It's all documented."

Mr. Cole leaned in close to Keith's face. "Here's the deal. You will sign the papers, or your marine career is over."

Keith's face turned red as he looked between Mr. Cole and JJ. The dude ought to take the deal, because if he didn't, JJ would help Heather do whatever it would take to wreck his life. He deserved to have nothing left.

"Enjoy the cold fish. If you had ever slept with her, you'd understand why I fooled around." Keith snatched the papers off the floor and took the pen out of Mr. Cole's hand. After signing the papers, he slammed them on the coffee table and stood inches from JJ.

JJ clutched his fist. He'd take the guy down.

Mr. Cole stepped between Keith and JJ. "How dare you disrespect my daughter like that. Get out of my house. Now."

"Truth is truth. Your daughter was a lousy wife. Probably learned it from Mrs. Cole."

Mr. Cole reared up his fist and punched Keith on the jaw.

Keith rubbed his face and grinned. "That didn't even hurt." He turned to the door and opened it. "You all better watch your backs. I signed those papers, but Heather and I aren't done. You mark my word—you aren't safe." He pointed at Mr. Cole then JJ. "Neither one of you."

Chapter Twenty

JJ, with Amelia and Zac by his side, stepped in behind a large line of people buying tickets for the high school basketball game against Danburg's biggest rival.

"Do you think we'll get tickets?" Zac asked.

"I hope we got here early enough. Most games sell out pretty quick though. It depends on how many tickets they presold." JJ tousled his son's hair. "If not, we can watch the game on the high school network."

"Yeah, but it's more fun to be here."

JJ nodded. "Fingers crossed. Only a few more people in front of us."

JJ caught sight of a brown-haired boy standing with a group of guys smile and wave at Amelia. She returned the gesture, and the boy winked.

"Who's that?" JJ asked.

Amelia's face turned pink.

"Is that the boy you can't stop talking about?"

She looked up at him from under her lashes.

He nudged her arm with his elbow. "Good-looking fellow."

"Dad. Shhhh."

"What?" JJ feigned ignorance.

"He's right over there."

JJ looked at him. "Okay. Do you want me to invite him to sit with us?"

"No, stop. You're embarrassing me. And I have my student-section tickets, remember? You just need get tickets for you and Zac."

"What's his name?"

"Why?"

"I want to know the name of the boy my daughter has a crush on."

"Stop. Shhh." Amelia's face turned a darker shade of pink.

JJ smiled. "Okay, then I'll have to call him Jim Bob."

"Dad!"

"I'm going to go introduce myself to Jim Bob."

"Daddy, if you do—"

He grabbed her into a bear hug. "Ah, I won't embarrass you like that. Go hang with your friends. I'll see you after the game. Hopefully, there are still seats left for me and Zac."

Amelia playfully rolled her eyes, then waved as she joined the teenagers standing with Jim Bob.

"Only two more people in front of us now." Zac pointed.

JJ looked in front of him and rubbed his hands. "Awesome."

The guy at the ticket table stood and announced, "Sorry, guys, but we just sold our last ticket."

"Ah man." Zac drooped his shoulders and hung his head low.

"It's okay."

"But I wanted to watch the game and go to the concession stand."

"I know. I tell you what. Let's stop by the concession stand and stock up on food to watch the game back at the apartment."

"I guess." The disappointment rang in Zac's voice. "Can we get lots of candy bars?" His eyes lit up.

"Of course."

They made their way down the hallway to the snack bar.

"JJ, what a surprise. I didn't know you were coming today." Mr. Cole stepped in line next to him and stretched his hand forward.

"We tried, but the tickets are sold out."

Mr. Cole nodded. "I have two extra seats next to me. The family we normally sit with is out of town, so they gave me their tickets. You want them?"

"Sure. That would be wonderful."

"Great. Heather and Anna came too. They'll be happy to see you guys." Mr. Cole handed JJ the tickets. "The seats are in the front row."

"Thanks."

"See you in there. I'm going to join the ladies."

"See you in a minute." JJ pointed toward the concession stand. "You want anything?"

"No, thanks. But tell Mrs. Cole I said hi. She's working in there."

"Will do."

Zac and JJ walked down the hallway to the concession stand directly outside the gym doors. Mrs. Cole waved at them from the popcorn machine

192

in the back corner of the small room, then made her way to the counter. The young girl working the window stepped over to help another customer.

"It's good to see you guys. Is Amelia here too?"

"She's with her friends."

"What can I get you?"

Zac put his hands on the counter. "What kind of candy bars do you have?"

"We've got lots." She pointed toward the assortment.

"I'll take that one."

"My favorite." She handed him the chocolate bar. "And you, JJ?"

"I'll take a popcorn and two Sprites. Mr. Cole says hi. He gave us the extra tickets next to him."

"Enjoy. They are great seats. The perk of being the Christian Athletes pastor."

JJ took the popcorn and drinks, then he and Zac went to the gym, which was already crammed with people and the chatter of the fans. The teams warmed up on their side, and the sound of balls dribbling amped JJ's soul, reminding him of the days when he'd played on this court and Heather would cheer for him from the stands.

The crowded gym didn't stop him from spotting her right away in her red Danburg High School hoodie, sitting next to Anna. She turned her head slightly and met his gaze. Following the fast beat of his heart, he picked up the pace and headed toward her.

She smiled. "Hey, guys. Zac, you want to sit next to me?"

Beaming from ear to ear, he ran around JJ and

193

took the requested seat. Anna slid down and patted the spot between her and Heather. JJ sat down and winked at Heather. She winked back. He nudged her with his shoulder, and she nudged back.

He held his popcorn over for her. "Want any."

She shook her head.

"Want a candy bar?" Zac asked. He held up an assortment for her to choose from.

"That's quite a selection." She tapped the top of each one. "I'm not hungry though. Thank you."

"I hear Indiana high school basketball is quite a thing to encounter," Anna said.

JJ grinned. "That it is."

"You haven't lived until you've encountered at least one Indiana high school game." Heather beamed. "Back in high school there was nowhere I'd rather be on a Friday night than at a game. Is Amelia here?"

"Of course. She's in the student section."

Anna took a few pieces of popcorn. "I'm glad Pastor Cole invited me."

"This was the best game to come to. Linville is our biggest rival," Heather said.

The teams headed toward the locker rooms, and the cheerleaders lined up midcourt as Mr. Cole entered the gym, waving at people and stopping a few times to shake hands. When he reached his seats, he kissed Heather on the head, gave Zac a fist bump, then waved at JJ and Anna.

The cheerleaders performed a dance routine, but JJ watched Heather instead. The routine ended, and the cheerleaders returned to their spot in front of the student section, where they faced the court waving their fingers in the air. An upbeat song played, and the crowd roared as the Danburg team busted through the gym doors and lined up at the top of the court.

"Welcome to Danburg High School. This evening's game features the Linville's Pirates and yourrrr Danburg Bulllldooooogs!" The commentator's voice echoed throughout the gym.

The crowd stood and stomped their feet, rattling the bleachers. The announcer recited the names of the opposing team's starters. The gym hushed except for a few claps.

"Here's your Bulldog starting lineup.

"Playing center at six foot four, number thirty-five, Michael Terry!"

The gym vibrated under the cheering and stomping. The player ran through the tunnel of players giving high fives, then he gave the referees and people working the scoreboard table fist bumps. Each player called did the same, and the crowd grew louder each time. The band played the school fight song, and the spectators chanted.

The teams lined up at the half-court line for the tip-off. Danburg got possession and took the ball down the court.

Touching her heart, Anna said. "Oh my. You guys know how to do it right."

JJ winked, then looked over at Heather. Her voice carried over the others as she sat cheering. He always loved watching her take in a game. She moved her feet up and down on the floor and clapped.

"Yes!" She pumped her arm in the air, then

winced and brought it down quick.

He turned to see what play he'd missed. A three-point shot. He looked back at her.

Her eyes, intent on the game, followed the ball. She rested her elbows on her knees and her chin in her hands. With every good play, she cheered.

Halftime arrived, and the cheerleaders again took the court for a routine. After they finished, the principal drew a seat number from the spinning cage sitting on the scoreboard table. "Section three, seat six. You've been selected for a chance to win fifty dollars if you can make a shot from the half-court line."

"Well, what do you know? That's me." Anna stood and hustled to the center line.

The principal greeted her with a handshake. "Are you up for this?"

"You know I am!" She stretched her arms in front of her and then behind her.

JJ looked at Heather and Zac. "Of course it'd be her, huh?"

Heather smiled, then spoke to Zac. "You think she'll make it?"

"Nah."

Anna took the ball and dribbled it a few times, then stepped back several steps. She dribbled the ball quickly and moved forward. When she reached the line, she bent her knees, and with perfect form she raised the ball to her chest, jumped, and shot the ball.

Swish.

Anna threw her arms in the air and did a celebratory dance. JJ and the crowd jumped to their feet and roared a collective "Ooooo!"

"You go, Ms. Anna," Heather yelled. "Woo-hoo!"

JJ looked over at Heather. She'd used her hands to push herself up, but she fell back down onto her seat. If she wanted to join in Anna's victory, he would help. He wrapped his arms around her waist and held her up.

"Thank you."

He smiled. She slipped a little, then wrapped her arm around his waist. He could hold her like this forever.

The principal shook Anna's hand. "Way to go. You surprised us all. Here's your fifty dollars." He handed her an envelope.

"Thank you."

The crowd cheered one last time, then the majority dispersed from their seats to the concession stand or to talk with other spectators. With her palms facing upward and looking at JJ and Heather, Anna sashayed back to the stands. "How about that?"

"That was awesome!" Zac pointed at Anna with both of his pointer fingers.

She tousled his hair. "Thanks. You want to go with me to the concession stand? I've got money burning a hole in my pocket."

Zac looked at JJ. "Can I?"

"Sure."

"You all want anything?" Anna asked.

"No, thanks," JJ said

"Me either." Heather shook her head.

Anna took Zac's hand, and they headed out of

the gym. Amelia met them along the way and gave Anna a high five. JJ helped Heather sit down.

"Can you believe Anna? She's amazing. A bad hip and all, and she sunk that shot."

Heather, looking down, smiled. "Pretty unbelievable."

Mr. Cole scooted down to the opposite side of Heather. "Who is Anna Ingram? Is there anything that woman can't do?"

"I couldn't have even made that shot back in the day." Heather laid her head on her father's shoulder.

"You feel okay?" her father wiped a sweat bead from her brow.

"I'm getting worn out."

She barked a deep cough, and her father held her up through it.

"I'm glad I got to come to one game at least, before I . . ."A single tear slid down Heather's cheek.

JJ wanted to hold her. *Take me instead.*

From behind them, JJ heard a woman say, "I heard it's lung cancer. Stage four."

"How awful," a man said. "I remember when she was a little girl sitting here watching the games. What a shame."

"I heard she up and left Keith."

"What's Dr. Jones doing with her?"

JJ turned around and looked at them. They looked away, as if they hadn't been talking about Heather or him.

"I guess more than just the church knows now." Heather looked at her dad.

"Gossip in Danburg flies out of the peoples'

mouths faster than a cheetah after its prey.'"

"Hmm. Isn't that true," JJ agreed. He knew that all too well. Last spring he'd been the talk of the town.

Heather sat in her wheelchair by the concession stand as her mom finished cleaning up, and Anna helped. The leftover smells of popcorn, burgers, and hotdogs gagged her, but she swallowed hard until the feeling passed.

From the corner of her eye, Heather caught sight of JJ shaking hands with a beautiful twenty-something blond woman by the gym doors. Who was she? JJ looked in Heather's direction and waved, then spoke to the woman again, and the two of them made their way toward Heather.

The woman held her hand out to Heather. "Hello. I'm Jenny, the tenth-grade language arts teacher and tennis coach. Your dad is the best."

"Yes, he is."

"All of us here are thinking of you and sending good vibes your way." She pointed behind her. "JJ's my neighbor. He says you two were friends in high school."

Heather's stomach knotted, and a bit of jealousy raced through her veins. That was all he'd said they were? "Yeah."

"You take care. I told your dad I'd stop by this week with my famous cornflake chicken and hash brown casserole." She turned to JJ. "I can make you one too and bring it by your apartment. I could hang out for a bit and get to know my neighbor."

Of course the beauty queen could cook. No doubt JJ would take her up on her offer. Heather held her breath, waiting for his response.

"Thanks, but I'm over at Heather's every evening. I'll grab a bite there."

In her mind, Heather pumped her fist in the air. But was it fair to him? She didn't have any intentions of having a relationship with him, so why should she hope he wouldn't want to have one with someone else? He deserved love and happiness with a woman for a long time.

"I don't mind making an extra and running it by no matter what time." Jenny's eyes twinkled as she gazed at him.

JJ glanced at Heather, then back at Jenny. "I'm just not home a lot."

Heather cleared her throat. "You can't be with me all the time."

Jenny dug around in her purse. "Here." She handed him a business card. "This is my number. Call me anytime, and we can hang out. I do want to get to know my neighbors."

"All right."

She turned back toward Heather. "I'll see you later this week. It was nice meeting you." She hugged JJ, then walked down the hallway.

"We were high school friends, huh?" Heather smiled.

He scrunched his nose and squinted. "Well, we were. I didn't want to get into all the details."

"Jenny seemed interested in you."

"There's only one woman I want." He stepped in

front of her and took her hand.

She looked down. He made her forget all the reasons she shouldn't be with him. But she had to stand her ground.

"I told you I'd wait as long as I have to." He ran his hand along her face, and she leaned into it.

Just give in.

Chapter Twenty-one

Amelia knocked on the Coles' front door, and it opened. She waved bye to Mark as he backed out of the driveway, then she stepped inside. Heather smiled from her wheelchair, and Amelia bent to give her a hug. She hoped that was okay.

"Was that your boyfriend?" Heather gave a sly smile.

"No, but I hope he will be soon."

"Details."

"He's a junior and the captain of the baseball team. He's on student council and takes all honors classes. And he *likes* me." Amelia placed her hands on her chest.

"Aw, young love."

"He's really cute too."

Heather laughed. "I'm glad you stopped by. I needed some girl talk."

"I've been going to the batting cage, and I've been practicing my pitching and throwing. It's felt wonderful, but I just don't know."

Heather motioned for Amelia to take a seat on

the couch, then she wheeled herself in front of her. "What don't you know?"

"If I love softball enough."

"Enough for what? You need to love it for you. No one else."

"Something really bad went down last year. And it made me hate softball, but then when I pitch or swing the bat, it brings back all the feels, you know?"

Heather smiled. "You mean you remember why you loved it so much. The feel of the ball in your hand, the laces on your fingertips, the winding of your arm, the release, and watching it glide through the air into the mitt."

"Exactly."

Heather closed her eyes. "I wish I could feel the feels again."

"Have you tried?"

"My shoulder is getting stronger, but I don't think I could ever move it the way it needs to so I could pitch."

Amelia slid her back pack off and dug in her bag. She pulled out a softball and put in Heather's hand.

Heather ran her hand along the laces and studied the ball, then tossed it up slightly and caught it. "It's thanks to your dad that I can even do that little bit."

"Speaking of my dad. He says you were his first love."

"He was mine too."

"You were friends first, right?"

Heather nodded.

"Can you tell me about him?"

"He made me laugh, he taught me to fish, he was

a great basketball player, and he wrote me the sweetest poems and songs."

"Did he sing them to you?"

Heather nodded. "He has a beautiful voice."

"He does, doesn't he?" Amelia smiled. She liked hearing these nice things about him. "We used to sing together all the time with the radio or silly songs I learned as a kid, and he'd sing Zac and me a lullaby before we went to bed, even though I was fourteen."

"He doesn't do that anymore?"

"He moved out."

"Is that why you don't want to play softball? Is that the bad thing that happened? Your parents got a divorce and he's not around as much to toss the ball with or sing you to sleep?"

Amelia sniffed back her forming tears, then held her hand out for Heather to toss her the ball. Heather lobbed it, and Amelia returned it. They continued to throw the ball back and forth.

Amelia swallowed hard. "It involves more than me. It's not really my place to tell the details."

"I understand. If you do ever need someone to talk to though, I'm here. I won't judge you or your mom or dad."

"I don't know about that. What do you think about my dad?"

"He's nice. Turned out to be a good guy."

"Boyfriend material?"

Heather laughed. "Why are you saying that?"

"Don't you see the way he looks at you?"

"Like a physical therapist treating his patient."

"No, like a love-sick puppy."

Heather shook her head. "No he doesn't."

"Yes he does, and you know it."

"I'm not girlfriend material."

"Why not?"

"I won't be here much longer."

"You don't know that. Dad says you're getting stronger every day."

"And my cancer's growing every day."

Amelia's heart dropped. She refused to believe that Heather would die soon. "But advances in medicine improve every day."

"I know my fate, and I've accepted it." Heather rolled the ball around between her hands.

It wasn't right. Heather was such a great person. "My dad says cancer doesn't discriminate. Otherwise he'd be the one with it."

"I'd rather have it than him. He has you and Zac." Heather threw the ball to Amelia.

"He's made a lot of bad choices."

"Haven't we all."

Amelia held on to the ball. *Not like him. Not ones that tear a family apart. Not ones that make a daughter not trust her own dad.*

"I guess." Amelia stared at the ball. "What kind of bad choices have you made?"

"I let my heartache make my decisions for me, then everything went downhill from there."

"Like what?"

"My grandma died, JJ and I broke up, and I dated his best friend's brother—and that tore their friendship apart. I left a full-ride scholarship to marry Keith, and I didn't leave the first time he hit me. Then I stayed, and I stayed, and I stayed until he almost killed me."

Amelia's stomach felt uneasy. She knew Keith and Heather were getting a divorce, but she never imagined that was the reason why. Heather seemed so strong, so together. She'd been a college athlete projected for greatness. How could she have been in an abusive relationship?

Amelia gulped. "But you're Heather Cole."

"First off, I feel like I need to tell you this because it can happen to anyone, even the strongest women. I never thought I'd be the kind of person who'd be in an abusive relationship. And I don't ever want it to happen to you. No one deserves to be hit for any reason. If he does it once, he's probably going to do it again and again. I thought Keith loved me. I thought he'd change, but the abuse got worse. Until eventually I was terrified to even open the front door. I was trapped."

"He almost killed you?"

"Several times. Thank goodness the last time someone heard, and she helped me escape while Keith was on deployment."

Amelia's heart rate sped. "He was here like last week, right? Are you worried he'll come after you?"

"I always worry, but he hasn't tried to call or come by again. I think he's gone back on deployment. But I don't know that for sure."

"I hope he did. I'm sorry you went through that."

"Thank you. Promise me if any guy starts to get possessive of you, threatens you, or hurts you that you won't stay in the relationship. You will find the one who will love and treat you like you deserve.

Don't settle."

"I promise. You know there's someone out there for you too."

"Who, your dad?"

Amelia shrugged.

"I'm happy that he and I are friends again. That's enough. I'm here with my parents. I've met you and Zac. I don't need a man to love me. I don't want to get all tangled up in those feelings and then have to let them go soon. Plus your dad and I have a past that I still have to deal with."

"Well, if you don't want to fall in love, what kind of things would you like to do before . . . you know?"

"Hmm." Heather looked upward. "Most of the things I'd really like won't happen."

"Like what."

"I'd love to go to the beach. It's my favorite place in the world, but traveling is really hard on me." Heather fiddled with a string on the bottom of her shirt. "I really wanted kids, but that can't happen. No husband and not enough time."

"I don't mean to be nosey, but why don't you have kids if you really wanted them? Could you not get pregnant?"

Heather wound the string around her finger. "Keith didn't want to have kids, so we didn't. Looking back now, I'm glad we didn't though."

Amelia laid the ball on the couch, then placed her hand on top of Heather's. "You would have been a wonderful mom."

"Thank you."

Chapter Twenty-two

Heather laid her back against her pillow and looked up at the ceiling. Pain oozed from every pore. JJ would be there soon enough. The massage would help, but hopefully the pain pill would kick in first. She whimpered slowly through her teeth. She needed another pill. She leaned over for the bell as her bedroom door opened.

Anna entered. "How are you doing?"

"I need more medicine please."

Anna looked down at her watch. "I can give you another one, but no more for three hours." She took a bottle out of her apron and opened it, then handed Heather a pill and a glass of ginger ale.

"Good evening." JJ walked in. "Look who came with me tonight."

Zac rounded the corner and waved.

With every bit of energy she had, she smiled. "Hey, buddy." Her eyelids felt heavy, and she closed her eyes.

Anna spoke softly. "Zac, would you like to watch cartoons with me? We can have popcorn with M&Ms mixed in if it's okay with your daddy."

"Can we, Daddy?"

"Yes, go ahead in the living room and wait for Anna."

"Okay."

Heather opened her eyes to mere slits and watched Zac leave, then she shut them.

"It hasn't been a good day. She's taken morphine around the clock. I'm surprised she's even coherent at this point. It started this morning with a five-minute coughing attack that she couldn't control. Then she's vomited several times, and she's had very labored breathing most of the day."

"Should I leave?"

"She needs to rest."

Heather needed to tell him to stay. She'd waited all day for him. *Please don't go.*

"I'll sit with her. You can go watch cartoons with Zac."

"All right. Let me know if she needs anything."

Heather opened her eyes and turned her head toward him. He smiled at her from the chair next to her bed.

"Go back to sleep. You've had a hard day. I'm going to sit here a bit."

"Where's Amelia?" she whispered.

"Softball tryouts."

"Wonderful."

His phone beeped. "Shoot. The pipes burst at the office. I've got to go. Sorry."

She reached her hand toward him, and he took it.

"I'll stop by later if it's not too late." He released her hand slowly, then walked out the door.

She closed her eyes.

Heather woke to the sound of a child laughing. Her body still hurt, but the pain had eased somewhat. She scooted to the side of her bed, sat up, then slid down to the end of the bed and climbed into her wheelchair. She made her way to the living room.

Zac sat on the couch by Anna, with a large bowl between them. Zac stuck his hand in, brought out a handful of popcorn, and shoved it into his mouth. Her dad came around the corner from the kitchen with a full bowl of popcorn.

"Hey, sleepyhead, you feeling better?"

"A little."

He lifted his bowl. "We're having popcorn for dinner. You want any?"

"No thanks. Mom at work?"

Her dad nodded.

Anna stood. "Don't let him fool you. We had potato soup for dinner. The popcorn is dessert. Would you like me to warm some for you?"

Heather's stomach growled. Soup would feel nice on her throat and chest. "Yes, thank you."

"We had popcorn twice." Zac's eyes widened. "With M&Ms. I love coming over here."

"Did Anna spoil you today?"

"I did no such thing." Anna walked toward the kitchen.

Zac giggled. "Yes, you did. And so did Granddaddy Cole."

Heather swallowed hard and looked at her dad. "Granddaddy Cole?"

"It has a nice ring to it, doesn't it?"

"But you're not—"

"It's symbolic. Like how your friends back in the day would call me Dad and your mother Mom."

It did have a nice ring to it. Her dad deserved that title. He would have been an amazing grandparent. "Okay then, Granddaddy Cole. What are you all watching?

"A new show on the Kid's Network."

Zac laughed. "It's funny."

"You want to sit on the couch?" Her dad got up and helped her out of the wheelchair and onto the couch.

"What time is it?" Heather's head felt heavy, as if she'd slept for ages.

Her dad looked at his watch. "It's 8:37."

Already. She'd slept the entire sunlight away. She feared more and more of her days would be that way. "Zac's still here? When's JJ coming back?"

"He called a little bit ago. He's stuck at work for probably a few more hours. Corrin's going to be by in a little while to pick up Zac."

Corrin's name echoed in Heather's ear. She hadn't seen the woman since Heather and JJ's high school graduation, when JJ introduced her. Like Heather had wanted to meet the girl who'd stolen JJ. The memory sat like a pit in her stomach.

"Okay." Heather planned to go back to bed before Corrin arrived.

"I could spend the night." Zac raised his eyebrows.

Her father laughed. "You heard Anna mention that Grammy Cole's making cinnamon rolls in the morning, didn't you?"

Wearing a huge grin, Zac nodded.

Grammy Cole. It would take Heather some getting used to if that was what her dad was going to allow Zac to call her parents. It was sweet, but to her it was a reminder of what she'd never have.

Zac put the bowl of popcorn on the coffee table, then laid his head on Heather's lap. "I'm really tired. Can I lay here?"

She ran her hand along the top of his head. "It's okay. Go to sleep."

He closed his eyes and breathed heavy, as if he'd already fallen asleep. Her dad turned down the TV.

"He's a sweet boy," her dad said.

"Yes, he is."

Anna entered with a tray and bowl of soup. Heather motioned with her head to Zac.

"I'll eat it later."

Anna winked, then whispered, "I'll put it back up. Let me know when you want it."

"Thank you."

As if her father disappeared and all sounds dissipated, Heather got lost in Zac's adorable face. She ran her hand along his hair. Every neve ending tingled. Heather would savor this moment forever.

The doorbell rang, and Heather looked to her father snoring in the recliner. When had he fallen asleep?

Anna came from down the hallway and opened the door. "Hello. You must be Corrin. Come on in."

Heather took in a deep breath and clenched her jaw. So many years had passed, and it was foolish for Heather to still dislike Corrin, but no matter the time, resentment resided in Heather's heart. She glanced at sleeping Zac and exhaled, then looked up at his mother, standing in the middle of the living room.

"Hello, Heather."

"Hey."

"Poor boy. He must have been exhausted. His bedtime is normally 7:30, but Amelia had tryouts until 8:00, and then I had to drop her off at home because she had a ton of homework."

Heather nodded and swallowed hard.

Anna closed the door and stepped in next to Corrin. "We are all proud of Amelia for trying out."

"Thank you. I am too. She loves it. But after last year, I thought she'd never even pick up a ball again."

"Did Amelia say how it went?" Anna asked.

"She said it went amazing, thanks to Heather and her pointers." Corrin looked at Heather "Also, thank you for giving her some perspective."

"Sure."

"It meant a lot to her that you shared such personal things with her." Corrin looked to the ground. "I'm sorry you went through all that."

Was she talking about the abuse? The cancer? Her realization that she gave up on her softball dream?

"Thank you."

Corrin's stomach growled. "How embarrassing. Sorry about that. I guess I haven't eaten since breakfast."

"That's not good." Anna motioned to the couch. "Take a seat. You like potato soup?"

"Yes, but don't worry about—"

"No, no, no. You take a seat. I'm getting you food." Anna looked to Heather. "You too."

Heather smiled and looked at Corrin. "There's no use fighting her. She always wins."

"Heather's right. Take a seat. Have a bowl of soup. I'm sure once you leave here you won't have time to eat again for a while. Let Zac sleep. You eat." Anna turned and walked toward the kitchen.

"Thank you." Corrin took a seat on the couch by Zac's feet.

Heather's father let out a large snore.

Corrin jumped. "I didn't even see him there. It's been one of those days." She took in a breath and let it out, then shook her head. "My schedule at work was nonstop. We had a two-year-old boy come into the hospital. His father accidentally shot him in a domestic dispute with the boy's mother. We tried to save him, but . . ." She looked past Heather to the picture window. "I've seen a lot, but today was awful. I haven't been able to get it out of my mind. Can you imagine a person being that enraged?"

Heather's stomach tightened. She knew all too well. She touched Zac's head. Thank goodness she and Keith never had kids. Children didn't deserve to be in the middle.

Heather reached across Zac and put her hand on top of Corrin's. "Are you okay?"

Corrin looked in Heather's eyes and nodded. "It makes me sick." She looked down at Zac's head in Heather's lap. "Thank you for watching over him. All day I couldn't wait to get to my kids and give them a hug and tell them how much I love them, but it was as if one patient after another came in, and I stayed late to help out. Then JJ had the issue at his office. He was going to keep Zac for me and pick up Amelia. I'm sorry I couldn't get here sooner."

"It's been no problem. My dad and my nurse, Anna, stayed with him most of the evening. I think my dad loved it. Even had Zac call him Granddaddy Cole."

Corrin straightened her back.

"I don't have any kids for my dad to spoil. He's really taken to Zac and Amelia."

"JJ says your parents are good people. My parents are Amelia and Zac's only grandparents. I'm sure my kids love having someone else to spoil them."

"I know JJ's dad died, but what about his mom?"

"She didn't stick around long after her husband died. JJ hasn't spoken to her in I don't know how long. I don't think she even knows about Zac. He tried for years to keep a relationship with her, but she didn't put any effort in. He'd be the one to call, and when she'd move to another state or house, she wouldn't give him her phone number and he'd go on a search until he found it. He went down to Texas to confront her once, but she'd moved, of course without telling him, so no conversation. He gave up after that."

"That's awful. I had no clue." Heather cringed inside. How could a mother abandon her son?

"Losing Bryson's friendship, then his dad dying, and to not have his mom around to help him through it all really messed with him. I tried, but we were young, and we didn't know how to deal with that on top of being a newly married couple. I made mistakes. He made mistakes. Until one day we were over. Don't get me wrong—we had wonderful years, but we had really dark days. If it weren't for Amelia and Zac, we probably wouldn't have stayed together as long. Look at me, spewing all this. Proof I need food. Sorry about that. I'm sure you don't want to hear any of this."

Nope. Heather didn't, but she wasn't one to tell people to be quiet. "It's okay. Kind of weird because of our history. You do know who I am, right?"

Corrin huffed. "Yeah. I know. I've always known who you were. When JJ and I first met, he talked about you all the time. It drove me crazy."

"Soup's on." Anna carried in a tray with a bowl. She sat it in front of Corrin. "Heather, you ready for yours?"

She looked down at Zac. "I'll wait still."

"Okay. And, Corrin, what would you like to drink?"

"Water works. Thanks."

"No problem. You ladies go back to talking. Sorry I interrupted."

Corrin lifted a spoonful of soup to her mouth. "Um, this is good."

"Anna makes incredible food. Do you like to cook?"

Corrin nodded. "Yes, but my potato soup isn't this good." She glanced at Zac. "You should eat. I can move him."

"I don't have much of an appetite these days. I can wait a bit. And I don't mind."

"Okay. Thanks."

Corrin ate the soup, and Heather stared at the TV. The woman who'd ruined Heather's life sat two cushions down from her. Heather had imagined hundreds of times what she'd say to her if she ever had a chance, but now the words stayed choked in her throat. And what good would they do now?

"You're a nurse?" Heather asked.

"I am. What are you? I mean, what did you do before . . . I'm sorry. I don't know how to ask it right."

"It's okay. I was a stay-at-home wife."

"Were you involved in all the military wife committees?"

"Nope. Keith didn't want me to. He was a homebody, so he expected me to be too."

"You guys didn't have kids?"

"We couldn't."

"I'm sorry."

"It was for the best. Did JJ or Amelia tell you anything about Keith?"

"Not really. I know he's Bryson's older brother and he's in the marines. And that you two are getting a divorce. Other than that, I don't know anything about him."

Heather nodded.

"I know this is super awkward to talk to me, of all people, about your divorce, but if you need to chat with someone who's been through it, I don't mind."

How nice of her, but Heather would pass. Corrin was right. This whole conversation was super awkward. "Thank you."

Anna returned to the room and set the glass of water on Corrin's tray. "Heather, do you need anything?"

"Not right now."

"Then I'm going to take a load off these feet." Anna took a seat in the high-back chair next to the couch. "That feels nice."

"Anna, this soup is fabulous. You'll have to give me the recipe."

"Sure thing. Next week I'm taking a cake-decorating class. Would you ladies like to join me? It's always more fun with a group of friends."

Friends? Heather wouldn't call Corrin that. Not even close. "I don't know if I'll be up for it."

Anna cleared her throat. "Today was a bad day. They won't all be that way. You have been getting stronger. Yesterday you walked from your room to the living room with a cane."

"But today I couldn't even get out of bed."

"Are you giving up then?"

"No."

"Then come join me. What about you, Corrin? You want to come?"

"Sure, if I'm not working. What day?"

"Tuesday at two."

Corrin pulled out her phone and scrolled through it. "Great. I'm off work that day. I'd love to. Heather, it would be lots of fun. You should join us."

"I don't know."

"I will sign you up," Anna said matter of factly.

Heather sighed. "Okay. I'll try."

Chapter Twenty-three

A melia sat on the couch next to Heather. She handed her a gift bag. She hoped Heather would like it. She'd spent last week's babysitting money on it. "For helping me with softball. Not only the pitching and batting tips, but everything else too. You reminded me how much I love it. And I'm playing for me. No one else. I wouldn't be on the team if it wasn't for you."

"Thank you." Heather stuck her hand down into the bag and took out the Jolly Ranchers first. "Awesome. You know me well."

Then she pulled out the journal. Amelia had found it yesterday and knew immediately she had to buy it for Heather. Inspirational quotes in different fonts took up the front cover.

Heather read the cover, then ran her hand along it. "I love it. Thanks."

"I thought you could write down your thoughts or make a list of things you'd like to do or places you'd like to go. Anna, Dad, me, your parents, even my mom can help you accomplish them. You know how you said you want to go to the beach. Maybe we can't go to South Carolina or Florida, but Mom said there are lots of lakes with sandy beaches in Indiana that are close. She said she could take us when it warms up."

Heather smiled. "That's sweet of your mom."

"She said you're as nice as everyone says. Don't tell her I told you, but she's actually excited to hang out with you and Anna on Tuesday."

"What's Tuesday?" Amelia's dad asked as he closed the front door.

"Hey, Dad, I didn't hear you come in."

"Hey." Her dad raised his hand at Heather. "How are you today?"

"Great."

Amelia stood up. "She walked to the door without her cane and opened it."

"Wow."

"To be fair, Amelia did have to go get the cane for me so I could get back to the couch."

"But you made it to the door," Amelia said.

Heather smiled.

"Where's Anna?" Her dad slid off his coat and hung it over his arm.

"She ran to the store real quick since Amelia's here and you were on the way."

He walked over to Amelia and hugged her. "Good to see you, kiddo. How did you get here?"

"Mark."

"Jim Bob?"

"Yes."

"I guess that's him waiting in the driveway?"

"He's taking me to practice. I brought Heather a gift."

"That was nice of you. Your mom said it was okay for Jim Bob to bring you here? I don't like you driving around with boys."

"She knows his mom. He's a good guy. You have nothing to worry about."

He raised an eyebrow.

"He is. I promise. And I actually better get going so I'm not late." She leaned over and hugged Heather. "Have fun tomorrow."

"I'll try. I don't know that my cake's going to look too pretty, but I'll try. Your mom and Anna are going to show me up."

"You are making cakes with Corrin and Anna?" Amelia's dad furrowed his brows. "How did that happen?"

Heather laughed. "Anna."

"Of course."

Amelia stood and hugged her dad, then headed to the front door. She caught a glimpse of him sitting next to Heather. There was no denying how much he cared for Heather. But she had that effect on everyone. One meeting and you loved her.

Amelia stepped outside and closed the door. A black truck pulled in behind her dad's car. The man rolled down the windows and glared at her, then drove off. A chill raced down her spine. She looked at Mark, who was sitting in his car in the driveway and bopping his head to the blaring music. She ran to his passenger-side door, jumped in, and slammed it shut.

"Did you see that guy?"

"What guy?"

"The weird creep in a black truck."

Mark looked behind him. "I don't see anyone."

"He already drove away. But he looked sketchy."

Mark backed up and pulled onto the street. "It was probably no one. This is a nice neighborhood."

"So?"

"I doubt anyone in this town would mess with Pastor Cole's house. Everybody knows the guy."

But what about Keith? Amelia's heart raced. What if that guy was him? What if he hadn't gone back on deployment? She closed her eyes and tried to remember the wedding photo that used to hang in the Coles' house. She'd never really paid attention to the portrait, let alone the groom. Should she say anything to her dad about the guy? She blew out a breath. Mark was probably right—it was no one. She was being paranoid.

Using her cane, Heather walked into the cake-baking classroom. Anna and Corrin followed. The smell of vanilla and sugar filled the area. She turned to her motley crew—the dying woman, her nurse, and the ex-wife. They sounded like a band name. "I can't believe I'm going to say this, but it smells amazing in here and I want a slice."

"Is that what I need to make so you'll eat?"

Heather laughed. "I guess."

They checked in and found a counter where the three could work together. They spent the afternoon laughing, sharing stories, and learning the craft of cake decorating. By the end, Anna's cake looked the best, followed by Corrin's, then Heather's. But

Heather had impressed herself—her cake actually didn't look half-bad. Now the question was, did it taste good? She'd followed the recipe the baker had shared. She slid a knife into it and laid the slice on her plate, then took a bite. It melted in her mouth. She had actually made this?

"You all have to try this strawberry crème cake. It's awesome." Heather dipped her fork into the cake and held it up for either one of them.

Corrin leaned in and took a bite. She spoke through the mouthful. "Incredible."

"I need a bite." Anna licked her lips.

Heather also fed her a bite.

"That is good. Way to go, Heather."

"Thanks."

"You should save a piece for JJ. He loves strawberry crème cake." Corrin smiled.

"I will."

"The way to a man's heart is through his stomach, and if JJ loves strawberry—" Anna laughed.

"Anna." Heather motioned with her head to Corrin, who was cutting a slice of her chocolate cake. "I'm not trying to win any man's heart with this cake. Especially not JJ's. This cake is all mine."

The ladies laughed.

"I agree I'd keep that yumminess all to myself too." Corrin winked.

The three of them cleaned the rest of their mess, boxed up their cakes, and slowly made their way out of the community center to the parking lot, Heather walking with her cane. Anna opened her sedan's back door behind the driver's side and placed her cake and Heather's strawberry crème on the floorboard.

Corrin opened the passenger door of her SUV and set hers on the floorboard.

Corrin hugged Anna and then Heather. "Thank you, ladies. I had a great time. We should get together like this every week for a girls' day. What do you all say?"

"Let's do it," Anna agreed.

"Yes, I'd like that."

Corrin waved as she slid into the driver's side.

Heather handed her cane to Anna, then scooted her feet across the ground as she made her way to the passenger side and opened the door. She caught sight of a black truck with dark windows pulling into the parking lot. She sat in the seat and closed the door. The truck slowed to almost a stop as it passed in front of Anna's car, then sped out of the parking lot.

JJ laid his wallet and cell phone on his nightstand, then reached inside his top drawer for the seashell he'd kept for twenty years. He ran his fingers along the grooves, then flipped it over and ran his thumb across the name Heather had written with a permanent marker when she was fifteen—*Cole*. He sat on his bed, leaning back against his pillow, and held the shell up to look at it. A knock from the door startled him. "Come in."

Amelia walked in and climbed onto the bed. "What's that?"

"It's a seashell Heather gave me when we were younger."

Amelia held her hand out, and he laid it in her palm. She flipped it over.

"What's the story with the shell?"

"Heather and her grandma went to a beach every summer, and they'd always come home with buckets full of seashells." He held up the seashell. "This was the last one they found together. Her grandmother died unexpectedly a few weeks after this trip."

Amelia frowned. "And Heather gave it to you? If Nana and I had found something together and then she died, I wouldn't give it away."

"She wanted me to have it. Heather told me she and her grandmother were getting ready to leave, but they decided to take one last stroll along the beach. They found this perfectly shaped purple scalloped shell. Her grandmother told her if someone comes across a scalloped shell without blemish and she gives it to the object of her affection, he will always love her and the two will be blessed with children."

"How romantic."

Nodding, he smiled. "We were undeniably in love. I was sixteen, but I couldn't imagine her not in my life." He flipped the shell over and rubbed his thumb across the name *Cole* again. "When we broke up, I thought about giving it back to her that way she could share it with the person she was going to marry, but I couldn't do it. It was special between the two of us, and I couldn't bear her giving it to anyone else. It reminds me of the time in my life when I was . . . worthy enough to be given something so special."

"Do you believe in the legend?"

"Nah, we both knew it was Aphrodite nonsense."

Amelia raised her eyebrows.

"She was the goddess of love and beauty who rose up from a scallop shell. I don't believe in myths or magic, but I believed in Heather's love, and at one time she believed in mine."

"You admitted to me you've always loved her."

"That I have."

"If you loved each other like that then why did you break up?"

"Because I met your mom."

"Did you love them both?"

"I did."

"Why did you choose Mom when it seems like you had this epic love for Heather?"

"Your mom was smart and funny. Strong and had a mind of her own. I liked that she was independent and not clingy. She had her own life, and I had mine. We met in the middle, and we clicked." JJ's heart warmed. He *had* loved Corrin. It wasn't always about meeting his carnal desires. They'd had a good life together when he wasn't screwing it up. "Regardless of what I've done, I loved your mother very much."

"As much as Heather?"

Wow. What a question. How could he answer that? "I loved them both in different ways. Heather was my first love, and your mom was my wife. Honestly, I didn't treat either one like they deserved."

Amelia took the shell back and traced the name. "Why does it say *Cole*?"

JJ smiled. "When I first met Heather, I called her by her last name, and it kind of stuck. Then after we started dating, I used the name *Cole* as code for *I love you*."

"Ah, Dad. You're a romantic."

"Heather does bring out the best in me."

"Is it weird that I'm rooting for you two?"

He turned on his side to face her. "No, why?"

"Am I being a traitor to Mom?"

"I don't think so, but if you're worried about it, you should talk to her."

She shook her head. "I don't think I can. You know she went on a date last night?"

A jolt of jealousy stabbed him. "She did? With who?"

"I don't know. Some guy she met through someone at the hospital. I think he's a lawyer."

"Good for her. Are you rooting for them?"

"I don't know. He's handsome and brought her flowers. That was nice, but I didn't really get to talk to him. I'm glad she's dating. She cried for months."

JJ's stomach dropped. He hated that he'd hurt Corrin. She had been a good wife, a good cook, a kind woman, and an excellent lover. Corrin had done nothing wrong. He'd been the one trying to fill a void every time he'd strayed from their marriage. She didn't deserve the heartache he put her through. "I know it sounds crazy, but I cried too. I do love your mom, and divorcing her was one of the hardest things I've done in my life. I want the best for her.

She deserves a man that will shower her with everything she desires. I'm happy she's dating."

"I'm always going to wish that man was you."

"I know."

"It won't happen though. Will it?"

JJ shook his head. "Too much bad history there."

"What about Heather? What kind of history do you have? Bad or good?

"Some bad, but I hope the good will overshadow all that."

"Me too."

Chapter Twenty-four

Heather stood at the mailbox with her cane in hand as Anna watched from the porch. She tore open the letter from the courthouse and stared at the words.

Divorced.

She'd wanted the divorce, so why did she feel this crushed? It hadn't been her fault. She'd done nothing wrong. She had no reason to feel like a failure. No woman should ever stay in a marriage like that. On the other hand, the law said she was officially free of him. Her heart couldn't keep up with the up and down emotions.

She flipped through the rest of the mail. A bill from the hospital lay on top. Insurance would cover the bills until Keith canceled her from the policy. How could she help with the bills? What about knitting baby blankets? Be a telemarketer? Sit at the desk at the indoor batting cages?

Underneath the bill, a red envelope addressed to her but without postage stuck out. She slid her fingers under the flap and pulled out a card. The words *I'm sorry* in a pretty font and a white rose decorated the front of the card. She opened it. Keith's large signature jumped out at her. Her heart stopped, and she looked around. How had he delivered it? Did this mean he hadn't gone back on deployment? She closed the card. Adrenaline pounded through her veins, and she made her way back to the porch.

"What do you have on the agenda for us this afternoon, Ms. Anna?"

"Today you're making chicken noodle soup."

"You are. Not me. I can't cook."

"Says who? Your ex-husband? I had your strawberry crème cake. You are amazing, girl. Start believing it. My husband told me I made the worst-tasting food he'd ever eaten. You know what though? I didn't listen. I kept cooking. He kept eating. One time, to prove him wrong, I entered my chicken pot pie in a baking contest at the state fair and won first place. It didn't keep him from complaining though. Sometimes there is no pleasing a person."

Heather made her way to the porch chair. "You don't talk much about your husband."

"Not much to talk about. He's in jail."

"For what?" she whispered.

"Murder."

How did Anna appear to have no emotions about it, like she was telling someone else's story and not her own?

"That's crazy. What happened?"

"It's a long story. I'll tell you about it another time. The important thing is, he's out of my life and serving time for his crime. Justice was served."

Anna reached for the handle on the screen door and froze. "My husband was very abusive also." She turned and looked at Heather. "But I didn't let it define me. I've left it in the past. You are a beautiful human being. Don't let what he did take away any of your light. Take pleasure in life like you did when you were a little girl. Like when you and JJ loved each other. And, sweetie, forgive like your number one on your bucket list says. It's the most powerful weapon you have. You can allow the anger and hurt to destroy you, or you can let it go and win."

"I don't know if I can forgive Keith."

"Forgiveness for Keith may come in time, but right now I'm talking about JJ. That man loves you with his whole heart. Can you see it?"

"Do you know why I'm not sure if I can trust him?"

"I do. He chose Corrin over you."

"He cheated on me with her."

"He feels awful about it. He's never stopped loving you.

"But if he hadn't left me for her, I never would have married Keith."

"*You* chose Keith. JJ didn't make that decision for you."

Heather's mouth went dry. She'd been blaming JJ for destroying her dreams, but she'd been the one to walk away and not fight for him. She left her softball career to marry a man she barely knew. She didn't find a way to run until someone gave her a way out. She was who she was mad at, not JJ.

"I know." A tear slid down her cheek.

"Then stop using the past as an excuse. Let go of what that eighteen-year-old kid did and allow the man he is today to love you."

"I don't want to be with JJ."

"I think we both know that's a lie. Trust him. He's not Keith. He never laid a hand on you. Think about giving him a chance before it's too late."

Corrin held the popcorn tin toward Heather as she sat next to her in the movie theater. "You want any?"

"No, thanks. My stomach's a little queasy today. I'm glad they had ginger ale." Heather took a sip.

Corrin was sure it wasn't a mistake that Heather had chosen the first wheelchair spot closest to the door. She'd coughed a lot on the car ride and had mentioned more than once she was nauseated. Hopefully, she could make it through the movie.

Anna leaned across Corrin. "If you want to leave at any time, let me know."

"You aren't getting off that easy, Ms. Anna." Corrin smiled.

"I thought you were taking me to a lighthearted comedy, not the tearjerker of the century. I like to laugh, not cry. I see enough heartache in my line of work." Anna winked.

Corrin saw it often too. Between the junk she witnessed at the hospital and the heartache she'd felt in her marriage, she found herself numb to most of life. A good tearjerker reminded her she could still feel something.

"Sometimes we need a good cry," Corrin said.

"I don't think so. I hold you responsible if this box of tissues is gone by the end of this. You will owe me another one." Anna held up the box.

Corrin laughed. "Why did you bring a box of tissues if you thought we were going to a comedy?"

"They make me laugh so hard I cry. I don't mind using tissues for that kind of crying. Heather, what do you think about Corrin bringing us to this depressing movie?"

"I'm not getting into the middle of it. You two can fight that one out. I'm going to sit right here and enjoy the fact that I'm out of the house. I haven't been to the movies since I was in college."

"Really? Why?" Corrin asked

"Keith."

"Did you guys ever do anything?" No wonder she'd divorced him.

"Not really. We rented movies at home. That was the extent of our exciting lives."

"He sounds like a bore. Good riddance. You enjoy our full movie experience."

"At twelve fifty a ticket and five dollars for a small ginger ale, I better enjoy it. Good grief. I remember back in the day paying five dollars to see a movie."

"It's a small price to pay for a ladies' afternoon out." Corrin smiled.

"Yeah, for a comedy." Anna pointed at Corrin.

Corrin rolled her eyes. "It's going to be great. At least we came to a theater with recliner seats. You can kick back and snooze if you like."

Smiling, Anna leaned her head against the

headrest and lifted the leg of her chair.

The lights lowered, and Corrin directed her eyes to the previews. Something—she assumed popcorn—hit the back of her head. She ignored it the first and second time, but the third time she looked behind her. Three rows back to the left, a group of college-age girls chatted quietly while showing each other their phones. They didn't have any popcorn. An elderly couple staring at the screen sat two rows behind the girls. They were too far back to hit her with anything. About ten rows behind her, a man wearing a baseball cap sat by himself. He lifted his popcorn tub, then tipped his head. She whipped back around. What a jerk.

Another one hit her. How was he accurately able to hit her from that far away? Was he doing it to everyone?

"Hey, Heather, is that guy back there hitting you with popcorn?"

Heather turned her head slightly to the left and then the right. "I can't turn my head enough to take a look, but I haven't been hit with anything."

"Anna, are you getting hit by popcorn."

"No."

"Well, he better stop, or I'm going to give him an earful."

Anna turned around and pointed a finger. "I'll give him one now."

But the guy had moved to the back row and the opposite corner of them. Good. He wouldn't bother them anymore. It took a real creep to come to a chick flick to pester people. Corrin turned back to the movie. Afterward she planned to question the man.

When the movie ended, Heather asked Anna to take her to the bathroom, but Corrin stayed to talk to the guy. She made her way to the back row and cornered him. He pulled the bill of his hat down.

"Why were you throwing popcorn at me?"

"You shouldn't talk bad about people's husbands?" He scowled and clenched his jaw.

He looked familiar, but she couldn't place him.

"What does that mean?"

"You called her husband a bore."

"How is that any business of yours?"

He took off his hat and glared at her. Who was he, and what did he care what she had to say to Heather?

"Don't you recognize me? My brother was the best man in your wedding."

"Keith?"

"Yep."

"What are you doing here? Heather said you were on deployment."

"Doesn't look like it, does it?" He puffed out his chest. "You better stop talking about me." He licked his lip.

"Are you trying to scare me? Because it's not going to work."

"Really? You should ask Heather how scared of me you ought to be."

Corrin held her composure, but she knew she should get out of the empty theater as soon as possible. "Are you following her?"

He raised his cheek in a grimace. "What I want to know is why she's hanging out with you? She doesn't like you. You're the hussy that slept with her boyfriend."

Corrin's stomach tightened. She'd go back and change it if she could, especially now that she knew Heather. Back then Corrin had her eyes on JJ, and she wouldn't quit until she got what she wanted.

He stepped closer to her. "You got nothing to say?"

"That was a long time ago."

"Thanks to you, I got Heather."

"It doesn't sound like you gave her much of a life."

"What do you know, Little Debbie cake decorator."

"You *have* been following her."

He raised his eyebrow. "What do you think you know about Heather and me?"

"She wasn't happy, obviously. You never took her anywhere, and you were a cheater."

"Sounds like your marriage. Not mine."

"Then why did she leave you?"

He smacked his fist into his palm. "I'm going to get her back."

"You think threatening me and calling me a hussy is going to win her affections?"

"Whatever. You tell JJ to watch his back."

Corrin had heard enough. She spun, and he grabbed her wrist. "You have a daughter and son, don't you? Amelia's quite the softball player, and Zac loves the tall slide at the playground. They seem to be getting awful cozy with Heather. Does that make you jealous?"

She yanked her arm away from him. "You stay

away from my kids and Heather, or I'll kill you."

"Who's threatening who now?"

"Stay away. Go back to California or wherever you were on deployment. Leave Heather alone."

He shook his head. "I can't do that. I'm on leave to watch my wife through her cancer, and that's what I plan to do."

Corrin ran down the aisle and the steps to the bathroom. Heather's wheelchair sat against the wall, and Anna stood next to it. Corrin ran into a stall and vomited.

"Corrin, you okay?" Anna asked.

"No, Keith's here." Corrin quivered. "He was the one throwing the popcorn." She walked out of the stall. "He basically threatened my kids. He's been watching them and Heather and . . ." She looked Anna in the eyes. "All of us."

Heather opened her door. With bugged-out eyes, she grasped on to the stall walls and trembled. "What did he say?"

"He was going to get you back and for JJ to watch out."

"I knew I shouldn't have come to Indiana. If I would have gone to Georgia like I planned, then he wouldn't be here and you all would be safe."

What was she talking about?

Anna took Heather's arm and led her to her wheelchair. "You wouldn't have had us in Georgia. He isn't going to hurt you ever again. We won't let him."

"I'm confused. I thought Keith was trying to act all tough. Is he really a threat?"

Heather nodded.

Chapter Twenty-five

JJ drove around Corrin's neighborhood searching for anything that looked suspicious. No one had heard or seen from Keith in a month, but JJ was sure the guy was lurking behind the scenes. He wasn't going to take the risk. He'd patrol his kids' neighborhood all night and every day if he had to—and he basically had.

He'd take care of the fool. Good thing Keith had taught him how to throw a proper right hook all those years ago.

His phone rang, and he pushed the Phone button on his car's display panel. "Hello."

"Hello." Heather's voice came through the speakers.

"What did Dr. Sutter say?"

"She was impressed with how well I'm doing. She couldn't believe I'm walking without the cane. My numbers are staying about the same, and it appears the cancer hasn't spread anywhere else."

"That's awesome."

"She says that could change anytime though and there still aren't any treatment options."

His stomach dropped.

"Did she give you a time frame?"

Seconds passed without her saying a word.

"Heather?"

"She didn't. I don't want to know anymore. Today I feel good, and I hope that tomorrow and the next day and the next I have enough energy to enjoy it."

"I'm still holding out for a miracle."

"Me too."

He pulled into Corrin's driveway and looked up and down the street one more time. Nothing suspicious. He backed up and headed toward his apartment.

"Do you think you'll be up for coming to Amelia's first game tomorrow?"

"I hope so. I haven't had a bad day for weeks, thanks to you and Anna."

"You've been working hard."

"I'm not ready to give up. I have a journal full of things left to do."

"Tell me one of them."

"Hmm, let's see. I want to see if I can still pitch or bat."

He wanted to see that too, and he wanted to make it happen. "I think you could definitely give it a try. Let's do it. Let's go to the indoor sportsplex after Amelia's game, and then we could catch a bite to eat after."

"Like a date."

"Yes. Is a date with me on your list?"

She laughed. "You don't give up, do you?"

"I told you I wouldn't. You should give in. What

could be better than time with me?"

"I'll think about it, but it's not a date."

Adrenaline pumped through Heather's veins as her dad pulled into Danburg High School girls' softball field parking lot. She climbed out of the car, and the smell of fresh-cut grass, burning charcoal from the concession stand grill, and sunscreen filled the warm April air. Heather inhaled. Softball season had arrived indeed. Her hands itched for a mitt and a glove.

"Welcome back," her dad whispered.

She smiled. "It's good to be home."

The bleachers outside the fence behind home plate on both sides already had several spectators. The dugouts, one red and the other black, had a bulldog painted on the back of each one. The Danburg girls warmed up the field, catching and throwing in the balls the coach hit. Off to the side by the dugout, Amelia pitched to a girl dressed in catcher's gear.

Heather followed her parents to the bleachers, and JJ met them at the bottom. He held her hand as he helped her up a few rows. Tingling sensations ran through her fingers, up her arms, and to her heart. Why wouldn't she give in to him? She couldn't deny she liked him.

Her parents took a seat, and Heather sat down next to her dad, with JJ on the opposite side of her. She looked at his hand still holding hers. She pulled it out and placed it in her lap. She didn't want to give him the wrong impression. They were just going to be friends.

He walked his fingers up and down her hand. She held her breath. If it wasn't for her death sentence, then she'd let her heart feel everything it wanted.

He slid his fingers between hers. She slowly slipped hers out of his and moved her hand between the two of them. His hand followed, touching the side of hers. That was the closest she'd let him get to holding her hand.

JJ nudged her shoulder with his and then winked. "I'm glad you made it. Amelia's excited you're here."

"I'm glad to be here." She looked around. "Where's Zac?"

"He and Corrin went to the concession stand for a—"

"Candy bar."

"Yep. You know that boy loves his candy bars."

Heather's mom leaned in front of Heather and looked at JJ. "That reminds me. I picked up that chocolate ninja Easter bunny from the store you asked me to get if I saw it."

"Thanks. I'll get it later tonight."

Her father tapped JJ's knee. "Can we take you and the kids out for ice cream after the game?"

"They would have loved that, but they are spending the weekend with Corrin's parents. She's taking them there after the game."

Her father nodded. "Next time then."

"Definitely." He turned to Heather. "Since I have the night free, I was hoping you'd go out with me.

Remember you said you'd think about it."

Her heart pounded hard, reminding her she was still alive. She had thought of little else since last night. *Live. Trust him. He loves you.* The words echoed in her mind.

"Like a date?" her mother asked with a playful tone.

"Not a date." Heather looked at her mom. "We're friends."

"You keep saying that." Her mom smiled.

"You can call me and our time together whatever you want. I love being around you." JJ put his hand on top of hers.

She looked into his eyes.

"Say yes to the date already." Her dad laughed.

Worry sat in her chest. She didn't want to get hurt again, but as she looked into JJ's eyes, she realized there was no going back. She'd fallen hard for him again. She'd either have to stop toying with the idea and tell him to quit chasing her, or she needed to go for it and trust her feelings for him. She wasn't sure she could do that though. She'd made such awful choices in her life. Who knew how much time she had left, and she wanted to enjoy it. She'd give him a chance. One date.

She grinned. "Let's see how I'm feeling after my physical therapist comes over. He can be brutal. I may be too worn out."

"I have it in good with that guy, and I think he'll let you off the hook today, if you agree to go out with me."

Trembling inside, she drew in a deep breath and slowly blew it out. "Yes, I'd love to go on a date."

He sighed and relaxed his shoulders. "Really?"

She smiled. "Really."

Zac jumped in front of JJ, and Corrin stood behind him.

"Look, Daddy. Mommy let me get the big Crunch bar."

"Cool, buddy. Say hi to Heather and her parents."

"Hi, Heather. Hi, Granddaddy and Grammy Cole." He handed the candy bar to Heather's mom. "Can you help me open this?"

"Sure. Do you want to sit by me?"

Heather's dad slid over, then patted the spot between him and Heather's mom.

Zac climbed over the bleacher and sat down. "Guess what I saw today?"

"What?" A grin spread across her father's face.

Heather smiled. She loved how close Amelia and Zac had gotten to her parents.

"How are you feeling?" Corrin sat down in front of Heather.

"I'm doing well. I don't even feel like a woman with cancer."

"You look good too. Even better than you did earlier this week."

"Thanks."

"On Tuesday, if you're still doing well, will you go dress shopping with me? That guy I told you about—the one I've been seeing—invited me to a swanky work dinner party. I'd love your and Anna's feedback."

"Of course, but I'll have to take the wheelchair for that outing."

"Please do. When I shop till I drop, I'll sit in your lap and Anna can push us around, like last time."

Heather laughed hard, remembering a few weeks back at the park when Corrin had playfully climbed in the wheelchair beside Heather and convinced Anna to wheel them around the walking path while they waved at people. The three of them had cackled like a bunch of teenage girls. It had soothed Heather's soul. Never in her wildest dreams would Heather have imagined she and Corrin as friends.

Corrin touched JJ's knee. "What did she say?"

He slid his fingers into Heather's, and this time she didn't protest. "She said yes."

"Good for you. It's about time."

What alternate reality was Heather living in where an ex-wife was happy for her ex-husband dating his old high school sweetheart? But add Anna into the mix, and they'd all become one strange, unexpected family.

The softball team took the field, and Amelia waved from the pitcher's mound.

Heather smiled, then looked down at JJ's fingers intertwined with hers. She was excited to watch Amelia play, but she couldn't wait until her date.

Chapter Twenty-six

Whistling, JJ locked his apartment door. *Why am I more nervous now than the first time I took Heather out?* He knew the answer as soon as the question popped into his head.

The day she entered his office might have felt like the end for her, but for him it was the beginning. A chance to start over.

He turned toward the parking lot and halted. Keith leaned against the hood of JJ's car, tapping a golf club against the palm of his hand.

JJ frowned. "What are you doing here?"

Keith took a step forward and swung the club as if hitting a baseball. "What I want to know is, what are you up to? You and that lying pastor told me Heather was dying. That means the Grim Reaper ought to be coming for a visit by now. But she looks healthy. She didn't even have her cane with her today. Not anything like that puny woman I saw back in February. I don't like being played." He pointed the club in JJ's direction.

Ready to defend himself if Keith attacked, JJ

planted his feet and clutched his tingling fist. "No one played you."

"Yeah, right. You got me to sign those divorce papers, and now the cancer suddenly disappeared?"

"She's fighting it every day. Through all the work she's done with Anna and me—"

Keith snarled. "I bet you've worked her up."

JJ tightened his fist.

Keith took a step toward JJ's car. "I didn't let Heather go so a lowlife loser could step in and take my place." He smashed the club into the driver's-side door. "Leave her alone, or next time that will be you."

"What are you doing? Are you insane?" JJ grabbed the club. "You don't scare me."

Keith yanked the club away and lifted it into the air, then slammed it downward. JJ raised his arms to block it, but with a brutal thud Keith wacked him on the back and JJ fell to the ground. Keith stood over him and brought the club backward, then swung toward JJ's head as if it were a golf ball. The blow blinded him, and he put his hands over his face and rolled over, attempting to stand up. Keith pressed him down to the ground with his foot.

"I told you to watch your back."

Heather sat on the front porch in her dad's chair watching the teenage boys across the street play a two-on-two basketball game while the sun set. The shortest boy went up for a lay-up, but the tall boy guarding him ejected the ball and sent it flying through the air into to the yard. The ball rolled into the street, and the short boy went after it.

Heather looked at her phone—7:30. Where was JJ? Two hours ago he'd run home for a quick shower. She'd send him a text to check on him.

JJ is everything . . .

A black truck with a dark windshield pulled into the driveway. Heather clutched the bottom of her chair, and her heart raced. The people who'd thought they'd seen Keith said he'd been in a black truck. She looked at the teenagers, then back at the truck.

The driver door opened, and a pair of cowboy boots hit the ground. Could she get out of the chair and inside fast enough? The door slammed, and her brother-in-law waved.

Her pulse slowed. "Bryson, what brings you here?

"Keith's done something."

"What do you mean, done something?"

"Keith went to confront JJ."

Her stomach tightened. "What did he do?"

"There was an altercation, and Keith's been arrested."

"What about JJ?"

"He was taken to the hospital."

Heather gasped. "What happened?"

"Keith beat him up with a golf club."

A tear slid down her cheek. "How bad is JJ?" She wanted to go to him now and make sure he was okay. Uneasiness weighed her down, and she rubbed at the pain in her chest. He had to be okay.

"I don't know. Keith called from the police

station. He told me what happened and that my truck was at JJ's. He's terrified that his military career is over."

Good. He deserved it. It was one thing to go after her, but another to attack the people she loved. She wasn't staying silent anymore. He needed help, and if that meant he lost his job, then so be it. Something had to get through to him. Let the police deal with him now—she couldn't worry about him. She had to get to JJ.

"My parents and Anna are out to dinner. Will you take me to the hospital?"

"Yes."

She stood and turned to go inside for her cane. A cough spewed from her lips, and she couldn't stop. She reached for the chair to hold her up, but she collapsed to her knees and continued to cough.

Bryson ran up the steps, put his arms around her, and helped her back in the chair. "Are you okay?"

She nodded through the coughing. "I . . . will . . . be."

He ran inside. She looked under her lashes at the teenagers across the street. They stood watching her.

"Are you okay, ma'am?" the neighbor boy asked.

She nodded and waved her hand, then looked down. The basketball dribbled again.

Bryson returned with a cup and handed it to her. "Here's water."

She took it, but her body shuddered, and she couldn't hold the glass to her mouth without water sloshing over the top. Bryson grabbed it and held it to her mouth. She took several small sips, then drew in small breaths and let them out. Her coughing stopped and her breathing steadied.

"Thank you."

"Of course." Bryson stared at her. "Keith said you were doing better. It doesn't look like it."

"Some days are better than others. Keith doesn't know anything. He assumes too much, and that gets him in trouble." She put her hand on top of his. "I know you love him, and you don't want to see it, but he's sick. You two lived the same childhood. Is it too hard to believe that it messed with him?"

Bryson looked down and shook his head.

"He needs help. Make sure he gets it before he hurts anyone else."

Heather clutched on to the arms of her wheelchair as Bryson wheeled her to JJ's room. "Thank you for bringing me."

Bryson nodded, then opened the door for her. "I'll come by later and get you if you need me." He rubbed his temple as he looked into the room.

She followed his gaze and gasped, then covered her mouth at the sight of JJ's swollen eyes, bruised face and forehead wrapped in gauze. He appeared to be sleeping, but she wanted to hear him say he'd be okay. But what if he wouldn't? She'd never forgive herself. She shouldn't have come to Indiana.

"I should go." Bryson touched the side of her arm.

"You can stay."

He shook his head. "Will you keep me updated?"

"Of course."

He gave her his number before he slipped out.

She wheeled herself beside JJ and put her hand on top of his. He didn't stir. "I'm sorry." A tear fell down her cheek. She wanted to deny it, but she loved him. He needed to know.

Arms wrapped around her from behind, and she looked up. Corrin frowned, and Heather squeezed her friend's arms. It comforted her to have Corrin there too.

"When did you come in?" Heather asked.

Corrin let go of Heather and scooted a chair next to her. "I've been here for about a half an hour."

"How did I not see you?"

"I was back here in the corner by the door, texting my parents."

"Amelia and Zac are with them, correct?"

"Yes. A few minutes after I dropped them off, the hospital called. I'm still his medical power of attorney." Corrin shook her head. "Can you imagine if the kids had been at JJ's this weekend?"

Heather's stomach churned. "Thank God they weren't. Do they know?"

"No. I didn't want to frighten them. I'll tell them when I figure out what to say."

"How is JJ?" Her shoulders tensed.

"He's in and out of consciousness, but the doctor said he'll be okay. He has a broken wrist and is bruised pretty badly over most of his body. When he came in, he couldn't see, but his vision is returning. He's also suffering from a concussion, but they don't believe there will be any permanent damage. Of course, they won't really know until he's fully awake."

This couldn't really be happening. He needed to wake right now and prove the doctors right. Keith could rot in jail for all she cared. "Bryson said Keith's been arrested."

"Yes. One of the neighbors called the police."

Heather put her hand on top of Corrin's. "Are you okay?"

"Yeah. How about you?"

"Really shook up. I knew Keith was capable, but I—I can't believe he went after JJ."

Corrin moved to the chair next to Heather. "I know you hinted at it, but Keith was pretty abusive, huh?"

Heather nodded, then spent the next few minutes telling Corrin what her life had been like—the abuse, the affairs, the stolen opportunity to be a mommy. But thank God they'd never had kids. What would he have done to them, or what would they have seen? Nothing a child deserved. Nothing she had deserved.

The grueling reality hit Heather like a swift blow to the stomach. As the words left her mouth, tears streamed down her face. That was her life. She'd lived it. Endured it. Survived it. Her mind had found a way to escape during the abuse, to take Heather somewhere else, to see it, to feel it, to live it, except somehow numbing it all as if she were watching it on a movie screen.

But sharing the truth again released her mind's hold on the repressed memories. More abuse and tirades flooded her mind. Other times that she'd been on the verge of death. How had she forgotten? Like finding a time capsule hidden for years, Heather couldn't believe all her mind had concealed.

She finished sharing, then wiped the tears from her cheek and sat straighter in her wheelchair. That life was over. Even if she only lived another few weeks, Keith would never control her ever again.

Corrin squeezed Heather's hand. "And now cancer. You're one strong woman."

"Only by the grace of God."

"I go to church, but I don't know if I'd been through what you have if I'd be giving God the credit. Seems to me he could have stepped in a time or two."

"Who's to say he didn't? I should have probably died the last time when Keith pushed me down the steps, and I should be dead by now, according to the doctors, and JJ very well could be too. It's in the moments that the worst is happening to us that God is right there. We never know how much worse it could have been without him."

"Now that's a positive twist on it. I want to be like you when I grow up." Corrin nudged Heather's shoulder.

Heather slid her arm into Corrin's and laid her head on her friend's shoulder.

"Hey," JJ whispered.

Heather turned to him and put her hand in his.

"I'll give you two a minute." Corrin touched the bottom of JJ's leg as she stood. "I'll be in the waiting room."

Heather watched her leave, then looked at JJ.

Blood sat inside the bottom of his eyeballs.

He lifted her hand to his mouth and kissed it. "Keith thinks we lied to get him to sign the divorce papers."

"Let him think whatever he wants. I'm sorry he did this to you. I should have gone where he could never find me." She touched his cheek.

"No. I don't care what he does to me. I'll take a million beatings. I love you, Cole."

Never again would she go another moment of her life not letting him know how she felt about him. "I love you too," she whispered as she kissed his temple.

Chapter Twenty-seven

JJ rolled to his side, onto his back again, then shifted his neck from side to side and stared at the ceiling. Everyone had left the hospital about an hour ago, but he couldn't sleep despite the dark and quiet room. His bruised body throbbed, and meds did little to alleviate the shooting pains in his wrist. It would be morning before the doctor could cast it. Breathing techniques and lying positions he'd taught his own patients didn't help either. And the fact that he couldn't get Heather out of his thoughts amplified the inability to shut his mind down.

He'd never been hit by anything worse than a hard bump against a corner or small trip up a step, but Heather had experienced pain like this regularly and without the help of doctors or narcotics. Talk about a strong woman. No wonder she was surviving and fighting through the cancer. She had the strength of Superwoman.

The dim lights behind his bed turned on as Anna entered the room, holding a disposable coffee cup. "How are you doing?"

"Not so hot."

"I can see that. You look awful."

"Thanks."

Anna grinned. "What are the doctors saying? How long will you be here?"

"I have surgery in the morning, then they will run a few tests. If all looks good, I should go home in the afternoon or the next day. The main concern right now is my eyesight. It keeps coming and going. You look pretty blurry. The doctor said worst-case scenario, I'll have slight vision loss and need to wear glasses. They'll know more tomorrow."

"Your eyes are pretty gruesome looking."

"You should see the other guy."

Anna winked.

"Heather said they arrested Keith."

"That's what I heard. I don't remember much." He cleared his throat. "How is Heather? She stayed here for a few hours. When Mr. Cole picked her up, she was exhausted."

"She was hurting really bad and had to take pain meds. She was sleeping when I left."

"She told me she loved me tonight."

Anna smiled. "Be careful with her heart."

Ouch. That hurt. "I will."

"Heather has been a strong opponent resisting Hydra's attack, but you are her Achilles' heel."

What was Anna talking about?

"I call the ability to continue even when all odds are against you *Resisting Hydra's Attack*."

"Who's Hydra?"

Anna tilted her head back and forth. "A Greekmythological creature with nine snakelike heads that each have sharp teeth and could kill men with their poisonous breath. For mere humans, killing the beast was an impossible undertaking because eight of the nine heads were immortal and would grow back in place when cut off. Destroy his one mortal head, and the creature would die. Hercules, the greatest hero from mythology, fought a great battle against Hydra and discovered the beast's demise. After cutting off the immortal heads, he scorched them with fire before it grew new ones. When he reached the last head—the mortal one and the most vicious—it was no match against the strength of Hercules."

JJ scrunched his eyebrows. What was Anna getting at besides telling him a crazy story?

"I've seen lots of attacks against the unsuspecting before, but it seems life goes after the Hercules of the world the hardest," Anna continued. "Heather's the first Hercules I've met. She's fought every attack, and though she's been down a time or two, she overcame. I'm afraid, though, that she's reached the most vicious obstacle. The one that might destroy her faith."

"Her cancer?"

"No, you."

Anna had seemed on board with the possibility of him and Heather. Why the change of heart, and why call him vicious? "I'm not Keith. I'm not going to hurt her."

"I know you don't want to, but losing you again will be the hardest battle she's going to face. If you can't stay strong through all this and you turn to another woman, it will hurt her worse than anything Keith ever did to her."

"She's not going to lose me. I want her."

"But you haven't always been faithful to the women you claimed to love. I'm trying to protect Heather."

"I respect that, but I'm telling you I'm not going to hurt her. I'm in it for the long haul. From now until always."

"I know you think your love for her is eternal, but I believe you could be her ultimate demise."

"No. I won't be. I can't be. I plan to give her an epic romance no matter how short. I will be sure she knows every day how much she's loved."

"What if she pushes you away because she realizes no matter how much you love each other, you won't ever grow old together?"

"I won't let her."

"I know you're familiar with what's going to happen to her body physically and mentally as she reaches her last day. Can you really handle watching her fade away? To see another person leave you? She's fighting the battle of her life and hanging on for dear life while the cancer continues to invade and tells her to give up."

"And I won't give up on her." He didn't want to believe it, but he knew she was right. Heather would leave him someday. And no matter how much he denied it, it would be sooner than later.

"What about when a pretty woman tries to catch your eye and Heather's frail body can't even support itself, let alone show you affection? Will you give in to the need for your desires to be met?"

"No. I don't care about that anymore. I only want her. Whether she's vibrant and laughing or whether she's comatose and moments from her last breath. I will choose her every day, every second, every moment." A tear slid down his cheek. "I wish I could go back eighteen years ago and choose her."

"Changing your past erases Amelia and Zac."

"I wouldn't trade them for anything."

"I know you wouldn't." She handed him the mug. "We can't change the past, only try to do better today." Anna touched his shoulder. "You are a good man."

"I'm trying, and I don't want to hurt Heather. What if you're right? What if I . . . can't stop being selfish? I didn't want to cheat on Heather or Corrin. I hated myself every time." He took a sip of the drink. "I know you say I can't change the past, but I've wronged and hurt so many people. Life would have been different if I'd have chosen Heather from the beginning."

"I don't know if that's true."

"I wouldn't have cheated on her."

"But you did."

"I mean, I wouldn't have done that to her again."

"Why did you keep cheating on Corrin?"

"I don't know."

"You aren't a bad person, JJ. You just need to fix what's broken inside, or you're going to keep on giving in to your flesh. No matter how much you love Heather this time around, you won't grow old together. You will lose her again. And then what? Are you going to sleep with every woman you encounter to try to fill that void? There's more going on, JJ. A night with a woman or a relationship with Heather is never going to make you whole."

"How do I fix me?"

"Pray."

"Pray? Anna, you know I don't—"

"Just try. What would it hurt?"

JJ shrugged.

"I'm only being hard on you now because you mean a lot to me, and I want the best for you and for Heather. She's fighting her battles and she's got the Lord on her side, so I'm not worried about her. But you, JJ, without the Lord it's nearly impossible to fight against Satan's schemes. He's got you in his web, and he's going to continue to trap you as long as he knows which situations and lies to weave you in." She touched his shoulder. "I'll leave you alone to think and hopefully pray. I added a little chamomile to the hot chocolate to help soothe the all-over aches and pain in your wrist."

"Thank you. And I hear you. I don't want to be that man who Amelia caught with another woman. And I don't want to hurt Heather or any woman in the future." He took a sip. "You really do make a wonderful hot chocolate."

"It has just an extra dab of this and a little bit of that." She winked. "I add and mix in simply what's needed for each moment. I better head out. I'm glad you're okay. Think about what I said. Be careful with Heather's heart."

JJ nodded as Anna left the room. He'd never hurt Heather again. He'd guard and protect her heart. *God, show me how to be the man Heather deserves. I've not always been an outstanding man, but I want*

to be. For Heather. For my kids. For . . . myself.
Anna seems to think I can't do it on my own, that
something is broken. Help me see what needs fixing.

An old rerun of *Walker, Texas Ranger* played
while he finished the drink. The pain had subsided a
little, and his eyes grew heavy. The conclusion of
the episode would be on after the commercial break,
but he couldn't fight the sleep knocking on the door,
and he closed his eyes.

He heard the door open and Anna speak.
"Perfect. The right amount to give him a glimpse."

What was Anna talking about? He lifted his head
to ask, but she shut the door. His eyes felt heavy,
and he laid his head back down.

JJ stood at the edge of a lake. A nine-headed green
monster with snakelike heads towering as tall as
treetops slunk out of the water. Its scales dragon-
like and its teeth as sharp as a Tyrannosaurus rex's.
With stealth, it moved toward Heather, who had her
back turned to the sea. She looked left and right, as
if suspecting trouble.

Around her waist, over a red battle skirt, she
wore a jewel-encrusted fringed leather belt. Dressed
in a golden breastplate and armor more impressive
than anything JJ had ever seen, she stood on her
feet, ready for battle in knee-high strappy leather
sandals. In her left hand she held a golden shield
embellished with diamonds, and on her head she
wore an open-faced helmet that matched the rest of
her armor. In her right hand she held a sharp sword,

the blade engulfed in flames that swayed like a spirit with her as she moved.

Hydra slithered along the ground behind Heather, but before it struck her heel, she swung around and brought the sword down on the head and used the flame of the sword to sear the spot shut before another head grew back in its place. Over and over the creature tried to attack, but she fought it off and defeated each head until one remained.

The last head was larger, and the mouth had sharper teeth. Heather lunged in the creature's direction with her sword, but it pushed the weapon away. She tried again, and it knocked the sword from her hand, then struck her on the shoulder.

JJ took a step forward, but vines growing up from the ground crept around his legs up to his waist, then around his arms. Trapped, he wiggled, but the vines wrapped tighter. A pool of water formed in front of him, and a singing mermaid emerged. Her beautiful long golden hair flowed over her breasts, and her aqua eyes looked as if the ocean danced in them. She ran her hand across his mouth, and his body desired her. He held his breath. She traced her finger down his neck, and the vines parted at his chest while she outlined his muscles. She leaned in toward his mouth, and he parted his lips. Her lips grazed his.

Heather.

He couldn't do this.

He pulled back from the kiss, and the vines returned around his chest. He looked around the mermaid to Heather lying on the ground, holding her bloody shoulder. The beast drew his head upward, then thrust its sharp teeth toward her, but she rolled away and seized her sword. She flipped herself up toward a stance, but midair the beast caught her belt with his mouth.

The mermaid grasped JJ's face with her hands. She sang a song, and he couldn't look away from her gazing eyes. She slid her arms behind him and drew him against her. "Join me."

"Where?"

"Into the water."

Yes. He'd go in the water with her.

A bright light burst from behind her, and he looked to Heather dangling from the monster's mouth by the illuminating belt. The monster gagged, and Heather whipped her shield around, then walloped it on the side of its mouth. It flung her out from its clutches against a rock. Her helmeted head hit the boulder, but she bounced off, as if she'd landed against a trampoline. She twisted and landed on her feet.

The mermaid sang and whispered in his ear while he watched Heather. "You don't want her. You want me. She'll be dead soon enough. No one survives Hydra. Come with me into the water."

Go with her into the water. Yes.

The creature wrapped its snakelike head around Heather's legs up to her neck, then tightened his squeeze.

"Heather!" JJ called

The mermaid moved his face to look at her, but he jerked his head away. He had to get to Heather.

"The water is nice. Join me."

Yes, he would join her.

"JJ . . . help . . . me." Heather choked with each word.

The creature stuck out his long snakelike tongue and hissed.

The vines released around his hand, and the mermaid took it. "Come with me."

He looked to Heather struggling to breathe. He had to help her. He tried to wiggle free of the rest of the vine, but it tightened.

"She's defeated. She can't win. I'll give you everything you want."

"No!" He pulled his hand out of hers, and the vine wrapped back around him. "I won't be under your spell. I love Heather."

"Then you shall die too." The pool of water swirled, and the mermaid dove in, splashing him with her tail.

Hydra sneered at JJ. "You're next after her."

Heather's face turned purple, and her eyes bugged out as she stared at JJ. She was going to die, and he couldn't do anything about it. He writhed inside the vine.

"Take me. Not her."

Heather closed her eyes, then her neck fell forward.

"I'd rather destroy you both." The beast opened its mouth, and a billow of rotten egg–smelling smoke filled the air. He dropped her from his grasp, and she fell limp to the ground. He blew a perfect circle of smoke that wrapped around her like ropes. "But I think I'll end you first." He slithered toward JJ.

A large trumpet blasted from over the mountain.

Hydra turned to look in the direction of the sound. "Wait here." He cackled. "Like you have a choice. Enjoy the little time you have left." Hydra crawled over the mountain.

JJ looked around. How could he get out of this? Heather's sword lay on the ground next to her.

"Heather. Heather," he whispered loudly.

She opened her eyes.

"Your sword. Can you reach it?" She touched it with her pinkie and scooted it toward her. She took it into her hands and slid it between her and the smoke rope. She cut through it, and it fell off. She ran to JJ and cut the vine. Once free, he threw his arms around her.

"Where did Hydra go?"

He pointed toward the mountain. "He went over it."

"How about a sneak attack?" She held her finger over her mouth, then ran over the mountain.

He chased after her but couldn't catch her. He reached the top of the mountain as a bright light from below filled the valley. He climbed down to find Hydra lying motionless and missing his last head.

Heather stood tall, sword in hand, standing next to the beast. "I won't go down without a fight."

No, she wouldn't.

Out of nowhere a thump walloped JJ in the stomach, and he fell onto his back. Something forced his eyes open. A brown-haired girl, about two, with Heather's green eyes and a smile, sat on top of JJ's stomach, pulling his eyelids open.

"Get up, Daddy."

Disoriented, JJ looked around at the large bedroom. Where was he? A large TV turned to the Disney channel hung on the light-cream walls above the fireplace directly across from him. To the right, French doors exposed a deck and the wintery outside, and to the left a small hallway led to a bathroom. Next to the fireplace, an opened bedroom door revealed a rail overlooking a tall-ceiling room below. The pillow-top king-size mattress not only held the little girl sitting on his stomach but a snoring, little blond-haired boy about seven, who looked similar to Zac and lay cuddled next to JJ.

He sat up and moved the girl off his stomach to the end of the bed. Carrying a laundry basket, Anna walked past the bedroom door.

"Anna, Anna." He climbed off the bed and chased her down the hallway.

"Good morning, sir. What can I do for you?"

Sir?

"What did you put in that drink?"

She looked at him with confusion in her eyes. "What drink?"

"The one you gave me last night at the hospital."

"At the hospital?" She put her hand on his forehead, like she was checking for a fever. "Are you feeling okay, Dr. Jones? I wasn't at the hospital last night." Confusion sat in her brows. "Is that where you were? Why you came home so late?" An unfamiliar tone of sarcasm dripped in her voice. "Heather was worried."

Heather?

"Am I having another one of those crazy dreams again?"

265

"Sir, I'm sure I don't know what you are talking about. Crazy dreams? You do feel a little hot. Maybe you should go back to bed."

"Are those my kids in there?"

She dropped her head and laughed. "Yes, those silly little critters are yours. Now go get in bed." She pushed him toward the door and into the room. "Abi, Sam, off the bed. Your daddy isn't feeling well."

Sam pulled the covers over his head. "But I'm tired."

Anna tugged the blankets down and pulled him into a sitting position and moved his legs off the side of the bed. "Now get up. You can get back in your bed."

"Why bother. I'm up now." Sam trudged out of the room.

"Abi, you too."

"But Daddy play?" She stood on the bed and jumped into his arms.

He caught her, and as if doing it out of habit, he kissed the top of her head.

"Daddy needs rest." Anna took Abi from him.

"I'm okay, really. Just woke a little confused." He rubbed a headache starting in his temples.

Anna's voice cut through the pain. "Maybe from your wild night."

"Wild night?"

"Don't play dumb with me. I know exactly where you were."

"Where was that?"

Corrin's, she mouthed.

Corrin's? Before he'd seen a glimpse of the past.

Was this a glimpse at the future? If that was so, then had God healed Heather of the cancer? The boy looked about seven and the girl two.

"What was I doing over there? Dropping off Amelia and Zac?"

"Who?"

"My kids, Amelia and Zac."

Anna rolled her eyes and huffed as she scooted Abi out the door. "The more I learn about you, the less I like."

"What's that mean?"

"That wife of yours and your four kids are amazing. How you can toss them aside for this week's flavor, I don't get. Heather hadn't told me about your other children. Which indiscretion led to them?"

"Led to what? I really don't know what is going on here."

"Heather's told me all about your affairs."

"My affairs. I didn't know she knew about them."

"Well, she does. You've broken her heart one too many times."

She was making his head spin. "Broken her heart? I never would hurt her. I made my mistakes with Corrin, but I've grown since then. And since Heather's cancer and Keith, I've only wanted to show her how a woman should be loved."

Anna gasped. "I don't know who Keith is or how you think you've shown love to Heather, but a man does not run around on the woman he loves. As far as the cancer, I thought she was waiting to tell you, but if you know about it and are still openly continuing the affair with Corrin, then you are a bigger jerk than I thought, Dr. Jones."

He slumped his shoulders. "I'm confused. Where is Heather?"

"At the doctor."

Just then a door alarm chimed, warning that the front door had opened.

"Mommy!" Abi yelled.

Heather. He had to see her. He ran out the bedroom to a rail that ran across the hallway and overlooked the downstairs. Heather sat on the step, pulling off her snow boots. She looked incredible and healthy. The front of her hair was pulled up into a large clip, and the rest dangled around her face and back. The loose-neck red sweater clung to her curves just right.

"Good morning, gorgeous." He waved down to her.

She looked up at him without a sparkle in her eyes. "Morning. It's like ten thirty. Are you just getting up?"

"Yes." He followed the rail down the steps and met her at the front door. He leaned in to kiss her on the lips, but she turned her head. The same move Corrin had given him many times. He kissed her cold cheek.

"I take it you stayed out too late and now you have Ken covering your day." She turned her back and walked into the living room. "That's not really fair to your patients." A hint of scorn trailed in her voice.

He followed her into the living room. "What did the doctor say?"

Heather shrugged. "Not much. Just to keep doing what I'm doing. I'm fairly healthy."

"Fairly? What's that supposed to mean?"

"You wouldn't care anyway."

"Heather, why do you say that?" He moved around to face her.

She met his eyes with a steely gaze. "It's true."

"No, it's not. I love you."

Heather rolled her eyes and blew out a laugh. "Give me a break, JJ. You stopped loving me a long time ago. You'd much rather be with Corrin. You don't even hide it anymore."

He grabbed her hand. "You've got it wrong, Heather. I don't want her. I want you. I've only ever wanted you."

She pulled her hand out of his. "You should tell your girlfriend that."

The anger in her voice struck JJ's heart.

A teenage girl walked down the steps, gave Heather a kiss on the cheek, and walked past JJ without a word.

"You are not on Lily's good side." Heather nodded toward the teenager.

"What did I do?"

She glared at him like he should know. He shrugged his shoulders, and she huffed loud enough the entire neighborhood probably heard it.

"What?" He shook his head.

"I swear, JJ. Your charm doesn't work on me anymore."

He looked up at her from under his lashes and cocked his head. Whoever the JJ was in this world was not him, and she needed to know that.

"Stop looking at me like that. It isn't going to work. I'm over you."

Over him? What did that mean?

"Which reminds me. The manager from the apartments called. Your unit will be ready the first of January."

"Unit?" JJ raked his hand through his hair. *What is going on here? Where am I? What kind of alternate reality is this?*

"Don't play dumb. You agreed to move out." She folded her arms across her waist and planted one foot firmly ahead of the other.

Move out? "But I don't want to move out. I want to be here with you and the kids."

"I stopped believing you wanted to be here with me and the kids last year when I found out you'd been cheating on me our entire marriage. The other women were enough, but the fact that the latest one is Corrin . . ." She shuddered and wrapped her arms around herself. "That was the final straw. Of course you know all this already. I'm done talking about it."

"But I married you. I've wanted to be with you my entire life. Why would I cheat on you?"

"Don't you remember? You blamed it on the fact that you never really got to sow your wild oats. We've been together since we were fifteen, and you'd never been with another woman. Oh yeah, and you said after having four kids, I just didn't give it to you enough." She huffed. "But you know what woman wants to sleep with her husband who is cheating on her? Makes you feel less than. But I don't have to worry about that anymore, because we're done."

JJ stared at her. He was ashamed of himself. He'd thought all these years that he'd cheated on Corrin because he was trying to get the thoughts of Heather out of his mind. But that wasn't true. He really was a jerk who had never grown up, who only thought of himself.

"I'm not leaving. I love you, and I'm going to change. I have to. Who will take care of you through the cancer?"

"Anna is here, and my parents live fifteen minutes away. Plus Lily and Michael are old enough to help around the house. I don't need you." She raised her voice, then paused. "Who told you I had cancer?"

"No one. I just know."

She rolled her eyes. "Whatever. I can't believe a word that comes out of your mouth."

"I could do your physical therapy."

"Uh . . . no. And besides, I don't need any physical therapy. It's just a small spot on my back. Melanoma. They'll cut it out and keep a close eye on my blood work to be sure, but they believe it hasn't spread anywhere else. They caught it soon enough." She rolled her eyes. "Thanks to you."

"Thanks to me?"

"Remember that dark spot you found?"

He shrugged.

"On my right shoulder?"

He shook his head.

She lowered her voice. "In the shower."

He raised his eyebrows. "When was this?"

"JJ, really."

"I'm serious."

"Last week when you handed me a warm towel from the dryer, you said you couldn't resist and had to join me. You found it when you were kissing my neck. Do you remember now? Or was I just another escapade added to the list for the week?"

The thought of kissing Heather in the shower made him shift. He hadn't kissed her since he was seventeen, and the most he'd ever seen of her body was what wasn't covered by a one-piece bathing suit, but he'd spent plenty of time imagining what she looked like underneath all her clothes.

"No, I remember," he lied.

"I was mad at myself for giving in to you that morning, but thank God I did because the doctor said if it hadn't been caught, it could have spread to other parts of my body."

JJ's heart sank. She had skin cancer. Was that the case in the real world? Had it all started with a spot on her back that no one caught? How could they have? Keith never let her leave the house, let alone go to a doctor. She was probably bruised so often he never noticed, or the way he said how fat she was, maybe he didn't even look at her.

He put his arms around her. "Despite what you think, I do love you and I'm sorry."

Chapter Twenty-eight

JJ woke but didn't open his eyes. The dream had been nice. He'd spent the rest of it playing cops and robbers with little Abi and Sam, throwing the baseball with his ten-year-old son, Michael, and made funny faces at the dinner table trying to make his oldest child, Lily, laugh. At least in that life he was still a good dad. Heather had seemed surprised when he told her and Anna to rest and he'd cook dinner and do the dishes. Then he'd ended the night giving Heather a massage before he headed to what he learned was his room and she went to hers.

He stretched his arms over his head and rolled his neck. Amazingly, his wrist didn't hurt, and neither did his body. Shouldn't he be in more pain? Did they cast his wrist while he slept? Were they pumping him full of morphine?

He opened his eyes. The TV above the fireplace played *Mickey Mouse Clubhouse*, but the volume was turned all the way down. Large snowflakes fell along the dark morning sky out the bedroom window, and Sam's feet pushed into his back.

How was he still here? It was morning, right?

Anna's crazy hot chocolate formula had to have worn off by now. He'd seen a glimpse of what could have been. He'd learned no matter what choice he would have made all those years ago, it wouldn't have changed the type of man he'd become. Knots tied in his stomach. He *was not* going to be that kind of man ever again.

Anna's humming carried through the house. He went downstairs. The sun had not risen yet, and the moon lit the kitchen. He flipped on the light over the sink and jumped backward when he saw Anna at the kitchen table.

"Good morning." She held her coffee mug up in a gesture of hello.

"Morning."

"Would you like me to make you some?"

"What is it, or rather what is in it?" He took a seat across from her.

"Hot chocolate with an extra dab of this and a little bit of that. An old family recipe."

"I knew it. Please tell me what's going on."

"What's going on?" She crinkled her forehead. "We are up early, and I'm going to make you my specialty drink."

"Right. A drink that reveals some kind of truth."

She shifted her eyes back and forth, like he was crazy. "Nope. I'm not a miracle maker, just a maid."

"I thought you were a nurse."

She laughed. "Maybe in another life. Here I'm a maid. You should know. You hired me."

"I did?"

This was all just too crazy. Maybe Anna really

had nothing to do with him being there. But what had and why? The last time, he'd seen four scenes before returning. Is that what would happen here too? Was he dreaming? These visions seemed too vivid and real to be a dream.

Either way he didn't mind spending time in this world for a bit. Maybe he could change things around. Here they'd caught the cancer early enough. Here she was his wife. He dropped his shoulders. But here she had more reasons to hate him, but maybe more reasons to love him. In this life they had been together for twenty years. In this life they had children. In this life he'd given her everything she wanted except for maybe his whole heart.

Why? Why couldn't he commit to one woman? Maybe that was why he was here.

JJ looked into Anna's eyes. Something told him she wasn't telling the whole truth. Anna had been in the past, in reality, and now she was in this life too. There had to be a connection between the three worlds and Anna and her specialty drink. All he knew was, every time he took a drink, it sent him to another time. He didn't plan on going anywhere. He'd stay here with the healthy Heather until whatever forced him back.

"You know I don't think I'll be having any of your 'this and that' drink. I'm fine right here."

Anna looked at him again like he was crazy. "Ooookay, Dr. Jones. Nobody's forcing it on you."

"Good morning," Heather's groggy voice said from behind them. She wore a short, silky pink robe and a pair of matching house slippers. Her hair was pulled up in a sloppy bun, and she'd never looked sexier.

Getting up from the table, he greeted her in the doorway with a kiss on the cheek. "Good morning."

She made a sound under her breath, as if annoyed by the kiss, but she didn't turn away. "What are you doing up? You're never awake before six."

"I couldn't sleep."

He pulled a chair out for her, and she sat down.

"Thank you." She scrunched her eyebrows. "What's gotten in to you? Dinner, dishes, pulling chairs out? And you were awesome with the kids yesterday?"

"Am I not normally good with the kids?"

"No, you are." She raised her mouth, but not to a complete smile. "Yesterday just felt nice. Almost like we were the picture-perfect family."

"We can be." He took her hand.

She looked down at their hands. "You know that ship has sailed. No amount of help around the house or attention is going to change my mind. You've given me the *I'm- sorry-I'll-change* speech a million times. I just can't do this anymore." She pulled her hand away. "You've broken every bit of trust I had in you." A tear fell down her cheek. "I can't forgive you anymore."

"I thought God said to forgive seventy times seven."

"I've probably forgiven you that many times. And since when did you believe anything the Bible said? I'm starting to agree with you and doubt its truth anyway. Forgive seventy times seven? That's just ludicrous."

What was she talking about? She was starting to believe the Bible wasn't true? It seemed even through her abuse she'd held on to God's goodness, but in this world . . . here with JJ, she doubted. He turned to look at Anna, who lifted a brow at him. Had his unfaithfulness finally destroyed Heather's faith?

JJ returned his gaze to Heather. "Well, I'm starting to think I might have been all wrong about God. Did I really cheat that many times?"

"I don't know . . . Between the actual women and the internet, it might be."

"I'm sorry."

"I know, but I can't let you break my heart anymore."

Chapter Twenty-nine

Three days later, JJ woke yet again in the alternate reality. How long would he stay here? Laughter from his children and Heather carried from downstairs. He rolled onto his back. He'd taken on the new life as if it were his own. He'd gone to work where, surprisingly, almost everything was the same. Same building and partners, same patients, and same receptionist, who apparently, he'd had a fling with recently. Why? Why was everything so eerily similar? He shook his head. Even his propensity to cheat.

He sucked in his lips. What a loser. What an absolute loser. He had the woman of his dreams, and he'd still blown it. What was wrong with him?

"Okay, kids. Let's hurry. I don't want you to be late." Heather's kind voice floated up the stairs and sang to JJ's soul. Watching Heather fulfill her most-wanted desire as a mother over the last several days made up for enduring the cold glares she threw his way.

Well, he was going to fix that. He'd prove to her he'd changed. That he wasn't the same man she'd known in this world. He was a better man. But . . . was he?

He got out of bed, showered and dressed, then joined his family in the kitchen. Heather handed him a plate of eggs, toast, and a banana, but her eyes never met his.

"Thank you."

Her skin glowed, and her healthy body's silhouette clung to her pajama shirt. A bit of her stomach showed just above her pants. Perhaps just a peck on the cheek, but she acted as interested in him as a lioness blinking away pesky face flies. Who cared? He leaned toward her, but ignoring him, she turned away and took her plate to the table.

Like a wounded puppy, he dipped his chin toward his chest and took a seat at the opposite end from Heather. Excited talk about it being the last day of school before Christmas break fluttered around the table, and then each child shared what they wanted for Christmas. How odd to engage in this conversations with his "children." He didn't know them well enough to have a clue what they'd want. Would he still be in this world that morning? Why was he here anyway? He looked to Heather. He could stay here forever, if here meant Heather was healthy and alive.

"What does Mom want for Christmas?" JJ winked.

Straight faced, she looked in his eyes. "Just for the kids to enjoy it." She looked away and kissed little Abi on top of the head.

"Ah, Mom. You say that every year." Michael laughed. "Just give us an idea. Please. So we know what to get you."

She glanced at JJ. "I don't need anything. I have everything I could want." Tears formed in her eyes. Then she looked out the window across from her.

JJ's stomach knotted. How could the JJ from this world not have appreciated her? How could he have broken her heart? Cheated on her?

A tear slid down her cheek.

"Ah, Mom, are you crying?" Michael touched her shoulder.

She wiped the crease of her eye and gave a phony smile, but the children didn't seem to notice. "I'm blessed to be your mother."

JJ winked. "You kids are pretty special."

Abi slid out of her chair and into JJ's lap. "Whatcha want for Christmas, Daddy?"

"To see your mommy smile." JJ gazed at Heather, but she stared at her plate.

Michael huffed. "You two aren't fun. Come on. What do you want?"

Heather slid her chair backward and grabbed the empty plates. "I'd like a locket with a picture of you all. Or maybe lotion or something. You know me. I'm easy. I'd like anything." She set the dishes in the sink. "Okay, kids, run upstairs and finish getting ready."

The children obliged. Heather leaned against the counter while JJ finished his last few bites. When he brought his dishes to the sink, she held her hand out for them. He left mere inches between them and gazed into her eyes while reaching around her to put his plate into the sink. Her lips were so close. So perfect. And if he didn't know better, he'd have thought she was waiting for a kiss. Her eyes stayed locked on his, and she stood perfectly still. Was she breathing?

He took a step forward and closed the gap. Her chest rose against him. She smelled wonderful. Like cinnamon rolls and vanilla. He tucked a strand of hair behind her ear, and as if the touch singed her skin, she flinched and slid away from him.

Without looking at him, she spoke as if the moment hadn't happened. "Don't forget we have that Christmas party tonight. Please be home a little early if you can."

"Where is the party at exactly?" Jumping into the middle of JJ's alternate life was confusing. Hopefully, soon enough he'd be able to get with the program.

"At Bryson and Claire's."

Bryson. Of course. In this life Keith hadn't dated Heather, so that meant Bryson and JJ's friendship hadn't ended. Did that mean Bryson didn't move away from Danburg either?

"JJ, I swear you've been weird the last few days." Her eyes met his again.

"I'm upset about us. I just can't think straight."

She rolled her eyes. "Have you called the manager back? You said it was *the* apartment you wanted. And I need you to get this all taken care of so we can move on."

He leaned in close to her face, almost touching her lips as he whispered. "I don't want us to move on."

She stepped back. "Come on, JJ. Stop this. I've had enough. I've given you plenty of chances. You haven't been fair to me. Please make the arrangements and move out. Let me deal with this the way I need to."

"I'm not giving up."

"Well, you're wasting your time. I said we could wait until after Christmas for the kids, but then we're done."

"Are you saying there's hope? I have until Christmas." He smiled. "How many days is that?"

She shook her head. "JJ!"

"I'm serious. How many days?"

She huffed and arched her neck backward. "Five."

"Please give me until then. If I haven't proven to you that I can change my ways by then, I'll leave." He grinned. "But if I can get you to kiss me under the mistletoe by Christmas at midnight, then promise you'll give me another chance." He lifted her hand and kissed it.

She closed her eyes and shook her head. "I swear, JJ. You make it impossible to say no."

Was that hope in her voice? Did she want it to work out?

Opening her eyes, she fixed them on his. "Okay, if you can prove to me that you have miraculously changed—which, believe me, will take a miracle—then I'll consider letting you stay and see if we can work through this."

Winking, he wrapped his arms around her waist and pulled her against him. "I'll buy you my favorite flavored lip gloss."

"Don't bother wasting your money." A small laugh escaped through her pursed lips.

His cheek brushed against hers as he whispered in her ear. "Um-huh, I can taste it now."

A smile spread across her face, and she playfully shoved him. Surprisingly, she didn't pull away from his arms. "Whatever."

Was she letting her guard down because she wanted him to make a move? He drew her against him and leaned in for a kiss.

She jerked out of his arms. "I don't think so, buddy." She looked at the clock above the sink. "You better head to work, or you'll be late."

Defeated, he nodded. Today he wouldn't get the kiss, but he was going to do everything in his power to get one under the mistletoe by his Christmas deadline. He opened the door to the garage. "I'll be home in time for the party."

"Okay. Thanks. See you later." She turned, then headed out of the room, but as she entered the doorway, she clutched it and said words that made his heart leap. "I'm rooting for you, JJ. Don't let me down."

Mentally, he pumped his fist in the air. "I won't. I love you. I will fix this."

Maybe he did have a chance after all.

JJ's heart sped as Heather walked down the steps. The tight red Christmas dress with the white feathery material along the neckline fit her snug in the right places, and the red pumps called attention to her legs. He took her hand when she reached the bottom of the steps and spun her around. "Mrs.

Jones, you look stunning."

How wonderful it sounded to call her that. She *was* his wife. Maybe only in this fantasy, but it felt real. Like he was really fighting for them.

"Thank you. You don't look too bad yourself." She winked.

She'd picked out his clothes—a black sports jacket, red button-down shirt, jeans, and cowboy boots. No denying she had a good eye for fashion.

"I had a little bit of help." He returned the wink.

She nodded while gazing deep into his eyes. The desire to kiss her invaded every part of him. Did she feel the same? Earlier, she'd backed away from his advances. Would she now? He wished he had the memories of their life together. The good times. The passionate times. The day he'd married her.

But her eyes didn't show years of joy, but rather sorrow. The same look Corrin held in hers after she'd endured years of his affairs. How could the JJ of this world do that to Heather? He didn't want those memories. The ones with Corrin were hard enough to bear. Why had he chosen to have an affair with Corrin in this world? He'd chosen Heather, but why had he kept Corrin too? What a fool. Why this strange twist of fate? What was the point? Why was he here? It appeared no matter what life held for him, he'd been destined to be a jerk, and if he didn't fix things in this world, he was destined to be alone here too.

He might never understand what was wrong with him. For now he'd enjoy the evening with Heather and convince her he'd changed.

He took her hand in his. "Let's get going."

From in the family room, Anna sat on the floor getting her hair fixed by Abi, and she shouted, "Have a good evening."

"Thanks for watching them tonight, Anna." Heather reached for her long black dress coat. JJ took it from her and helped her slide into it.

"Not a problem at all. You have good kids. They make it easy."

Heather smiled. "Thank you. We shouldn't be out too late."

JJ zipped up his jacket. "Unless we decide to not come back."

"Ha-ha. We're coming back. I've got a weekend ahead of cookie baking starting in the morning."

"Fun," Anna said.

"You're welcome to join us." Heather kissed Abi on the cheek, then yelled bye to the kids upstairs. "We'll see you later."

Holding Heather's hand, he led her out to the car and opened the door for her.

"You're pulling out all the stops." She smiled and slid into the seat.

After starting the engine, he turned the radio to the Christmas station, backed the car out of the driveway, then took a glance at her legs. What he wouldn't give to run his hand along them. Would she let him?

He shifted into gear and started down the street. "It Came upon a Midnight Clear" played on the radio, and she sang along. He'd forgotten what a beautiful voice she had before cancer had tainted it.

Her legs called to him, *Touch me.*

Biting his bottom lip, he fought the urge and kept

his eyes on the road.

The song ended, and the Chipmunk version of "It's Beginning to Look a Lot like Christmas" came on. JJ joined in, and Heather laughed. This felt nice. The way a marriage and friendship should be, but this wasn't real.

He turned left on Bryson's street. He'd memorized the directions from Google Maps that way he wouldn't have to ask Heather how to get there.

As JJ parked the car along the street, Bryson, full beard and all, hurried down the driveway. Crossing his arms and looking around like the getaway driver, Bryson waited as JJ opened the door for Heather. What was up with Bryson?

Bryson hugged Heather. "You look amazing."

"Thank you. How is that new wife of yours?"

"She's great. Although I think she's feeling a little overwhelmed with the whole throwing-a-party thing."

"I'll go in and help her."

"That would be great. You should be able to find her somewhere in the kitchen surrounded by all that food."

Heather laughed. "I'll find her." She touched JJ's arm. "I'll see you in there."

"Okay."

When Heather was out of sight, Bryson hugged JJ with a back slap and whispered, "Dude, I didn't know Heather was coming. Corrin said she was thinking about stopping by, and I told her to come on. I thought you and Heather were just going through the motions for appearances around the kids until after Christmas."

The knots returned. He'd have an ulcer by the end of this.

"We were, but now I'm not sure. She's given me until Christmas to prove to her I've changed. I don't want a divorce."

"But what about Corrin? Are you ending it with her? She said you had to choose, and you chose Corrin. You said things have been blah with Heather for years."

"I'm learning that was my fault. I love Heather."

"But I thought you said you couldn't live without Corrin."

"I did?"

"Yes. We were standing right here the night you told me. You said you'd fallen out of love with Heather years ago and that you needed a woman who made you feel alive. And Corrin was exciting and adventurous."

Corrin adventurous? The most exciting thing she'd ever done was take her seat belt off during an airplane ride to walk to the bathroom. Heather had been the adventurous one. She enjoyed hiking, skiing, jumping off the high dive, ziplining, snorkeling with sharks. You name it—she'd try it at least once.

"Well, I was living a fantasy. Heather is real. She *is* the love of my life. Maybe I forgot that along the way. We got in a rut or something. I can't let her go."

"Okay, do you want me to tell Corrin not to come now?"

"Yeah. If Heather sees her here, that will be the

end of me convincing her I want only her."

"It might be too late." He pointed to a black Toyota Celica parking across the street. Corrin waved and opened her door.

JJ rushed over to her before she exited the car. Hopefully, he could send her away before Heather saw. "Hey."

"Hey. You look good. Love the boots. Turn around. Let me see how those jeans hug your backside." Passion filled her eyes.

He hadn't seen that look from her for years.

"Look, Corrin. Don't get out of the car. Heather's here—"

Corrin rolled her eyes. "Why is she here? I thought you said she was staying home." Anger sounded in her voice. "I was pumped about the party. I even bought a new dress." She opened her coat and revealed a slinky black dress that barely covered her thighs. Any man would have a hard time keeping his hands off her. "I even got something a little special for the after party."

The words escaped his lips before he had time to think of the consequence. "Ummmm, you look *fiiiine*." Memories of what it felt like kissing her, and more, flooded his mind. He drew in a deep breath and blew it out. He wanted her and she wanted him.

But what about Heather?

JJ bit his bottom lip. This wasn't real life, only a dream or something. What would it hurt? It had been too long since he'd been with a woman. Not even a little kiss for months. He was a man, for goodness' sake. He leaned his forehead against the roof of the driver's-side door and looked down at Corrin still sitting in the seat. He had needs. And Corrin was willing. The women were always willing. He shook his head.

That was the problem.

He was weak. He surrounded himself with woman after woman who didn't care if he had a girlfriend or a wife or children. He'd known every time where the relationships would lead.

Corrin wrapped her arms around the back of his legs and pulled him closer. "Come here."

If in the real world Heather fought like Hercules, then here in this alternate reality, he'd fight too. For her. For himself. For whatever life God had planned for him. Being an adulterer wasn't who JJ wanted to be.

But could he put his trust in God?

"Come on. Get in the car. Let's go back to my place." Her long nails traced circles along the side of his thighs.

God, I'm weak. I need you. I don't know that I'm strong enough. I love Heather, so why am I considering this?

JJ looked toward the house. Bryson had disappeared, and hopefully Heather wasn't watching him from a window.

A thought from deep inside him spoke. *Grow up, JJ, and stop your selfish ways. Do not conform to the patterns of this world, but be transformed by the renewing of your mind. Then you will be able to test and approve what God's will is—his good, pleasing, and perfect will.*

Had that come from God? It sounded familiar,

like a Bible verse maybe. But he'd never memorized any.

"Are you joining me?" Corrin's seductress voice drew his attention as her hands ran up his backside.

"I can't." He stepped away from her roaming hands. "Heather's my wife. I can't do this anymore." He would fix everything the JJ from this alternate world had damaged. And when he returned to his real life, he needed to make things right with Corrin and Heather.

Corrin huffed. "If you go in that house without me, we are through. Do you hear me? We are done. I'm tired of being strung along by you. It's been seventeen years of this. Seventeen years I've waited for you to choose me."

"Seventeen years?"

"Are you kidding me? Don't you remember all of the times you ran to me instead of Heather when you tired of the current fling? You know she's boring. How many times did you tell me she's not interesting? Why are you acting like this?"

"Well, I was a fool. I don't want to hurt you, but I want to make this work with Heather. Loving her isn't always about the fun and interesting moments, but all the others in between too."

Corrin looked toward Bryson's front door and gestured at it with a nod. "I see. Heather wore that little *Santa baby* dress, and you couldn't resist her in it."

JJ turned slowly. Heather stood in the doorway. When he caught her eye, she looked down at the porch. His heart plummeted into his stomach, and his pulse raced.

Corrin continued her tirade. "That's what it always comes down to, huh? Who looks hotter? Guess your little sweatpants stay-at-home mama got herself fixed up to win her husband back."

JJ whipped his head back toward Corrin, and his blood boiled as he spoke. "No, as a matter fact, it was when Heather was coughing up blood, fighting for her life, and showing me that through cancer she was the strongest woman I know that I realized I'd forgotten who she really was. She hadn't changed. I'd been selfish. I'd changed from the boy she'd met."

Corrin scowled. "What are you talking about? You were ready to leave her just last week. Cancer? This is the first I've heard of it?"

Sarcasm oozed from him. "Well, maybe I don't tell you everything."

He shoved his hand into his pocket and clutched the seashell. How had it gotten there? "I missed out on what could have been an amazing life with Heather because I was driven by my sexual desires. I'm done with that. I'm not losing the rest of the life I can have with her. I'm sorry if that hurts you, but she *is* my wife. And I can't do this with you anymore. We're done." He slammed her door shut.

Corrin squealed her tires as she pulled out from her parking spot and sped away. JJ didn't like the Corrin from this world. She'd never been that self-absorbed. That cold and cunning. That needy. The way life happened here had probably caused it. He felt bad for how mean and straightforward he'd been with her, but after he'd watched Keith abuse Heather and call her names and spit and throw food on her in the other strange twist of reality, he couldn't take letting anyone disrespect Heather, ever. Even if the Heather in this world had never encountered a life with Keith.

He walked toward Heather, and she met him halfway down the driveway.

"Why was Corrin here?"

"She just showed up, but I wasn't . . . I was—"

She put her arms around his waist and hugged him. "I know. I heard. Thank you."

He wrapped his arms around her and pulled her closer. How nice it felt having her against him. Cinnamon and vanilla filled his nose. He inhaled her intoxicating scent again. "I do love you, Heather, and I promise I'm going to spend the rest of my life showing you that."

"JJ?" She tilted her head upward.

"Yes."

"Why did you tell Corrin you watched me suffer from cancer? I'm having the spot removed. The doctors aren't really concerned about it."

He gazed in her eyes. "I had a dream. An awful dream where it wasn't caught early enough. It moved to your lungs, and I had to watch you die." A tear rolled down his cheek. "It was the worst nightmare of my life." He shook his head. "I can't live in that world. I want to be here with you and the kids. I can't live without you."

She wiped the tear from his cheek. "I don't want to live without you either, but I . . . I don't know if I can ever trust you again."

"I know I don't deserve it, but please give me a chance. Have faith in us."

Taking in a deep breath and then letting it out, her chest rose against his. "I don't have much faith in anything anymore."

Chapter Thirty

JJ sat in the waiting room of a psychologist Anna had recommended. Two days—that was all he had left to prove he was going to change. What was wrong with him? Why did he do what he didn't want to do? Hopefully, the doctor could help him figure out why he hurt the hearts of the women who loved him and the women he'd loved.

A cylinder-shaped fish tank full of large, colorful fish sat in the middle of the room, running from the floor to a few feet below the ceiling. A small girl, rocking back and forth, sat in a fetal position in the chair next to a woman reading a magazine. A man called the girl's name, and she and her mother followed him to the other room. Two TVs hung from opposite sides of the room. PBS channel's *The Cat in the Hat* Christmas episode played on one, and *The View*'s Christmas deals and steals on the other. He opted for *The Cat in the Hat*. Minutes passed, and his eyes grew heavy.

"Dr. Jack Jones."

JJ stirred from his seat. Had he fallen asleep? He wiped the corner of his mouth and followed the white-haired balding man down the hallway. The doctor's office was furnished with a dark-colored desk, a cream couch, two royal-blue armchairs, and mind-game puzzles hanging on the wall.

The doctor held his hand out for JJ. "Hello, I'm Dr. Miller. Please take a seat. What brings you here today?"

No need to hold anything back. JJ cut to the chase. "I continually commit adultery. The thing is, I love my wife, yet I've cheated over and over. She wants a divorce. I want to prove to her I won't do it again. And I really want to change. I just don't understand why I keep doing it."

The doctor nodded. "Tell me a little bit about you. Your childhood, etcetera."

JJ sucked his lips in. His childhood was normal. It was his late-teen years, the years when he'd become a man, that were messed up. He took in a big breath and blew it out. "Life was fairly normal." He shrugged. "I was happy. I had everything I could want. Great friends, a wonderful girlfriend. I played on several sport teams. I was popular, did well in school, and had prospects to go to several top colleges."

JJ paused and stared at the doctor's desk. Then one day his life crumbled. "My dad had a heart attack and died two weeks after I graduated from high school. Shortly after, my mother found a boyfriend and ran off with him. She doesn't come around or call ever, but I've dealt with it. That's the way things go." The hurt ran deeper than JJ wanted to admit. He shook the thought away.

The psychologist cleared his throat. "Is that

really how you feel about your absent mother?"

JJ scoffed. "No, but what can I do about it? I tried for years to reach out. She'd answer when I called, and we'd have nice conversations. But for whatever reason, she would never bother to give me her new phone number any time it changed. I'd search for it, call, and she'd act as if I'd had it all along. Then one day—I guess thanks to cell phones—I couldn't find her number anymore. I sent pictures of the kids to her last known address, but she never replied. I don't even think she lives there anymore." He sniffed. "Okay, I know she doesn't. I flew there last year to confront her. The young couple who answered the door said they'd bought the house from her a few months prior, and they thought she moved out of state, but they weren't sure. How can a mom not care about her only son and his family? I mean, I know I'm not a good husband, but my kids . . . I could never hurt them."

A jolt stabbed JJ. Hadn't he done just that when Amelia caught him with the other woman?

"The actions of others don't always make sense to us, but we can't let their mistakes wound us." Dr. Miller jotted down a note. "Tell me about the first time."

"The first time?"

"The first time you cheated on your wife." The doctor bit the end of his pen.

JJ swallowed past a lump in his throat. "It was when we were dating."

"Was this before your father passed?" The old man cocked his head sideways.

Ashamed, JJ stared at the floor. "Heather and I

were friends for years, then started dating when we were fifteen. I loved her, but I thought I needed more. I cheated the first time nearly three years after our first date. My dad didn't die until a year later. The night I cheated was the biggest mistake of my life. It's a part of me I don't want to remember."

Dr. Miller pushed his chair back, came to the front of his desk, and sat on the edge. "But your cheating didn't stop that night, and if we are going to get to the root of the problem, we have to dig a little deeper. Are you willing to do this?"

JJ's leg trembled. Since the first moment he'd given in to another girl's advances, he'd wanted to forget, to erase his mistake, but instead he'd let his desires consume him, leaving stain after stain on the heart of so many. Heather. Corrin. Amelia. Not anymore. He'd go to hell and back for Heather, for himself, to stop the madness that drove him to be a cheater. "Yes, I'll try my best."

For the next hour, they talked about JJ's exploits—the acts of betrayal he'd committed against Corrin. The doctor wouldn't know the difference. Every time JJ told another story and replaced Corrin's name with Heather's, his heart lurched and stomach churned. How could he have disregarded Corrin's feelings? His action made no sense, much like his mother's, who hadn't seemed to care if she hurt him.

When JJ finished sharing, the doctor looked at him. "Well, the good news is that you aren't broken. You *are* fixable."

JJ sighed. *Thank God.*

"Bad news is, this is like an addiction for you.

Even though you love Heather, you got away with it once. It felt exciting. According to you, she's given you everything sexually, physically, and emotionally you could want. She was your dream girl."

"Still is."

"Yes, but you have given in to your lust. A pretty woman shows you that she's into you, and you play along. Sometimes your toe dangles over the edge to see how far you can get with a woman, and other times you dive right in. The problem is your self-control. Even though you know it will hurt your wife, you do it anyway because you think you can get away with it. It makes you feel good about yourself. It's exciting and new. A relationship, no matter how attracted you are to each other, can get stale after a while. You get into the same old routines. Kids and work and life take the place of running away for a sexy weekend. Blend that with lust and self-control issues, and voilà, you give in to your temptations even knowing you might ruin your marriage."

"Why do I keep doing it though?"

"It boils down to you thinking of your needs over that of your significant other's. It doesn't mean you don't love her or care for her. It just means that in the heat of the moment, lust takes over and you aren't thinking of the woman you love, only the needs your body is telling you it wants."

"Can I fix this? I don't want to hurt anyone anymore."

Dr. Miller nodded and folded his hands over his crossed legs. "Yes, and admitting you need help is the first step. Then you need to go to your wife and talk when there are no other distractions. Admit your mistakes and ask for forgiveness."

"She doesn't want to forgive me, or at least I think she's afraid to."

"Of course she's afraid." The doctor barked out a laugh. "You've given her every reason to doubt you. She may not ever be able to forgive you, and she may still not want to be your wife. If you love her and want this relationship to work, then you need to show her you've changed, continue to work on yourself, be the man you want to be." The doctor paused. "Are you a praying man, JJ?"

"Not really."

"Well, start to be. Pray that God will restore your relationship."

JJ laughed inside his head. Of course Anna would send him to a doctor who believed in God. JJ nodded.

The psychologist continued. "Know, though, that if and when Heather does forgive you, she won't forget everything. There will be days in the future when she cries for no reason or brings up what you've done. You need to be gentle with her and not defensive. You're the one who messed up. You're the one who ruined your marriage. You broke her trust, and it may take years before she believes where you are going, what you're doing, or who you are with. Show her she *can* trust you. Be an open book. Let her see your cell phone, email, your social media accounts, whenever she wants. Let her feel she can stop by at your office unannounced anytime. From time to time, come home early to show her you want to be with her. Plan trips and date nights. It boils down to showing her you respect and love her."

The doctor raised an eyebrow. "JJ, when the temptations come your way, you have to fight them. You led yourself to believe you didn't have to hold yourself accountable. Satan's got a hold on you, and he isn't going to let go without a fight. Ask God to take the temptation away. And let him know you need him to fight for you when you aren't strong enough."

JJ stretched his neck side to side. He could be an open book for Heather. He could fight against his temptation, but . . . "I don't know that I believe in God. Well, I believe in him. I know he's the creator and all. It's just I don't buy into the idea that he cares about the things of our lives." He tapped his hands on his knees. "He's allowed things to happen to Heather that just make it seem he doesn't care too much for his children."

The doctor furrowed his brows. "Like what?"

"There was a time Heather and I weren't together, and she was with a man who treated her like a prisoner and brutally abused her almost every day. And now she has cancer. And only has months to live. She's the best person I've ever known. How could God have allowed all that to happen to her? Why didn't he . . . why doesn't he step in and intervene?"

"How do you know he doesn't?" Dr. Miller paused, waiting for a response. When JJ didn't answer, the doctor continued. "This world is tainted by sin. Poverty, war, death—"

"If all things are supposed to be possible with God, why doesn't he just stop it all? Create peace again? Keep bad things from happening to good people." JJ rolled his eyes.

Appearing unfazed, the doctor grinned. "That I can't answer, but I do know that he uses all of our experiences to shape us into individuals who can lead others to him. Satan doesn't want that, and even the best of us can get caught up in Satan's schemes. He wants to wipe out all that God has made good. Satan uses our weaknesses and perverts everything. Like sex in marriage. He whispers in your ear how attractive the girl at work is, and you find yourself lusting over her, almost obsessed with her, thinking you have to have her. Then more lies enter your head. Your wife is boring. She doesn't give you what you want or need anymore. It's her fault you want this other woman. It's Heather's fault you're bored with her. It's her fault you want to sleep with the woman giving you attention. You're a successful, attractive man. You deserve a woman to give you what you want. You don't even fight against the lies anymore. You believe it's what you want in the moment. You let Satan win."

The vision of Heather fighting against Hydra in the dream flashed through his memory. The beast attacked Heather over and over, but she fought back with everything she had, using every piece of armor, just like she'd done in real life. For a while she'd been knocked down, her spirit nearly broken, but JJ had watched as she fought her way back. Satan would not defeat Heather. "Satan's trying to destroy Heather by using cancer, the abuse, even my infidelity?"

"Yes. He uses everything he can to attack us. Our strengths, our weaknesses, our fears, our hopes, and the things meant for good."

"I've been blaming the wrong guy? All the awful things that have happened to Heather aren't because of God?"

"Yes. If you want to fix this with Heather, you are going to have to make things right with God first."

Dr. Miller finished the session with JJ by giving him a few more things to work on and set him up in an accountability group with men recovering from pornography and sex addictions, along with men reconciling with their spouses after extramarital affairs. He recommended JJ and Heather come for counseling and wished JJ a happy holiday season.

JJ unlocked his car door, climbed into the driver's seat, took in a deep breath, and exhaled.

God, I can't do this without you. I need your help. Please help me show Heather I'm sorry and I only want her. Help me to change. Take the lust away for other woman, and fill me with passion for only Heather. And, God, show me how to believe in you.

Christmas Eve arrived. JJ spent it baking cookies with Heather and the kids—something he'd never done with Corrin, Amelia, and Zac—and nothing, according to Heather, he'd ever done with them. Heather teased that in the past he'd sat around watching Christmas movies and only devoured the cookies rather than help. He looked around the table at "his children and wife." How could he have missed out on this every year? How could he not have done this with Amelia and Zac either? He missed them.

Sitting on JJ's lap, Abi shook a mound of sprinkles on the top of a blue star cookie. Sam, frosting a Santa cookie with red icing, sat on his knees in the chair next to JJ. Lily took a fresh batch of cookies out of the oven with Heather's help. And Michael, Picasso-like, sat on the opposite end of the table, frosting his gingerbread boy cookie.

"Dude, you've got mad skills. Let me see that." JJ winked at Michael.

Michael held up the cookie.

"That looks too good to eat." He turned to Heather. "Hey, babe. Can you get my phone and take a picture of this cookie?"

She walked over to JJ and put her hand on his shoulder. "What's that? I didn't hear you."

The gesture made JJ smile. Maybe her heart was softening. "Over there on the fireplace, I believe, is my phone. Can you get it and take a picture of Michael's masterpiece?"

"Sure." She squeezed his shoulder.

"Daddy, I happy you help." Abi turned and kissed him on the cheek.

"Me too, sweetie."

"Can I eat this?" Sam held up his cookie.

"Only if I get a bite first." JJ grabbed it out of his hand and pretended he was about to take a big bite.

"No, Daddy."

JJ handed it back. "Okay, I'll just eat this one." He picked up Abi's, and a rainbow of colorful glitter-like sprinkles fell onto the table and JJ's hand.

"Daddy, you look pretty. You can eat mine cookie."

Acting like a hand model with pouty lips and batting eyelashes, JJ displayed his hand against his jaw. The family laughed. This was the life he'd always wanted. What if he never had to leave it?

JJ knocked on Heather's bedroom door.

"Come in."

She sat on her bed in a cute red zip-up Santa suit pajama top and bottoms. "You look festive."

"Well, I wear these every year. You gave them to me the first Christmas we were married."

He smiled. "I remember." He wished he did. He sat down on the end of her bed. "The kids are all sleeping, and I was hoping we could talk."

"Sure."

"Today was nice."

"It was."

He reached across for her hand. "I don't know how much longer I have here, but I want you to know I love you. I'm sorry for thinking of myself over you. You did nothing wrong. You are an incredible wife and mother, at thirty-five you are even more attractive than you were when we were teenagers, and you satisfy my every need." Even though he'd never actually slept with her, the JJ in this world had, and there was no doubt in his mind that she more than satisfied him. Just her touch drove him wild.

A tear rolled down her cheek. "Then why would you cheat on me? I'm sorry I wasn't giving you what you needed."

"Heather, you have given me everything I've ever wanted. Look at our family. Four beautiful children, a gorgeous, loving wife, the opportunity to own my physical therapy practice." He looked at her from under his lashes. "And earn your forgiveness?"

"JJ, it's not that easy."

"But it is. I'm sorry I was selfish. None of the other women meant anything. You mean everything. I want you only. I was stupid and only thought about what I wanted in the moment, not how it would affect you. I felt horrible afterward. I was weak, but I'm done letting my failings control me. I want to be strong for you. I want to be the man you deserve. The father our children need." The words flowed as easily as if he'd been the actual man who did these things to her. He didn't remember the women in this life, but he remembered the ones in reality—the ones he'd hurt Corrin with.

"You have been incredible the last few days, and I've tried to be open to it, but I don't know. It's not like it was just once. It's been over our entire marriage. I don't know that I can trust you."

"I understand that. But I'm willing to let you look into my whole life if that's what you need to trust me. I'll tell you everywhere I'm going and who I'm with. You can look at my cell phone with freedom and my internet and email activity."

"Wouldn't that make me a crazy stalker wife?"

"No, and I don't care." He put her hands on his heart. "I want this. I want you, and I don't care what it takes to get you back. I'm willing to do it."

Tears ran down her face.

"Please don't cry." He wiped her tears with his thumb.

"I just don't know that I'll ever be enough for you. I'm not a crazy woman in bed."

"You are more than enough. I don't need wild. I just need you. Together we are awesome."

"That's what hurts the most. I thought that part of our life was pretty amazing."

He wished he had experienced it with her. "It is amazing."

"Let me think about it over the night. Then let's not talk about it tomorrow. Let's just enjoy Christmas with the kids."

"But what about the kiss under the mistletoe? I don't want my time to run out." He smiled.

"When I agreed to that, I was sure I'd say no. And now . . . I don't know. But I don't want the added pressure to answer you by tomorrow. I just want to spend the day as a family. If I don't kiss you under the mistletoe, it doesn't have to mean no. Just give me more time. Okay?"

"Okay." He slid his fingers into hers. "You want to check and see if Santa left the presents yet or ate the cookies?"

She smiled and let him hold her hand as he led her downstairs.

Chapter Thirty-one

In the morning, JJ snuck downstairs and hid a present in the end table. He lay down on the couch, waiting for the kids and Heather to join him.

Anna stuck her head around the corner from the kitchen. "Merry Christmas, Dr. Jones."

"Merry Christmas, Anna. Please call me JJ. I thought you weren't coming back until tomorrow."

"My father had other plans today. Is it okay if I celebrate with you guys?"

"Of course."

"Great. I figured I'd surprise Heather and make pancakes and other goodies for a big breakfast. Do you think she'll mind?"

Would she? Did she like cooking a big breakfast on Christmas? What he wouldn't give to have the last seventeen years of memories.

"I think she'd be okay with it. Gives her more time to hang with the family. Thank you."

"No problem." She headed toward the kitchen, then turned back around. "JJ, enjoy today in case tomorrow doesn't bring what you're expecting."

"Do you know something? Is she not going to forgive me?" His heart raced. Why wouldn't Anna just tell him what was going on? If she had answers, especially ones that told why he was here in this alternate world, then why did she pretend to be the maid and give no more than subtle hints? Enough was enough.

She frowned. "Leave tomorrow's troubles to worry about themselves."

He couldn't stay here and not be with her, and he couldn't go back and lose her to cancer. God had to intervene.

"Hey." Heather's beautiful voice almost sang as she walked down the steps. "What are you doing up? Usually the kids and I have to pounce on you to get you up on Christmas morning."

"I couldn't sleep. I'm too anxious. I'm hoping you've made a decision."

She followed her halfhearted smile with a frown. "Not today. Remember? Let's talk about it tomorrow."

Did the sadness in her voice and on her face mean she'd made her decision? Had he come to this world for nothing? Did he come here to be all alone? To get the punishment he deserved? Had he died a few days ago at the hands of Keith, and this was his hell—a life close to having it all with Heather but then having it ripped away?

His voice shook as he spoke. "Does that mean you know what you're going to do?"

She sighed. "JJ, please. It's going to take a lot of prayer and consideration, and I just can't devote any time to that today. Please honor that."

"Okay." He stuck out a pouty lip. Maybe he still had a chance. Maybe this wasn't his hell after all.

"I guess I'll go get breakfast started, then we can go wake the kids." She ran her hand along the side of his arm and squeezed his hand before walking toward the kitchen.

"I almost forgot. Anna wanted to make us a big breakfast."

"How sweet." She grinned and rubbed her hands together like a mischievous child ready to open her presents before it was time. "You want to go wake the kids?"

"Let's go." He grabbed her hand, and they ran up the steps to Lily's room first, then Michael's, Sam's, and finally Abi's.

The children ran down the steps and jumped into a seated position around the tree. Santa had left each child an unwrapped present. Abi went first—an American Girl doll. Sam—a dinosaur almost the same height as him. Michael—a remote control sports car. And Lily—a karaoke machine. The children each helped hand out the rest of the presents, then sat down and waited as each person opened his or her gifts. Anna, waiting for the family to finish, put the food in the oven to keep it warm and joined them. She too had a lap full of presents.

JJ slid his finger under the wrapping paper of a present from Abi. "I love how we do this. Amelia and Zac always just rip into their presents at the same time, and nobody can see what anyone else gets."

Everyone looked at JJ. "Who's Amelia and Zac?" Michael asked.

Shoot. He'd blown it. Anna thought she knew who Amelia and Zac were—children from an affair. How would he explain that they were his children from another life? That would sound insane. "Children I know."

"Are they your patients?" Sam asked.

"Kind of. I have given them physical therapy from time to time."

"Cool. I think I'd like the way they do it better. Then it wouldn't take forever to see all I've gotten." Sam tilted his head to the left in an act of boredom.

"Nah, I love this way." JJ ruffled Sam's hair.

The family unwrapped the presents until only the hidden one for Heather remained.

"Okay, kiddos, clean up the wrapping paper. I'll go get the Bible and we can read the story of Jesus's birth." Heather walked over to the bookshelf.

The kids picked up the paper and threw it in a trash bag. Anna left the room and returned with a tray of hot chocolate for everyone.

They all told her thank you and sat down on the floor around JJ. Heather climbed into the spot next to him. She flipped open the Bible.

"Can I read it to everyone?" JJ took it from her hands.

With widened eyes, a smile formed at the corner of her mouth. "Of course you can."

She tucked her feet underneath and wrapped her arm around his.

She pointed to Luke 2, and he read. When he finished the chapter, he prayed for his family and thanked God for sending his Son.

At the end of the prayer, Heather squeezed his

arm. "Thank you."

He winked.

Heather picked up her coffee mug. "I don't know about you guys, but I'm ready for hot chocolate. It looks delicious."

Everyone picked up their mug and toasted to a wonderful Christmas, then took a drink.

"Anna, this is wonderful. What did you put in it?" Heather asked.

Anna looked at JJ, who had just finished taking a sip. "An extra dab of this and a little bit of that, with just a touch of something special."

No.

JJ's heart stopped. Did this mean he was going back? Not now, not when it looked like things might work out and he could have the life he'd always thought he'd have with Heather.

"Well, it's the best hot chocolate I've ever had. Don't you agree, JJ?"

He stared at Anna.

"JJ, what's wrong?" Heather put her hand on his back.

"Nothing, I just don't want this day to end."

"Me either."

He set the mug down and didn't pick it up again. Maybe one sip wouldn't be enough to end the illusion.

When Heather turned on *It's a Wonderful Life*—another tradition they apparently did every Christmas afternoon—everyone napped together in the living room instead of watching the movie, except JJ. He studied the film as if it would reveal how to keep him in this alternate reality, but George hadn't wanted to stay in his twist of fate. Clarence had guided him to the realization that he wanted to live.

JJ wanted to live too. He wanted to live with peace in his heart. He needed forgiveness from Corrin and from Heather. The real ones in his real life. Until then he'd always think of himself as a sleaze.

From the TV, ZuZu said, "Look, Daddy. Teacher says every time a bell rings, an angel gets his wings."

And George said, "That's right. That's right. Attaboy, Clarence."

JJ looked over at Anna, who had fallen asleep in her chair. Was she an angel?

After dinner, JJ asked the family to join him in the living room. "There's one present left." He opened the end-table door and pulled out the tall rectangular box wrapped in shiny red paper topped with a white bow and ribbon.

Heather smiled as he handed it to her. "What's this?"

"Just a little something."

She carefully slid off the bow and ribbon, then unwrapped the paper. On the top of the cardboard box he'd written, *A memory from the past.*

She ripped off the packing tape and pulled out a glass jar layered with seashells and sand. On the top layer of sand, JJ's purple seashell lay in front of a picture of Heather and her grandma from their last summer at the beach.

Heather's face lit up, and a tear ran down her cheek. "I love it. Thank you. Where did you find all this stuff?"

"Remember that time capsule we buried in your parents' back yard?"

"You dug it up?"

He nodded. "I only took out the photo then I buried it again, so we could go through the rest together someday. I found the seashells in a box in the garage, and I don't go anywhere without the one you gave me."

"This is the sweetest thing you've ever done. I love it so much."

She grabbed his hand and pulled him over to the doorway. She pointed up to the mistletoe, then wrapped her arms around his neck. "You really are trying, aren't you? I was on the verge of losing all my faith in you and in . . . JJ, I couldn't understand why God had put us together for you to break my heart over and over again. I thought he wasn't listening to my prayers. But he was, wasn't he?"

A single tear fell down his cheek. "Please, forgive me. I'm sorry."

She studied his face. "I love you, JJ, but . . ."

His heart raced and his body trembled.

But what?

She let out a long, slow breath. "JJ, you have to promise me you'll never betray my trust again."

Of course. Never again. He wouldn't hurt her ever again.

"I promise. You have my complete heart."

"I forgive you."

Anna walked past them and caught JJ's eye. As if time stood still, all sounds vanished. Something in her eyes told him it was time, but he wasn't ready. He wanted to hold on to Heather. To be with her forever. To live a life with her. With children. With healed hearts ready to love. He wouldn't go. He wouldn't leave. He looked back at his wife. Heather pulled his neck forward and leaned toward his mouth. He parted his lips, ready to receive her kiss, when the room spun and blackness swirled around him.

"No! No! Please, Anna. No!" he shouted as the darkness turned to light.

Lying propped up in his hospital bed, pain surged through his body, and his wrist felt heavy. The pressure in his eyes felt like his head was about to explode. Bright sunrays penetrated through the windows, and he could barely keep his eyelids open. He blinked a few times, then a black haze settled over his eyes. He closed them tight and opened them again, but everything had gone black. Had the blood pooled more? But his eyesight had returned yesterday. What was going on? He blinked several times again and looked around. Through cloudy vision he could see the TV hanging on the wall in front of him, the door across the room, the IV machine next to him, and the empty chairs sitting around the room.

Yes, he was back in reality. His heart tore through his chest and stomach knotted. Heather was dying in this world.

He looked down at his wrist in a cast? When had he gone to surgery? The last thing he remembered was Anna visiting him and the dream that seemed to last all night.

The door to his room opened, and Corrin entered. "Hey there. How are you feeling?" She sat in the chair next to his.

"Like I've been run over by a truck."

She touched his arm. "The doctors said you are very lucky you survived and that your damage isn't worse. Your surgery went well. They said your eyes will feel added pressure from lying flat during surgery, but it should decrease throughout the day if you stay propped and don't lie flat."

"Were you here during the surgery?"

She nodded.

"Thank you for staying."

"Of course."

"Is anyone else here?"

She smiled. "You mean is Heather here?"

"Yeah."

"No. She wanted to be, but Anna called and said Heather isn't doing too well. It appears the stress of everything has taken a toll on her. She's too weak to even lift her head."

He should be with her, not stuck in this hospital bed. "Did they say when I could go home?"

"Remember, they need to run a few more tests, but hopefully later today. The nurse did mention you'll have to see an eye doctor every day for a week or so for him to check the level of pressure." She touched his face next to his eye. "I can't believe

Keith did this to you. Can I do anything for you?"

He put his hand on top of hers. "Corrin, I'm really sorry for everything I put you through in our marriage. You deserved better."

"Thank you." She moved her hand to her lap.

"No, seriously, you are incredible. I've watched you with Heather, and you amaze me."

She looked down. "I'm not going to deny that it hurts seeing how much you love her. But I've always known your heart belonged to her. And now that I know her, I can see why. I was the main reason for her heartbreak all those years ago, and the guilt has eaten away at me ever since—even more so now that we're friends. She has every right to detest me, yet she's never made me feel that way."

"I'm glad you two are friends."

"Me too. And I'm really happy our kids love her and that they have Mr. and Mrs. Cole too. Don't get me wrong. I was super jealous at first. But look at Amelia—she's playing softball despite what happened."

"Heather has a special magic about her."

Corrin smiled. "It's like you can't help but love her."

"You're like that too." JJ touched her hand.

Corrin shook her head. "Thank you, but I'm not. Heather has such a good heart despite all she's been through. Last night she was talking about how she hoped this would force Keith to get help and that deep down he was a decent person whose father had broken him a long time ago. I kept thinking about all the horrible and tortuous ways I could make him pay for what he did to you and her."

"I'm right on board with you. He's done awful things to her. He deserves everything he has coming to him."

"See, that's why Heather's better than us."

"Do you wish terrible things would happen to me? I was such a scumbag."

"I did. I hated you. You hurt me really bad, and you *were* a scumbag, but I see you're trying."

"It kills me that my wake-up call came at Amelia's expense."

"Me too."

"I hope you're happy now."

"It's taken time, but, you know, I am. Max and I are hitting it off."

"Max?"

"My new boyfriend."

Good for her. "You let me know if he doesn't treat you right and I'll take care of him."

Corrin smiled.

He had a lot to make amends for. "I want the best for you. I really do."

"What did I do wrong? Why did you sleep with those other women?" Tears sat on the brim of her eyes.

"You did nothing wrong. It was all me. I was trying to fill a void. It felt good being wanted."

"Because I wasn't enough?"

"It wasn't that. My own mom abandoned me. If she didn't love me enough to stay, then surely you wouldn't stay either."

"I wasn't going to go anywhere."

JJ shook his head. "It wasn't fair to put that on

you, I know. But I was hurting. I'd lost Heather, my dad, Bryson, and then my mom. I was numb, and I needed something to help me feel."

"You should have talked to me."

"I know, but I couldn't get hurt again. It was safer to stay guarded. Instead of distancing myself, I should have clung to you. I know that now."

"I believed I didn't deserve you because I took what wasn't mine."

JJ huffed. "Don't be crazy. You most certainly deserved to have every piece of my heart. You loved me and took care of me. Our house ran smoothly because of you. And our kids know how much you love them. You're amazing."

A tear slid down her cheek. "I wish you would have seen that back then."

"I did. I tried to ignore it because . . ."

"Because I wasn't who you really wanted."

"I loved you."

"Not as much as Heather."

He opened his mouth, and words left him.

She touched his arm. "I've always known I was two rungs below her, and truth be told I knew you'd been sleeping around for years. But what right did I have to say anything? And I didn't want to lose you."

"You were my wife. You had every right to call me out. Our past is our past. We were dumb kids. Stop chastising yourself for it."

"The guilt won't go away. Has yours?"

"No."

Corrin drew in a breath, then blew it out slowly. "I have to ask for her forgiveness."

He nodded. "Will *you* forgive *me*?"

Corrin's eyes darted back and forth as she looked at him. "I need time. There were more women than Kerri. Do you even know how many?"

He shook his head. How could he have been that dumb and reckless? "I'd change it if I could."

"I believe you." She wiped her face with her palm, then stood up. "I better go. I need to let the kids know what's going on."

"How are they?"

"They don't know yet. I'm heading over to Mom and Dad's now."

"Tell them I love them."

"I will."

She grabbed her purse next to the chair, then walked out the door. He'd been such a fool. His heart ached thinking of the possible life he could have had with Corrin if he'd not been selfish.

The door opened, and a golden-haired beauty with her hair flowing over her shoulders entered. His stomach tightened. What was she doing here? "Kerri?"

"I heard you were assaulted. I know I said I'd stay away, but I had to be sure you were okay."

"No." JJ shook his head. "Please leave. You shouldn't be here. I'm fine."

"I saw Corrin."

His heart leapt violently. "Did you talk to her?"

"No. She didn't see me."

"Good. Now please go before someone does see you."

She stepped toward him. "But I miss you."

"We're done."

"But you're divorced."

"No. We will never be together, and even if I wanted to, I wouldn't do that to Amelia."

"She's a big girl."

"Please leave. I made a mistake."

She ran a finger across his chest. "You poor thing. You look awful. I could take care of you."

"Stop this." He grabbed her arm. "We. Are. Done."

Chapter Thirty-two

Heather woke with her head pounding and her body aching. She coughed up blood, and nausea weighed heavy on her stomach. But no matter. She'd go to the hospital and wait during JJ's surgery. She fought through the pain and sat up.

Anna entered with a food tray holding a plate of cinnamon rolls and bacon. "Good afternoon, sleepyhead. You snoozed the morning away."

"What time is it?"

"Eleven thirty."

"Wasn't JJ's surgery at nine?"

Anna nodded.

"Why didn't anyone wake me? I wanted to be there. Has anyone heard how it went?"

"I didn't wake you because your body needed to rest. You were too weak to even get out of the wheelchair last night, and besides, there is no reason to expose yourself to unnecessary germs by visiting the hospital again. Corrin called and said the surgery went well and he should be home today. I'll take you to his apartment later if you want."

"Okay." Heather lay back down. "Can I get pain medicine? I'm hurting really bad."

Anna nodded, laid the tray on the dresser, then left the room. Heather stared out the window at the beautiful spring day. Hopefully, by the time JJ got home, she'd have the energy to leave the house. Right now she wasn't even up for a trip to the bathroom.

The nurse wheeled JJ out of the hospital entrance to Corrin's SUV, where she, Amelia, and Zac waited for him. The natural light from the setting sun entered JJ's eyes, and he couldn't keep them open even with the dark sunglasses the hospital had given him.

"Dad, can I drive you home?"

JJ looked at Amelia through squinted eyes. She playfully gave him pouty lips and batted her eyelashes.

"You know I have my permit now, and I've driven Mom around a lot, but not you yet. Please."

Pretending to think about it, he tapped his lips. "Hmm. I don't know."

"Come on, Dad. I'm a really good driver. I drove here all the way from Grandma's."

He smiled. "I guess, but could you take me to Heather's?"

"Yes! Thank you." She ran around to the driver's side.

Corrin opened the passenger door for him as the nurse kicked the footrest up. She held her hands out for him to take, then helped him into the car. "Now remember, the doctor said to rest your eyes as much as possible. We don't want you to strain them. Even cover them with the patches if it will help you not overwork them."

"I will. Thank you."

The nurse shut the door, and JJ was able to open his eyes fully again. "I'm glad your windows are tinted. I could barely see outside."

Amelia gripped the steering wheel tight and looked straight ahead.

"Amelia, don't wreck," Zac said from the backseat. "We don't want to hurt daddy more than he already is."

"Don't make me nervous." She pulled the SUV forward and made her way out of the parking lot and onto the street.

Ten minutes later they'd almost reached Heather's house and Amelia hadn't made one mistake. "You are doing a great job."

"Thank you, Dad." She turned onto the Coles' street.

"I appreciate you all picking me up from the hospital and for taking me to Heather's. I want to check on her before I go home. Anna said she's not doing well today."

Amelia pulled into the driveway, and Zac asked, "Can I see Heather too?"

"I think we should let your dad visit," Corrin answered. "We'll come another time when she's feeling better."

"Okay." Zac blew out a breath, vibrating his lips.

JJ opened his door. "Great driving. I'm proud of

you. Be safe driving back to Grandma's."

"I will."

"I love you guys." He winked at Zac, then Amelia. "I'll see you at your game on Monday."

Corrin got out of the car and moved to the front seat. "After I drop the kids off at my parents, I'll come get you."

"Thank you." He closed the door for her, then watched them drive away as he walked up the Coles' front steps and knocked on the front door. Would it be odd to see her? It had only been twenty-four hours in real time, but after the reality swap, it seemed like a lifetime.

Mr. Cole opened the door. "Hey, JJ. Nice surprise. How are you feeling?"

"Not great, but I'm surviving. The cast should come off in about six weeks. The bruises should heal in a few weeks." He followed Mr. Cole through the doorway into the living room. "I'm more worried about Heather though. Is she okay?"

"She's pretty shook up about the whole thing. She thinks it's her fault and feels guilty more than anything."

JJ shook his head.

"She says this never would have happened if she didn't come home and force Keith to sign divorce papers."

"Well, of course it wouldn't have. But I'd take a million beatings at the hand of Keith just to keep her away from him."

He followed Mr. Cole through the living room and down the hallway to Heather's room.

JJ gazed at her sleeping frail body. "If you don't

mind, I'm going to sit in here while she sleeps."

"I'll be down the hallway in my office. Anna's off for the rest of the day, and the missus is at work. Holler if you need me."

"Sure thing."

JJ sat in the chair next to Heather's bed. Moaning, she twitched and contorted her face. She looked different than the Heather he'd just left. That Heather had color to her cheeks, thicker hair, and a healthy twenty-five extra pounds. What he wouldn't give to rid her body of cancer.

A text notification chimed, and JJ looked at his phone. Anna had sent him a message. *I thought you'd like this.*

Below the text, she'd sent a photo of Lily, Michael, Sam, and Abi standing in front of the Christmas tree. A knot formed in his throat, and he swallowed hard. He loved those kids that he'd never really have. Those kids Heather could have had.

You did have something to do with my dream. How?

We'll talk later.

"Hey there." Heather's raspy voice startled him.

"How are you feeling?" He took hold of the end of her hair and twirled it between his fingers.

"Not too good today." She gave a slight smile. "I'm sorry I didn't make it to the hospital."

"You didn't need to be there." He leaned in close to her face.

She removed his sunglasses, and he squinted. He'd forgotten they were on. He blinked a few times as his eyes adjusted. She touched his cheek. "You look awful."

Pain shot through his face, and he grimaced.

"How do you feel today?" she asked.

"I'm not going to lie. It hurts, but I'm fine."

"I'm sorry."

"There's nothing to be sorry about. Keith's a jerk. We've already established that. I'd take anything for you." He took her hands and rubbed her fingers. "I love you."

"I love you too."

He'd never tire of hearing that. He kissed her hand. "Do you ever wonder what our life would've been like if we ended up together?" He looked at the photo again.

"All the time. What are you looking at?"

"A photo of these kids I know. They're pretty great."

She gave a slight smile. "Can I see the picture?"

"Sure." He handed her the phone.

She studied the photo. "They look familiar. The younger boy kind of looks like Zac. Are they related?"

"Yes. They're from my side of the family." His heart sunk. There would never be a time where the six children would actually be siblings. "What do you think our life would have looked like?"

"I always picture us with four children."

"Me too. Two boys and two girls."

Heather yawned. "Exactly."

"One of our girls would be Abi, since that's your favorite name."

"You remember that."

He nodded then yawned. "You are the love of my life. I really messed up. I know I can't change the past, but what if we could? Would you have wanted to marry me? Flaws and mistakes and all?"

"Of course. I told you I would have forgiven you."

He slid his hand into hers. "Do you forgive me now?"

"Yes. You aren't that boy anymore."

"I made a stupid decision in the heat of the moment." He lifted her chin and looked into her eyes. "I've done a lot of soul searching lately. I'd do anything if I could go back and fix it all. I'd have chosen you, and I'd be the man and husband you deserved. I'd be sure we played together and continued having fun. I'd try with everything I had to show you every day how important you are to me and that no other woman could possibly compare to you."

He took her hands. "I'd do it all. I would have noticed when something wasn't right about your body or your cough or raspy voice. We would have caught the cancer early enough and then . . ." A tear ran down his face, and he choked up. "You would have lived a long life . . . if I would have just been there for you."

One wrong choice. One moment of giving in. One dumb seventeen-year-old brain believing he had to have sex and then supposing the feeling that came with it was love. Love meant saving yourself for the *one*.

"I'm sorry, Heather. I'm sorry I ruined your life." He laid his head in her lap.

She stroked his hair. "I ruined my own life, JJ. I rushed into a relationship with Keith. I didn't know him. I was desperate to feel what I had with you that Keith and I were married in less than a year. I stayed with him even after all he'd done to me. If I had been stronger, I would have left. I could have called someone. I could have run before I finally did. But I was worried what my parents would say, what God would think, if Keith would hurt someone I loved to get at me, if someone else would ever love me. I believed for a long time if I loved him enough, if I cooked better, lost weight, gave in to what he asked for, then he'd change. But he never did. When I started feeling bad, I should have found a way to go to the doctor." She kissed the top of JJ's head. "You didn't do this. Keith did. I did. But *you* did not."

She lifted his face to look at him. "It's okay that you chose Corrin. If you hadn't, you wouldn't have had Amelia and Zac. God has a plan and purpose for them. I was mad at you and blamed you for my unhappiness for a long time. Even that day I walked into your office, I thought if you had chosen me, I wouldn't have been abused, I wouldn't have missed the chance to have kids, and I would have married the love of my life."

He looked into her eyes.

She smiled. "But having you in my life again and getting to know your kids put it all in perspective. When you and Corrin ended up together, you were doing what God intended. Maybe you made some mistakes along the way and didn't actually start your relationship with Corrin how He would have wanted, but he allowed you to have children together."

"But what if there was a world out there where you and I had children?" He held up the phone. "Children like the ones in this picture."

She shook her head as tears filled her eyes. "That is not reality. This is."

"But I want to go back and change every choice I ever made. I want a life where we end up together."

"What about Amelia and Zac? They wouldn't exist. You can't have both."

"You're right. I can't. But I also feel the loss of the children we never had. They are amazing."

"I imagine they would have been."

"I wish you could have met them."

"Me too." A tear slipped down her cheek.

"You were a great mom. We named our kids Lily after your grandma, Michael after my grandpa, Sam after your uncle, and Abi just because you always wanted a girl named Abi." He smiled.

She squeezed his hand. "I know you mean well, but talking about our hypothetical children hurts more than you can imagine. I'll never know what it feels like to be a mom."

"I'm sorry." He dropped his head to her lap again.

"I should have left the second he hit me the first time."

"I wish you had. I wish you'd fought for yourself. I don't want you to die. I love you."

He sobbed in her lap, and she leaned over him and put her arms around him.

"Why didn't you? I'm so mad." He lifted his head. "I'm so mad at you."

"I'm mad at me too." She ran her hand through

his hair.

JJ sat in a chair in the empty waiting room of his practice. He'd sent Missy and Ken home a few minutes earlier, and ever since he'd been staring at the screen, contemplating whether to spy on Anna. She'd come in to his office that first day with pain in her hip, then she'd recouped faster than most women her age, and over the last three months she hadn't complained about it once. Who was she?

He typed *Anna Ingram* into the Google search bar along with the name of her hometown, where she'd once said she was from. *Lemon Grove, California.*

The title of an article with her name and picture came across the screen: *Anna Ingram murdered by husband John Ingram.*

What? No, that was impossible. His heart hammered hard against his chest.

A cold breeze blew past, and a chill ran down his spine. All the lights were off in the building except the small corner lamp on an end table next to him. It suddenly seemed incredibly dark. He stood to flip on a light, when a knock on the door startled him.

He turned slowly. Anna waved from outside. He took small steps as he made his way to the door. The article had to be incorrect. He unlocked the door. "What are you doing here? Come on in."

"We need to talk."

"Yes, we do."

"With your wrist broken, can you recommend

someone else for Heather until it heals?"

"Yes, Ken has already taken over for me for a while. He retired a few years back, but he covers for me when I need someone. I trust him completely, and of course I'll be around. And he agreed to help Heather also." He scratched his head. "I need to ask you something, and I need you to be completely honest." Would she?

"Okay."

"Who are you?"

"Anna Ingram."

"From Lemon Grove?"

"Yes."

He picked up his laptop and stared at the article. "What was your husband's name?" The question barely escaped JJ's lips.

"John."

"Where is he now?"

"He's in jail for murder."

With mounting dread, he asked the question he hoped didn't have the answer he envisioned. "Who did he murder?"

"Me."

That was preposterous. Even though he'd predicted her answer, his mind couldn't comprehend. "You? So you're telling me that you're a ghost?"

"Not a ghost. More like a spirit." She chuckled.

His cheeks rushed with heat. "What? None of this makes sense. Who are you really?"

"JJ, I know this seems like a crazy tale, but it's true."

"Let's say I believe you. Then why did you show

me all those things?"

"I wanted you to see, to remember, to be certain, to give you a reality check that you must fight your desires to be the man you want to be. And lastly, you needed to see that you can overcome your temptations if you deal with your past."

"I want to go back and be with Heather and our children. I fixed things there."

"I know you did, but I can't make that happen. It's not needed anymore. That's not the life you were meant to live."

He shook his head. "I'm confused. It was a perfect dream and a perfect life. Put your potion or whatever it is in your specialty drink and let me go to a world where Heather is healthy."

Anna sighed. "Believe me—I know the real world isn't always what we expect or desire, but we have to live it anyway."

He rolled his eyes. "Really? Like I don't know that I'm watching Heather die. Sure she's gained some strength, but I'm fully aware that there's nothing anyone can do about her cancer. Only a miracle can save her, and let me guess—you don't have an extra dab of this and a little bit of that to help her."

Anna looked to the floor, and his heart dropped with it.

He clutched his good fist. "Why are you even here?"

Her eyes met his. "I go where I'm sent. I landed on Heather's apartment doorstep with the knowledge she needed an escape, and I provided it. Next I was outside your office with pain I hadn't felt since the day I died. Then you and I were both at Heather's house, sent to help her until the end. I don't know the plans any more than you do. I go because that's where I'm placed."

"Who sends you?"

"God, my father. I'm not sure why I'm still on earth and not in heaven. He knows the plans he has for us, and I'm blessed he's asked me to do this."

JJ squeezed his eyes shut. He couldn't believe all this nonsense. Anna was a crazy con artist who'd stolen the identity of the real Anna Ingram and was playing mind tricks on him. But what about the picture on the internet article? And the photo on his phone?

Anna touched his shoulder. "I know this is all hard to believe, but it's true. I'll spare you all the gory details, but my husband was very abusive. One day he went too far, ran me over with our car, then shot and killed me. Now I'm doing this. I don't know why. I help where I land. Normally to women who need redemption of the spirit—to women who've been abused or cheated on or who are . . . dying."

Her gentle words, the kind expression on her face, and his knowledge of how wonderful Anna had been to Heather told it all. Anna had come for Heather.

Chapter Thirty-three

With the little bit of energy Heather had she'd made lunch, and now she washed the dishes, careful not to drop them. She leaned against the counter for support, but her arms were starting to get weak. She placed the plate in the sink and blew out a breath. She could do this.

"This is delicious. You make an excellent BLT." JJ sat at the kitchen table.

"Thank you. I try." She giggled. "Next time I'll do grilled cheese." She winked.

"How about meatloaf? It's my favorite."

"I can try, but I'm not guaranteeing it'll be any good."

"It will be fantastic. You are an incredible cook." JJ got up from the table with his plate, and she held her hand out for it. He left mere inches between them and gazed into her eyes while reaching around her to put his plate into the sink. This felt like déjà vu, but they'd never had a moment like this. Had they?

His lips were so close. So perfect. His eyes stayed locked on hers, and she stood perfectly still.

He took a step forward and closed the gap between them. Her chest rose against him. He smelled wonderful, earthy and woodsy. He tucked a strand of hair behind her ear, and she trembled on the inside. She'd longed for his kiss for way too long.

"You want to go to a dinner with me and Amelia's team tomorrow night? It's for all the players and their families. I believe Max is coming with Corrin."

"Sure."

Winking, he wrapped his arms around her waist and pulled her against him. He leaned in close to her face, almost touching her lips. "I won't let anything ruin this date. I'll buy you my favorite flavored lip gloss."

Again the feeling of déjà vu.

"For what?" A small laugh escaped through her lips.

His cheek brushed against hers as he whispered in her ear. "Our first kiss on the doorstep when I bring you home. Um-huh, I can taste it now."

A smile spread across her face. "What flavor?"

"Strawberry." He breathed heavily in her ear.

She turned her head and looked upward. His mouth was inches from hers. "Why wait?"

He crashed his mouth against hers, and as if time hadn't changed a thing, she kissed him back. The familiar way he gently took her face into his hands and the sweet way he ran his hand along her jaw and ears made her feel young and alive.

"I love you." His words muffled between kisses.

She lost her breath, and afraid she'd collapse, she

grabbed ahold of his arms. "I think we need to take it slower."

He lifted her into his arms and cradled her. "I'm sorry. One kiss and it was like I was sixteen again."

JJ's heart sped as Heather walked down the hallway. The black dress accentuated her curves normally hidden under baggy clothes. He took her hand. "You look stunning."

"Thank you. You don't look too bad yourself." She winked. "I like the glasses."

He touched them. "I keep forgetting about them. Doctor said I need to wear them for a while."

"They look good on you, Dr. Jones." She gazed deep into his eyes.

"Dr. Jones, is it?"

"Yes. You look more like a doctor in them. Very regal and handsome."

The desire to kiss her hard on the mouth invaded every part of him, but since Mr. and Mrs. Cole and Anna sat on the couch, he gave her a small one on the cheek instead. He took her hand in his. "Let's get going."

"Have a good evening. You take good care of my girl," Mr. Cole said.

"I will, and thanks for watching Zac tonight. Corrin should be here shortly with him."

"No problem. We love having him over. He's a good kid. Makes it easy."

Heather smiled. "We shouldn't be out too late."

JJ turned into a parking spot and looked in his rearview mirror. A dark-haired man pulled up in a car in behind him, and Corrin sat in the passenger seat.

JJ got out of his SUV and opened the door for Heather as the man did the same for Corrin, then Amelia. A bit of jealousy ran through him. From what JJ had heard, the fellow seemed nice enough, but seeing Corrin with him felt odd. What right did JJ have to feel this way?

"Hey, guys." Heather waved to them.

Amelia ran over and hugged her. "I'm glad you came. My team is really great."

Corrin and her date stepped next to JJ. "This is Max. Max, JJ."

He shook Max's hand. "Nice to meet you."

"Likewise."

Amelia led them up to the door and opened it for everyone. Her coach stood in the waiting area and directed them to the back. One table for the girls and another for the parents.

"Please take a seat," the coach said.

The few parents already at the table waved to Corrin, then JJ. Corrin took a seat next to one of the moms they'd known through softball since Corrin was seven. Max took the spot next to her. Heather sat next to Max, and JJ next to her. More parents entered and took seats. Soon all the teammates and their parents arrived, but the girls ran off to the bathroom. Whispers and stares went around the table, directed in Heather's direction.

"Excuse me." A woman of one of the older girls on the team looked at Heather. "Are you Heather Cole?"

"Yes."

"I'm Kendall's mom. She said Amelia told her you had given her pitching pointers. It's great that you could be here tonight. I heard you have cancer. I'm sorry."

"Thank you. I'm glad I could be here too." She squeezed JJ's arm. "I'm glad he invited me."

The woman's eyebrows drew together, and she titled her head slightly and opened her mouth, as if about to speak. Then she closed it.

"Are you dating JJ?" Another woman a few chairs down asked.

Heather smiled. "Yes."

"You two dated in high school, right?"

She nodded.

The woman raised her eyebrows and looked away.

JJ looked at each person in the room. All of them knew what he'd done and why he and Corrin were divorced. Everyone except Heather. Whispers continued around the room.

The coach, scrunching her brows, looked behind JJ, then rose from the table.

Her voice carried from outside the party room. "What are you doing here? You need to leave," the coach said.

JJ turned his head and saw the coach shaking her head but couldn't see whom she was talking to.

"Do it on your own time, not here. We're having a team dinner. You aren't invited."

The coach continued to shake her head as the person spoke.

"Kerri, go home."

All the adults in the room looked at Corrin and JJ. His stomach twisted in knots. What did Kerri want?

Kerri pushed the coach aside and entered the room as Amelia and the other girls returned to the table. Amelia stopped laughing and glared at Kerri. All the girls looked at Amelia.

She held her arms across her stomach and flared her nostrils. "Why are you here?"

Kerri took a step toward Amelia. "I want to say I'm sorry."

"I don't care."

"You've pitched a great season so far."

The coach stepped in front of Kerri. "Go or I'm calling the police."

JJ should talk to Kerri, but all eyes were on him, Corrin, and Amelia.

Kerri looked at the girls, then the adults. "I'm sorry I let your girls down."

Amelia turned and ran down the hallway. Corrin stood and went after her.

Yes, JJ should do something. He looked at Heather. "I'll be right back."

"Come on, Kerri. Let's go talk." He grabbed her arm.

She followed him out the door as he heard the murmurs start. The knots in his stomach pulled tighter.

The adults whispered and glanced back and forth at Heather. Enough was enough.

"Who was that woman?" Heather asked anyone who'd answer.

The man sitting across from her cleared his throat. "That's Kerri Johnson. She was the head middle school softball coach last year and the high school assistant coach." He ran his hand over his mouth.

The rest of the room remained silent. Would someone tell her something? How had Kerri let down the girls? And why did Amelia, Corrin, and JJ seem to be in the middle of it?

"What did she do?"

She looked at each parent, but no one would look at her other than the woman with the man who'd spoken.

"She had an affair with JJ, and Amelia caught them in the act."

Heather gasped and threw her hand over her mouth. She couldn't breathe. What? They had to be wrong. No. JJ wouldn't have done that to Corrin. He'd changed. He was a well-educated, compassionate man. "Are you sure?"

"Kerri quit her job, and Amelia left the team," Corrin said as she entered the room. "It was a hard time for everyone involved."

Heather swallowed hard and clutched the edge of her chair. What was she doing? How had she been stupid enough to trust him again? She didn't know him at all.

JJ walked down the sidewalk with Kerri next to him. "You should leave. This isn't fair to the girls."

She stopped and turned toward him. "I miss you." Her eyes fixated on his.

He drew in a deep breath. "What are you doing here?"

"I wanted to apologize to the girls. I shouldn't have quit. I should have stuck out the season no matter how embarrassed I was."

"No. You made the right decision."

"For Amelia, but she still abandoned the team even though I left. I could have kept coaching if I knew she was going to quit."

"She was fourteen years old, and her coach had an affair with her dad. Can you blame her?"

Kerri slid her arm inside his. "I've missed you. Let's go back to my place." With her fingernails, she traced circles along the side of his forearm.

He pulled his arm away and looked toward the restaurant. "I can't."

Kerri huffed.

Had anyone told Heather the truth about him and Kerri? Would she still want to be with him now? "Look, I already told you we were done the moment Amelia walk in that door."

"I've waited nearly a year since your divorce. I thought we had something and you'd come back to me. Why are you acting like I meant nothing?"

"I don't want to hurt you, but I love someone else."

"Who?"

"Do you know Heather Cole?"

"Who doesn't? I heard she has cancer. You love her?"

He nodded

"You're going to be brokenhearted soon. Don't come running back to me." Kerri looked toward the restaurant and gestured at it with a nod. "She looks all skin and bones. Why would you want her? She probably can't even please you the way I can."

"I'm sorry that I hurt you, but we're done. Please leave me and Amelia and the rest of the team alone."

She stormed away toward the car, her heels clacking on the sidewalk.

He walked toward Heather, who'd apparently followed him out, and she met him halfway.

"Who is she?" Her wide eyes waited.

Shame filled his bones. He should have been honest about his affairs from the beginning. She'd told all her secrets, and he'd kept his hidden. Would she forgive him?

"JJ, who is she? I need to hear it from you. Everyone inside says—"

"She was Amelia's softball coach. I had an affair with her."

Her lips quivered. "Why?"

He shook his head. "I don't know."

"Was she the only one?"

He shook his head. "No."

She turned her back. "You aren't who I thought you were."

He wrapped his arms around her waist and pulled her against him "I'm sorry I didn't tell you. I love you. I should have told you, but I'm not that man anymore."

She pulled away from him. "How am I supposed to believe you? You cheated on me, and then from what I've heard, you were unfaithful most of your marriage. And now you say you've changed?"

"I have. I saw what it did to Amelia. When my eyes were opened, I realized how badly I hurt Corrin." He grabbed her hand. "I've always known I broke your heart. I'm sorry."

"I had forgiven you, but I can't anymore. I'll have Corrin take me home."

A tear rolled down his cheek, and he shook his head. "No. I'm sorry. I'm sorry I didn't say anything. Please believe me. I've changed."

"I poured out my heart about Keith and how he'd cheated on me and how abusive he was, and you kept your past locked away. I can't trust you. Since you can't do my PT right now anyway, don't bother coming over. I don't want to see you."

"No, Heather. I can't live without you."

"You will have to soon enough anyway. Why not start now?"

"I know I don't deserve it, but please give me a chance."

She took in a deep breath, then let it out. "I can't risk it. I've been through enough heartache already, starting with the moment you decided to sleep with Corrin."

"I've changed."

"Don't you understand? I can't be with someone I don't really know. I thought I knew you. I was seeing what I wished for."

He caught her hand. "Don't end us before we even have a chance to begin. I can't live another moment without you a part of it."

She pulled her hand out of his. "I can't."

The finality in her whispered words hurt as if a hand had reached inside his chest and crushed his heart.

Chapter Thirty-four

A month later, Heather leaned her cane against her leg as she sat on a bench at the edge of the pond. She tore off a piece of bread and threw it to the ducks. A few feet back, Anna set up a picnic lunch for the two of them. The wind quietly blew past her and moved her hair in front of her face. She tucked it behind her ear, and the memory of JJ doing the same and then their kiss flashed through her mind. She touched her lips. Her heart ached. She missed him, but she couldn't make another bad choice in men. This time her brain needed to make the decision, not her heart.

"Lunch is ready," Anna called.

Heather took her cane and lifted her body from the bench. Her arms and legs felt heavy, and she didn't know if she'd make it to the picnic table. She took four steps, then collapsed. Anna ran to her, lifted her to her feet, and helped her walk to the table.

"Should we pack up and go?"

Heather shook her head. "No. I'll be okay. I wanted to feed the ducks and spend the day at the park. Number twenty-two."

"Okay."

Heather looked at the turkey sandwiches, chips, and fruit salad. It looked lovely, but her stomach felt full even though she hadn't eaten a thing all day. She ate a strawberry and swallowed it slowly.

"I visited with JJ yesterday," Anna said

"How is he?"

"Not too good actually. He said his wrist is really bothering him and has had to take more pain pills than he'd like, and his eyes aren't improving. He still has to wear the glasses. He sounded really depressed. I think he could use a friend."

"I guess it's a good thing he's got you to talk to."

"He needs you, my dear."

"I can't, Anna. I thought he'd only cheated on me, but he'd done it to Corrin throughout their whole marriage. I know what that feels like. I can't be with someone like that."

"I understand, but if it's worth anything, I do think he's changed."

It didn't matter.

Amelia looked at herself in the mirror. Mark would be there any minute to take her out to the movies. She couldn't wait. Her first official date. She touched the softball charm on the bracelet Heather had given her yesterday. She hated that Heather wasn't talking to her dad, but Amelia got it.

That night had been crazy, but it did her heart good watching from the restaurant window as her dad rejected Kerri. But then equally as heartbreaking to see Heather walk away from her dad.

The doorbell rang, and she ran down the steps. Her mom opened the door for Mark. He took her breath away. Perfect surfer hair that he ran his hands through, red polo shirt—the front tucked into his dark-blue jeans—and his hand holding out a bouquet of roses.

She smelled them as he handed the bouquet to her. "Thank you."

"I'll put them in water," her mom said. "You two have a nice time."

"We will, Ms. Jones."

Amelia passed the flowers over to her mom, and Mark opened the door. Once outside, he slid his hand into hers. Be still her heart. He opened the car door for her and kissed her cheek. "You look good."

"You too."

"No, like I mean . . . wow. You are gorgeous."

Her checks rushed with heat, and her heart raced. "Thank you."

She looked down at her light-blue floral cold-shoulder dress. She had thought she'd looked cute, but gorgeous sounded good too. She took her seat, and he shut the door, then ran around to his side of the car. He stared in her eyes and smiled.

"What?"

"I can't take my eyes off of you." He looked down at her legs, then back at her face.

No one had ever looked at her like this, and her stomach fluttered. He put his hand on her knee, and she lost her breath for a moment. He backed out of the driveway, and they spent the drive talking about baseball, softball, school, their friends, and everything she could think to bring up. With him, it always seemed natural and perfect.

He pulled into the parking spot and turned toward her. He ran his hand along her face, then leaned toward her mouth. She opened her lips, and his met hers. Her heart pounded, and she put her arms around him. His put his other hand on her back and pulled her closer.

"I love you, Amelia Jones."

She drew back and looked at him. Love? She liked him an awful lot, but love already?

"You don't feel the same?" He stuck out his bottom lip.

A shiver ran from the tip of her fingers down to her toes. Mesmerized by his good looks, she couldn't think straight.

He took her hands in his. "I know we've been talking a few months and this is our first date, but I've had my eye on you for a long time. It took me a while to get the courage to talk to you."

"Me?"

"Yeah, you." He tucked her hair behind her ear. "You're incredible."

She licked her lips. "I . . . think you're wonderful too."

He slowly moved toward her mouth and lightly kissed her. Her body rushed with heat, and she kissed him back.

"We better go in, or we'll miss the movie," he said between kisses.

"Would that be so bad?"

He pulled back, and his eyes searched her face. "You are more than I ever expected." He sat back in his seat, pulled at his pants at the thighs, then held on to the steering wheel. "You don't know how much I love you and how much I want to take you somewhere more private."

She gulped. No, she wasn't ready for *that* kind of relationship. "I . . . I . . ."

"Don't worry. I'm more of a gentleman than that. I want to. I really, really do, but—"

"I don't want to do that for a long, long time. Like not even until I'm married."

"Okay. I'm totally cool with that."

"You'll wait for me."

"For you, I'd wait forever."

"Are you sure? I mean, you're a guy."

He grabbed his heart and rubbed it. "That hurts. What's that supposed to mean?"

She shook her head. "I'm sorry. I know some guys find it elsewhere if their girl won't . . . you know."

He looked in her eyes. "Not me. Not ever. I've found my forever."

His forever? The thought didn't settle well in her gut. She was almost sixteen, and he was seventeen. He was awesome, yeah, but finding her forever right now seemed like an eternity away.

Chapter Thirty-five

Bugs flew around the bright lights illuminating the softball field, and the stands had a few empty spots left. The warm breeze of the last day of May felt nice on Corrin's face. Amelia's boyfriend sat next to Zac behind her, and Max sat next to her. She kept her eyes open for Heather and her parents.

Zac wrapped his arms around her neck and squeezed. "When is she going to be here?"

"Buddy, they had to drive two hours to get here like us, but it could take longer for them with Heather."

"Why?"

"Traveling is hard on her. Look, there they are now!"

Corrin waved, but Heather didn't appear to notice. She wriggled her neck and shoulder back and forth as her dad wheeled her in front of the bleachers. Her dad waved and headed toward them with Mrs. Cole and Anna following behind.

Mr. Cole put his arm around Heather's back and took her hand in his to help her out of her wheelchair. She grimaced. She looked thinner than last week, when Corrin had visited her.

Mrs. Cole opened a portable stadium seat for Heather and placed it on the bleacher next to Corrin. Heather took her seat and smiled at Corrin. "Hey."

Corrin put her hand on Heather's "You look like you aren't feeling too good. You okay?"

"I'm having more bad days than good lately, but I wouldn't miss Amelia's state championship game for anything." Her voice sounded hoarse, like she had trouble speaking, and Corrin couldn't help noting Heather was fading fast.

She patted Heather's hand. "Amelia's glad you could be here."

"Me too."

"Hey, Mr. and Mrs. Cole."

Heather's parents waved and took the seats next to Zac and Mark. Anna sat on the other side of Heather.

"Hey, Anna."

"Hello, dear."

JJ and Amelia came out of the dugout and exited the field. Amelia motioned for Mr. Cole to come to her. She whispered in his ear, and he smiled the biggest grin Corrin had ever seen a man make. He nodded his head and wiped a tear from his eye.

JJ winked at Corrin.

"What's going on?" Heather asked Corrin.

She shook her head. "I have no idea."

"Heather, will you come with me?" Amelia smiled.

"Okay."

Amelia and Mr. Cole helped Heather back into

her wheelchair, and Mr. Cole wheeled her away, with Amelia following.

"What's happening?" Corrin whispered to JJ.

"Number two on her list."

Heather sat at the back end of the dugout, out of the way of the girls and their equipment. It meant the world they'd invited her to hang with them for their championship game. Each girl hadn't stopped smiling and talking to her since she'd entered their domain. Her dad stood next to the coach at the opening of the dugout.

The umpire looked at her dad. "You're on."

Her dad followed the umpire out of the dugout and went to home plate.

"Come on, girls. Let's line up," Coach said.

The girls ran out of the dugout and lined up on the first base line. Amelia remained and threw something at Heather. "You too. Come join us."

Heather looked down at the red jersey in her hand. She held it up. Her old number and *Cole* on the back. A tear slipped down her cheek.

"Come line up with us."

Heather nodded, and Amelia slipped the shirt over Heather, then wheeled her out.

"Tonight, we have a very special treat," the announcer said. "Danburg High School's alumni and Indiana state record holder for pitching the most shut-out games in one season, Heather Cole has joined us tonight, and she's going to throw our first pitch."

The crowd cheered.

What? Another tear slipped down her cheek. Amelia wheeled her to the pitcher's mound.

"Her dad, the Christian Athlete pastor at Danburg High School, will be catching for her."

Heather looked at him all suited in catcher gear. He lifted his helmet and blew her a kiss. The crowd again cheered.

Amelia handed her a glove and a ball.

"Thank you for this." Heather took Amelia's hands

"I didn't do it. My dad did." Amelia looked to JJ in the stands.

He'd do anything for her. Wouldn't he?

"I don't know if I can do this. It's not even going to make it past the mound." Heather looked up at Amelia.

"It's okay. We all love you here. We aren't judging."

She looked at the spectators. All eyes on hers. Surely the word had already spread that she had cancer in her pitching shoulder.

"You can do it, Cole," JJ yelled from the stands. "Cole. Cole. Cole." He stood.

The crowd followed his lead and rose. "Cole. Cole. Cole. Cole. Cole."

To the crowd they shouted her name, but to Heather, with every chant she heard JJ's louder than the others. *I love you. I love you. I love you.*

"Cole. Cole. Cole."

"Please help me stand up," Heather whispered. "Are you sure?"

Heather nodded. She hadn't been able to stand

on her own for a month, but for this moment she had to try.

Amelia put the mitt and ball on the ground, then put her arm around Heather's waist and took her hand. Heather steadied her balance and held on to Amelia's arm. "Will you help me put on the glove?"

Amelia slid it on Heather, then still holding on to Heather, bent down for the ball. She placed the ball in Heather's hand. Heather's legs wobbled, and she fell back into her wheelchair. The crowd hushed.

"Let's try again." Heather wanted to do this more than anything now.

Amelia helped her stand again, but she couldn't give Heather the support she needed. Heather fell back into the wheelchair again. She looked to the crowd. A pitch from her wheelchair would be fine.

JJ ran from his spot around the fence, through the gate into the dugout, and out onto the field to her.

He knelt down. "Can I help you?"

"Please."

He helped her stand, then moved behind her and held her waist. "Lean back on me. I'll be your support. I've got you."

She leaned against him and let him hold her up with his strong arms and body. Why had she made him stay away? She missed him.

"You can do this, Cole," he whispered in her ear.

She met the ball in her glove at her chest, then winding her arm back, she hopped forward, pointed her glove as she twisted, and turned back. Her arm circled, and she flicked the ball from her hand. It soared through the air slowly but landed in her dad's glove. Pain raged in her shoulder.

The crowd went wild, shouting and stomping their feet and jumping up and down. Her dad leapt from his crouched position and ran to her, tears streaming down his face. JJ hugged her waist. "You did it, Cole."

She squeezed his arm, and Amelia hugged her from the side. "You are a legend!"

Heather's dad threw his arms around her. "Way to go, kiddo!"

JJ released her, and her dad held her up. Winning the championship game hadn't felt this good.

Holding on to her dad, she turned to JJ. "Thank you for this."

He nodded, and her legs gave out. She started to fall forward, but JJ swept her into his arms. "I'd give you the world if I could."

Chapter Thirty-six

Amelia lifted her blue cover-up over her head and adjusted her matching bikini top and bottoms. She tossed the cover-up in her bag, then laid her beach towel on the sand next to Mark.

He smiled at her from his towel. "It's not the actual ocean, but this lake is pretty nice, and I'm liking that bathing suit too." He leaned down and kissed her.

"Enough of that now. My mom, Anna, and Heather will be here soon."

"I'm glad they let me crash your girls' day out."

"My mom said you could hang for a little while since you picked me up from my dad's."

He scowled. "I wish she'd let me stay longer. You know I could, but not actually be with you guys. It's a public beach. Your mom can't tell me what to do." He laughed.

"Are you going to do that?" Uneasiness settled in her gut.

"No. But I could. Then I'd be able to be sure no guys are checking you out in that bikini."

"They aren't. Not to worry."

"They are. You're too beautiful not to look at."

He leaned in for a kiss as she caught sight of her mom. She moved back.

"What's that about? You don't want to kiss me." He curled his lip.

"I do." Amelia pointed toward the grassy picnic area behind them. "My mom and them are here."

He put on a huge smile and turned his head, then waved. "Hi, Ms. Jones. Anna. Heather."

The ladies waved. Her mom scooted Heather's wheelchair next to the picnic table, then she and Anna went back to the SUV.

"Let's go over with them." Amelia smiled.

"But we just got here, and I'd like a few more minutes with you before your mom kicks me out of here."

"Come on. We can help her get the food and stuff out of the back."

Mark jumped to his feet. "I'll race you."

He darted off. By the time Amelia stood, he'd already made it to her mom. He grabbed the cooler and carried it over to the picnic table, then grabbed the bag her mom was carrying and took it to their spot.

"What a gentleman. Thank you," her mom said.

"No problem. Anything else I can get?"

"I think we've got it all."

Amelia reached the picnic table as everyone else sat down around it. She hugged Heather. "I'm glad you're here."

"Number five." Heather's voice sounded strained. "Your mom got me to a beach. Not the ocean, but good enough. Sun, breeze, sand, and water."

Heather coughed, and everyone looked at her.

"I'm okay." Her voice sounded strained. "I could use a blanket though."

"Of course." Corrin ran off toward the SUV.

A blanket? It was mid-June and like ninety-something degrees. A dip in the water would feel nice, not covering up with a blanket. Heather barely had meat on her bones anymore and looked almost skeletal. How Amelia wished for a miracle.

Everyone else cleaned up the mess at the picnic table while Heather held on to Corrin's hand and stood barefoot in the sand. She squished her toes between the grains and closed her eyes, feeling the sunrays beat down on her face. Small waves crashed from the boats that had created them farther out in the water. A perfect day and wonderful sensations that brought back memories of days with her grandma on the beach. She wouldn't trade this moment for anything.

"I was jealous of you," Corrin said.

Heather opened her eyes and looked at Corrin.

"You were the love of his life, and I was always second best."

Heather shook her head.

"It's true. He was cute and funny. And a charmer." A tear rolled down Corrin's cheek. "I had my eyes set on him, but I wouldn't relent. He told me he loved his girlfriend and he was going to marry her. I told him I didn't care, and I didn't stop pursuing him until I got what I wanted. Afterward I heard him crying in the bathroom. I felt like a . . . well, you know the word. I asked him if he was okay. And all he said over and over was, 'I ruined it. I ruined her wedding night.'"

Heather dug her foot farther into the sand. "Why are you telling me this?"

"Because I want you to know how guilty I've felt for eighteen years. He chose me, but it was your heart he wanted. It was *you* he wanted. I opened that door and showed him he could get away with it. I deserved him to cheat on me. You never deserved any of it." Corrin struggled to catch her breath through the tears. "I'm sorry."

Heather squeezed Corrin's hand. "I forgive you, and you didn't deserve it either. He was a jerk."

Corrin hugged Heather. "I'm glad we're friends. Who would have ever thought it?"

"I know, right? Your friendship means the world." Heather laid her head on Corrin's shoulder.

"Amelia says JJ's crushed. He's not sleeping. I do think he's changed. Kerri was over a year ago now. And that was my story, not yours. That was in his past when you came back into his life. Could you possibly give him a chance?"

"I don't know. Would you?"

"It's not me he wants, but yes, I see he's changed, and if he wanted to, I'd try us again. He's the father of my kids, and I do love him."

"He's going to need you soon. I don't have much time left."

"Consider giving him what you do have left. He

adores you. I mean, look at the amazing thing he planned for you. And he held you so you could pitch. How much more romantic can you get?"

"Hmm, it was. I'll cherish it forever."

"I was waiting for the big screen kiss."

Heather put her hand over her mouth. "I do love him, Corrin."

"I know you do. Tell him before it's too late."

Amelia slid into bed and tucked the covers under her neck, then yawned. She couldn't imagine a more perfect day for her mom, Anna, Heather, and her to have enjoyed at the lake, but now Amelia was exhausted, and she closed her eyes.

A text notification chimed and woke her. She checked her phone and saw Mark had texted her.

Are you awake?

Yes.

How long you been home?

An hour.

Why didn't you text me?

I came home, took a shower, and got in bed

Can you come outside and talk to me?

You're here?

Yep

I don't think I should come out. My mom would freak if she found out.

It's late. What took you so long?

We took Heather home

And that takes all night?

We spent most of it at the beach, then mom and I hung at Heather's and talked to Anna for a while. Why does it matter?

Cause I wanted to be with you, but your mom wouldn't let you.

We had a girls' day planned with Heather. You knew that.

Whatever. You don't care that you couldn't hang out with me. I bet you didn't even go to Heather's.

Then where did I go?

I don't know. Some guy's house. You probably met someone at the lake.

I didn't.

Now you don't even want to come out here and talk to me.

Good grief. I'll come out there. Let me be sure my mom's asleep.

She snuck downstairs to her mom's room and put her head to the door. "Mom?"

No answer.

She opened the door and peeked in. Her mother lay sprawled out on top of the blanket. Amelia closed the door.

She's asleep. I'm coming out.

She opened the front door. Mark stood there with his arms across his chest and his jaws clenched.

"What's with the attitude?" she asked.

"I'll tell you what's with the attitude. You wore that little bikini that shows off your body to everyone at the beach. I don't want you to wear it again."

"What?"

"I'm your boyfriend. You don't need to be

flaunting yourself."

"I wasn't. I was at the beach with my mom and her friends. And you were there for part of it. So chill."

He grabbed the back of her hair and yanked it. "Don't tell me to chill." He seized her jaw between his other hand. "You're my girlfriend, and you won't wear anything like that again. You hear me?"

Who did he think he was? She tried wiggling free, but he pulled her hair back more and grabbed her cheeks harder. "Did you hear me?"

How badly would he hurt her if she didn't play along? She nodded.

"Good." He let go of her.

Her cheeks throbbed, and the roots of her hair stung. She reached for the door handle. "You don't control me." She rushed in the door, slammed it shut, and locked it. "Don't ever call me again!"

He banged on the door. "I'm sorry. I love you. I go crazy when I think of another guy looking at you."

"I don't care," she yelled through the door. "We are through. No one will touch me like that!"

Her dog ran down the steps and barked at the door.

"I won't do it again. I promise."

"Amelia, what is going on?" her mother's voice said from behind her. "Who's at the door?"

She turned and fell in to her mom's arms. "Mark. He hurt me."

"What did he do?"

"He pulled my hair and grabbed my face."

"Mark, go home or I'm calling the police. You

leave Amelia alone."

"Ms. Jones, I'm sorry. I didn't mean it."

"My daughter is not allowed to see you anymore. Leave now."

Her mom looked out the sidelights.

"Did he leave?" Amelia shook in her mom's arms.

"Yes, he's heading to his car."

Amelia squeezed her mom tighter. "I can't believe he did that to me."

"How did you react?"

"I told him what he wanted to hear so he'd let me go, then I ran inside."

"Has he done this before?"

"No. He's gotten a lot more jealous lately, but this is the first time he did anything like that."

"Don't you get back together with him. I mean it. No matter what he says, you are forbidden to date him. He will only get worse. Trust me."

"I won't go out with him again, Mom. I know what happened with Heather. She said Keith would apologize and make nice for a few days, then start the abuse again. I don't want to be with anyone like that."

"If he bothers you in any way, you tell me and your dad."

"I will."

"I'm proud of you, Amelia."

Chapter Thirty-seven

Walking toward his apartment after a long day at work, JJ looked up at the bright evening sun. He hadn't seen Heather since the night at the ball game two weeks ago.

JJ raked his hand through his hair, then slid his key into his front door and paused before unlocking it. He slammed the door and went to the living room. He sat in his recliner and propped his feet, then pulled out his phone and opened the photo of Amelia and Heather at Amelia's first game. He ran his thumb along Heather's cheek. Emptiness filled the pit of his stomach. He missed her.

A bright light appeared in the corner next to the fish tank and morphed into the shape of a woman. He squinted, then blinked several times. Were his eyes playing tricks on him? Was that Anna? He went over to it and swatted, but nobody was there. He went back to his chair and sat down. He needed sleep. He hadn't gotten nearly enough since Heather walked out of his life again. He hated not seeing her every day. Anna and Amelia kept him updated, but he needed to see her for himself.

His cell phone rang, and he answered. "Hello?"

"Heather's in the hospital," Ken said. "She would like to see Corrin and the kids."

"Is she . . ."

"I don't think it will be long now."

JJ dropped the phone and fell to his knees. He'd known the day would come. She'd hung on for nearly six months, but that didn't help the pain exploding his heart. "I'll be there as soon as possible."

Heather struggled to breathe even with the oxygen mask. It was time. Time to let go. Her parents sat in chairs next to her hospital bed, and Anna stood looking out the window. She wanted to fight for them and fight for Amelia and Zac, but her body couldn't take much more pain. She needed rest.

The nurse came in and adjusted her mask. "How are you?"

Heather smiled. It took too much energy and hurt too much to talk.

The door swung open, and JJ stood there wearing a scruffy beard and sad eyes under his glasses. Despite what she said or tried to convince herself, she loved him. She didn't want him to remember her like this. She closed her eyes and pretended to be asleep.

"We've missed you," her mother said. "She hasn't been doing well the last month, but she really went downhill two days ago."

"What happened?"

"Heather collapsed this afternoon. She woke about two hours ago, but she's been in and out of consciousness since." Her mother sniffed. "It could be a matter of days or weeks, more if we're lucky. They're sending her home tomorrow. There's nothing more they can do for her."

"Ken said Heather wanted to see the kids. They're in the hallway with Corrin. Can they come in?"

Someone tapped Heather on the shoulder. "JJ brought Amelia and Zac," her mother whispered. "Do you want to see them?"

Time to stop pretending. Heather opened her eyes and nodded.

JJ stepped toward her and opened his mouth, then closed his lips.

She smiled.

"Heather." Tears sat on the brim of his eyes.

"Hey," she whispered.

A tear slid down his cheek. "I'll go get the kids."

Thank you, she mouthed.

He stared at her, his eyes searching her face, then he turned and went into the hallway.

Heather looked at her dad, and he said, "Would you like to sit up?"

She nodded.

"Sure thing, darling." He helped her sit, then adjusted the pillows behind her.

JJ returned with his children and Corrin. Amelia held her mother's hand. Zac had the same fear on his face as the first day he'd met Heather.

Heather's mother stood and looked at Corrin. "You guys can sit here."

Her mom and dad moved to the other side of the room. Corrin let go of Amelia's hand and sat in the chair closest to Heather. Amelia sat next to her, and Zac climbed in his sister's lap.

"Hey, friend." Corrin grabbed Heather's hand.

Heather smiled.

"Was our beach trip too much on you?"

Heather shook her head. She didn't want Corrin to think that. That day had meant the world to her.

Heather looked at Amelia and Zac, then whispered, "I love you guys."

"I drew this for you." Zac jumped out of Amelia's lap and held out a picture of a ninja kicking her foot into the air, surrounded by people.

She'd hang it in her room so she could look at it all the time and remember this precious boy she loved.

"It's you doing that ninja move I taught Daddy. The one you said you'd do one day when you get stronger."

"It sure is." Heather grinned.

"I know you can't do it here. This is you in heaven, and the crowd back here watching you are the angels. And this is Anna."

"Why am I in it?" Anna turned from the window and went to Heather's bedside.

"'Cause you're an angel."

"I am, am I?"

Zac nodded.

She looked over Heather's shoulder. "Well, isn't that something. Good drawing."

Heather kissed him on the forehead. "Thank you. I love it."

"Can I talk to Heather alone?" JJ asked.

Mr. Cole stepped toward him and patted the side of JJ's arm. "Sure. Come on. Let's give them some time."

Everyone followed him out, and JJ sat in the chair next to her. His eyes stared into hers, and she smiled.

"I've missed you." He took her hand. "I'm really sorry that I didn't tell you about everything."

She nodded. "I forgive you. Will . . . you . . . forgive me?" she whispered.

Wrinkles formed in his forehead. "For what?"

"For making you stay away." She took in a deep breath. "I . . . love you."

He leaned forward and moved a strand of her hair. "Can I kiss you? Will it hurt?"

She moved the oxygen mask. "I don't care if it does."

He cradled her face in his hands and kissed her. She gasped, and he pulled back.

"I'm . . . okay . . . Kiss me."

He put his lips to hers again. "I love you." He pulled back, keeping her face in his hands. "I know this seems sudden, but I haven't stopped thinking about it." He kissed her cheek. "I love you, Heather Marie Cole. We may not have long, but will you marry me?"

Marry him? No matter how much time she had left, she wanted to spend it with him. She slid his glasses off his face and kissed him. "Dr. Jones, nothing would make me happier."

Two days later, Heather held on to the arms of her mom and Anna as she looked in the church's long mirror at herself in a strapless ankle-length wedding gown. She smiled as excitement flip-flopped in her stomach. Soon she'd be married to JJ, and it couldn't come fast enough. If it weren't for the oxygen tubes sitting under her nose, then she'd have looked like any other happy bride.

Heather's legs shook. "Can you help me sit back down?"

Anna and her mom helped her to a chair, then her mom pulled out a square box from her purse and handed it to Heather. Heather opened it and found a diamond necklace and matching earrings.

"I wore them in my wedding. I thought you could wear them for yours."

"Yes. Please."

Her mother draped the necklace around Heather's neck and clasped it. She put the earrings in Heather's ears. "You look beautiful."

"Thank you. I hope I can make it down the aisle without tripping." Heather winked. She wasn't even going to attempt it with her cane. She'd take her wheelchair down the aisle.

"That reminds me." Anna ran out of the room and returned with Heather's wheelchair.

White linen covered the front and dangled down the back to the floor, like a train. A bouquet of sunflowers, daisies, and violets hung from linen on the back of the chair.

"Anna, it's lovely. Thank you."

"Amelia helped. She did all the flowers for the

wedding."

"What a talented girl. Everything looks beautiful," Heather's mom said.

From down the hallway, instrumental music began, and her father opened the door. "Okay, ladies, it's showtime."

He lifted Heather and carried her to her wheelchair, while Zac and Amelia came in the room. Zac, the best man, wore a black tux, and Amelia, the maid of honor, wore a peach summer dress.

Anna blew a kiss to the kids as she walked out of the room. "I better go get a seat."

Amelia handed Heather a bouquet that matched the one on the back of the wheelchair.

Heather smiled. "You did a wonderful job with the flowers. Thank you."

"I loved doing it for you."

The door opened, and Anna returned. "Look who I caught sneaking in the church doors."

JJ's mom waved at Heather. How did she know? What was she doing there? Heather waved back.

"Hey there, stranger," her dad said. "We were worried you wouldn't make it in time."

Heather pointed at her dad. "You knew about this?"

"Sure did. Anna arranged it. Found her number somehow."

"I've been living out in Vegas. It didn't surprise me when Ms. Anna said my son was marrying you."

His mother leaned down and gave her a kiss. "It's about time. That boy's loved you his whole life."

Heather wanted to ask how she'd know since she hadn't been around, but Heather would enjoy the moment instead. Those issues could be discussed another day. His mom was here now.

"He misses you." Heather looked into Mrs. Jones's eyes.

His mother nodded. "It's been too long." She looked over at the kids and gasped. "Amelia. Zac. You kids are old. I've seen pictures of you, but I can't believe how big you are. I'm your Grandma Jones."

Zac giggled. "We know who you are, Grandma Jones." He took a mini Hershey bar from his pocket. "Want one?"

"Yes, thank you, young man." She looked at Amelia. "You, young lady, are gorgeous."

"Thank you." Amelia hugged the woman she'd never met. "Dad's going to be happy to see you."

"I hope so."

"Ladies, you better get out there. JJ's going to wonder if Heather has cold feet." Her dad motioned toward the door.

"We don't want that," JJ's mom said.

Heather's mom kissed her on the cheek. "I'm happy for you, sweetie. I love you. Enjoy your day."

"I love you too, Mom."

Her mother slid her arm in JJ's mom's, and they walked down the hallway. What would JJ think when he saw his mom walk down the aisle? Heather wished she could see his face.

"Okay, Zac, take Amelia's arm and follow your

grandmas up to the front of the church. Then go stand by your dad. Okay?"

"All right, Granddaddy Cole. I got this." Zac tugged at the collar of his tux.

"You do, do you?"

"Um-hum." He removed an opened mini Hershey bar from his pocket and took a bite, then placed it back. "Let's do this, sis." He held his arm out for her and then led the way down the hallway.

Heather's father wheeled her through the church into the foyer. The instrumental music stopped and then Mendelssohn's Wedding March began. Two church members opened the sanctuary doors, and her father wheeled her inside. A white runner ran down the aisle to where JJ, Amelia, and Zac stood on the stage waiting for her. Her mother, his mother, Corrin, Anna, relatives, friends, and many of the church congregation sat on either side of the room.

She saw JJ and held her breath. He wore a dark-blue tux, a pink rose-colored tie, and a white daisy boutonniere. He smiled, and her eyes met his. Everything other than him disappeared. When she reached him, he took her hands.

From behind, her dad lifted her under the arms, and JJ pulled her against him and wrapped his arms around her waist, and she did the same to him.

"You look stunning," he whispered in her ear.

Heather's limbs ached and her head spun. She took in several labored breaths, then gasped. A tear rolled down her cheek. She couldn't do it. She wanted to stand with him, but she couldn't. She pointed to the wheelchair her dad had moved to the side of the room, but JJ swooped down and lifted her up into his arms.

"Don't worry, Cole. I've got you."

JJ carried Heather over the threshold to his apartment with her oxygen tank slung over his shoulder. He kissed her cheek, then carried her back to their bedroom and laid her on the bed before lying next to her.

She closed her eyes and took a deep breath as she removed the tubes from her nose. "Aren't you . . . going to kiss me?"

"Yes, if you want me to."

"Of course I do."

He ran his thumb along her cheek and across her lips, then down her chin. He slid his hand up to her ear and traced it, then back down to her chin and lifted it slightly. He parted his lips, slowly moving toward her mouth, then softly kissed her. His heart raced. He wanted to do more, but what about her fragile body, and he didn't want to take too much of her oxygen.

She giggled. "Kiss me like you mean it."

"Oh, I mean it all right."

"I know, but don't be afraid of breaking me. I want this. I want you. You're my husband . . . finally."

That was all he needed to hear. He kissed her hard, then moved down to her neck. She ran her hands up his shirt onto his abs and chest. "I didn't know you had these muscles under here."

She opened her eyes, and he unbuttoned his shirt, then threw it on the floor. She ran her hand over his chest as she looked at it. Fire flashed through her eyes. He knew the look well, but it was finally from the only woman he'd ever want to see it from.

JJ's skin tingled, and sweat dripped from his brow. He looked at Heather's bare shoulder and kissed it. He wanted her again. He moved his mouth to her neck. But could she?

If Heather could make him feel this amazing when she was not 100 percent, then what would it be like if she were healthy?

She ran her hands up and down his back. "Again."

He breathed heavier and pulled her against him.

Heather rolled to her side and watched her sleeping husband. He breathed heavily, and she kissed his lips. He kissed back but remained asleep. She smiled. He was hers. Her JJ. Her husband.

Being intimate with him had been incredible. It was exactly like she'd dreamed it would be. The way a wife and husband should be together.

She rolled onto her back and let out a happy sigh.

JJ stirred. "Good morning, Mrs. Jones."

"Good morning, Dr. Jones."

"Lots of people call me Dr. Jones, but not with that raspy voice. Say it again."

She giggled. "Dr. Jon—" A cough sent excruciating pain through her head.

"Are you okay?"

The back of her throat felt thick with salvia, and she gurgled. She coughed hard, and her hand filled with blood.

"Let me get a towel." He jumped off the bed and ran to the bathroom.

Darkness surrounded her. "I can't see."

JJ touched her arms. "I'm right here." He wiped her hands off.

"I don't feel right." Her chest felt heavy, and she gasped for air. "Help . . . me. I . . . can't . . . breathe." Her heart tumbled and raced. Was this the end? Not already.

He stopped wiping her hand, and something brushed against her as the mattress slightly bounced under her. She sensed he'd moved off the bed. Feet moved heavily on the floor, and something knocked against the wall.

"Could it be your oxygen tank?"

The dark started to turn to light, and a loud noise pierced her eardrum. At least God had given them a chance to begin again.

Chapter Thirty-eight

JJ paced the waiting room floor. Would the doctor come out already and tell him what was going on? Mr. and Mrs. Cole rushed into the room, and Mr. Cole grabbed JJ's arms. "What's going on?'

"Her oxygen tank ran out, and I didn't realize it until she passed out. I transferred her to another tank immediately, but she didn't wake up. The doctors haven't come back out yet." He raked his hands through his hair. "I knew we should have been more careful."

A young dark-haired doctor entered the waiting room. "Heather's awake," he said. "She's doing well. Her numbers are up, and she's asking for you all. Other than this little scare, everything's the same as it was three days ago when she decided to go home. If she still wants to be there instead of here, I'll get the paperwork in order. She'll be out of here shortly. Keep her comfortable."

JJ's mother sat at his dining room table, eating the spaghetti he'd made for them. Heather slept in their bedroom, with Anna keeping watch over her.

"I'm glad you came for the wedding. Thank you."

She finished her bite of food and wiped her mouth with a napkin. "I was happy to be there. It's been too long. I'm glad to see you followed your dreams and became a doctor."

"I have a medical degree, but I'm not a doctor. I'm a physical therapist."

"Anna told me you're one of the top PTs in the country. Is that true?"

He nodded. "I put the work in, that's for sure."

"Why did you stay here in this little town? You could have gone to Chicago or New York City. Even joined me out in Vegas."

"You're in Las Vegas now?"

"Yep. We've been there for a year or so, I think."

"You and Charlie?"

"Heavens no. That lasted two years. I was on my own about ten years, until I met Derek. I love it there."

He pursed his lips and glared at her. Why hadn't she picked up a phone once to check on him or to learn about her grandchildren? Guess she'd rather live her best life without him a part of it. Anna shouldn't have invited her.

"What is it, JJ? You look like you want to say something."

He clenched his jaw. He had an earful for her. "I don't get you. I really don't. A son should know where his mom lives. I gave up and stopped looking. I figured if you cared, you'd try. You never did."

She stared at her plate.

"I got married, then Dad died, so you thought you'd sow your wild oats and leave me behind and never look back again."

"You could have come with me."

"Right, Mom. Give up school, force Corrin to quit her new job to follow you and a man you didn't even stay with across the country. No, you should have stayed and been here for your son."

"I couldn't stay. There were too many memories. Everywhere I went in this town, I'd run into people who knew your dad. I'd lie in bed at night and stare at his empty spot. It was harder than you can imagine. You don't understand now, but you will."

JJ threw his napkin on the table. "Was I too hard to look at? Is that why you left me? Why you never called? Why you didn't bother to visit or get to know Amelia or Zac?"

His mother stared at him, but he couldn't read her.

"I couldn't do it again," she said. "I couldn't look at the sympathetic faces anymore. I had to go where no one knew me."

"I get you wanting to get away from Danburg, but why did you walk away from me?"

"I was selfish. All right. Does that make you happy? I was sad and selfish, and I didn't know how to deal with my grief. Then the years passed and passed and passed, and it got easier to stay away."

"To ignore me?"

"I'm sorry."

"Sorry? Why did you even come to the wedding?"

"I took it as a sign. I've missed you. When you stopped looking for me, I thought you never wanted to see me again. But then Anna called, and I wanted to come make amends. I want to start over. I want to know Amelia and Zac. I want to know you again."

She put her hand on top of his, but he pulled it back.

"I could never do to Amelia and Zac what you did to me. No son should feel unloved by his mom. I've made my fair share of mistakes, but I do everything in my power to be sure my kids know I'm there for them." He stood and pushed his chair in. "I can't do this with you anymore."

"I'll prove it to you. I've rented a little apartment here in Danburg. Derek can work from anywhere. He's going to join me, and we're going to stay here for a while. I want to fix things. I really do."

"I'll believe it when I see it."

Heather lay in her bed watching TV, and Anna sat in a chair across the room, knitting. JJ's raised voice carried from the dining room.

Anna set her yarn and needles in her lap and looked at Heather. "It sounds like he's upset."

Heather nodded. "I hope he's okay."

"He will be. He needs to talk with her. He can't keep letting it fester."

Heather's throat tickled, and she cleared it away. She tried clearing it away again, but it wouldn't back down.

"Grab me a towel!"

Anna ran to the bathroom and threw a towel at Heather.

She held her breath trying to hold the cough back, but it burst through her lips, and her body thrashed back and forth and up and down against the bed. She grabbed the towel over her mouth to catch the blood. Pain intensified in her ribs and shoulder with every cough.

Anna jumped onto the bed next to Heather and held Heather still in a propped position. "JJ!"

Now that Anna had ahold of her, Heather coughed without thrashing back and forth, and the pain lessened.

Between coughs, JJ and his mother ran into the room, and Anna barked out orders.

"Meredith, get her water. JJ, come hold Heather. I need to check her oxygen tank."

Anna slid off the bed, and JJ held Heather up with one arm as he scooted behind her. His legs sat on either side of her, and she lay back against him as he wrapped his arms around her. She coughed again, and he held her still.

His mom came back into the room with a glass of water and held it to her lips. The water slid down and soothed her throat. Her cough relented. Exhausted, she turned her head to the side against JJ's chest while his mother wiped her mouth.

JJ kissed her head. "Are you okay?"

Heather nodded, and then whispered. "Can I

break a rib from coughing too much?"

"Yes. Are you hurting?" JJ's hold around her lessened.

She nodded. It felt like a truck had rammed into her.

"Should you take her to the hospital?" Meredith asked.

"Even if she broke a rib, there isn't much they can do. It's best to let her rest and give her pain meds and avoid the germ-filled hospital. If the pain gets unbearable, I'll take her." He looked down at Heather. "Are you okay with staying here?"

She nodded.

"I'm staying behind you for the rest of the evening. If you lay down, it could hurt worse. Take slow, steady breaths."

His hands touched her sides, and he lightly rubbed her rib cage. The gentle massage eased some of the pain.

"Let's let her rest," Anna said to JJ's mom as the two women left the room.

Heather closed her eyes. "That feels nice." She let out a sigh. "You have incredible hands. Having a physical therapist for a husband comes in handy. Dr. Jones, I could stay here in your arms forever."

"I wish you could."

Chapter Thirty-nine

"If you won't let me take off this blindfold, will you at least turn down the heat? You covered me in so many layers that I'm afraid sweat will get in my oxygen tube." Heather sat in JJ's Mustang while he drove who knows where in the dark.

"Sorry, but this is the coldest Thanksgiving we've had in a while. I want to make sure you're warm."

"Where are you taking me?"

"Uh-uh."

"Give me a clue. Please? I'll call you Dr. Jones."

He laughed. "As tempting as that is, no. No clues."

She laid her head back against the headrest. She'd found love and happiness. Something to live and fight for. She'd never walk again or get off the oxygen tank, but she was enjoying every moment until the end.

The car stopped, and JJ got out. He opened her door, then lifted her into his arms and slid the blindfold off. "Ta-da."

In front of her stood a two-story, cream-colored Mediterranean-style house with a driveway leading to the back. She looked around at the surrounding homes designed to look like a Florida neighborhood.

"What's this?"

"Our house. Ours and Amelia's and Zac's."

"How?"

"Anna met the owner at the grocery store. And of course, they got talking. She found out the woman was selling her house, and Anna suggested I come by to see it. I bought it on the spot."

"Really, why?"

"Because it reminds me of the house from a dream I had when I was in the hospital. We were married and had four kids. And Anna was our maid."

"Our maid?"

"I guess in my self-conscious, I couldn't imagine Anna not in our lives, and in this dream you didn't have cancer. I guess that's why Anna was the maid."

"I didn't have to cook or clean? That's my kind of dream."

"I don't really know why we had a maid. I hate to burst your bubble, but in the dream you washed the dishes, folded the laundry, and cooked dinner. I really don't know what Anna did, other than talk a lot and make her specialty drink."

"Specialty drink?"

"Ask her about it. It's pretty tasty, but only drink it if you're ready to have crazy dreams." He unlocked the door. "Come on in." He carried her over the threshold.

The vaulted entryway opened to a rounded foyer. To the right, stairs led to the second floor, and to the left the living room looked up at the banister running along the hallways upstairs.

JJ carried her through the living room to the French doors into the kitchen and family room.

The house seemed familiar, as if she'd lived in it in another lifetime. She closed her eyes and pictured the children JJ had once described to her. She'd never forgotten their names: Lily after her grandma, Michael after his grandpa, Sam after her uncle, and Abi just because she'd always wanted a girl named Abi. The mirage of the children similar to the ones in the picture of the mystery kids on JJ's phone, who were somehow related to Amelia and Zac, waved at her from the table. In her mind, she blew each one a kiss, and they vanished as her breath puffed over them.

Laughter came from the living room. JJ turned around and took her there. Her parents, Anna, Corrin, Amelia, and Zac held a *Welcome Home* banner and balloons.

"What do you guys think? Do you like it?" JJ asked.

"It's beautiful, Dad." Amelia beamed. "This is our house?"

"Imagine all the candy bars I can store in a place like this?" Zac jumped up and down.

"Buddy, sounds like you have an addiction going on here." Heather's dad tousled Zac's hair.

"Granddaddy Cole, I've got it under control."

Her dad laughed. "Let's check out the rest of this

joint."

Heather kissed JJ. "Thank you."

"For what?"

"For the house. For loving me. For everything."

Chapter Forty

The doorbell rang, and Heather wheeled herself from the kitchen into the dining room. JJ was at work, and Anna had run to the post office to mail a last-minute Christmas present.

Heather peeked out the window and didn't see a car. Neighbors stopped by all the time to bring baskets of Christmas goodies or to say hi. Without looking out the sidelights first, she opened the door.

Her ex-husband stood tall. Keith? Heather gasped, and her heart flew. She reached for her phone in her wheelchair bag. "What are you doing here? How do you know where I live?"

"Bryson."

Why would he do that? Heather hadn't worried about Keith since the day the marines transported him—restraining order in hand—straight to California to serve time in the brig. And when she and JJ moved to the new house, her mind eased at the fact Keith wouldn't know where to find her.

Keith took a step forward. "He and Sissy are waiting for me in the truck."

She glared at the opened front door. "Why are you here?"

Keith shifted back and forth on his feet. "I . . . I brought something for you. It's in my truck by your garage. It's nice back there. JJ's kids will have a good time in that pool in the summer."

Heather glared at him. Why was he making nice? She wanted him to leave. "You opened the gate to the driveway into my backyard. Why?"

"I thought it would be easier."

"For what? Me to not see you?"

"No."

"What did you bring?"

"Come back with me and see?"

"Yeah right. I'm not going anywhere with you."

She closed the door, but he stuck his foot in the doorway. "Please. Listen to me."

It seemed like a lifetime ago since she'd been his punching bag. She was weak and riddled in a wheelchair, but never again would Keith break her. "You know, what you meant to harm me made me stronger, made me a fighter. I should have been dead in April, but Christmas is in two days, and I'm still here. You made me your prisoner, but you were the one in chains. What kind of man would ridicule, spit on, kick, hit, throw, and force himself on his wife? One so wrapped up in his own self-hate and insecurities that he believed that's the way to keep her."

She clutched the arms of her wheelchair, waiting for a slap across the face, but it didn't come. Instead he stared at the ground.

"What, you have nothing to say?" she spewed.

He shook his head.

"Why would you threaten Corrin and her kids and attack JJ? You are insane. I thought you were in the brig." She clutched the armrest again.

He looked up. "I was for several months. Now I'm in counseling. Don't worry. I'm not going to hurt you."

She glared at him. "Good. 'Cause it would take a real coward to beat on a woman in my condition."

"How are you?"

"It's not your business anymore."

"I'm worried about you. I still love you. I know I was wrong."

She glared at him. What did he want from her? "Please leave."

"You're right. I was a coward and insane. I became someone I hated. Exactly like my dad. I swore I would never be like him. Ever. I joined the marines to get away from the abuse, but ignoring the beatings and the cruelty didn't take away the memories. And I ended up being worse than my old man. The first time I hit you, I went in the fetal position for hours."

"I remember."

"You were good to me after that. Understanding and forgave me. I knew I didn't deserve you. Then the first time a guy in my unit mentioned your curves and how good you looked, I played it off, but after more of them made crude comments, I snapped. I believed you must have been seeing some of them on the side when I was at work or at the gym. I didn't know how to keep you from them."

"You didn't believe me, but I didn't even know the guys in your unit. Then you made me think I was worthless in every area of my life." Heather paused, then waved her hands in front of her and shook her head. "I don't want to rehash it all. We both know what it was like. It's over. And I'm happy now. So please go."

The longer he stared, the more frightened she became. Would he take the oxygen tubes out of her nose and smash the tank over her head before slamming it against the floor in a fit of rage? Then leave her gasping for air until she died? No, she had not fought this hard to die at the hands of Keith.

He bent to his knees and looked in her eyes. He looked too composed to be unruffled. Almost like a tiger about to pounce on his prey. Should she call 911? Scream like a maniac until he fled or a neighbor heard her?

His hand lifted to her face, and she flinched. Instead of ripping the tubes off her face, he ran his thumb along her cheek. "In counseling I'm dealing with the abuse at the hands of my father and the abuse I inflicted on you. I don't ever want to be like that again. And whether you believe me or not, I'm sorry for it all. I'm glad you're happy. You, more than anyone, deserve it."

Tears welled in her eyes, but she refused to let them fall in front of him.

He stood and wiped his pants off. "You said something I can't stop thinking about it. You told me they didn't know where the cancer started and if I'd let you go to the doctor, they could have found it in time before it got this far."

Heather nodded. Why did she feel bad for him? The spreading cancer probably was his fault, but she believed he was remorseful for the abuse and was hurting over her cancer. "The doctors said it could have all started as a small melanoma on my back, but there's no proof of that. By the time it was found, it was in my lymph nodes, the lungs, and in my shoulder and spots on my back. It was too far to determine where it actually started. Now it's in my bloodstream and probably my brain next."

He choked back sobs. "I'm sorry."

Bryson and Sissy walked up behind him. Sissy raised a hand and whispered, "Hi."

Heather nodded.

Bryson touched Keith's shoulder. "Come on. Let's go."

"But—"

"Let her be. You said your peace."

"I love you." He reached his hand toward her and pulled it back. "I should have gotten help the first time."

"Let's go."

"But what about the—" Keith looked at Bryson.

"Sissy and I unloaded it. Come on."

Keith nodded, then stared at her.

Her heart ached for the man she knew he could have been. The man she'd originally fallen in love with. The life they could have had.

She grabbed his hand. "Keith, there are many what-ifs in life. But no matter, this was my life, as unsuspecting as it was." She let a single tear fall. "Remember me when I'm gone and when you feel yourself on the edge and unable to control your rage. Remember who you want to be. And please let me die in peace. Don't come here again or threaten my loved ones."

He nodded. "Goodbye, Heather. I won't bother you or anyone else again." He let go of her hand, then turned and walked away. Bryson and Sissy put their arms over Keith's shoulder, and they rounded the corner behind the bushes.

Shaking, Heather shut the door, then let out a sobbing exhale and held her hands over her face.

Heather lay on the couch and flipped the TV to the Hallmark Channel. The scent of chicken and rolls wafted into the living room. It was nice to be able to smell again. She inhaled. What was that other smell? She couldn't quite place it. Sweet? Spicy? Pumpkin Pie?

The garage door opened and closed, then JJ entered the living room from the kitchen. "Heather, do you know why there's a mirror in the driveway?"

"Mirror? No. That's weird."

"Should I toss it?"

"What does it look like?"

"It's a cheval mirror. Looks like an antique. It looks kind of familiar, but I'm not sure."

"Will you take me out there to see it?"

"Sure." He wrapped a blanket around her and then carried her to the driveway.

She gasped. Her mirror stood in front of the garage. "That's my grandma's. What's that?" She pointed at a white envelope taped to it.

JJ stepped close enough for Heather to grab the envelope.

I know how important this mirror is to you. I wanted you to have it back. —Keith

"Was Keith here?"

Heather nodded. "I don't know how I forgot that."

"Did he hurt you?"

"No."

"What did he want?"

"He apologized. Said he was getting help. I guess he came to bring me the mirror?"

"If he ever comes back again, call me."

She nodded. "I can't believe I forgot that he'd been here. How could I forget that?"

He put his forehead to hers. "Are you feeling okay? You feel a little warm."

"I've felt weird the last few days, but nothing I can put my finger on. Earlier I couldn't place what I was smelling, and I keep forgetting things people have said to me."

His smile dropped.

Chapter Forty-one

W hile she sat in her wheelchair and examined her reflection in her grandma's mirror, a gray cat jumped onto Heather's lap and purred. She ran her hands along its soft fur. What had they named her? Abi . . . That was it. Abi. Because she always wanted a cat named Abi.

Zac's reflection ran across the hallway, then stopped at the doorway and peeked at her through the mirror. "What are you doing?"

The cat jumped off her lap and ran past Zac. "Grab Abi. I don't want her getting out the front door."

"Who's Abi?"

"The cat, silly."

"When did we get a cat?" He ran down the hallway. "Dad, you got us a cat! Is that our Christmas present? Here Abi, Abi, Abi!"

Abi jumped back in her lap, and she held it up toward her face. "Did that boy scare you? He's harmless." She hugged the cat, then placed Abi in her lap and petted her.

Through the mirror, JJ walked up behind her and

placed his hands on her shoulder. She smiled at his reflection while petting Abi.

"Sweetie, there's no cat."

What was he talking about? She looked down. Where did Abi go?

JJ massaged her shoulders. "Anna's got everything set. Are you ready to make Christmas cookies with the kids?"

"It's Christmas?"

"No, Christmas Eve."

Blackness crowded the light in her eyes, and she squeezed them shut, then opened them repeatedly until the blackness disappeared. Fear crept into her heart. Why was she so confused? "Are you sure we don't have a cat?" Her stomach knotted.

He nodded.

"Then who's Abi?"

JJ sat at the kitchen table across from Heather. She decorated a star cookie with Zac, who sat next to her, and Amelia sat on the opposite side. Anna pulled out another tray of cookies and laid them on the counter. Christmas music played from the intercom speakers, and all seemed perfect.

But JJ knew better. He took in a deep breath. If he was right, she had days left. He sniffed back tears. It couldn't be happening already. He needed more time. She'd made it nearly a year since her diagnosis, but knowing that didn't make it easier. He was going to lose her.

At least let her make it through tomorrow. God,

please.

She smiled at him, and he smiled back. He'd fill her days with joy and laughter. He grabbed the tube of blue icing, got up from the table, and squeezed a glob onto her nose.

"Hey." She wiped it off with the back of her hand, then grabbed the tube from his hand.

She gestured with her finger for him to come closer. She took the icing tube to his mouth and drew an icing mustache, then filled his chin with more icing.

She dropped the icing and laughed. "My masterpiece."

"Do I look pretty?"

"Always."

"Look at me, Dad." Amelia held her phone up.

He smiled, then grabbed Heather's face and kissed her. Then leaned over to Zac and kissed his check, then did the same to Amelia. He looked over at Anna.

"You better not." Anna pointed a pot holder at him.

"You know I will." He ran toward Anna, and she ran to other side of the island. He darted to the left, but she moved to the right. He chased her around the island, and she laughed.

"You can't catch me."

He faked left, and she went the same direction as him. He caught her in a hug and smeared icing on her cheek from his chin.

"You're in for it now, buddy."

JJ ran into the family room. "I am, am I?"

"Don't underestimate an old lady and her posse."

Anna looked to Amelia and Zac. "Come on, kids. Let's get him."

Anna grabbed a spatula full of green icing off the table and chased JJ over to the couch. She knocked him down. Zac climbed on top of his legs while Amelia sat on his stomach and held his arms down. He wouldn't put up a fight. He let Anna cover his face with icing.

"Heather, toss me the red sprinkles," Anna shouted.

Heather threw the bottle, and it landed halfway there. "Sorry. I couldn't get it all the way to you."

Zac jumped off his legs. "I got them." He handed the container to Anna, then sat back on JJ's legs.

Anna sprinkled them over him.

"The human Christmas tree," Amelia shouted. "We have to take a picture."

Amelia and Zac got up, and JJ stood, saying, "How about a selfie with Heather?"

They followed him over to her and smiled as Amelia held out her phone and took several pictures.

Amelia laid her phone on the table and reached for a cookie, but JJ grabbed her into a giant bear hug and smeared icing onto her face from his.

"Dad, stop."

"Uh-uh. Paybacks."

"Mom, tell him to stop."

Mom? JJ pulled back and looked at Heather, smiling.

"I was going to say it tomorrow as a Christmas present, but I couldn't wait any longer. Is it okay? Can I call you Mom? My mom said she didn't mind."

Heather held her hands out, and Amelia stepped in front of Heather and kneeled down. "Of course it's okay." Heather put her hand around Amelia's back and beckoned for Zac to join them. "I love you two as much as if I'd given birth to you. I'm blessed."

In that moment watching Heather and his icing-stained children, he saw the goodness of God. He had seen glimpses over the years, but right now he understood everything Heather and Anna had tried to tell him. God was good all the time. All the time God was good.

Christmas morning JJ carried Heather into the living room and set her down on the couch, then scooted in next to her.

"Looks like Santa's been here."

"It sure does."

"I can't believe he ate all the cookies and drank all the milk." He winked.

"I'm sure he enjoyed them."

"I think he did. You guys made wonderful cookies."

"What's that?" Heather pointed at a red box with a white ribbon sitting on the coffee table.

"It's for you."

Heather smiled. Her eyes looked heavy and tired. Exhaustion sat on her face.

The doorbell rang. Within minutes Corrin, Heather's parents, JJ's mom, Derek, and the kids filled the living room.

"Presents! Presents!" Zac chanted.

JJ laughed. "In a minute, buddy. Let's read the Christmas story first."

Zac ran to the bookshelf next to the fireplace and grabbed the Bible. "Can I read it?"

Heather nodded. "Yes, please. Come sit by me, and I'll help you with the words."

Zac climbed between Heather and JJ.

Anna slipped into the room from the kitchen and took a seat in a folded chair near the tree. "Zac, since you are holding the Bible, am I to assume we are reading the Christmas story first?"

Nodding, Zac smiled. "Daddy said I could, and Heather's going to help me with the big words."

"Wow. I'm sure glad you're going to start the morning out reading from the Bible. My father just loves when people remember to think of Jesus's birth before ripping into presents on Christmas morning. It's sad many can't even take a moment to reflect on the reason for the season." She winked.

"Okay, Zac. You ready to read?" JJ flipped through the Bible until he reached Luke 2.

Zac ran his finger along the words as he read. "In those days . . ." He looked at Heather.

"Caesar Augustus."

"Caesar Augustus . . . Uh, Heather, maybe you should read this."

"You can do it, buddy. How about we read it together?"

Zac agreed, and they read together. Heather read slowly and had to catch her breath several times, and when they came to a word Zac didn't know, he'd repeat it after her.

When Zac and Heather finished, Anna clapped her hands and sang "Go Tell It on the Mountain." Heather's parents joined first, then Heather, followed by Zac and Amelia. Corrin raised an eyebrow at JJ. He shrugged and joined in. A few seconds later, Corrin did too.

"Hallelujah, amen," Anna shouted. "We're having church in here."

"That we are, Ms. Anna," Mr. Cole said.

JJ laughed under his breath. At this time last year, he and Corrin had gone through the motions for the kids, but there'd been no joy in the celebration. He'd been sure this Christmas he'd be alone. But now he had Heather's, Amelia's, and Corrin's forgiveness, Zac's respect, his mom back in his life, and friendships he never imagined with Anna and Mr. and Mrs. Cole.

"Daddy, can we open presents now? Please?" Zac grinned.

"Do you mind if I give Heather one first?"

Zac made a grumpy face, then smiled. "Go ahead, but a kid can only wait so long."

Heather kissed Zac on top of the head. "Thank you, buddy. I'll hurry."

JJ handed Heather the present. She ripped off the paper and pulled out a glass jar layered with seashells and sand like the one from his dream. On the top layer of sand, JJ's seashell with the word *Cole* faced outward in front of a picture of Heather and her grandma from their last summer at the beach.

Heather beamed. "I love it. That's the shell I

gave you a long time ago. You kept it." Heather kissed his cheek. "Thank you so much."

Heather pointed to the doorway leading to the kitchen. "Will you take me to the mistletoe?"

He lifted her into his arms and carried her to the doorway between the living room and kitchen.

"I love you, JJ. I guess my grandma knew what she was talking about. I gave that seashell to the object of my affection, and we're married, have children, and maybe it won't be as long as we'd like, but it's sure feels like a lifetime of love."

This day couldn't come to an end. His body ached understanding that tomorrow would bring doctor visits and the knowledge her time had run out. No miracles. No more months to hang on.

He swallowed hard. He'd give anything. He'd trade his own life if he could. She couldn't be leaving him, but her poor body couldn't give anymore. He'd have to say goodbye.

He brought his mouth to hers. He couldn't pull away. He kissed her again. This couldn't come to an end.

Tears raced down her cheeks, and she grabbed his face. Pressing hard against his mouth, she whispered, "It's in my brain now, isn't it?"

He nodded. "I'm afraid so."

She kissed him over and over. "I'm not ready, but I'm afraid there's no fight left in me. I'm tired."

Her words punched JJ in the stomach. "Cole, you've fought hard. Take your rest. You've earned it."

"But I can't leave knowing you don't have faith in God. You won't be with me someday."

Planting a hard kiss on her forehead, the realization spilled over. "But I will."

She raised an eyebrow.

"I've blamed God for everything wrong in my life, but finally last night something clicked. Things don't always have to be the way we planned. God's goodness comes in the mighty and the small moments. Mighty like in you—a warrior. And small like last night with icing wars and days like today with family. But most of all those moments of forgiveness. I didn't deserve it, but it was given."

She kissed him. "I've never loved you more."

Heather looked up at the mistletoe, then back at her husband. She kissed him again and kept her mouth on his. "I'll love you forever."

He drew her closer, and his hold around her tightened.

She touched his face and whispered, "Let's join our family."

She looked at them sitting in the living room watching her and JJ. Each one meant the world to her. What a year she'd lived. Moments to cherish. Love unending. And friendship she'd fought to live for.

He carried her back to the couch.

"Can I open my presents now?" Zac looked at Heather with wide eyes.

"Yes, buddy. Go ahead."

He ran to the tree and checked the tags. He grabbed one and ripped it open. "A car track! I love it. Thank you." He ran to the tree and looked for another.

"Go find you one, Amelia," Heather said. "That green one with the gold bow is from me."

Amelia jumped off the couch and picked up the green package, then returned next to Heather. She took off the paper and opened the box.

Heather anxiously waited to see Amelia's reaction.

Amelia pulled out a picture frame and turned it for everyone to see the picture of Heather and Amelia at the softball state championship.

"That's a great photo," Corrin said. "What's the inscription say?"

Amelia turned it around and read it out loud. "My dearest Amelia, my best friend, I love and adore you. I didn't give birth to you, but in my heart you are forever my girl." She choked up. "Our bond was like no other. Stay strong, for I'm not far. Find me in our precious memories." She put her arms around Heather. "I love you, Mom."

Heather kissed her cheek. "I love you too."

JJ went to the tree and handed the rest of the presents out. Heather watched each person carefully as they opened their gifts, thanked each other, laughed, and told stories. Her heart overflowed with peace. They would miss her, but they had each other. They would be okay.

Anna left the room, then returned with a tray full of coffee mugs. She held the tray out for Heather to choose a cup, then JJ and the rest of the family.

"Is this your specialty drink?" Heather asked.

Anna grinned. "Not today. It doesn't need

anything extra. Today everything is perfect just as it is."

Chapter Forty-two

A cardinal landed on a snowy picnic table two down from JJ. He tossed a handful of birdseed in its direction. After finishing the snack, the bird flew over the lake to the trees on the other side. JJ pulled his collar up around his neck. January in Danburg was normally cold, but this one felt more frigid than normal.

A shadow moved on the ground in front of him, and he turned. Corrin held her hand up. "Anna told me you were probably here. Can I join you?"

"Sure."

She sat next to him, and JJ looked back at the water. "Whether Heather was here at the lake or the ocean, the beach was her favorite place to be. I can't leave. It's like she's here."

His insides felt ripped to shreds. Corrin's hand touched his back. It meant a lot that she was there with him.

He looked at her. "I knew it was coming, but nothing prepared me for watching Heather's body give out." He covered his face with his hand and whimpered, then wiped at the tears and stared out at the lake. "The days after Christmas passed more quickly than I thought possible, and it's all kind of a blur. She faded fast. First the confusion, then the blindness settled in. After that the inability to speak, followed by unconsciousness."

He'd repeated these words many times over the last few hours, and every time it hurt worse. "I held her the entire night, and I told her it was okay to let go. I kissed her goodbye and said I loved her one last time, then she stopped breathing. Her fight was over."

Corrin rubbed his back. "I'm so sorry. Is there anything I can do?"

"Sit with me for a while."

"I'm here as long as you need me."

"That might be a long time."

"It's okay. I don't mind." She laid her head on his shoulder, and he placed his head on hers.

"Thank you. I know this is hard for you too. You and she became really close."

"We did."

He smiled. "It's quite a miracle that you and I found our way into Heather's heart."

Corrin slid her arm into his. "We're lucky she loved us."

Chapter Forty-three

How had this day arrived? JJ couldn't possibly be old enough to have a daughter graduating from high school. Amelia sat in the front row, first seat on the gym floor, and smiled up at him. He pulled out his phone and took several photos.

"Dad, come on. Stop taking pictures of Amelia. You're embarrassing me." Zac smirked from his seat next to JJ.

"I don't care. It's not every day your daughter graduates as the valedictorian. I'm one proud papa."

Corrin climbed up the bleachers, then patted JJ on his chest. "Hey, old man."

"Old man?" He winked. "What does that make—"

She looked at him from under her lashes with wide eyes and raised brows.

He grinned. "Doesn't Amelia look beautiful, just like you?"

"She does. And thank you." She took the seat next to him. "Max and I were wondering if you'd like to come over for dinner tomorrow."

"Are you and your husband trying to set me up on a blind date?"

Corrin smiled.

"What a bummer. I have plans."

She swatted his arm. "You do not. Come over. Meet her. She's nice."

JJ looked at his feet. He wasn't ready. "I can't."

"JJ, it's been three years. It's okay to move on."

He knew that.

"Fine. Ignore me, but I'm not giving up."

"I'm not ignoring you. I'm not interested right now. I'm good. I don't need a woman's affections to make me happy anymore."

"Heather really brought out the best in you."

"That she did." He looked around. "Where *is* Max?"

"He'll be here soon. He wanted to get Amelia flowers. Isn't he sweet? It's kind of their thing."

"I've noticed. I'm glad she has him." He nudged Corrin with his shoulder. "You too. You deserve a man like him."

Her smile said it all. Max brought out the best in Corrin too.

The Coles slid in next to JJ. Mrs. Cole reached across her husband to hand Zac a candy bar.

"Thank you, Grammy Cole."

JJ's mom walked up the bleachers and took a seat in front of him.

"You made it."

"I wouldn't miss it for the world."

JJ looked down at Amelia, then back at his family. He wished Heather could be there. His stomach turned a knot. Emptiness still sat in his gut.

She would have been proud of Amelia.

JJ stepped into his kitchen from the garage and threw his keys on the island. They slid across the counter and landed next to a steaming mug of hot chocolate and an envelope with his name on it. He pulled out a note.

An extra dab of this and a little bit of that. Enjoy. *–Anna*

He dropped the letter on the counter and looked around the room. She wasn't there.

He lifted the mug to his mouth and took a sip. Rich, smooth, hot liquid slid down his throat. He took it to the couch and finished it. His eyes soon grew heavy, and he yawned.

JJ opened his eyes, and a brunette woman, wearing a red bathing suit, stood with her back turned to him and her feet in the lake.

"Hello," he shouted as he walked toward her, but she didn't turn.

When he made it to her, he touched her shoulder, and she spun around. Heather's eyes lit up, and she put her arms around him. "You made it."

"I miss you."

She pulled back, her skin healthy and glowing. "I'm right here." She touched his heart. "I haven't gone anywhere."

He put his hand over hers. "The ache won't go away."

She patted his chest. "It will continue to ease, and a new woman will come into your life."

"I only want you."

"It's okay to let me go. I know you love me."

"I always have and always will."

"Me too. Amelia looked beautiful today."

"You were there?"

"I'm always with you." She kissed his cheek. "I have to go now. I asked Anna to let me see you. She's training me to do what she does. She said this was a one-time thing and I had to be quick. Her drink is to be used to reveal what needs shown for healing. I told her I needed to tell you goodbye and that your heart still needed a little healing."

He kissed her lips, and she kissed back. "Don't go yet."

"I have to. My time is up. I love you." She took his hands. "It's okay. You can let go."

"I can't."

"It's time. You are who you always wanted to be. I will be with you always. I must go."

He let go of her hand, and she walked out into the water and then slowly faded until she disappeared.

Chapter Forty-four

After getting Amelia settled into her dorm room, JJ walked toward his car as a black cloud loomed overhead. He checked the radar on his phone. Noting the rainstorm would be quick but fierce, he opted for the small campus coffeehouse across the street rather than his car.

A raindrop landed on his head, followed by more. He crossed the street into the shelter of the building, and the aroma of brewing coffee filled his nose. A warm cup would really hit the spot. He put in his order, then took a seat on the sofa across from the fireplace. A hint of hot chocolate swirled around him, reminding him of Anna. He looked around as if expecting her to be there. He hadn't seen her since Heather's funeral.

"JJ." A hand touched his shoulder.

Anna handed him an insulated cup from the coffeehouse. Where had she come from?

He gave her a quick hug. "Anna, it's good to see you. Come. Sit down. How have you been?"

"I've been well and busy helping those I can." Anna came around the sofa and sat next to JJ.

JJ looked down at the cup. "Now, is this your specialty drink or what I ordered?"

She grinned. "No, that's your boring cup of joe. You had your last bit of my hot chocolate."

"Thank you for that. How is Heather? She said you're training her."

"She's going to do a great job."

"Will I ever see her? I mean, I can see you."

"She isn't allowed to visit anyone she knew before."

"Why?"

"It's a rule. Something about messing with the natural world."

"What if I search for her? You know I won't give up."

Anna raised an eyebrow.

He took a slow sip of his coffee. "Okay, truth be told. I already found her. She's in Alabama, and I plan to drive there tonight."

"I'm sorry, JJ. She's there to do a job, not to be with you."

"But I have to try. It's Heather."

She shook her head. "The father will prevent it. Yes, she's out there somewhere and she's not suffering anymore, but you can't go to her. God has given her a new healthy body, and he's created her to be so much more than you can imagine."

A warm sensation filled his heart, and the emptiness in his stomach vanished. "Is she happy?"

"Yes. Very."

He took in a long breath and blew it out. "I can't ever see her?"

She nodded.

"Please tell her I love her."

"I will."

He stared out the window at the rain pounding the ground. He couldn't promise he wouldn't ever try to see Heather. He looked back at Anna. "What are you doing here besides warning me about not messing with the natural world?"

"I have an assignment in the next town over. And I wanted to see how you are."

"I'm doing well now." JJ took a sip of his coffee, then studied her face. "Thank you, Anna, for coming here for Heather. For helping her see how strong she was."

Anna grinned. "That wasn't me. I provided the money and the car. She did the rest all on her own. She was an incredible woman."

"Yes, she was."

Anna put her hand on his knee. "JJ, I didn't come for Heather. I was sent here for you."

For him? He ran his hand over his mouth and down his chin. "Why?"

"Redemption was in God's plan for you. And you needed a reminder that you were more than your mistakes. I've always known you were a good man."

"Thank you for believing in me. And for showing me all I needed to see."

She placed her hand on top of his. "It was my pleasure."

ACKNOWLEDGMENTS

So many incredible people have followed me along on this journey. Thank you.

My mother, Linda Robison has read the worst of my writing and cheered for me every step of the way. My dad, Steve Robison Sr. believed in me and made me feel like I could be or do anything. My brother, Steve Robison Jr. spent many late nights when we were children letting me read him my made-up stories.

My husband, Jason Young gave me the time to write, and he listened to me talk endlessly about Heather, JJ, and Anna. My children turned the volume down, gave me my space when I needed it, or sat behind me in my chair and fixed my hair, rubbed my back, or were just present and quiet so we could be together while I wrote.

My mother-in-law, Sharon Moore reminded me that even when I'm down and feeling alone, I am loved. When my world turned upside down during a difficult time in the journey of getting this book published, my Aunt Donna spent hours as an ear to listen.

Thank you, Uncle Shawn Robison for helping me with Heather's softball stats and Aunt Debbie Robison with the proper pitching terms. Jennifer Dillman, thank you for giving me one of my favorite lines in the book. "I may look like I have lots of miles, but on the inside I'm just getting started."

Several friends and family have given of their time to read my books and give their feedback. Amanda Dickerson, Brooke Thomas, Angie Dunn, Pat Cooper, and Addie Decker have stuck by me when the stories were rough and in the first drafts. Angie Dunn, Shannon Williams, and Malinda Dalton proofread The Unsuspecting Heather Meyers in its final stages. Thank you for being that extra pair of eyes.

I would not be where I am if it was not for my first critique group. Mikal Hermanns, Teresa Tysinger, Holly Michael, and Angela Jeffcott, thank you for all your input and help in the beginning stages of this book.

Crystal Caudhill, Voni Harris, Angela Carlisle, and Carol Rapp Sherman your friendship has seen me through many days of doubt in this scary author world.

Thank you to my wonderful launch team. It means so much that you would take the time to help promote my book.

Dori Harrell, my editor, is one of the most outstanding individuals I know. She was an encourager while making this story shine and letting me know what needed tweaked and what parts made her hold her breath in anticipation and the times she was so wrapped up in the story she had to go back to edit. Most of all she believed in this story and the way God placed it on my heart. A unique way to tell a difficult story.

And most importantly, thank you to my Lord and Savior Jesus Christ. He has led me every step of the way and I'm blessed beyond all measure.

About the Author

Shawna Robison Young enjoys writing a little bit of the unexpected. Why be normal? In a world of conformity, a touch of something out of the ordinary can make a work of art astonishing. Shawna loves all things chocolate especially a warm cup of hot chocolate and sea salt caramel truffles. She is the mother of four, a preschool owner and teacher, a former children's minister, and the wife of a veteran.

Visit her website: shawnarobisonyoung.com
And find her on Facebook, Twitter, Instagram, Pinterest, and Goodreads.